HOUSE OF DESIRE

N. E. BUTCHER

Book Cover by Lucy M of Cover Ever After

Developmental Editing by Makenna Albert of On the Same Page Editing

Line Editing by Sarah Lamb of Sarah Lamb Writing

Proofreading by Courtney Reynier and Paige Schmidt

First Edition: September 2024

Identifiers: ISBN 9798987991633 (print) | ISBN 9798987991626 (ebook)

Also by N.E. Butcher

<u>Contemporary Romance</u>
House of Deceit
House of Desire

<u>Paranormal Romance</u>
Breaking, Gracefully

Content Warning: Mention of spousal abandonment, divorce, child illness and death. Sexually explicit language and scenes.

DEDICATION

For those that have had someone walk away and stayed standing.

To Dani.
For reading every word and listening to every voice memo just so that this book could become a reality. I love you.

To Kendra Hybertson,
For giving me my first review of my author career. I sat on my floor and cried tears of happiness.

PROLOGUE

D INNER WAS AWFUL, SILENCE owning the space. The boy I loved sat across from me but never saw me. Never even looked at me. His dusty jeans and dirty boots left behind a trail, just in case he needed to find his way out.

But he doesn't need to find his way out.

I do.

My floral bag is packed and tucked into the coat closet. The closet he rarely uses because he almost never puts his *fucking* boots away. The bag has been there for over a week and yet, he hasn't found it. Hasn't seen it.

I don't know why I picked that closet. It'd only take him opening it once to discover my plan. Why didn't I pick the linen closet? He never goes in there. Maybe I want to get caught? Maybe I want to fight. To yell.

To live.

But there's no fighting. There's no yelling. There's no good-night kiss.

There's no sex.

Of course there's no sex.

There hasn't been for one year, seven months, and six days. I look over at the clock and see it's crossed over midnight.

Correction, seven days.

Parker snores softly beside me, but I know it's more from the start of the season change than anything. There are three weeks when summer starts to turn to fall that make his allergies go crazy. And during those weeks? The softest snore.

I don't mind it, really, listening to the sign of life. At least it tells me I haven't gone deaf. That the silence is of our own making and not some sudden onset medical condition.

My fingers *tap, tap, tap* out the seconds as they go by, my eyes watching the fan blades spin above me through the darkness.

I keep waiting for the right time. The right time to throw back the covers. Slip from the bed. Grab my bag.

And leave.

Leave and never come back.

Maybe I'm a coward for it. There's really no maybe about it. I am a coward. And he deserves so much more than this. Than me. Than the pain I'm about to put us both through.

But this is all I have left to give.

The second hand on my bedside clock ticks and I feel it. The perfect time. When my determination crystallizes and I know if I don't leave now, I never will.

And I'll have to walk by that bedroom every day for the rest of my life.

Looking at Parker's back, I slide out from under the covers, trying not to make the bed move too much, but I shouldn't be worried. Nothing can wake him.

I creep from the bedroom, gently shutting the door behind me and move on silent feet through the house. Stepping over the squeaky boards of our ranch-style house, I make my way to the closet, pulling out my bag. The keys to my car threaten to jingle, but I clasp them firmly in my hand, lifting them off the hook.

Looking back at the house, I take a moment to soak it in before letting myself out one last time.

CHAPTER ONE

PARKER

Jewelry stores are the seventh circle of hell. Between the price tags and pressure, sweat is already starting to bead along my forehead despite the excessive air conditioning. The last time I was in a jewelry store, I was eighteen and had no money and the sales associate knew it. Embarrassment coursed through me as every ring I picked was above my price range.

My hands were shaking as I paid for the simple gold band.

But this trip is much different.

First, this store is not located in a mall. Second, I'm not the one buying a ring.

"Hello, how may I help you?" the sales associate asks kindly, her white hair tied in a demure knot at her neck.

"Good evening, I'm here to pick out a ring for my hopeful fiancée," Alec, my best friend's soon-to-be fiancé, says, a giant grin on his face.

I met Alec's other half when we were costars on a reality TV show. The moment he decided to propose to Charlie, he called in reinforcements to make sure he bought her the perfect ring.

Unlike the guy who helped me, this woman does not sniff at his exclamation. Instead, her face softens as her thumb gently touches the ring decorating her left hand.

"I'd be happy to help you and your companions. And might I say, congratulations." She directs this last bit to Courtney, Charlie's best friend from childhood.

"Oh, no, I'm not her. I'm here to make sure he doesn't fuck up," she says with a large smile while I snort with laughter.

"Sorry, I should have been more clear. I'm Alec, and this is Courtney and Parker who are here for moral support," Alec says, clapping me on the back.

"It's nice to meet you all. Is there anything in particular you had in mind?" the woman behind the counter asks.

Alec and Courtney go over the various things they were hoping to see while I make my way around the cases. Diamonds are tucked into their soft, velvet beds. The light shines off the different jewels. I'm happy for Charlie and Alec and the love they've found. Yet, as I look at the rows and rows of rings, I'm almost angry.

All I see lining the cases are broken promises and all the days that were supposed to be lived with Brittany by my side. I don't think about my ex-wife much anymore, but sometimes a memory makes its way from the ether and it's like she's left all over again.

"What's your budget, Cowboy?" Courtney asks the ex-wrangler while eying one of the biggest diamonds I've seen in person.

On *House of Deceit*, our wranglers were a production assistant in charge of interviewing us for confessional footage and giving us a confidant to brainstorm strategy with. The hours Charlie and Alec spent together during filming led to an attraction neither of them could deny. And now here we are.

"Let me worry about that. You're here to help me find the perfect ring."

She leans over the glass with a critical eye while Alec looks at the two rings the woman has already pulled at his request. I make my way around the store, trying to tamp down my anger. Looking at slightly less traditional options, a particularly beautiful emerald ring with leaves twisting around the band catches my eye.

"What about this one?" I ask, pointing at it.

Courtney attempts to nudge me out of the way to see what I'm pointing to, her small stature no match for me once I set my feet just to annoy her.

"Move, you giant sequoia," she says, putting her whole body weight against me.

"Make me, small fry," I taunt, smiling down at her, my anger fading.

"Ugh, you are such an *asshole*! I'm gonna tell Charlie on you." She grunts, trying to push me, and my anger fades. Courtney is one of my favorite people who has come into my life over the past few years, all thanks to being on the show.

"You can't or you'll ruin the surprise."

I consider moving away and letting her fall, something I know I'd pay for later once she came up with a suitable punishment, but I decide against it letting her edge me away from the display.

"Wow, that's beautiful," she says, squatting down to look at it from a different vantage point. "I'm not sure that's the—" She sucks in a breath as her eyes snag on a ring slightly to the left. "Alec," she whispers, calling him over.

She simply points to a ring as he squats next to her.

"Can I see this one?" he says, the associate following him around the store.

Unlocking the case, she reaches in and pulls it from its place and as she sets it on the black cushion for us to look at it, I know it's the one.

The ring looks like a flower with a sapphire in the middle, the exact shade of Charlie's eyes. The petals surrounding the stone are covered in diamonds that continue down the band.

Alec's eyes brim with tears as he tells the woman it's the one, while painful memories eat away at me.

The therapist's office feels like I'm in the interview room with my wrangler from *House of Deceit*, once more.

Minus the camera.

As always, I make my way to the leather chair. I never sit on the couch. The couch makes this feel too personal. Plus, I never know if I'm supposed to lie down on it or not.

It took Charlie suggesting therapy a few times once we were back in the real world before I finally found myself here.

Sharon shuts the door behind her, setting her usual tea on the table next to her chair. The dark gold of her dress pops against her brown skin. Bracelets on her arm jingle as she readies her pen and crosses her legs. She's a few decades my senior. Her nurturing air combined with her no-bullshit attitude reminds me of my mother in a way that makes me able to talk to her.

Some people would probably not like her delivery, but it's exactly what I need. Someone who will tell me how it is, and call me on things, so I can be better.

"Alec picked out a ring for Charlie the other day. He asked me to help him. And Courtney, of course. He asked me and Courtney to help him," I tell her without preamble.

We learned early on in our sessions together small talk just made me edgy and irritated.

"That's wonderful," she says noncommittally.

She knows there's more to it, but she doesn't push me. Sharon is happy to sit in complete silence for our entire hour, if that's what it takes.

Our first session was a disaster, and I was sure as I stormed from her office she was going to fire me as a client. The questions were simple enough at first.

"Tell me about yourself."

"What brings you here today?"

"How did your time on *House of Deceit* change you?"

But then they weren't so easy.

"When's the last time you dated someone?"

"What made you pick up and leave everything behind?"

"How does the leaving of your ex-wife continue to plague you?"

It was the last one that made me mad, unable to articulate what the moment did to me. Six weeks passed before I made another appointment, but eventually I did, at Charlie's insistence that growth is never comfortable.

"It is wonderful and I should be happy for them, but all I wanted to do was tell him how much marriage is a lie." I push up from my chair and start pacing, a usual occurrence. Keeping my body still is almost impossible when I have to talk about my emotions.

"And how is marriage a lie, Parker?" she says, her face thoughtful.

The wall behind her is littered with all of her different degrees, magazine covers, and various awards she has won. I'm lucky she was willing to take me on as a client, but that doesn't change the fact that I have no desire to rehash all the pain of my past.

"People say it's forever, but how many even last a decade?"

"Every relationship is a leap of faith. You're handing your heart over to someone. But even if it doesn't last forever, does that really mean it'd be better if it never happened?" Sharon asks.

"I don't know," I say, but my body knows I'm lying. "Maybe," I hedge, sitting back down in my chair.

With purposeful movements, she uncrosses her legs and leans forward, resting her arms on her knees as she makes direct eye contact with me.

"If you ever want to have a successful relationship, one day, very soon, you're going to have to come to terms with your wife leaving you."

"What makes you think I want a relationship?" I ask her, crossing my arms over my chest like a petulant teenager.

"Don't you?" she asks, her tone all knowing. "Being in a relationship doesn't just mean sexually. Meaningful friendships, for example."

"I have Charlie, Alec, Courtney, and Mitchel. Those are meaningful, platonic friendships."

"And who else?" she asks, but she already knows the answer, so I sit there in silence. "Maybe you should go on a date and just see how it feels? Didn't Alec's sister," —she flips through her notes for a second—"Lorelei offer to set you up with one of her friends? The sister of one of her husband's teammates or something? I think it could be good for you to just *try*."

"And if it is awful?" I ask.

"Then obviously you should give up after one try and remain alone for the rest of your life," she deadpans and I smile, trying to hide the fact that even the thought of going on a date makes my stomach hurt.

Mitchel snaps in front of my face, shaking me out of replaying my session with Sharon again over a week later.

"I would be offended you're not listening to me, but I'm used to it. What's the deal, man?"

Looking at the plans he has in front of me, I double check the numbers for the tile order before signing off and sliding the papers back toward my friend and right-hand man.

When I came home from *House of Deceit* and sold my business and almost everything I owned, all he asked was where we were going. Could I have built another business without him? Yes. But I didn't want to. The fact he was willing to uproot his entire life at the whim of a friend was more than I've ever expected since Brittany walked out the door.

"Do you think I should date?" I ask him.

He straightens the papers, making sure they go back in the appropriate folder in his stack. We have thirteen custom houses in the works and management of all the different details is a full-time job, plus some. I make a mental note to hire Mitchel an assistant, someone he can train up and make into his protégé the same way I did with him.

"I don't think it'd hurt you to get laid," he says with a smirk, causing me to roll my eyes.

"I'm not asking about sex, dude."

He straightens his tie, the result of him having a meeting with some clients later today.

"Listen," he starts, leaning back in his chair, "far be it for me to talk about anyone's healing process, but just because you left everything behind doesn't mean you turned in to a brand-new person."

"Thanks, Yoda."

"It's been over a decade since she left. You haven't heard from her. You had to divorce her in absentia. I know you thought she was your soul mate. I can't even think about how hard it was after she left. But eventually you have to move on." Sometimes, it sucks having a friend that's known you since high school.

I lay my head back on my chair, looking at the ceiling. "That's what Sharon said, too."

"Sounds like I need to up my hourly rate, then."

"I don't think that's what I said," I joke. My phone vibrates in my pocket and I see it's a text from Charlie asking me to stop by the house on my way home. "Do you need me for the last meeting of the day?" I ask, knowing I'm not going to be any help to him with my head so distracted.

"No, go. I've got this. But you owe me."

"Put it on my tab," I say, texting Charlie I'll be there in about an hour, then grabbing my keys from my desk drawer.

"Your tab is getting long," he says, shuffling all the folders into his arms, breaking off to his office as we make our way down the hall.

I make my way out to my car, the last conversation I had with Alec playing through my mind. He offered to put my name forward for the dating show that's owned by the same network as *House of Deceit*. Although he never worked on the show himself, he knows plenty of people on the production team.

Every year, I vehemently reject the offer.

But maybe Sharon is right.

Maybe I should go on some dates.

I roll my windows down and throw my hair into a knot to avoid it blowing in my face before reversing out of my spot. I make my way in the snarling, snaking traffic toward the hillside where Alec and Charlie had me build their sprawling mid-century modern house. Looking out at the ocean, I sing along to the radio.

The land was a perfect choice, and owned by Alec's family from when they had first moved to the region back in the 1800s. They could have sold it for an astronomical price, but it was passed down from generation to generation. Upon the death of his mother, it was held in trust for both him and Lorelei. Married to a professional football player who makes millions a year, she gave her brother her share of the land with the express purpose of building the house he wanted to make into a home for Charlie.

"Knock, knock!" I call out, letting myself into the richly painted foyer with the key they gave me.

They have only been living here for a few weeks. Boxes are still scattered in a few places, but they've made fantastic progress.

"Back here," Charlie calls, from what I believe to be the vicinity of the library she uses as her office.

She stretches to put a book away, her shirt riding up to show a small sliver of skin above the yoga pants she is fond of wearing when she writes, claiming no good ideas can come if she's wearing uncomfortable clothes. Considering the success of her book, I decide to believe her.

Her red hair is streaked with blonde from being out on her pool deck every day. She turns and gives me a smile that draws one from me, no matter my mood. The sister I never had, we bonded in a way only people who went through an experience no one else could understand would be able to.

"Hey, thanks for stopping by," she says, padding over to me in her bare feet. I wrap her in a bear hug as she lays a quick kiss on my cheek.

There was a time I was attracted to this woman, but in the same way someone is attracted to a painting or a symphony. The beauty of the art draws you in and drowns you as it pulls emotion from the well of your being, but you know it's not something you can ever own. Only experience. That was Charlie for me.

The experience of feeling my heart beat again.

It never bothered me she went for Alec. I knew I wouldn't be able to offer her everything she deserved.

But feeling something again. Even if it was just a flicker.

Made me remember I'm still alive.

I put her back down on her feet and make a decision. Or really let an impulsive thought take over.

"Is Alec around here?" I ask.

"He's taking a nap. They had a day of reshoots at two in the morning and then wrapped about an hour ago. He mumbled something about making a daytime thriller next time as he tumbled into bed. Dinner is in an hour and he'll be up by then for sure," she says, smiling up at me, the freckles on her nose having grown in number. "You're welcome to join us. I think Lorelei is stopping by."

"Next time. What did you need me to come by for?"

"Let me show you," she says, wrapping her arm around my bicep and leading me out to the pool.

They have the wall of window doors pushed open, allowing the outside and inside to meld together. That was Charlie's request and has been increasingly popular with every build Mitchel and I have done. Moving toward the left side, I see the daybed she had me custom build slanting slightly to one side.

"So, Alec and I *might* have been a little acrobatic the other night and I don't know what happened, but all of a sudden it just dropped on one side."

I get down on my knees and look around. If she needs to me to fix something, that's what will happen. Pushing pieces this way and that, I find the problem.

"It looks like you guys shifted it off the base just enough to drop it. It'll be easy to fix and I'll stop by this weekend with better tools and anchor it so it doesn't happen again." I straighten up and jostle her with my elbow, teasing, "I wasn't expecting *Cirque de Soleil*, but I see that was an oversight."

Her blush is pretty as she smacks my arm.

"I see you brought in the best to fix the bed," Alec says as he saunters out, kissing Charlie firmly.

His hair is tousled and there are bags under his eyes, but he seems happy. The movie he's finishing up has a lot of potential and Charlie and I can't wait to see it.

He sticks his hand out for me to shake, which I do, as he settles his arm around her. I remember when Brittany used to lean into my side as Charlie is doing right now and it strengthens my resolve once more.

Without any buildup, I jump in. "Hey. Are they still looking for a lead on *House of Desire*?"

Charlie's mouth drops open in utter shock. A fair reaction.

"Um, what?" she asks, but I ignore her.

He looks at me, almost a bit skeptically. "It's funny you ask. They were going to reach out to their choice for lead this week. I could give my old boss a call. I know they'd jump on this chance, so you need to be positive."

"If it's not too much trouble," I say, rubbing my quickly reddening face.

My legs itch to run from the scrutiny with which he looks at me until finally he says okay, and begins dialing a number. Ringing immediately sounds from the speakerphone as we wait.

"What, Alec?" The woman's voice is harsh with the demand the second the call connects. I immediately note the difference in his body language. His spine is straighter, his face more closed off. He's wrangler Alec right now.

"Parker is interested in being the lead for *House of Desire*," he says simply.

"Are you shitting me?" the woman asks. "Last time we asked, I believe he said 'I'd rather stand in the middle of I-5 naked'."

"I want to do it," I say, cutting in. "Can you make it happen?"

"I'll make the call. They'd rather you than this other guy, anyway."

She hangs up abruptly and I turn toward Charlie.

"What brought this on?" Charlie asks, her hand touching mine, her brow wrinkling.

"Sharon told me I should get back out there, so that's what I'm doing," I tell her.

"I doubt she meant in a dating competition show with twenty contestants all fighting for your heart, Park."

"Why wade in the kiddie pool when I can jump in the deep end?" I joke, trying to hide the apprehension and regret I'm already feeling. But it's too late. The water is already covering my head and now there's nothing left to do but push off the bottom and swim for the surface.

Alec's phone vibrates and he reads the message. His gray eyes lock with mine. "Congratulations, you're in."

CHAPTER TWO

ANYA

MY GLITTER SHORTS WEDGE themselves so far up my ass as I squeeze past people on my way to my seat, I'm afraid I'll have a sparkly asshole for the rest of my life. Before I can make it, the crowd jumps to their feet, screaming their love as the football sails over the goal line and into Tank's waiting hands in the end zone. The guy claiming the chair I'm standing in front of lurches to his feet, causing my balance to become precarious. Without thought, I wrap my arms around the shirtless man, his painted chest pressed against my cheek.

"Woah there, honey, what do you think you're doing?" he asks, grabbing my arms and unhooking them from around himself.

"Sorry!" I shout, trying to be heard over the crowd. "I thought I was going to fall!"

"Well that doesn't mean you get to grab onto The Clint, now does it?" He looks down at me with such self-importance, I almost laugh. Instead, I simply apologize again, pull myself from his grip, and continue on to my seat.

"I didn't think you were going to make it," Lorelei says into my ear as I kiss her cheek in greeting. Unlike the other players' wives, she enjoys being in the throng of the crowd.

"Sorry I'm late. My friend at the bank called. Apparently, I'm going to be rejected for the loan to expand. Again. What have I missed?"

As I settle into the space in front of my seat, prepared to stand for the duration as no one seems to be sitting after the last touchdown, I try to discreetly dislodge the shorts from my ass crack.

"Oh, I'm sorry, babe. That sucks. Do you want me to talk to someone?" She claps as the ball soars through the uprights for the extra point.

"No, that's alright. Thanks, though. I just might need to push back my plan to expand and start teaching classes."

"You'll figure it out. You always do."

Looking around the sideline, I scan the different jerseys I can see, looking for my brother's. Seeing what I'm doing, Lorelei points over to the left of the group.

"He's over there," she says and I feel myself smile as I find Dominic.

"How's he been playing today?" I ask.

"Two touchdowns so far."

She laughs as I cheer, belatedly, for my brother's offensive prowess on the field. I know she understands.

Lorelei is obsessed with Tank, her husband. Her love for him is obvious. It's so different from some of the other spouses. She doesn't care about his ranking in the league or how he plays. She simply enjoys supporting her partner in his passion. She is at every game. Every event. Cheering every play and accomplishment. Whatever he needs, she's there. And he does the same for her during the off season. You can see deep down they are best friends above all else.

As the top ranked tight end in the entire league, Tank could have gone anywhere when his contract was up last year, but instead of following the money he was being thrown, he signed a less lucrative deal to stay here, near Lorelei's brother.

Selfishly, I'm glad she stayed.

Three years ago was Dom's rookie season. The quarterback's wife, Sasha, set up a dinner for the significant others of the entire team so they could all meet the new members of their exclusive club. Being the spouse of a professional athlete is a position that requires you to sacrifice everything for the betterment of a team. Holidays, birthdays, anniversaries, weddings. If it's not in the off season, it's like it doesn't exist.

When asked for a name for this dinner, my single brother gave mine, knowing I've been struggling to find a good group of friends. Our family moved here my sophomore year so Dom could play for the best high school football coach in the country. It was worth it for his dream, but I never seemed to click with any of the girls in my class.

Sasha welcomed me at the dinner, but I could tell she was not thrilled at Dominic's blatant disregard for the nature of her request.

Lorelei Carlston sat next to me that night, and as they say, the rest was history. We quickly bonded over the fact we didn't feel like we fit in, uncaring of the unspoken ranking of the spouses based on the ranking of their husband on the team. We joked and laughed all night long as we shared stories about Tank and our brothers.

As we watch the game today, we talk of small things. Nothing deep, but I enjoy the conversation all the same.

"No, I'm serious. There was one season Alec's contestant refused to wear anything except swim trunks as shorts, which is weird but whatever. The problem was they were always light colored and you could almost always see his penis through them!" Lorelei giggles as one of the guys in front of us turns and gives us a dirty look.

We both love watching the games, but we aren't going to only talk about football the entire game.

"What are you wearing to the benefit next week?" Lore asks at the next break in the action.

The holiday benefit is planned for the bye week after the team's last home game in December. Private dinners with the players are auctioned off to raise money for whatever cause Sasha has picked out for the year. The guest list is extensive, with friends and family of the team staff, top-tier season ticket holders, and various sponsors.

The whole affair is the bane of my existence because the evening attire we are expected to wear is so expensive. And the last thing I will ever do is ask my brother for money.

"The same dress I wore last year," I say, keeping my gaze on the field, my lack of dresses and formal attire embarrassing me.

"Why don't you come over to my house? You can go through my dresses and see if there's anything there you like?" She claps her hands in excitement.

I grimace. "That's a very nice offer, but there's no way I'm going to fit into anything you own."

While we both have black hair, that is where the similarities between us end. Even in high heels, Lorelei barely reaches my chin. She is slender, with gentle curves, and almost everything in a clothing store is made for her.

On the other hand, I'm an inch shy of six feet without shoes on and my curves are more like a road winding its way up a mountain, all thanks to my mother. We all tower over my already short father who seems to be shrinking with every passing year.

She looks at my long legs and my ample breasts and nods in agreement.

"You're probably right. Charlie has a close friend who designs clothes and is also crazy tall with giant tits," she says, mentioning her brother's girlfriend. "I'll call her for you tomorrow and we'll get you all squared away."

I've never met Charlie, but Lorelei has only had good things to say about her.

"You're like a fairy godmother," I tell her, clapping for the field goal we just scored.

"Don't I know it."

Flour dances in the air as the sun crests the horizon. The early rays break across the bakery case, bathing the various offerings in morning light. The blue and pink walls are bright, more like a toddler's bedroom than a bakery. I have a lot of plans for the space, wanting to bring in some sophistication and expand the menu to include coffee drinks, but there's only so much I can afford at the moment. So the pink and blue walls from the old ice cream shop that used to inhabit the space remain.

Liam, my shop boy, walks in at six on the dot, slinging his backpack on the floor behind the counter while running his hand over his tightly coiled hair.

"Anastasia! Guess what, guess what."

Rolling my eyes, I grab the backpack and hang it from the hook Dad put up right inside the kitchen for exactly this.

I tripped over the bag one Monday morning, losing an entire tray of fresh croissants in the middle of our morning rush. And I almost broke my ankle in the process. After we got through all the customers, throbbing ankle be damned, I called my dad and he rushed over to make sure it never happened again.

"What? What?" I ask, mimicking his excited tone.

"I asked out Sophia!" he says, tying his apron around his waist.

Sophia is one of the popular girls at Liam's high school whom he's had a crush on since she wore a yellow polka dotted bikini to the community pool on the first day of summer over a year ago.

"And?" I ask, pointing to the sink silently reminding him to wash his hands, excited he finally worked up the nerve. If I tried to count how many hours we have talked about the various dating dynamics of teenagers during our time in the shop together, I would lose my mind.

"We are going to get ice cream on Saturday!" I try to remember the last time I went on a date as he soaps up, no closer to the answer when he turns off the water and begins drying off. "Which reminds me, is it okay if I cut out a little early? That was the only time she had available." As he finishes drying his hands, he clasps them in front of his chest, giving me a smile full of braces and guilt. Knowing I'll never be able to say no, I decide to tease him a little.

"Saturday is our busiest day, you know. And you're giving me less than two days' notice." I cross my arms over my chest and pretend like I'm thinking.

"What if I promise to buff the floor on Sunday? We haven't done that in a really long time and it could use it."

I cock an eyebrow at the unexpected offer.

"You would do that? You know it can't be done until the shop closes."

Buffing the floor requires the chairs and tables to be moved around as well as a loud buffing machine I was able to get second hand. The intention had been to do it every Sunday before heading off to the football game since we close at ten a.m. during the season so I can watch Dom, but there was always something else needing to be done.

"My mom doesn't need me to babysit this week."

He hasn't put his hands down the entire time, but now he adds on big, round eyes.

"Okay, fine. And I'm taking you up on your offer to buff the floor even though I was going to say yes without that," I say, smiling as I move to the front of the shop, turning on the neon 'Open' sign.

His mouth drops open, arms fall to his sides, and my smile widens even further.

"You were going to say yes?" he asks.

"Yup," I say, popping the 'p'.

"So, I don't have to buff the floor then?" He holds still in expectation and I *almost* give in. Almost.

"No, that was the agreement I accepted. You leave early on Saturday and I get a freshly buffed floor on Sunday."

"But you were going to say yes!"

"Sounds like you learned not to put all your cards on the table until you see what the other person is going to do," I tell him, jokingly, but it's an important lesson. One I had to learn through similar trial and error. I'll never forget the four weekends I had to spend helping Mom with the gardens to go on a school canoe trip.

His shoulders slump and I feel a little bad for him, so make a mental note to talk to my father and see if he can come help him with the buffing. The whole family loves Liam, but Dad especially.

"He's a good kid," he tells me every time he sees him, like I don't already know.

Liam joined my shop last school year as a way to earn credit for a business class. It meant his first class period of the day on Mondays, Wednesdays, and Fridays were spent here with me, opening the shop and helping our early morning guests. When the school year came to an end, he asked if I would take him on as part-time help. Considering I wasn't the only person to fall in love with him, my customers and family did too, I happily agreed. His presence allowed me to take on a few additional custom orders a month, covering the expense of paying him.

"Don't look so sad, kiddo. Sophia is going out with you!"

His smile is as dazzling as a disco ball. The bell above the door tinkles as our first customer of the day walks in, and we prepare ourselves for a busy morning.

I rush into Lorelei's bathroom where a makeup artist is dusting my friend's face with some sort of powder.

"Sorry! I'm so sorry. I was finishing up a cake for a client and then I got some inspiration for another one and anyway, here I am."

I had rushed home to shower and change before coming over to take advantage of the glam team Lorelei hired for herself. My boobs are tapped in almost every direction under my t-shirt in preparation for the backless, deep plunging dress Lore had picked out from the designer friend for me. Lore said she had many stunning pieces from her time on the awards circuit with her various projects, and was happy for them to receive a night out, but they both agreed this one would show off my assets the best. I happen to agree, even with the inconvenience of the tape. I pull my phone out, answering Dad's text I received while driving.

Dad: *Liam ran out of polish. Small section to go. Where?*

My parents remain unconvinced they have unlimited text messages no matter how many times I've called their phone company and had them explain it. Because of this, my father uses as few words as possible to keep from sending more than one text. Normally, I can figure out the message. Other times, I just have to call him and ask.

Anya: *There's more in the back closet, on the bottom shelf, behind the mop bucket*

I told Liam he would have some help with polishing the floors and he said he'd change my name in his phone to "The Benevolent Boss". Originally, I was simply "Bakery Lady" so I feel like it's an improvement.

Anya: *Is everything going okay?*

My father sends a thumbs up emoji, his favorite, and I put my phone away.

"It's okay, babe. I told you earlier than you needed to be here in anticipation of this. You're right on time." Lorelei smiles at me.

I would be offended, but she's right. More often than not, I am going to run late. I do my best, but sometimes creativity strikes at the worst time. Unfortunately, the disorganization and changing plans for cakes at the last minute has led to some lost business.

"Did Liam tell you how his date went?" Lorelei asks as the hairdresser curls her tresses, while I plop into the chair next to her.

The week after we met, Lore stopped by to grab a variety of cookies and desserts from the shop for the executives at her job. Liam had stopped by after school to make a few extra dollars, and his eyes almost popped out of his head when Lorelei came strutting in.

With the shameless optimism of a teenager, he flirted with her as he filled her order. Hearts were bouncing around his head like in a cartoon. Lore has had a soft spot for the boy ever since, talking to him about his life whenever she comes into the shop.

"From what he said, his ice cream fell to the floor when he licked it a little too hard. He was convinced she'd never be attracted to him after that. But she gave him a kiss on the cheek at the end of the date and her phone number, so I think he'll survive," I tell her as my makeup artist begins working on my closed lids.

"Good for Liam! Alec never orders cones for his ice cream after a similar event. Our mom refused to buy him a new one since she had warned him against the double scoop."

"Always have to listen to Mom," I tell her, laughing. "Dom never did either, and he suffered the consequences a time or two."

She doesn't respond, and I open my eyes, looking over at her. Her eyes are downcast, no smile on her face, and I know I stuck my foot in it. One night, sharing a bottle of wine, Lorelei and I sat cuddled under a blanket on her outdoor couch, looking over her and Tank's backyard. As we talked, the topic turned to family, and she shared how her mother tragically died while she was in high school.

"Lore," I say, but she picks up the pieces of her broken smile and fits them back together on her face. Not quite the same, but a good approximation.

"It's fine. Don't mind me," she says, waving away my guilt. "Are you bidding on anyone tonight?"

Her change of subject is as subtle as a tornado siren, but I let it pass.

"Dominic forced me to take some money to bid on him in case no one else does." Lore snorts, looking at me with a real smile this time and I roll my eyes. There's no way my brother won't be bid on. He's told he looks like a young, dark-haired Jensen Ackles constantly. I don't see it, but then again, he just looks like Dom to me.

"I can tell you which players I know are single," she says, with a suggestive wiggle of her eyebrows making me roll my eyes.

"You know I don't have any time to date. I think in the last month I've left the bakery on time twice. Dates don't really like to wait because I've been struck by inspiration or have a deadline. Plus, if I have one more guy serenade me trying to prove he's going to be the next big thing, I might scream."

She turns toward me. The hairdresser followed her movements with the practiced ease of a professional. "You should go on *House of Desire!*"

"The dating show with the candles? Where twenty people compete for the hand of one? Pass." I give a dismissive flick of my hand and hold my mouth steady as it's painted.

"I know for a *fact* Parker, the guy from season ten of *House of Deceit,* the tall blond one that Charlie flirted with? He's going to be the lead. You could be one of his flames! He's a really great guy. Truly. I wouldn't lie to you about this. He's not a wannabe actor or aspiring musician. Plus, I've always thought you two would be a good match."

I can't respond as my mouth is painted, but my mind is working through every excuse in the book.

"*And*," she continues, "my brother can get you in. They just started going through the women's applications. I could give Alec yours, personally. Some of the wranglers from *Deceit* have moved over to *Desire*."

Dating has been hard in LA. Between the wannabe actors and aspiring musicians, I've taken a bit of an unintended hiatus. That, and the store keeps me busy. I perk up a little. If I went on *House of Desire*, I would have the ability to talk about the bakery. That could be incredible marketing. Plus, maybe there is some merit to trying something different.

"I'll think about it," I say, surprising both of us.

CHAPTER THREE

THE HOTEL BALLROOM IS decorated in the colors of the team. Of course. Lord knows we can't have a color palette that isn't gold and red. A runway shoots out from the center of the stage into the middle of the room for the players to strut down when it's their turn to be bid on. A podium stands on stage left with a microphone waiting for the auction to begin after dinner.

Christmas trees, glittering sentries, stand around the edge of the room, adding to the ambiance.

"I already see at least three guys I have to punch in the face for checking you out," Dominic says, looking around the crowd, his eyebrows in an angry slant. His obliviousness to the stares he's getting from numerous women in the crowd makes me want to laugh.

"Oh relax, you overprotective bear. If I want to go out with someone on this team, you're definitely not stopping me." I smile up at the hostile face staring down at me.

As my brother has found his place among the team, the little boy I knew has faded away into sharp lines and a hulking body he's trained into athletic perfection.

Our father's dark eyes and sharp jawline stare down at me and I bend. Just a little.

"How about I promise not to make out with any of your teammates while I'm here?" I say, partially joking. There are a few men I wouldn't say no to, if given the chance.

He sighs heavily before leading me over to our table, just left of center in the room. Lorelei sits tapping out a message on her phone while Tank talks to one of the other offensive team members. Outside of uniform, it's hard for me to remember the names of the entire squad but when he turns, I know it's Miles Lawson, a wide receiver I've had a crush on since I saw him for the first time walking to his car after a game.

Tank notices us out of the corner of his eye, and raises his glass in greeting.

"Reynier," he says, clapping Dom on the back in that manly way guys do. He leans in and brushes a kiss against my cheek. "Anya, you look mouth watering. Lore, are you sure she wouldn't want to be a third for us?" he asks, getting an immediate rise out of Dominic.

"If only, babe," Lore says without taking her eyes from her phone.

"Pity. Miles, let me introduce you to Anastasia, Reynier's gorgeous sister. Anya, Miles."

The man turns toward me and I think my heart stops as he smiles. He is stunning with eyes that are a deep, warm brown drawing you in and telling you to lay your secrets bare at his feet as an offering. The dimple on the left side of his smile is perfect, and I inexplicably want to lick it.

Much like the other men in the room, his suit is eye catching and perfectly tailored. The brocade jacket takes the team colors and darkens them, bringing out the richness missing from the decorations. The black pants hug his thick thighs and I almost gulp at his impressive package as my gaze takes him in.

"Anastasia, the pleasure is all mine. And might I say, that dress is utterly enchanting on you." His voice is deep like the cosmos above us. I want to hear him say my name for the rest of my life.

He takes the hand not wrapped around my brother's bicep so I wouldn't trip and fall on my way over here, and gives the back a soft kiss.

I think I hear Dom scoff, but I'm too busy swooning over Miles.

"Your dress, too," I stumble, my brain having melted out of my body. "I mean, you look amazing, as well," I manage to stammer out, the heat of my blush making sweat bead on my lower back.

Still holding my hand, he looks deep into my eyes. "I hope you'll place a bid on me," he says with a wink. "Guys, I'll see you later. Anya, would you excuse me? I need to mingle, but I hope to speak with you more this evening."

"I'll be around," I say with much more finesse this time.

As he saunters away, I take a moment to appreciate the hard work he's put into sculpting his backside.

"Stop ogling my teammate," my brother whispers in my ear.

"I would hate for all his hard work to go unappreciated," I tell him, not removing my eyes, or bothering to keep my voice down.

I hear Tank and Lorelei snort, but ignore them until my eye line is broken and I am no longer under a trance. "Is he single?"

"To my knowledge," Dom says with a heavy sigh.

Lore laughs, pulling my attention to her.

"Can I be the fifteenth person tonight to tell you how great you look? I can't keep my eyes off your boobs!" Lorelei had left the room before I was in my dress. She motions for me to do a little spin, which I do as my brother huffs for the hundredth time, mumbles something about needing a drink, and abandons me.

"Are you sure we can't take you home tonight, Anya? It'll be a night you'll never forget," Tank says, all promise in his voice.

His wife swats him as unease runs through me, not because Tank is making me uncomfortable, but because Lorelei is the only best friend I have and I don't want to ruin our friendship. In high school, my best friend's boyfriend tried kissing me at a farm party and she never spoke to me again even though I immediately ran away.

"I already told you she isn't interested. Leave the poor girl alone and go get us some drinks. Anya, what do you want?"

"A vodka soda with a lime," I tell her. Tank nods before making his way through the crowd.

"I hope you know he's just teasing you," she says, pulling me down into a chair next to hers.

"I didn't realize you guys, you know." I make some indelicate gestures that would make Dom swallow his tongue.

"Only sometimes, and it's never with friends we don't believe can maintain the friendship without awkwardness after. There are a lot of NDAs involved, because of his position, but it's something we enjoy. You're drop dead gorgeous and both of our type, so he would love to watch us together and vice versa," she tells me without a hint of joke or embarrassment about the things they enjoy.

"Wow, that's incredibly flattering," I say with relief she's not mad her husband finds me attractive. "I'm going to pass tonight, but it's definitely something I'll keep in mind." I give her a wink and she smiles, but we both know that's not something I'll take them up on. However, I can't promise the thought won't come back to me as I'm wrapped in my sheets tonight. All alone.

Tank brings us our drinks before disappearing again.

Lorelei and I talk at our table as various players and other people at the event come to say hi or offer a word. I notice as the evening goes on, most of the single players have made their way to our table, letting me know they hope to receive my bid tonight.

Eventually we get up and make our way around the room. Tank and my brother periodically find Lorelei and me in the crowd, depositing fresh drinks in our hands before moving away to converse with someone else until I'm tipsy.

Sasha walks up to us looking perfect in a red dress, her blonde hair styled over one shoulder.

"Hi, I'm Sasha Donovan. Patrick Donovan's wife." She holds her left hand out for me to shake, her giant wedding ring glinting in the low light. I take her hand in mind, shaking it.

"I'm Anastasia, Dominic Reynier's sister. We've met about ten times."

She pulls her hand from mine, looking down her nose at my dress, making me shift under her intense gaze.

"Your brother must not have shared the 'elegant' memo in regard to the dress code," she sneers. As Lorelei opens her mouth to respond, the lights blink, telling us the dinner is about to begin. I grab Lorelei's arm and pull her toward our table without further acknowledging Sasha.

"I can't stand her," Lore says and I just nod in agreement.

Everyone moves in a dance of bodies through the ballroom, making our way back to the designated table. I take my seat next to Lorelei, Tank on her right, my brother on my left. We are sat with another couple who are a sponsor of the evening, as well as two players who have come stag.

At the table to our right, in the center of the room, sits Sasha, her husband the diamond of the team, Miles, the head coach and his wife, and the owner with his eldest daughters. The hungry gleam in their eyes as they listen to Miles talk lets me know I'll have a lot of competition when it comes to bidding on him.

Not that I blame them.

Waiters in all black bring out the dinner. Course after course flood the tables as plates are swept away and deposited with perfect efficiency until finally, the last dessert dish is cleared.

The food is luxurious and it's all I can do to keep from licking my plate. As dinner comes to an end, Sasha moves up to the podium, calling for the players who will be auctioned off to make their way to the back of the stage. The younger, less well-known players will be auctioned off in groups at the beginning. The stars like Tank and our quarterback will be auctioned off individually and bring in the most money.

An arm, clad in red and gold brocade, reaches past me, setting a vodka soda with lime in front of me. I look up and Miles is smiling down at me as I thank him for the kind gesture. He makes his way to the stage, but his eyes stay locked on mine while Sasha finishes her speech. She thanks everyone for their attendance and the bidding begins.

Sasha has hired a professional auctioneer and the energy is electric as the price goes up and up. Looking at the young guys, I think about their muscles and the work I need done around the shop.

"Do you think, instead of a date, the guys would do some work around the bakery?" I ask Lorelei in a low whisper.

She shrugs. "I think most of them would do pretty much anything you wanted. What are you doing to the bakery?"

"I've been wanting to rearrange the kitchen equipment to make it more efficient for me, but all of that stuff is heavy."

"Why didn't you ask Dom and Tank?

"You mean before or after their practices, meetings, and games?" I snark, making her laugh.

"Dom did force you to take some money and made you promise to spend it on someone."

"On him! Not some random guys."

"Pfft," she says, waiving away my objection.

"You're right," I say as I raise my paddle that was placed at my dinner setting, all the alcohol in my system blowing through my reservations about using Dom's money. Before I can blink, the gavel is dropped, making me the winner of five strapping, young, football players. Everyone claps as the next round of guys are brought forward and the entire thing begins again.

And then, Miles makes his way to the front of the stage.

The bidding becomes a frenzy as the players with more prestige come to the stage one after another. Miles goes for ten thousand dollars to the wife of the owner. I bid a few times so he knew I was interested, but even the opening bid was outside my spending limit.

As Dominic walks onto the stage, I make sure to hoot and holler, making his cheeks red with a blush. The bidding starts at two thousand dollars and the blonde daughter of one of the coach's pounces, lifting her paddle before the auctioneer is even done announcing the price. With a giggle, I raise mine, increasing the price by two hundred. He glares at me from the stage and Lorelei leans over.

"I think he has designs on that blonde," she says as the girl in question raises the bid again.

"I think you're right," I say as they make eyes at each other. "I sure hope the coach is oblivious or he's going to easily pick up the tension there."

After another hour or so, the auction comes to a close. As a winner, I go and provide the payment for my bid and give my contact information. A little over heated from the booze and number of bodies in the room, I make my way to a side door hoping to get some air until, suddenly, one of the younger guys in one of the groups I didn't win cuts me off.

"Hi there. I'm Aaron. How's your night?" His blond hair, blue eyes, and pale skin give him the look of every high school quarterback in the movies.

"Hi Aaron. Would you excuse me?" I try to move around him, but he moves in front of me.

He runs his fingers down my arm and every instinct honed by years of lessons learned from overly pushy men puts me on high alert.

"You should have bid on my group. I would have made sure you had a *good* time," he says, pushing into my space and backing me against a pillar, blocking us from view of the room.

"I have a boyfriend," I lie.

"I know you don't. Your brother told me." Suddenly, his grip around my arm is bruising and painful until his mouth is pressed roughly against mine. I try to break out of his grasp, but it's too firm. I bite his tongue as he shoves it into my mouth and he pulls back.

"Ow, you stupid bitch!" His hand comes up and he grabs my face.

"Stop, get off me!" I yell. Right as his angry face comes closer to kiss me again, Miles Lawson rips him off me and shoves him to the ground, shielding me with his body in the process.

"What do you think you were doing? She told you no. That doesn't mean keep going." Anger darkens his voice as he stares down at the kid slowly getting back to his feet.

"You see how she's dressed? She was practically panting in my arms, *begging* for me to fuck her. I was just going to give her a little taste down here before I took her back to my room," he says, tucking his slightly too large shirt back into his pants.

The commotion has drawn eyes and now my brother is barging over, realizing I was in the ruckus.

"Anya, are you alright? What's going on, Lawson?" he demands as he walks up to us, but pitching his voice in order to avoid a scene. I understand. Everyone who's anyone to the team is watching us right now.

"This little shit stain was making a pass at your sister. She said no, he didn't retreat. She didn't do anything wrong." He turns toward me and addresses me only. "Anastasia, you're well within your rights to press charges for assault. I'd be happy to get my lawyer for you, no cost to you."

Not only is this man tough and smart and funny and incredibly handsome, he's kind and caring. My heart skips a beat.

I look at the guy and I know men like him are given a slap on the wrist and nothing more. But that doesn't mean I shouldn't try to have him held accountable.

"Yes, I would like to press charges."

Aaron tries to turn and run, but my brother lunges for the young guy, horse collaring him and pulling him down to the ground once more.

"You'll stay there until the cops come," he tells him, his voice full of threat and danger.

Miles pulls his phone from his pocket and dials a number from memory, running a gentle finger down my arm.

"Hey, I have someone who needs you," he says when they answer, moving off to the side.

The head coach and owner make their way to our group, as well as Lorelei and Tank. Once Miles is off the phone, he repeats the story to their coach.

"Effective immediately, you are no longer affiliated with the Thunderhawks and have no access to team resources, including in-house counsel. Your locker will be cleaned out and your things mailed to you. You are not to set foot in the stadium again," the coach declares, red faced. Aaron pales further and a small part of me is happy at his discomfort.

About forty-five minutes later, Aaron is led from the room by one of the cops and Miles's lawyer promises to call me in the morning.

"Would you like me to drive you home?" Miles asks after everything is done.

"No, thank you. I have to go over to Tank's house to get my car. Plus, my brother is about to have an aneurysm and I know leaving right now wouldn't be helpful," I smile shyly up at him. "But maybe we could get dinner some time?"

Despite the awful end to the evening, I've felt butterflies talking to Miles all night long. Right as he opens his mouth to speak, his phone rings, pulling his attention.

"Would you excuse me? This is my girlfriend," he says before moving away, answering the call.

I freeze momentarily like a marble statue, my mouth dropping open. My mind skips through the night, wondering if I misread all the signals I thought I was picking up. If he had a girlfriend, why was he flirting with me? Was it just to increase how much he'd go for in the auction?

As I come back into my body, betrayal is all I feel. For the first time in years, I was looking forward to possibly going on a date with someone and spending some time away from the bakery. Maybe finding someone who could be a partner.

Lore talking about the guy who is going to be the lead on the dating show pops into my head. How great she thinks he is. And my hurt takes control of my mouth as I turn toward her.

"Do you really think your brother can get me on *House of Desire*?" I ask.

Her smile is evil. "Hell yeah."

SIX MONTHS LATER

CHAPTER FOUR

PARKER

60 DAYS UNTIL PROPOSAL

R EGRET HAS BEEN A constant thorn in my side over the past five and a half months as I've gotten ready for my time on *House of Desire*. My days become constantly filled with meetings, fittings, and filming for commercials and other various spots, causing the regret to crystallize more and more. I can almost see it walking through my house like a ghostly shadow.

Why would I go from not dating anyone to dating twenty women? I must have had a stroke. That's the only explanation.

"I don't understand why you're packing. You're the principle of the show. Alec said they have a whole wardrobe for you," Charlie says, laying on my crisp white bedding while flipping through the edits on her book that her agent sent her. After the raging success of her story based on our time in the mansion, Charlie finally picked up her novel again and finished it.

"Who wants to wear underwear someone else bought for them?" I ask her, shoving said underwear into the bag in my hand. The bottles of cologne on the top of my walnut dresser clink together as I shut the drawer with my hip. I pull open my sock drawer and begin shoving them into my bag without any regard for order.

She looks up at me, tapping her pen on her chin.

"You might just have a point there. Did I ever tell you that you won me a hundred dollars by agreeing to do this?"

"A few times." I smile over at her. "Is Courtney still pissed?"

"She'll get over it," she says, making a note on the page she's looking at.

"Why did I do this again?" I ask her, zipping up my bag.

She must hear something in my tone because she sits up and puts a cap on the pen, moving her book off to the side. I drop my bag and turn to lean against my dresser.

"Because you deserve to have someone love you and love them in return," she tells me, her sapphire blue eyes earnest.

"I did have someone, though. Do you think we only get one shot at this thing? Maybe I used my chance up on someone who,"—I struggle to find the words without spilling my entire sob story—"didn't want me, in the end."

Dating experience is not something I have a lot of. And my brief foray into online dating when I returned from *House of Deceit* didn't go well. As I would sit with girl after girl at dinner listening to their stories, my mind would turn back to the place that always wondered if Brittany and I were *supposed* to be together or if circumstance just pushed us together.

Charlie gets off the bed and moves over to me, wrapping her arms around my middle. My arms go around her automatically and I rest my head on top of hers, which is hard considering she's taller than most women.

"You didn't use up your chance, Parker."

"Well, you did pick your wrangler over me, so I don't know if that's true," I joke.

She pulls back from me and gently flicks me on the nose. "We weren't really dating!" she says, fake outrage coating the exclamation.

"My heart didn't know that!" I protest, grabbing my chest like I'm in pain and falling on the bed. "Call the paramedics. I think I'm dying of a broken heart."

"You're so dramatic, you oversized Viking man." She falls onto the bed next to me, giggling.

I'm lucky to have Charlie as a friend.

Basically, everyone called me crazy when I came home and told them I wasn't going to pursue Charlie in the real world. No matter what I said, they didn't believe me that it was all for the show. Is she gorgeous? Absolutely. Was I attracted to her initially? Yes. I think most people were. But there was one day when we were talking on the sun bed when she mentioned Alec and I saw it. I saw the spark I felt when I first met Brittany. Back before she pulverized my heart into such small pieces you'd need a microscope to see them.

Which always seemed amazing to me. The pieces were so small and yet the pain felt as though I was buried alive. Every time I would open my mouth to scream, the dirt would fall in, further suffocating me. Being in the mansion during filming was the first time it felt like the pressure was starting to ease.

"I'm going to miss you," Charlie tells me, knocking me with her elbow.

"You know I'll miss you, too."

Jacob Jacobson sits in the makeup chair next to me, a man I never thought I'd see in person again. His perpetual tan makes him glow even though it's May and the day is cold and rainy. My skin feels itchy in the unfamiliar routine. The pressure of day-to-day life fading away into a new pressure of picking the right person settles on my shoulders.

Rain splatters against the tent roof where we are getting ready before filming starts. The hairstylist stands behind me, trying to tame my hair into a more manageable mane, the humidity making their job harder.

"You can pull it back, if that'd make your life easier," I tell the person after they have struggled for a good ten minutes.

"Unfortunately, they want it down for the first night. They feel like it will make you look more debonair," they say. I can see the stylist's trepidation, but I'm sure they are up to the task.

"I didn't realize you were going to be the host this year, Jake," I say, trying to make small talk with the man beside me.

"It was a last-minute change. The usual host was moved to a morning show for the duration of her pregnancy. She didn't want to travel since she's in her third trimester," he says as the artist pats powder around his face. "Too bad about a few years ago. You would have been a phenomenal winner for *Deceit*."

"Thanks. I'm glad it was Charlie, though, since it wasn't me."

A production worker pokes their head into the tent, warning us there is only thirty minutes until we are needed.

It's amazing how different this show feels than *House of Deceit*. With that show, once we were in the house, we never saw any production members except our assigned wranglers. But even before we made it to the house, the number of people we met from the show were minimal.

But with this one? There are all sorts of assistants rushing around for their given department. Not only that, but I'll be living separately from the women in a pool house behind the mansion.

Desire also doesn't have live eliminations. Nothing about this show is live due to the filming schedule. One week to the audience will only be five days to us. While intense, it allows for filming to only take nine weeks instead of twelve.

The schedule sounds grueling, but there's nothing to be done about it now.

Once Alec confirmed I would be the new lead, I watched a few seasons of *House of Desire* to determine what I was in for in regard to the dates. Over the course of nine weeks, I will be dating twenty women who will be competing to be the flame of my desire. Their words, not mine. There will be group dates and competitions for solo dates. And many meals where we aren't allowed to eat because no one looks attractive eating. And then, at the end of the week, I'll send home one lady.

Tonight, I have to meet all twenty contestants, speak to everyone during what will probably end up being a ten-hour cocktail hour, and then I will send home five women. I'm not quite sure why I have to get rid of five people right off the bat, but this was a sticking point with the show. I suggested keeping the majority of the ladies until we hit week six and *then* kick seven people to the curb. By then, at least, it wouldn't be a snap decision, allowing everyone to settle into the show and show their true colors.

But they wouldn't hear of it.

Once my hair is complete, the stylist switches places with the makeup artist. She stands in front of me, her hand under my chin turning my face this way and that. I've long gotten used to the random touching from strangers before being on TV.

"You have a gorgeous bone structure," she tells me before grabbing her brushes.

"Thank you. I worked hard chiseling it," I joke.

She snorts as she gets down to work. We have five minutes before I'm needed in front of the camera, but she moves like Quicksilver and I know it'll be no problem.

Jacob Jacobson leaves the tent as I stand, straightening my suit in the mirror. As I push through the flap, I notice the rain has let up, leaving the world clean and sparkling.

Unlike my time on *Deceit*, there are cameras and crew all over the set. Lights shine down where Jacob stands in front of the mansion, waiting for me. Sitting around the monitors, the show runner, Jane, sits with a gaggle of her helpers.

A production assistant walks up to me.

"The first limo is about to arrive. The women inside are Mary Ella, Persephone, Drew, Carmen, and Anastasia," he tells me before quickly stepping out of frame. I try to hold the names in my mind, but they are like water through a sieve.

I stand on my mark, having been walked through what would happen tonight earlier in the day, as the first limo pulls up. My heart starts racing, nerves taking control. Until this very moment,

I was unflappable. With the grind of getting Mitchel an assistant squared away to manage without me, filming the various promos, and fittings for wardrobe, I didn't have time to really think about what I was doing. Now, weeks of preparation have given way.

But it's too late to bow out now.

A member of production counts us down and Jacob Jacobson is cued in.

"Hello, everyone. Welcome to the first night of *House of Desire* where Parker will be looking for the woman who lights the flame of his desire." He turns toward me, his smile welcoming and warm. "How are you feeling?"

"Nervous," I tell him honestly, "but also excited. I could be meeting the woman of my dreams." I make sure to hit the last point as I was directed, knowing they will extend the moment in post-production with prerecorded snippets of my background and what I'm looking for in a partner.

"Well, here comes the first group of women. Let's see if one of these ladies is the one."

He steps away from me as the limo comes creeping over the cobblestones, parking at a strategic angle. The driver gets out of the limo and moves to open the door for the first woman.

A tan, slender leg appears from the dark depths. The light catches the glittery red heel. It looks like Dorothy's red slipper if it was a high heel. The woman emerges in a white dress that hugs every curve, the hem falling to the ground as she stands. Mary Ella sees me and the demure smile on her face turns into a giant grin.

Shock takes over before a smile lights on my face, matching hers.

"Parker!" she exclaims, her southern drawl pulling me back to the *House of Deceit* mansion and another first night of filming. Walking far quicker than I believe possible over the cobblestoned drive, before I can say a word, she's in my arms, kissing my cheek with red lips that match her red shoes.

"Mary Ella, stunning, as always. Congratulations on being Miss Alabama," I say, nodding to the sash running diagonally over her dress. "Charlie and I watched the pageant."

"That's so sweet of you to say! I'm so surprised to see you standing here. How have you been?" she asks, her sweet earnestness pulling at my heartstrings. The girl I knew three years ago has grown into a beautiful young woman.

I see the signal from the producer to wrap it up, but I take a moment more.

"We'll catch up later, I promise. But it's so good to see you. It looks like third time's the charm, yeah?" I say, hinting at her multiple attempts to get on the show.

"It seems so. I'll see you inside." She hugs me again before striding into the mansion.

We take a moment to reset and the limo door is opened again.

The next woman looks like a twin of Gemma Chan from *Crazy Rich Asians*, a movie night favorite of mine and Charlie's.

She moves toward me with sure steps. How these women move in these high heels will never cease to surprise me, while I'm simultaneously glad society has not deemed them a requirement for men.

I lean in to give her a quick hug, brushing a kiss on her cheek as I introduce myself.

"Hello, I'm Parker. Thank you for joining me on this journey." The crew really emphasized the use of 'journey' instead of 'show' or 'game'.

"Parker, it's a pleasure." Her posh English accent makes me want to listen to her talk all evening. Ever since I was a kid watching any Julie Andrews movie with my mom, I've been obsessed with the accent. "My name is Carmen."

"The pleasure is all mine," I say, but then my mind goes black. I have two minutes with each woman as they come out of the limo. I didn't expect this to be a difficult amount of time to fill, but here I am letting the silence stretch between us. "Tell me about yourself."

The second the statement leaves my mouth, I want to kick my own ass. But like an angel, Carmen saves me.

"I'm a nurse at a hospital made specifically for children with cancer. It's a cause that's been very dear to my heart since my childhood best friend passed away from Hodgkin's Lymphoma."

So, not just an angel for saving me, but a literal angel.

"Wow, that's amazing. I'm so sorry about your friend, but what an amazing way to honor them."

The two minutes are up quicker than I expect and Carmen is ushered into the mansion as I promise to catch up with her later. My time with Drew and Persephone goes smoother as my brain finally assists and regurgitates the list my assistant, Philip, provided of about fifty introduction questions I can ask.

Taking a deep breath, I settle in for the last woman in this limo. The door opens again and my mouth drops. Even in this group of stunning women, the most beautiful woman I've ever seen stands before me. Her dress is a vibrant crimson. The V-shaped neckline shows just a hint of cleavage causing my mouth to water. She runs her hands down her hips, adjusting the bodice of her dress.

With a smile that feels like the sun breaking through the clouds after a hurricane, she begins walking towards me. It feels like an eternity as I listen to her heels clack against the stones with each of her steps.

I scan down her body again and I see it. Her ankle turns and before I can do more than unclasp my hands, her entire body slams into the wet cobblestones, bringing her in a sprawling heap near my feet.

CHAPTER FIVE

ANYA

MY KNEES CRACK AGAINST the cobblestone, pulling a cry of pain from my throat. Of course, this is my first impression with a man. I realized for a split second before I became intimately familiar with the ground, he was even prettier in person than he was on TV. I pray no one saw my fall. A frivolous, unanswered prayer.

Strong hands hoist me from my rock laden home, and I die a little inside.

"Are you okay?" the deep voice asks me. I know it's not Jacob Jacobson. His voice is like a summer drizzle against warm ground. Quickly dissipates and is forgotten.

But this voice.

His voice is everything. It is the wave crashing against the shore. It is the tumble of thunder within the sky. It is the beauty of the brush stroke on the canvas.

It is all encompassing.

"Please tell me you didn't see that," I beg him to lie to me, looking up at his concerned face.

"The bright side is you will be the one I remember most from tonight," he says, a soft smile on his lips.

I dust off one of the many dresses Charlie's designer friend sold me at cost, which still made my credit card cry. He reaches out and I think he's going to cup my cheek. My face heats, but he pulls a leaf that inexplicably got tangled in my hair, dropping it down to the ground.

"While you're getting to know the other ladies, I might be having a bonfire out back to destroy these shoes and send them to hell where they belong," I tell him.

He gives me a small laugh, which pulls a smile to my lips.

"Should I have production get some sage? Smudge the space of the bad fall energy?"

His knowledge of smudging surprises me, easing my embarrassment.

"I wouldn't want to put them out." One of the people with a headset makes a hurry up motion with their hand and I know my time with Parker is coming to an end. "Come find me later?"

"The second I can," he promises, his voice earnest.

I hold eye contact with him as long as I can, accepting the arm of one of the production assistants. As I cross the threshold of the mansion, all the aches from my fall make themselves known as if they were waiting for me to be done talking to Parker.

Very considerate of them, honestly.

My limo ladies are waiting inside with a glass of champagne for me. I accept it but only take a small sip.

"Ladies," Carmen starts, lifting her glass, "to us and all the hell we will be put through. Let us remain friends despite trying to attract the attention of the same man."

We all toast, taking a drink and as the bubbles burst across my tongue, I try to gauge how much of a disaster this is going to be.

Drew sits next to me on the couch. Her face has looked familiar since we were in the limo, but I still can't place where I recognize her from. She doesn't say anything as we sit together. The moment has the barest hint of awkwardness around the edges, but it's to be expected in such an unusual situation. Camera people walk around the room, filming various groups, telling us not to look at the camera when we inevitably do.

Every five minutes or so a new woman enters the mansion and joins in the mingling until the evening has the air of a party while we wait for Parker.

Alcohol is flowing freely at a bar set up in the kitchen by production. I watch from my perch, nursing my original glass of champagne, watching the group get progressively more and more drunk. One thing Lorelei drilled into me after I was cast was to watch how much alcohol I consumed.

"Just remember, everything you say or do can be cut and edited out of context. And no matter what you do, don't get drunk. You will *regret it because it will inevitably be the footage they choose."*

It's obvious this advice is accurate as I watch camera people follow those who are imbibing the most.

"Do you think they will serve us dinner?" Drew asks.

"No, there's no dinner," I tell her, watching Persephone tell a story, her body moving in an animated fashion while all the women around her stare, enraptured.

Hours tick by and I wonder why I'm here for the millionth time. Dating has never been my forte and there's no way love can really be found in this situation. Once my embarrassment at Miles's rejection wore off, I deeply regretted telling Lorelei to give her brother my name. However, since I'm not one to back out of a promise, when I received the call, I accepted the casting.

When I told my parents I would be needing to take time off, they were extremely worried about me. I haven't focused on myself since I opened my bakery. Once I explained where I was going, they were excited. They are hoping I come home with a husband while I just hope I make it past night one. More to avoid the embarrassment at being let go the first night.

Mom and Liam immediately agreed to take over the bakery for me while I was gone, which will help me to avoid losing any customers I have. It also allowed me to continue taking cake orders during the time I'll be out. While a great cook, my mother's decorating skills are limited. I made sure to only accept the types of orders we had discussed.

It took twenty minutes for Dom to stop laughing when I told him. If he had been in the room, I would have thrown a shoe at him.

I'm going to miss being at my bakery, but hopefully this turns into the best choice I could make.

Bethany H, the fashionable accountant, plops down on the couch, sloshing her martini out of her glass and across my arm.

"Whoops!" she says giggling. "You're beautiful." Her hand is slightly sticky as she runs it down my face.

"Oh, well, thank you so much. Can you stop touching me?" I try to pull my face away from her, but she wraps her arms around me, pulling it back toward her. For a drunk girl, she's surprisingly strong.

"Can I tell you a secret?" she whispers in my ear, her spittle making me cringe.

"Only if you get away from my face."

"I'm only here because I want to become a leading Hollywood actress. Don't tell, okay?" She hiccups before giggling.

"Ladies!" a production assistant calls, clapping his hands loudly. The noise diminishes immediately. "Parker and Jacob are about to come in. There should be a lot of excitement and cheers. Everyone please be standing and mingling during this time." He looks pointedly at Drew, Bethany H, and me until we all stand awkwardly.

"Also," he continues, "Jacob will reintroduce Parker to you all and then he will say a few words. There will be a toast at the end, so everyone please have a glass in your hand. Everyone will need to talk to Parker tonight. Have fun!"

A few camera people come into the room, adding to the visible cameras that are placed around the room. This entire situation makes me feel like it's the first day of school where no one really knows what's going on and I'm just following the lead of others.

An unseen production assistant calls out a countdown to the doors opening. When she hits zero, Jacob and Parker push in and we all cheer as instructed. They both smile at us until the noise settles down.

"Ladies, welcome to *House of Desire*!" Jacob says, causing another round of applause. "This season is going to be a great one, I'm sure. As a reminder, five of you will be going home tonight. Parker, would you like to welcome the women fighting to be the flame of your desire?"

"I'd love to," he says, taking half a step forward, smiling at us. "Ladies, I can't wait to get to know you all over these next few months and for you to get to know me. Thank you for your willingness to be here. I already know I'm the luckiest man alive."

Everyone claps politely as he looks around the room. Locking his gaze on me, he shoots me a wink. Confused, I look behind me, thinking maybe he meant that for someone else, but there's no one else there. I point to my chest, just to confirm. He nods and winks again.

This time, everyone turns and looks at me. Some women with confusion, others with outright hostility, and I know this singled out attention is going to hurt my ability to make friends.

"Parker will now choose the woman he'll have a one-on-one moment with first," Jacob Jacobson says.

Parker looks at me and I can tell he's about to call me out again. My eyes widen, worried everyone is going to hate me if I get his attention again. I shake my head infinitesimally. Confusion colors his expression, but he seems to understand and calls on another woman.

She's the shortest of the group, barely coming up to Parker's chest, but her boisterous laugh and sunny disposition more than make up for her lack in stature. He leads her outside and the rest of us break up, mingling more.

An hour into the night, I have settled back onto the couch, trying to be comfortable as we wait to cycle through our time with Parker.

"Cletus is my thoroughbred. He's the most *beautiful* chestnut color," Leslie says to the small group of us. She is everything I would expect from a debutante, something she told us about within the first minute of her joining our group. Her long, blonde hair, blue eyes, pale skin, and slight southern drawl pair perfectly with the string of pearls clasped around her neck.

She has shared the name of every horse on her family's farm and their various pedigrees like it means anything to us. My eyes glazed over around the fourth horse, unable to follow the conversation, never having been near horses in my life.

There was a girl in our town who was the designated "horse girl" growing up. She was a nice girl, but the deep obsession took up her entire life and a good portion of her wardrobe. In elementary school, she would often whinny when teachers would call on her. Luckily, she grew out of the habit and once she developed boobs, the guys in our grade quickly learned to ignore her dedication to the animal.

By the time high school rolled around, she would participate in competitions, winning the majority of them. Her love of the horses took her all the way to the Kentucky Derby as part of a now famous trainer duo.

While Leslie seems to love her family's horses, I don't get the impression they are anything more than an accessory to her.

My empty water glass saves me and I excuse myself from the conversation, moving to the bar.

"Can I get a rum and coke?" a blue-haired girl asks the bartender. "It's shocking to me they don't have food at this little shindig. I'm Zoey," she says to me.

"Anastasia, but you can call me Anya. I agree about the food. I am starving. I would kill for a chicken fried steak and some mashed potatoes and gravy right now."

She takes a sip of her drink while I gulp down my water, sure I'm dehydrated at this point.

"That sounds delicious. Is that your favorite meal?"

"Just what I'm craving right now. I've been eating healthier the past few weeks in preparation for this, and I started dreaming about everything being smothered in gravy."

"That sounds like a very sexual dream."

I laugh, genuinely enjoying this woman. "It definitely was."

"Anastasia," a member of production calls, reading off a list on their clipboard.

"Yes?" I say, turning toward them.

"You're up," they say and move on with no care to the bomb of nerves that just exploded in my stomach.

CHAPTER SIX

PARKER

MEETING TWENTY WOMEN COMING out of the limos has been overwhelming to say the least. A member of production let me know they would have cards for me with each girl on them and a few facts so I can work on memorizing everyone in these first few days.

The only one I don't need a card on is Anastasia, the one who ended up in a heap at my feet. I'd be lying if I said her rejection at being the first person I talked to didn't sting, but thankfully, I was able to pivot to Mary Ella, the familiar face a welcome respite from the endless parade of strangers.

She leads the way through the Tuscan inspired house and through the sliding back doors to the patio.

"How ya doin'?" she asks, her twang just as strong as it was three years ago. "This must be extremely overwhelming for you."

I smile at the girl, appreciative she's not looking at me like a bull on auction.

"It's pretty intense, but I'm sure everything will be fine," I tell her, my eyes flitting to the camera man across the patio. "I'm lucky to be here."

She takes her sash off, and settles onto the couch like we are two old friends catching up. Taking a sip from her wineglass, she looks at the backyard. The twinkling lights remind me of the finale at *House of Deceit*.

"What have you been up to since we left the house?" I ask Mary Ella, a small piece of guilt breaking off and floating along inside me, infecting me with the feeling. "I'm sorry I didn't keep in touch."

She waves away my apology. "Don't think anything of it. I know you've been busy. Charlie and I email," she tells me. "I won Miss Alabama, as you know. I've tried dating, but it didn't work out for me. Other than that, I just graduated my master's program and now I'm doing my clinical hours. I'm hoping to become a therapist."

Her entire face lights up, passion seeping from every pore as she talks about her plans. The girl who was fresh faced and new during *House of Deceit* now has an aura of peace around her that wasn't there before. She's radiant in her happiness.

"That's amazing," I say, knowing she'll be able to do wonderful things for her clients. "Mary Ella—" I start but she cuts me off.

"Parker, it's okay. I know you're going to send me home tonight. I was so excited when they announced you were going to be the lead, but I knew that would be the end of my time on the show. You know, I actually considered pulling out so one of the alternates would have a chance, but I wanted to see you." Her smile is small but warm. "But I also wanted to give you a friendly face. Someone who is here just because you're,"—she takes me in for a second—"well, you're *you*. Not because they are fighting to win a show."

Her words are the sun on my sno-cone of a heart, melting me in her warmth. I didn't deserve to have Mary Ella here. She deserves someone who will see all she is instead of a pseudo little sister. I just can't be that guy for her. No matter how much I know having her in my life would make me a better person.

"If they aren't completely dumb, they'll let you have your own season. They'd have to beat all the men off with a stick," I say.

Her laughter is like a tinkle of bells and as she lays her hand on my forearm, I feel nothing but the warmth of her skin.

Heels clack against the pavement and I know our time is coming to a close. Grabbing her hand, I pull her to standing, wrapping Mary Ella in a hug. She grips me, tighter than I'd expect, before pulling back.

"Good luck, Parker," she says, giving me a gentle kiss on the cheek.

"You too, Mary Ella," I say, the next woman stopping right outside of my peripheral vision, but I can feel her there.

"I hate to interrupt," she says, trailing off.

Mary Ella and I hug once more, but then we separate and I know I won't see her again until I have to send her home at the end of the night.

"Hello," I say smiling at the woman. I know her name is a Greek goddess, but I can't remember which one at the moment. "Take a seat."

"I'm Persephone," she tells me, kindly. "How's your night going so far?"

She runs her fingers through her reddish-blonde hair and pulls it all over one shoulder as she looks at me with light green eyes expectantly.

The amount of small talk required for this show is extreme. I don't know why I didn't realize it would be, but it's been quite a jolt.

"My night has been great, thank you. Meeting all of you has been really amazing and I just can't wait to deepen our connections."

As I was getting ready, my personal production assistant gave me a list of statements to try to work into conversation the audience seems to enjoy and expect. I mentally tick "deepen our connection" off the list. The falseness of this exchange grates on my nerves, but this environment is not conducive to spending hours getting to know these women.

"Ah, yes," she says, with a secret smile. "I can't wait to see what this journey holds." Her eyes are sparkling with humor as I realize that was another on the list.

A bark of laughter leaves me as a small wisp of embarrassment dissipates through my body.

"Sorry, I'm a little tense tonight. It's already been a lot, to put it nicely, and I got in my head," I tell her, apologizing.

I can feel my body relax as she lets out a giggle, something I didn't think I'd hear from this sophisticated woman.

"It's alright. I actually am a huge fan of the show. My grandmother and I would watch it together until she passed away last year."

"I'm sorry to hear that. I'm sure she will be watching over you this season with great interest."

"I'm sure she will be."

I give her a moment to collect herself.

"So, Parker, tell me about yourself," she jokes and I laugh.

"I feel like there should be a single spotlight on me. What would you like to know?" I ask. A few of the greeting conversations from the limo I had started this way, making it feel more like an interview. But it was almost better than the ones where they thought they knew me. Knew who I was, what I was like. My passions. My flaws. All from my time in interviews or on *House of Deceit*.

They don't know me at all.

"Everything," she says, shrugging, like it's obvious.

"My parents conceived me after a game of strip poker." Her jaw drops and I want to laugh, but I widen my eyes, just a little, making my facial expression earnest. "My dad always pretends I might belong to his best friend. Apparently, he stole my mom from the friend, but I look just like him," I tell her, my voice dripping with innocence.

"Well, that's, um." She tries to take a sip of a nonexistent drink, seeming genuinely surprised there's not a glass in her hand. I make a motion to the production crew just to the side of us and silently ask them to bring us both something. Her hands fall to her lap.

"I'm not really sure what to do with the information you just shared with me," she says, clearing her throat.

I bark a laugh and she stares at me, a quiet smile on her face.

"I'm sorry for messing with you," I say. "Not that the story isn't true, I just wanted to be a smart ass."

A man in all black with a headset perched on his head walks toward us, a glass of white wine in one hand and an old fashioned in another. I should have specified water, but anything would be better than nothing at this point.

Without a word, he holds the glasses out to us, which we take, and he departs, fading into the shadows like he was never here.

"To the journey," Persephone says, holding her glass.

I touch mine to hers, a clear bell sound echoing around us.

"To the friends we make along the way." We both take a sip and I set mine on the coffee table in front of me. "If you weren't here, what would you be doing right now?" I ask her.

"When I got the call I was cast, I actually had to cancel the safari I was planning. Some friends and I were going to go down to Kenya, Botswana, Tanzania, and Namibia for a month. We had some adventures planned like skydiving at sunrise. It was going to be magical."

"That sounds so incredible. I'm sure it was difficult to leave that for this. I've never left the States, but I've always wanted to. We never had a lot of money growing up. We were comfortable compared to a lot of people, but we never really vacationed. It's always been something I've wanted to do."

"Oh, you must do it one day! I try to take a quarterly trip. I'll have to give you the name of my travel agent. She's the best. Hikes, bungee jumping, swimming with sharks, any sort of adventure you'd want, she can find. Plus, she makes sure everything is first class and five stars."

I almost laugh, but I choke it down. Even though I can afford first class and five stars, it's not a normal part of my experience. Growing up, my parents instilled in me a love of hard work and living modestly. It took Charlie *months* to convince me I could buy a house that was larger than five hundred square feet even though it's just me.

As Persephone recounts her last adventure, a memory swims out of the depths of my mind, assaulting me. Suddenly, Brittany is sitting in front of me. Telling me how our life is too small. Too caged in. Too *predictable.* She'd talk about how we should ditch everything and backpack across other countries. Work our way around, and have a grand adventure.

But adventure has never been my strong suit.

A hand touches my forearm, but it's not my ex-wife's.

"Parker? Are you alright?"

I shake my head, coming back to the present. "Yes, sorry. Got lost there for a second." I give her a smile before reaching for my glass. The smoky bite of bourbon coats my throat, bringing me back into my body. "Do you do those types of trips often? What do you do for work?"

"I'm head of the board for my family's philanthropy division. We meet quarterly, so I just have to come back to vote on various matters. It helps me keep track of the year, really. One time, I was in a village that doesn't use cellphones and my assistant had to show up and get me when it was time for me to go home."

This woman, while magnificent, isn't for me. I would stifle her. Just like Brittany always told me I did to her. I wouldn't be able to travel with her for months on end. And I most certainly wouldn't be going skydiving and the like.

"I'm sure that was a great trip. Every once in a while, I consider throwing my phone out into the ocean when it won't stop ringing."

She laughs, harder than the joke warrants, running her hand down my arm.

"What do you do for work?" she asks, taking a sip of her wine. Her eyes have gone glassy since we've been sitting here and I doubt it's her first drink.

"I build homes," I tell her simply. I open my mouth to explain more, but she cuts me off.

"Oh, that's precious! I've always thought manual labor is *such* charming work. It must be nice to work with your hands."

And that's the nail in the coffin. Manual labor isn't *charming* work. It's hard, backbreaking work. My people work tirelessly to build homes they will probably never live in. While I pay everyone extremely well and provide the best benefits possible, when you build custom homes, there's a steep price tag.

I could expand my business into developments. Building two hundred of the same five types of houses. That is where I got my start on understanding the process, after all. We were expected to throw houses up as quickly as possible in the blistering summer heat. Not only that, but the company was wanting to build everything cheaply instead of lowering the profit per house and using materials that would last centuries. But it was consistent work for a kid with a wife.

After Brittany left, I quit.

And I started my own business. It took a long time to get the first contract and I made basically nothing, but seeing a family move into something you put your blood, sweat, and quite a few curse words into?

Priceless.

"It's very rewarding to build things, but I doubt anyone on my team would consider it 'charming' work."

"Oh, no, I didn't mean it as a snub," she tries to backpedal. But as I listen to this woman who has probably never missed a rent payment because her hours were cut at her job, I strike her from my mental list of women to continue on after tonight.

I've talked to fifteen women when *finally,* the one in red who fell out of the limo catches my attention from behind the woman currently sitting on the couch across from me. Her long, black hair looks even darker in dim light.

She points to herself and then to my companion, and I guess she's asking if she can interrupt. I want nothing more than to talk to this woman who captured my attention from the first moment I saw her, so I give her the barest of nods.

As the woman I'm speaking with finishes her sentence, her name lost to the recesses of my mind, the woman in red walks up, her hips swaying, and I have to force myself to look away. She gently sets her hand on the other woman's shoulder, pulling her attention up.

"I'm so sorry to interrupt, but you would mind if I stole him for a moment?"

"Oh!" she turns and looks back at me. "I've taken up too much of your time. I look forward to seeing you later," she says as we stand. I make noises of agreement and then she's off. I've forgotten her before she was fully inside the house as my tired, scratchy eyes drink in the other woman before me.

"I don't think I ever gave you my name," she says with a smile on her face as she comes to a stop before me. Her eyes are like honey.

"No, I don't think you did." While I already know it from production, I want her to tell me. "You were too busy falling for me,"

I say, and she snorts. Not a soft delicate thing, but a loud, shocking sound.

She slaps a hand over her nose and mouth, her eyes wide with shock. "Holy fuck, I just snorted on national TV."

It's small at first, my laugh. Just a tiny blip of a thing. But then it grows until I'm bent over, tears streaming down my face as my entire body shakes with laughter. At some point, she joined in, thank goodness, and is equally lost in mirth. Eventually my laughs subside, a few last chuckles bubbling to the surface.

"I needed that so badly," I tell her as we both settle down.

"I can only imagine how much of a zoo animal you must feel like. I can blend in with the other girls, but you're the only one. The name is Anastasia, by the way."

I shake my head. "There's no way you could ever blend in. But I get what you're saying. And that's a beautiful name." She crosses her legs, pulling my attention to them. "I see you're still wearing the traitorous shoes."

She rolls her eyes, giving me a smile.

"I doubt they would be okay with me walking around bare-footed during cocktail hour."

"You're probably right, but so long as you're with me, you can take them off. If you'd like."

"If I take them off right now, I won't be able to put them back on. My feet are perfectly numb, but I appreciate the offer." I watch her as she seems to struggle with something for a moment. "We have some people in common."

Confusion covers me. "We do?"

"Lorelei Carlston? I'm friends with her. She's told me a few things about you. All good," she reassures me, "but I wanted you to know."

My shoulders relax as I smile. "Lorelei is amazing. And if you're her friend, then I know you're a good person. She is an astonishingly accurate judge of character. How did you meet her?"

"At an event for the Thunderhawks. Then she came into my bakery, the Whimsical Whisk, one day and kind of"—she searches for the word—"adopted me, I guess? She's been great."

I laugh, knowing exactly what she means. "That sounds like her. She adopted my best friend Charlie when she started dating her brother and, by extension, me. How have I never seen or met you before, is my question. They love having get togethers, and if I know Lorelei, she would have invited you."

"Oh, I thought she was going to kidnap me this last time to force me to go, but after a long day baking and the fact I have to get up early in the mornings to make pastries fresh, it never worked out. I'm regretting it now, though."

"Maybe we could have avoided this whole thing if you had come over," I tell her, honestly. When Lorelei mentioned trying to set me up with a friend, I always blew it off, never liking being set up before. Regret runs rampant through me now.

"Maybe we are meeting exactly when we were supposed to? Like fate."

"You believe in fate?" I ask, being reminded of Brittany for just a second.

"Fate. Karma. I believe what you put out is what comes back to you when you're ready for it. Maybe we wouldn't have been ready before."

I nod, considering her words. Considering if maybe now is the right time.

"I would agree. I think you can meet the right person at the wrong time." Maybe Brittany was that for me. I know we could have made it, but maybe fate had other plans. But I want to share myself with this woman, if even just a little piece. "You gave me honesty and I want to do the same. I'm divorced. I know for some people that can be a deal breaker, but I hope for you it's not."

"We all have pasts, Parker," she reassures me, but I resist.

"Mine has some heavier moments than others." I refuse to divulge everything here, on camera. My past is not for public consumption, no matter that I signed up for this show.

Sadness weighs on me, until her hand grasps mine, her skin soft, dragging my eyes back to hers.

"Good thing I'm strong, then," she says with a smile.

With five words, I know I need more time to get to know Anastasia.

"Would you be the spark to my flame?" I ask her, hoping she can't hear the nerves in my voice. That's not quite the right phrase I'm supposed to use when asking one of the women to continue on the show with me, but I don't care.

I see a member of production talking rapidly into their headset, covering their mouth. A part of me wonders if they are going to deny me this chance to give Anastasia a candle outside of the elimination ceremony. No one has stopped the moment, so I'm assuming it's been deemed acceptable.

"I'd love that," she says, taking my hand and squeezing it.

One of the many assistants comes rushing out with a candle for Anastasia and another for me, before instructing us both to stand. When my candle is lit, they disappear again. Nerves start to take over again as I put myself on the line and ask the first person to continue in this circus with me, but I push through them.

"Anastasia, will you be the spark to my flame?" I ask her in a serious voice.

She stifles a laugh and tilts the unlit wick of her candle into mine. It smokes and then catches. Taking a step back, in an equally serious voice, she gives me her agreement once more.

"I thought you'd never ask."

CHAPTER SEVEN

THE SKY THROUGH THE windows is painted in the first morning rays of light as I look over framed pictures of all the different women, their names on plaques. My eyes burn with exhaustion and my stomach sings out my desperate hunger as I look from picture to picture. Anastasia's name plaque is missing from her frame, already in the yes pile. The memory of her snort followed immediately by her cursed surprise makes my face split in a grin once more.

Grabbing Mary Ella and Persephone's names from their frames, I put them in the no pile. There is one woman I don't remember talking to named Bethany K. While she looks nice, I can only take those who made an impression. I look at the pictures with remaining names and pick Scarlett's, adding it to the elimination pile.

But all I can think of is Anastasia.

While falling definitely grabbed my attention, there's a warmness about her that calls to me, as if I'm walking into the home I've always wanted.

The ones I want to keep are easy. Four or five of the women made lasting impressions. I didn't think the hard part would be deciding who to eliminate. When I had signed up for the show, I knew I would just eliminate those I didn't have a connection with. Did I think I would have a connection with everyone except the ones I needed to ask to leave at any given time? That would be a lot of women to be attracted to.

And it's not that they aren't attractive.

They are, as I knew they would be. The show isn't exactly known for bringing on average looking contestants. What I didn't anticipate is there would only be a handful I'd want to really continue with.

While I haven't dated much, one thing I refused to ever do was lead someone on. Standing here in front of these pictures, I realize that's exactly what I have to do.

The show will not allow me to go from twenty women to five in one night. What kind of season would that be? So I have to call out names of women I know I have no interest in.

Drew's picture shows a pretty woman. One I've recognized from tabloids.

The actress has been making headlines for her over the top antics on set, as well as the affair she had with a married director. Having been in the spotlight a small amount after *House of Deceit* and having my continued relationship with Charlie scrutinized by, what feels like every news outlet in the country, I have a great amount of sympathy for her.

Charlie took on the brunt of the speculation around us, people saying she was sleeping with me behind Alec's back. One of our favorite covers, that made us laugh for hours, said she was in a relationship with both of us. But they could never substantiate any of the claims, since they weren't real.

I think about how it would feel to be Drew and thrust into the spotlight in that way again. The placard is heavy in my hand but I add her name to the pile of eliminations, wanting to protect her from the scrutiny this show could bring.

"I'm finished," I tell the cameras sitting in the room, recording my deliberation for the audience. Production assistants swoop in, making note of the names in the pile, and they begin directing me on what will happen next.

The ladies' voices flow to the hallway I'm standing in waiting for my cue. Jacob Jacobson talks to them, explaining how the ceremony will go, something he'll do before every elimination. As if anyone in this house will forget.

"And now, ladies, please welcome Parker." Jacob turns toward me and I move from my hiding spot.

A forced smile is on my face. My hair rests against my neck. With all the lights, cameras, and people in the room, I wish for what feels like the hundredth time I could put it up. I take my mark next to Jacob and put my hands behind my back.

"Hi, again, ladies," I say, and a few of them swoon. A little intense reaction for the situation, but I'm sure the cameras picked them up well. "I want you all to know this was a really hard decision and even if you get sent home tonight, it was a pleasure meeting you. I hope you are all able to find the flame of your desire, even if it's not me."

Production moves around us, signaling when we need to take a pause. Luckily, they seem to have what they need for this shot and we are ready to go.

A podium is brought out to me with a single lit candle on it.

"Ladies, if you don't receive a candle tonight, you will be eliminated," Jacob says, his smile perfectly in place like the sun is not about to crest the horizon outside. "Parker," he says, indicating I should start.

Anastasia stands in the crowd, holding the only lit candle. There seems to be a slight gap between her and the rest of the girls, and I feel bad for putting a target on her with my attention this evening.

I take the first candle from the basket next to me and light it from my candle. Staring out at the ladies, I take a breath.

"Carmen," I say, and the statuesque woman gives me a demure smile and comes to stand in front of me. Her caring nature intrigues me, and the thought of spending more time with her is exciting. The feel of the cameras on us pulls me from my thoughts. "Carmen, will you accept this spark of my desire?"

She smiles at me and it does something in my chest. "It'd be my pleasure," she says, taking the candle from my hand before returning to her spot in the lineup.

Grabbing another candle, I repeat the process of lighting it.

"Aisha," I call out. A woman with black hair cut to her chin steps out of the crowd. Her physique reminds me of a dedicated yoga instructor. "Aisha, will you accept this spark of my desire?" I ask once she's standing in front of me. Her smile is much smaller than Carmen's was. Shy, almost. But it's endearing.

"I'd love to," she whispers so quietly I barely hear it. My hand reaches out to offer her the lit candle, but production stops us.

"Wait! You need to speak up. Let's take it again from you asking her, Parker," the faceless guy from the wings says.

"Aisha, will you accept this spark of my desire?" I repeat, hoping my face doesn't show any annoyance from having to repeat myself.

"I'd love to," Aisha replies, this time loud enough to be heard. Production allows her to go back to her position in the group and I grab up another candle.

Woman after woman presents themselves to me and I ask each one if they would like to be the spark of my desire until, finally, I'm at the last candle. Before I can grab the candle, Jacob Jacobson steps up, as expected, and addresses the ladies once more.

"Parker, ladies, this is the last candle of the night." He melts back into the shadows and I grab the candle, lighting it.

"Mia," I say and the tall, blonde, California girl with beautiful hazel eyes walks forward. She comes up to my shoulders. Not short, but not tall. "Mia, will you accept the spark of my desire?"

"I'd like nothing more," she says before stepping forward. Instead of grabbing the candle, she grabs my face, pulling my lips down to hers.

The kiss is nice, if not a little aggressive. Taken aback, my eyes stay open and I am able to see the outrage on some of the other women. But it's the slight look of hurt on Anastasia's face that makes me pull back.

Clearing my throat, I hand her the candle without further comment. Jacob steps forward once more and brings the elimination ceremony to a close.

"Ladies, if you have not received a candle tonight, you will not be continuing on in the *House of Desire*. Please say your goodbyes."

All the women are broken from their stances they've held for the better part of an hour and start mingling. Mary Ella walks up to me, her arms outstretched for a hug, which I give her.

"This is going to be a fun season, I can already tell. Beware that some of them might be pretending, Parker. Presenting only the most perfect version of themselves in front of the cameras can be overwhelming as we know," she whispers into my ear. I give her a kiss on the cheek in thanks.

"It was great seeing you. When I get out of here, maybe we should organize a *House of Deceit* reunion."

"I'll text Charlie when I get home," she says, waving as she steps away. Production leads her through the house, but my attention is quickly grabbed by another woman.

Persephone's anger is written in every line of her face and body.

"Well, Parker. I'm glad you eliminated me because if you didn't I would have removed myself. I just don't think you'll be able to keep up with me. I require quite a lot from my paramours. Plus, you just seem so bland," she says, looking at her nails, a haughty smirk on her face.

I know she's lashing out from embarrassment. No one ever wants to go home on the first night, but that doesn't matter to my brain.

Brittany's voice comes back into my head, just like it did when I was speaking with Persephone earlier, and I don't regret sending her home, no matter how much of a catch she probably is.

"I'm glad it worked out the way you wanted it to, then." I stick my hands in my pockets, unsure of what I should do with them. She moves past me, shoving her shoulder into mine roughly and I smile at the childish display. Maybe she wasn't as much of a catch as I thought she was.

It's finally just the women I kept and me. For the final shot, everyone has a drink. Holding my glass in the air, I address them all.

"I can't wait to deepen my connections with all of you. Lucky doesn't even begin to describe how I feel about having the chance to get to know all of you amazing women. This is going to be the season they talk about for years to come. Here's to *House of Desire*." We all clink our glasses and the ladies cheer. Some take sips, others just stand there.

The second the cameras get their shot, a member of production bleeds from the shadows.

"Cut! Great job everyone," they say.

My assistant, Philip, magically appears at my elbow.

"Parker, your suite is in the pool house. I will take you there now. Ladies, if you'll follow Sam"—Philip indicates a man standing off to the side of the room—"he'll show you to your rooms."

The women begin shuffling around while I follow Philip out the back door. I wish I had a chance to talk to Anastasia more, but exhaustion slams into me like a linebacker and I can barely keep my eyes open. A hand at my elbow guides me around the pool, the first vestiges of dawn on the horizon.

"You won't have anything to film today, so sleep as long as you want because tomorrow, the real fun begins," Philip says. Words fail me, all my energy focused on putting one foot in front of the other, the air like molasses around me, making my movements sluggish.

He unlocks the pool house for me and flips on the lights. He tries to take me on a short tour but I ignore him, making a mental note to apologize for my rudeness later when I go straight down the only hallway to where the bedroom must reside. Kicking off my shoes, I flop down on the bed, asleep before my face hits the pillow.

CHAPTER EIGHT

ANYA

54 DAYS UNTIL PROPOSAL

ALL FOURTEEN OF US stand in a circle, dressed like we are about to go to war. My hair is tied into braided pigtails at Zoey's instance. The blue-haired girl is a force of nature when it comes to styling my hair, and sometimes it's easier to bend like a willow than stand firm against her gale force winds. Except when she tried to convince me over dessert to let her tattoo me.

There was no way I was giving into that request.

"Ladies, you have all drawn numbers. This will determine your opponent. One will play two, three will play four, and so on," Olivia says as she points to the whiteboard with the bracket taped to it, all of our names written down.

The twenty-eight-year-old fashion designer was bored and decided an elimination style ping pong tournament would be a great way to pass some time. All of us are thrilled except for Victoria, Meghan Markle's lookalike. When we are not doing individual diary style interviews, most of us enjoy the various available games. The attorney, however, has decided to be the referee and make sure all rules are followed despite it giving us uneven numbers since Amber was eliminated the other night.

"Numbers one and two, please step up to the table," Victoria instructs.

I walk up, picking my paddle up off the table. As number two, I am playing Jasmine, our resident wildlife photographer. Her face is flushed with excitement as she steps up to the table opposite me.

"You're going down, Anya!" she taunts. The first few days, I received some cold shoulders after being the recipient of Parker's attention that first night. Thankfully, being together all day and night warmed them to me quickly enough.

"We'll just have to see about that!"

We play a quick round of rock, paper, scissors to determine who serves first. Anticipating Jasmine is a paper first kind of girl, I throw scissors and win.

She sways back and forth like she's waiting for the opening serve at Wimbledon from Venus Williams. Not letting her get into my head, I knock the little white ball over the net and into the rectangle opposite me. She returns it and the ball spins away.

My mouth drops open while I stare at her. Her predatory smile lets me know exactly how much I underestimated this cat loving woman.

"Point," Victoria calls out.

"What the hell? Are you some sort of ping pong prodigy or something?" I ask Jasmine.

"No. But it was one of my brother's favorite things to play growing up. He didn't have anyone else to play against."

I just look at her.

She shrugs. "I got tired of losing."

Now that was something I understood. I always hated losing to Dominic. He was the worst. Not only was he a sore loser, he was a sore winner! If I won, he would whine and cry, but if *he* won? You'd think he cured cancer, solved world hunger, and reversed global warming. "I would have stopped playing with him."

"That wasn't an option. He did go to the Olympics one year and medaled so I like to say it's all because of me."

"You have got to be shitting me. I feel like I deserve a redo against someone else," I say, exasperated and ready to have my ass beat.

"No. No redos. You knew the rules when you agreed," Victoria says from her judge's chair.

Jasmine serves the ball right past me and I groan. Luckily, she decides not to toy with me, quickly racking up point after point. Saying she won removes the flavor of how badly I lost.

She decimated me.

The paddle clatters against the table as Victoria stands, drawing a line through my name and advancing Jasmine's. I slump down into the empty chair next to Zoey while Aisha and Emily get up to play the next game.

"Sorry you lost," Zoey says as the girls play their quick game of rock, paper, scissors.

"It's okay. I have a feeling a few more people are going to lose to her, too. It always feels better to lose to the one who wins the championship."

The door to the rec room opens and the butler, Sam, walks in carrying a silver platter with a dome on it. Aisha's return volley is completely ignored, Emily staring at the man.

"Excuse me, ladies. I have a card for Ms. Lucy Swan," he says, his free hand tucked behind his back as he offers the country singer the card.

Lucy stands from her chair squealing, rips open the card under the silver dome in the butler's hand, and clears her throat as we all gather around.

"Lucy, the night is singing its sweet song for us. Please pick five other women and get ready for our group date in one hour."

We all wait for who she's going to pick.

"Um. Let's see. Izzy, Emily, Mia, Leslie." She looks around at the rest of us. Weighing us all. "Anya."

The others who are picked squeal, while those who weren't grumble. Not only will they not get to see Parker, they'll be stuck at the house for the entire day. The butler produces another card for them as those of us picked run from the room to get ready.

I pull out the bands holding my hair and look at my disheveled appearance, nervous to see Parker again. Not sure what to do with the strands, I throw it up into a bun for the time being and make my way to the bathroom to shower. After a quick rinse, I rub my favorite lotion into my skin, making sure I smell of warm vanilla and tonka bean for the date.

The dressing room is awash in activity. Every woman has their own vanity with a lighted mirror as well as a closet and dresser. My face is dewy from my shower so I slather on various serums, trying to keep it that way. One benefit of Lorelei's friendship has been learning about fabulous products she recommends. In anticipation of the hot night, and not wanting to look like I'm melting, I apply minimalist makeup. A makeup artist friend of Lorelei's taught me how to highlight my eyes, cheeks, and lips in a way that makes it look as though I've put in a ton of effort without weighing down my face in layers.

"I'm going to put some texturizer in your hair. Lean into the waves the braids gave you," Zoey says as I finish lining my eyes.

"If you make me look stupid, I'll shave your head in your sleep," I warn.

"Please, like I've never had a shaved head before. And I rocked it, FYI."

The disembodied voice of a production member floats out of the house-wide speaker system, announcing we have ten minutes to be at the entrance of the mansion for our date. Izzy squeaks with stress as she tries to untangle her bracelet that has somehow attached itself to her curls. One of the other girls assists her, but she quickly slaps them away. They seem to be doing more harm than good, so I can't say I blame her.

Zoey deems my hair finished, and I move to the closet in my towel. I grab my white midi halter dress, espadrilles, and a few pieces of gold jewelry, aiming for the understated and sweet look.

"Olivia, can I borrow your black dress?" Lucy asks, grabbing the garment and holding it up to herself.

As a fashion designer, Olivia's clothes are perfectly tailored to her body. While they will fit others, you can tell they weren't made to do so. It also doesn't help Olivia has about four inches on Lucy.

"Sweetie, are you sure you don't want to wear something else?" Olivia asks. "That dress won't really hit you in a good spot. It's meant to be above the knee. And for bigger boobs." She whispers the last bit, but since I'm the only one close to her, I don't think anyone else hears.

"No, I think it's gorgeous! Plus, I hate everything I brought with me," Lucy says.

Shrugging, Olivia turns away and looks through her closet, planning her outfit for the group date for the other girls tomorrow. While production made it clear everyone will get a chance to see Parker each week, everyone wants to be on the first one. To be picked instead of left for the second date.

"Everyone to the entrance, please," the voice says over the speaker.

Everyone takes a final look and then moves to the front of the house. Only six of us are going on the date tonight, yet everyone is expected to come to the front of the house, with the ones left behind waving us away. It seems silly to me, but there's not much we can do about it.

Lucy climbs into the limo first while I say goodbye to Zoey.

There are a few camera people moving around us as we get into the limo, capturing the various angles as well as the other women being left behind.

"This isn't fair!" Victoria cries, stamping her foot. The cameras swing to her, focusing on her anger.

"Not everyone is going to go on every date. You knew that," Leslie says before she climbs into the limo.

"I should be going. He'll want to see me!" Tears start streaming down her face and I know this will be airing, their goal to create the most dramatic show possible.

I climb into the car, the reality I'm dating the same man as thirteen other people hitting me. I want to see Parker. The man is extremely attractive and seems very charming, but a part of me wonders how much is for the cameras and how much of it is *him*. So far, I've not seen or talked to him when cameras weren't around. Lorelei promised he's a great guy, and I trust her, but I think of Miles and how he seemed like a great guy. Kind and attentive.

Who's to say that the person I'm meeting is the person that any of us are deep down inside? With the cameras there, everyone is going to try to present their best selves, me included.

Taking care to smooth out my dress as I sit down so I'm not a wrinkled mess when we arrive at the date, I slide into the limo, taking the seat next to Lucy.

"What do you think we are doing?" Leslie asks the group, smoothing down her pin straight hair.

"The card was sent to Lucy and mentioned singing. We are going to do some sort of karaoke or something," I say.

The other girls explode into conversation.

"If we have to stand in front of people and sing, I might quit on the spot," Leslie says and I nod my head in agreement.

There are few things I would rather do less than sing on national television.

The limo door swings open, giving me a peek at Parker standing there with cameras all around him before Lucy's butt blocks my view while she climbs from the car.

Nerves hit me as it's my turn to exit, counting to five like production told us before we left the house, and I pray to anyone who can hear me I won't face plant again. Walking across the pavement, everyone stands and watches me. Parker's green eyes feel heavy on my skin, but it's a weight I enjoy, unlike the cameras.

"Hey, Anastasia," he says. The way his voice caresses the vowels and consonants makes me think of stolen moments and hidden desires.

"Hey, Parker," I say, trying to keep my voice even. I hope everyone thinks the blush I can feel coloring my cheeks is from the heat and not his attention. "You can call me Anya."

I may not know anything about the man, but he is definitely sexy as sin.

He offers me his arm, which I take despite knowing it will further separate me from the other girls. Except Zoey. She doesn't care if Parker shows interest in someone who isn't her. She's just here to 'meet a cool person, and see if we click.'

Before anyone else can take the opportunity, Emily grabs on to Parker's other arm as he turns me toward the building.

We all walk in, the cameras following our every moment, making sure to pick up on any last-minute reactions we might have. I try to make sure my face is showing serenity, but based on Dom's jokes when he caught me practicing facial expressions in the mirror before I left, I'm not sure it's working.

Inside the rather nondescript building, a red carpet is laid, leading us toward the people who presumably work here, waiting at the end.

The woman standing in the center of the group, dressed in an impeccably ironed suit, steps forward.

"Hello, Parker and ladies. Welcome to Born to be a Star, where everyone gets to pretend to be a musical star. We are so excited to have you." She motions to the men on either side of her. "We will be helping you this afternoon as you try your hand at being a rock star!"

Instructed to clap after the welcome by a member of production riding in the front of the limo, we do so now. Despite the clapping, I know we are all freaking out.

Except Lucy, our semi-professional singer.

I have done some embarrassing things in my time dating.

I've driven a date home because he didn't want to take an Uber after ignoring me the entire time to check scores on *ESPN* when I said I didn't want to talk about my favorite sexual position. I had helped a man catch his loose chicken instead of going to our dinner reservations.

Somehow, I ended up conned into taking a kitten home with me despite the fact Dom lived with me at the time and he was allergic.

I have even baked a last-minute cake for the birthday of one guy's mom, only to find out he had a girlfriend when she came with him to pick it up. He was so pale, I thought he was going to pass out.

But this will take the cake.

I'd think being on *House of Desire* would be the most embarrassing since it basically announces to the world I'm the worst type of single.

Desperate.

But no.

Singing in front of, minimally, ten strangers probably tops the list.

"Ladies, if you'll follow me," the woman says, leading us to the right while one of her assistants takes Parker to the left. Isabella waves goodbye to Parker, blowing him a kiss. He merely smiles at the gesture and as she turns from him, I see her face fall ever so slightly.

We are led down a short hallway and through a door labeled 'Costumes'. Once we are all inside and standing in the middle, two of the camera people direct their lens at us while one records the woman giving us instructions.

"Tonight will be a lot of fun and a chance for you all to showcase your talents. You may wear any of these costumes. They are separated by genre and then in order of size. Each genre has two outfits in every size from XS to 5XL. There are mirrors around the room, as you can see. There are lockers and changing rooms through that door," she says, pointing to the door on the left. "If anyone is musically inclined, we have a few instrument options, just let one of us know. I also have this for whichever one of you is Lucy?" She holds out an envelope with Lucy's name on the front. It looks exactly like the one Butler Sam brought to us in the game room.

Lucy snatches the envelope out of her hand, thanking her as she rips it open.

"*Ladies, it's time to show me the song of your soul. The winner of this event, as determined by a panel of judges and myself, will get to go on a solo date with me while the others go back to the mansion. Make sure to bring your best,*" Lucy reads.

I vaguely wonder if I'm allowed to sit out of the game or if Parker would be required to send me home. I don't want to go home. Not only because of the chance to show off my bakery during the hometown visits that air during week eight when the remaining four contestants will take Parker home to meet their families. But also because the initial spark I'm feeling for Parker might turn into a crush.

However, part of me knows this group date is more a waste of time than anything. Being forced to listen to me sing will be the quickest way to kill any spark Parker might be feeling toward me.

"You have ten minutes to get dressed, starting now!" says one of the workers of Born to be a Star.

Like a bomb went off in the room, we are all blown away to different areas, the camera people following us around as we go to look at the various costume offerings. Sucking it up, I move over to the rack of clothes with 'Folk' over them. The clothes are subdued earth tones and simple designs. I find my size on the rack and look at the two options available. Grabbing the russet red dress, I move toward the changing room door, my camera person abandoning me to change in peace.

Before I know it, we are standing in the wings of a theater. I am trying to convince my body that passing out is more embarrassing than singing in front of a crowd. It doesn't entirely believe me. My vision dances with little spots, but at least I'm remaining upright. For the time being.

People in the wings usher us out onto the stage with little care for the panic attack I'm actively having. When I turn to look at the audience, I almost have to sit down and put my head between my legs.

"Everyone, please welcome the ladies vying for Parker's heart! Lucy! Isabella! Emily! Anastasia! Leslie! And Mia!" the MC announces from the middle of the stage.

Easily two hundred people roar a welcome, the sweltering heat of a thousand suns raining down on me from the lights. Sitting in the fourth row with a table in front of them, are the judges who look very familiar.

And Parker.

Who dares to look calm as a cucumber.

I want to wring his neck until his eyes pop out of their sockets. The violent desire would shock me if I wasn't in such an intense state of fight or flight.

The host of the evening begins introducing the judges and I realize why they look familiar.

They are the judges of the ever-popular *Star Search* reality TV show that has singers audition for a chance to win a recording contract and to work with some of the biggest names in the industry. So not only am I about to embarrass myself, they are going to tell me exactly how bad of a singer I am.

A dream come true.

My nervous system understands there's nothing else to do and so, to protect myself, my brain shuts off.

CHAPTER NINE

PARKER

OTHER THAN LUCY, THE women all look to be in various states of distress at the activity for this date. But Anastasia, in particular, looks like she's having an out-of-body experience. All color has washed from her face and I'm almost afraid she's going to collapse. The desire to take her away from from all of this makes me antsy. But I know that's not an option.

The fact none of them have quit on me is truly astonishing. I would have walked away by now.

Granted, I never would have filled out the application to be a contestant in the first place, and yet, here we are.

The crowd cheers for my girls and the judges as the host of the show introduces everyone. I stand when my name is called and wave, wondering what would drive someone to want to come to an evening like this.

Karaoke is not my thing. There's something about the experience that has always put me off. I never intend to be critical, but the sound of an off-pitch note has always grated on my nerves. Brittany would purposefully sing off key in the car, knowing it drove me crazy, even though she was the star of our school's choir.

While I would rather hang out at the mansion and get to know all of these women, that's not an option when you're on *House of Desire*.

Everyone shuffles off the stage except for Mia, who will be singing first. The beautiful blonde is dressed in a rocker outfit. Tight, ripped, black jeans. Spiked heel boots with studs all over them. A black t-shirt is cut so low I can see the lace of her bright pink bra peeking over the neckline.

She steps up to the microphone. After a slight pause, music begins pumping over the speakers. Down low and pressed against the stage are three monitors with, I'm assuming, the lyrics of the song so she can see them no matter where she moves.

Her first notes are unsure and shaky, nerves coating her tone. But the crowd encourages her when she hits a high note and with a smile, she smashes out of her shell. My eyes follow her as she shimmies and shakes across the stage.

The final notes of the song play around the theater. I clap along with the crowd as the judges write down their notes.

"Mia, that was such a fun performance. You really had great energy," the judge, Lennon, says. Their long hair is dyed a neon pink that shines even in the dim room.

"I appreciate that," Mia says, her breathing heavy in the microphone after the intensity of her performance.

The bald judge, Hank, is next. "While a little pitchy in places, you did a great job. Going first on something like this is always hard. I applaud you for staying calm under pressure."

"Thank you," Mia says.

The third judge is a man named Steven that I know, despite not watching the show they judge, is a jerk to contestants. "Mia. That was possibly the worst performance I've seen. The audience was applauding so you'd get through it, not because it was good. If I were you, I would stick with whatever your career is."

Even from where I'm seated, I can see her chin tremble with the threatening tears. Boo's echo around the stadium and I want to hit him for making her listen to that diatribe.

"Mia, I loved your performance," I say in a controlled tone, pulling her tearful gaze to me. I smile at her and her lips tilt in response. "It can be hard to receive negative feedback, especially from someone who's never done what you just tried." I glare at Steven and he scowls at me. "Don't let those people tell you jack shit because I thought you were mesmerizing."

I don't care that my face is going to end up on magazines for calling out this asshole when this airs. I will always stand up for the women who are trusting me with their hearts.

She mumbles a thank you into the mic while swiping at a tear. The host comes back onto the stage, thanking her.

"Next up, we have Anastasia," the host announces and everyone claps politely.

Anastasia walks out in another red dress that goes down to the floor. Unlike the one from the first night, this one looks like she should be frolicking in a field but her wooden movements make it seem like she's walking in front of a firing squad, and knots start to form in my stomach on her behalf.

The opening notes start and I recognize the song immediately as one Charlie has listened to in the car. On repeat.

Her voice is husky and carries a warmth that makes you think of home and comfort. And love. She misses a note here or there, but I don't care. I'm enthralled, despite her standing on the stage like one of Medusa's statues. The song ebbs and flows, the lyrics about a woman telling her partner how undervalued and unloved she feels in their relationship. It's beautiful and haunting.

She holds the last note perfectly as the recorded band concludes the song. As if pulled by an invisible string, I stand from my chair and clap in awe. Anastasia's voice had a way of crawling into the cracks and crevices inside me, taking root despite the minor imperfections.

Steven goes first this time with his critique. "You were a little wooden in your stance, but you had a few moments where the song sounded good." His feedback is nicer than it was to Mia, but his words still set my teeth on edge.

Anastasia doesn't respond and I wonder if she heard a word from his mouth.

"That was beautiful. Your lower register is very strong," Lennon says.

"That's one of my favorite songs and you've done it a great service. Well done, Anastasia," the last judge, Hank, says.

I decide to keep my comments short. It's obvious that Anastasia is ready to be off the stage as quickly as possible.

"It was perfect. I loved it," I tell her, putting all the feeling her singing triggered into my voice. She gives me a small smile, the most acknowledgement she's given any of her critiques and she all but sprints off to the wings.

Lucy comes out with a guitar in a simple jeans and t-shirt and blows the entire crowd and judges away with her original song. Every note is pitch perfect. Every lyric is full of meaning. But for what she has in technical ability, I find it all missing any sort of passion.

The other girls have various successes with their performances and after what feels like hours, the show finally comes to a close.

The host comes out on the stage with all the women once more.

"Let's give the girls another round of applause for entertaining us today with their great performances," they say and the crow cheers. "Now, to announce the winner."

He slides his finger under the flap of the white envelope and pulls out the card.

"The winner of this special edition of *Star Search* and the solo date with Parker is Lucy!"

Hot air balloons surround the open field as I wait for Lucy to arrive. A camera is pointed in my face as one of the members of production asks me questions. There are appointments for confessionals later tonight where I'll have to go more in depth about my feelings for the various women, but these will be aired between the two dates on the episode, specifically.

"How do you feel the women did singing today?" he asks, looking down at the list of questions on his clipboard.

"I think they all did a fantastic job. That's something I could never do, so I commend all their bravery."

"You got in a bit of a tiff with Steven. How did it feel to hear him criticize the women?"

A shadow of the anger I felt listening to his critiques burns through me again.

"I was pissed. They didn't deserve to be talked to like that. They weren't there to try and participate on his show. Other than Lucy, most of them had probably never received a day of training in their lives and yet there they were, singing in front of all of us and doing a damn good job, and he was sitting there criticizing them for it. I don't care if he's the judge of a singing show. He didn't need to talk to them like that."

He makes a note on his paper while I try to rein in my protective instincts.

"How do you feel about your first solo date with Lucy?"

"I am really excited to get to know Lucy more and deepen our connection. This journey of getting to know these impressive women has been such a pleasure." The canned answer falls from my lips without input from my brain. I wonder how the audience doesn't get tired of these responses. I'm already tired of repeating them. And of lying. I'm sure Lucy is a wonderful woman, but the desire to get to know her further seems to be missing entirely.

But she won the judges' votes and now here we are.

"That's enough for now," he says. "She'll be here in five minutes. Take a moment to get ready. The ride will be about an hour."

He walks off while the cameras get set up around where I'll be waiting for Lucy to arrive so they can make sure to get all the appropriate angles.

"Parker, to your spot!" someone on the team calls out and I make sure to hit my mark they taped out of me. My left foot is on the tape as instructed.

The black SUV comes over the grassy hill before stopping. Lucy pushes the door open, stepping from the inside. Her dress is the burnt orange of the setting sun burning behind her. Thankfully, she's wearing cowboy boots so her heels don't sink down into the grass.

"You look lovely," I tell her as she nears. It's not a lie. She is lovely. But I'm not overly attracted to the woman, despite her beauty. Other than her incredible singing voice, she hasn't stood out to me.

"Thank you," she says, and I lean down to give her a hug. "You look great. But you always look great."

The rosy blush of her cheeks as she tries to keep herself from babbling is cute.

"Are you ready to go on an adventure today?" I ask.

She looks at the riot of color behind me and smiles. "I've always wanted to go in a hot air balloon."

"Let's go make your dreams come true."

Lucy threads her arm through mine, and I lead her to the balloon. The chevron pattern is done in the colors of the rainbow and glowing beautifully.

The operator steps up to us as we get closer, reaching his hand out to introduce himself, first to Lucy and then me.

"Hi, folks. My name is Jim. I'll be handling your flight tonight. We don't want to waste any time, so if you're ready, we'll go ahead and get started."

He opens the door on the basket and holds a hand out to Lucy. Once we are all settled in, his assistant goes around and unties us from the stakes in the ground.

The roar of the fire above our heads is deafening. Lucy squeals and wraps her arms around my waist, the balloon beginning it's assent. Attached to the ropes leading up to the balloon are cameras, ready to catch every minute of our date.

"You have to see this," I tell her, awe in my voice.

She pulls back before spinning around in my arms, my hands settling on her slim hips and she gasps. "It's stunning," she says and I can hear tears in her voice at the sight of the sunset and the glowing balloons.

If this was a movie, I would be staring at her and say something like "It is," her thinking I'm talking of the view, but the audience knowing I'm talking about her. When she looked up at me, our eyes would lock and we'd be trapped in a passionate kiss soon after. But this isn't a movie, despite the circumstances of our situation. Luckily, Jim steps in before my silence can linger for too long and he begins pointing out different landmarks on the horizon.

Twenty minutes into our flight, I pull the champagne and glasses from the basket in the corner provided by production. I know they are probably tearing their hair out watching the live feed during, what I'm sure is, the most awkward date on the planet.

"How did you get into singing," I ask, picking an easy topic.

"My parents pushed me into the child beauty pageant circuit when I was three. When I won, they pushed me into even more. As a teenager, I had to pick a talent." Sympathy blooms for the younger Lucy and growing up being judged for everything about her. "It quickly grew from a love of singing to writing and composing my own songs."

"You have a beautiful singing voice. Do you have a record deal or anything?"

She snorts. "No, I don't. I've had a few over the years, but they dropped me, typically due to low sales. The industry is crazy difficult to get into."

"I met a record executive when she hired me to design and build her home. To say she was the most hardworking person I'd met at that point would be an understatement."

She looks at me, sharp eyes taking in my face. "What was her name?"

"I can't really tell you that. Discretion is part of our business."

Wheels turn behind her eyes and I watch her scrutinize me to determine if there's a chink in my armor she can exploit for this information and it makes me think of Mary Ella's warning about how not everyone is here for me. She must sense I'm not going to be backing down.

"I wouldn't want to make you compromise your morals. That's one of the things I like about you."

Her hand is warm on my forearm, but it doesn't feel as natural this time. Not wanting to shake her off, but needing the contact to end, I busy my hands with tying my hair back out of my face.

"Lucy," I start, "you're a great woman. Anyone would be so lucky to call you theirs."

"But you don't want to, right?" She looks up at me with a mixture of understanding and disappointment.

"I just don't think this would really work out. For either of us. I'm sorry."

She sniffles with unshed tears, blinking rapidly trying to keep her emotions at bay.

"It's okay. If you don't feel it, you don't feel it. I think I could have loved you, with time, but I'd rather know now than get to the end and be sent home."

Tension drains from my body. The part of this process I hate the most is letting these women go. While I know they signed up for this knowing there was a good probability they would be eliminated, I don't want to hurt anyone.

"Friends?" I ask, holding my arms open for a hug.

She scoffs, rolling her eyes, and jumps out of the basket the moment Jim opens the door.

"What would even be the point?"

My arms fall to my sides in shock at the abrupt change in tone and wonder how much of her personality I enjoyed was for the cameras. And how much was really *her*.

"I think, maybe, you dodged a bullet there, son," Jim mumbles and I can't help but agree.

CHAPTER TEN

ANYA

49 DAYS UNTIL PROPOSAL

"Marco!" Maya calls out, her eyes closed.

"Polo!" we all chorus back to her.

She spins in a circle toward Carmen's voice that is closest to her. The stunning woman everyone treats like she's personally trying to cure childhood cancer by working at a children's hospital, tries to move slowly to avoid making noise. Maya lunges and Carmen squeals before slipping away in a flurry of waves. Maya tries to follow her, but she's slightly disoriented with the echoes of the rest of us laughing and misses Carmen entirely.

"Marco," she calls out again when she realizes her prey has slunk away to safer waters.

"Polo!"

"I don't think I've played Marco Polo in about ten years. I forgot how much fun it is," Zoey whispers, trying not to call Maya's attention to us.

"I would have played almost anything today. I was getting really bored. I didn't think about all the downtime included in this show," I say.

Looking over at her, I notice a tendril of her blue hair has escaped her bun. Reaching over, I tuck it back up for her so it doesn't dip into the chlorinated water. Dyed mere days before we came to the mansion, she doesn't want it to fade too quickly since she'll be unable to touch it up and that means avoiding the harsh chemicals in the pool. She considered asking for a swim cap on the first day but discarded the idea, sure they would include the footage in the show.

"I did and it was still what I expected. Did you hear about Olivia and Victoria's fight the other day?"

"Which one?" I ask. While I have no desire to be a part of any drama, with no access to television, I'm desperate for entertainment. There are only so many games we can play.

She snorts as we move away from Maya, skirting around the edge of the pool. "Apparently little Miss Lawyer Barbie Victoria was screaming about Olivia breaking her four-hundred-dollar hair straightener and how she was going to take her to small claims court if she didn't pay for it."

"Why would a hair straightener cost four hundred dollars? What does it do one costing less than a hundred dollars doesn't? It'd better give me a scalp massage at that price point," I say.

"Fuck if I know, but Olivia ended up sitting on the floor crying about how she can't be taken to court."

"Did someone tell her the likelihood Victoria will actually sue her is extremely low?"

"Once they could get her to uncurl from the ball she'd rolled up into, yes."

"Boredom and this many different personalities isn't exactly a great mix."

"Maybe not, but it's definitely entertaining. For those of us staying out of the drama, that is." She lifts her hand out of the water for me to high-five as Maya finally catches someone, ending her turn as Marco.

"Oh my God!" Leslie squeals from her sun chair as Sam the Butler comes out with his usual silver domed tray.

"Pardon the interruption ladies, but some of your presences have been requested by Mr. Parker this evening." His white glove clad hand grips the dome, pulling it off with a smooth, practiced grace.

Leslie rushes over, the gold bangles on her arms tinkling as she grabs the white envelope from the tray and rips it open.

"*Gorgeous ladies. I have been able to think about nothing other than seeing you all again. Will Anastasia, Carmen, Zoey, Leslie, and Maya please join me today? Your taste buds will never be the same,*" Leslie reads out.

"Looks like you and I are competing against each other today," I say, grinning to my friend.

"As if I'd ever consider you competition," she jokes as we lift ourselves from the pool.

The kitchen at the culinary school we are taken to is cold and clinical feeling compared to mine. Everything is perfect and pristine. There is no chip on the corner of the workbench from it being dropped when the installers were bringing it in. There are no stains from dye incidents. Everything matches. And everything is white or stainless steel.

"Ladies, today you will have one hour to create a home cooked meal for Parker. Whomever creates the best one will be the winner of a solo date," Jacob Jacobson says, from the monitor on the wall.

We haven't seen Jacob in person since the first night. Since Lucy was sent home after their solo date, the elimination was just a time for us all to hang out. My guess is most of these messages were recorded beforehand since he's dressed in the same suit in them and eliminations are the only time he's live.

"Parker, do you wish to say anything to the ladies before they begin?"

He stands before us in tight jeans and a black t-shirt, leaving his bulging biceps on display. His black boots are scuffed and well-worn while his wrists are littered with leather bands and simple beaded bracelets. There is one simple, metal ring around his middle finger. His blond hair is wavy and kind of a mess but he looks perfect.

The desire to snuggle into his broad chest is strong. But so is the desire to lick his neck.

Luckily, I have enough self-control to keep myself from doing both of those things.

But only just.

Two of the camera people move around, recording us and Parker from different vantage points. I keep my eyes glued to him, having been yelled at not to look in the camera one time too many.

"Ladies, I'm not terribly picky. All I ask is there is no cilantro. It tastes like soap and I will die on this hill," he says, and I laugh.

Dominic has been telling me the exact same thing his entire life. I don't agree, but I've gotten so used to cooking any meal without it, that it's not something I have in any of my kitchens.

"On your marks. Get set," Jacob says, pausing for dramatic effect. I hate to say it works, but my heart rate picks up noticeably as I feel like I'm standing on the starting line of a hundred-meter sprint. "Go!"

We're off. Everyone scrambles around the kitchen, grabbing various ingredients and kitchen tools. While baking is my passion, cooking is a little different. Baking tends to be more precise than cooking. With cooking, a little extra of something can typically be dealt with while still having an edible result at the end. In baking, a result can be different because of something as simple as weighing your ingredients versus scooping them.

One of my favorite meals to make for Dominic whenever we want something comforting, delicious, and easy is a creamy sausage tortellini dish.

Making my way over to the ingredient area, I mentally run through the recipe. Heavy cream, tomato paste, sausage, various spices, and cheese filled tortellini. Normally, I would make the tortellini by hand, but with only an hour, I just don't have time.

Production provided us baskets, but they are off to the side of the ingredient station and unnoticed by the majority of the women. I snatch one up, not wanting to make multiple trips, and begin shopping. The basket is heavy on my arm as I make my way to my cooking station.

Carmen is in the station next to me and already measuring things into a bowl, her perfectly chic outfit covered by an apron. After winning a one-on-one date with Parker during a group date a few days ago, she came home talking about how good of a kisser he is, I've been annoyed by her.

Her hair is too perfect.

Her face is too beautiful.

Her voice is too captivating.

In every way I can see, she's perfect, and all I want to do is fake trip and spill a glass of wine down the front of her dress.

What's even worse is Parker's eyes are glued to her movements.

Pushing my childish thoughts from my mind, and ignoring the stunning man with his sharp eyes, I put on my apron and get to work. This is a recipe I don't need a card for. It's also one where precision isn't required and things can, generally, be measured using my eye. After watching my mother make this dish all throughout our childhood, I know if I have the mixture correct based on the color of the sauce.

Once I have all the ingredients ready, twelve minutes have disappeared from the clock. A bead of sweat runs down the side of my face from both the heat of the stoves and ovens as well as the stress of the competition and wanting a chance to spend more solo time with Parker since night one.

I want to get to know the man Lore thought would make a good match for me.

My deep skillet sits on the stove warming over medium heat with a drizzle of oil, waiting for me to add the sliced sausage. As the meat cooks, I look at the other ladies.

Carmen is cool and collected as expected. On her other side, Zoey is a tornado of movement. I can't tell from here what she's making, but there's a particular scent of burning coming from her pan as she turns the dial on the stovetop. On my other side, Leslie stirs at something in a pot. From what I can gather, it seems as if she's making a soup of some sort.

On Leslie's other side is Maya who, much like Zoey, is a blur of motion. But where Zoey feels chaotic, Maya feels like a performer hitting their mark, moving like the dancer she is.

Minutes tick by as we all finish making our dishes. As I finish spooning mine into the bowl, Jacob Jacobson comes onto the screen to announce our time has run out.

"Contestant number one, please present your dish to Parker," Jacob says before the screen goes black once more.

Zoey picks up her plate, and carries it over to him with a grimace on her face. She sets the plate in front of Parker.

"Well, I tried to make fried chicken, but I don't know if the oil was too hot or what. It shouldn't be black." She rubs at her forehead and I feel a little sorry for her.

"It looks great, Zoey. Thank you for making this for me," Parker says with a gentle smile and a touch of her hand. His tenderness melts my insides and I try not to turn into a pile of goo on the floor.

Parker's face shows nothing but enjoyment as he eats the overcooked chicken, soupy mashed potatoes, and soggy roasted broccoli. For each item, he finds something to compliment, and I melt even more at his treatment of my friend.

The chicken was moist.

The potatoes were well seasoned.

The broccoli had good flavor.

Despite knowing her food was lackluster, Zoey beams at him as he thanked her again for her effort.

The TV turns back on and Jacob calls for contestant number two, Carmen. She strides across the floor, not a hair out of place despite all the activity for the last hour.

"Darling, I made you my favorite things since I've moved to this country. A steak with honey sriracha Brussels sprouts."

Her accent grates on my nerves as he tells her Brussels sprouts are his favorite vegetable now. Apparently, he hated them as a child with the passion of a thousand suns. Which seems completely reasonable to me.

As he compliments her on how amazing her food is, I wonder if I should have subverted expectations and done a dessert instead of a meal.

Desserts for me are a love language.

But, despite them being my living, they aren't all I am. And that's what I was trying to show with this dinner. Maya presents her dish as I continue to berate myself for not sticking to my strengths, but when my number is called, I let it go, unable to change the choice I made.

I walk over, and stare down at the simple bowl, letting my hair fall in my face.

"This is my mom's famous one skillet tortellini dish. She makes it in the fall when all you want is comfort food," I tell him, but keep my eyes down on the bowl I place it in front of him.

I can't look at him when I share this meal with him. What if he doesn't like it as much as my family does? Or what if it's not fancy enough? I should have baked for him.

His large hand reaches out, but instead of grasping the bowl, his fingers barely grip my chin, raising it, forcing me to look at him.

He lets go, tucking one side of my hair behind my ear, his fingertips gently brushing my neck as he pulls back.

"Please don't hide from me," he whispers so no one can overhear us. But we are wearing microphones so no matter how private of a moment we might be having, I know it's being recorded.

"Parker, you need to speak up," a member of production instructs, but he ignores them.

"Sorry," I say, a little embarrassed.

"I'm surprised you didn't bake for me," he says louder, trying to lighten the mood.

"I considered it, but I figure if you want to taste my baking, you'll have to keep me here until the hometown dates."

"Will you teach me to bake something if I do?"

"Yes."

"Promise?"

"I promise."

He nods and then grabs the fork, stabbing a few of the tortellini as well as a slice of sausage. Plopping the bite in his mouth, he hums as he chews and my face heats in pleasure.

"This is amazing. It reminds me so much of something my mom would make. The slight spice is really nice," he says, taking another bite.

He's only taken one bite of the other girl's dishes so far, so I can feel myself preening under the compliment.

"That's my brother's and my favorite meal."

"I can see why. Okay," he says, setting the fork in the bowl and pushing it toward me, "you need to take this away from me. Thank you for cooking for me. And I'll be holding you to your promise."

I grab up the dish and float across the room back to my station as Leslie goes last.

My mind races a mile a minute at the implications that if he expects to hold me to my promise, he intends to keep me until the hometown dates at least. Despite my desire to show off my bakery, my first thought is of getting to spend more time with Parker.

Metal chair legs screech across the floor as Parker pushes back and stands, shocking me out of my thoughts. Suddenly, I want nothing more than to run from this room and not hear his judgment. But my obligation to the show keeps my feet rooted in the spot like an aged oak tree.

"Thank you all again for such lovely meals. I know cooking for another person, especially a food that holds sentimental value to you, is a precious gift. Carmen, the technicality of your dish won me over. Will you do me the honor of going on a date with me?"

Hope sours into hurt and I have to quickly avert my tear pricked eyes. For the first time during this entire endeavor, I realize that I am not the only person vying for Parker's attention.

And how much I want that attention for myself.

"I'd love to," Carmen tells him and at his smile, I die.

CHAPTER ELEVEN

PARKER

"DID YOU GET ENOUGH to eat?" Philip asks, rolling a lint roller down my arm. I want to protest, but I know it's easier to let him do his job. The black car turns on a gravel driveway that turns into a paved driveway the closer we get to the winery.

"I did, thank you."

While the audience is told we go straight from the group date to the solo date, that's not actually the case. We are always given an hour or two to get showered and changed before we are expected at the next event. If the date is going to include eating, they also give us time to eat beforehand as well.

We park and the van with the camera equipment and two different camera people pulls up beside us. They are out of the van and grabbing up their cameras before the driver can open my door.

One immediately begins to get setting shots while the other gets ready for Carmen's arrival. Philip tells me what we will be doing. Everyone but the camera people clear out as the car pulls up. The door opens and my palms begin sweating.

Carmen is smart and beautiful. And intimidating.

A part of me wishes I had chosen Anastasia's meal. But Carmen's was just as good. And my attraction to her is just as strong.

It was like flipping a coin on who to pick.

"You look gorgeous," I say as she makes her way to me. Her dress is a deep plum with strappy gold high heels that make her legs look a mile long. She looks as if she was going on a sultry date to a Michelin star restaurant.

"Thank you. You look wonderful."

I'm in a soft pink button-down and light khakis with loafers. I look like a member of a golf club. Carmen mentioned liking preppy looking men on our first solo date. But I feel like I'm wearing a costume.

Her arms slide around my neck as she gets close. My hands automatically go around her and pull her body against mine. Soft lips press against mine. The kiss is nice, but the cameras being present keep me from deepening it. I pull back and give her a smile so as not to hurt her feelings.

"Hi," I say.

"Hello. Thanks for picking me." Her voice is coy.

"I'm glad we can spend more time together."

Our first date was a little awkward, as all first dates are, but by the end it felt nice and relaxed. The heat of her body is replaced by the cool air around us when she retreats.

"Tonight we are going on a short tour of this beautiful, family-owned vineyard and then our host, Amelia, is going to let us do a tasting. Sound good?" A rhetorical question, since it's not like production would allow us to abandon the date if we didn't want to do it.

"Sounds perfect," Carmen says, demurely. "I love wine."

"Me too. My best friend introduced me to it and I've been hooked ever since."

We all turn and walk into the winery. Amelia is small but well honed for work. Like a sharpened sickle.

"Welcome to Grape Expectations. You are going to regret those shoes," she says to Carmen who just laughs.

"Don't worry, I'm a professional walking in them."

"Sounds good. Let's get started."

We traipse all around the winery. From the pressing room, the storehouse, and the bottling area. All in all, we probably walk around for about an hour and a half while Amelia talks. The part that's surprising is Carmen's engrossment in everything Amelia says. When she's thinking of a question, she will crinkle her nose and with each crinkle, my interest in her deepens.

"This will be our last stop and then we will head to the tasting room. You can't use your lighting equipment to record as it can damage the wine." Amelia directs the last piece to our camera person, who simply nods and stops to take care of whatever adjustments they need to do. "Meet us down there."

Amelia turns and begins going down the stairs, Carmen behind her, and I bring up the rear.

"This is our rare bottle room. I think you'll enjoy some of the history in here," she says as she keys in a code to a locked door at the bottom of the stairs.

Carmen smiles up at me.

"You're so beautiful," I tell her. Her face softens and I bend down, pressing my lips against hers in a silent kiss. A kiss that's just for us.

No cameras.

No audience.

No production.

We separate, but Carmen links our fingers and we make our way into the rare bottle room, the spark of attraction burning even brighter inside my chest. For twenty minutes, I watch Carmen and Amelia discuss the various wines in the room. And then finally, our tour is done.

Despite her shoes and Amelia's concern, Carmen doesn't show an ounce of pain as we are led back up the stairs and into the tasting room. Soft music plays through the room.

"We have six beautiful wines for you all to taste today," she says over her shoulder.

"I don't think I'll ever need to know how the grapes are grown and harvested for wine again, but it does give you a new appreciation, doesn't it?" Carmen asks me.

"I'll almost feel bad when I drink a glass now, thinking of all the work put into creating every ounce I drink."

She nods as I pull a seat out from the bar while Amelia pulls down glasses and bottles. Music plays gently in the background while Amelia tells us about our first wine.

Carmen moans at the first sip, the sound drawing all of my attention to her mouth.

"That's sinfully decadent," she says, crossing her legs, her dress hiking up her thigh. My mouth waters at the display. "Try it."

I raise my glass and take a sip, humming in approval. "It's very good."

If someone asked me right now what this wine tasted like, I'd be unable to name a single note.

"The last time I was in France, I went to the Champagne region and toured with some girlfriends. It was beautiful. Maybe we should take a trip and visit the winemaking regions," she suggests. "Do you like to travel?"

"I never really had the opportunity growing up and now, if I travel, it's more to go visit my family."

"Family is so important. That's something I learned early on." Her voice holds a note of sadness. She busies herself listening to Amelia's explanation of the second wine.

"Did you learn that while your friend was sick?" I ask. While she mentioned the loss the first night on the show, we haven't talked about it since.

"His name was Logan and he was only three months younger than me. One of his parents was always at the hospital. My parents took me after school every day, and on the weekends I basically there with him. Our families were friends. We traveled together over the summers. Went to the same parties. He was my brother, for all intents and purposes. And I lost him at thirteen."

My heart breaks for her loss and the pain I can see written in the lines of her face. It doesn't matter it's been more than a decade. She can feel the loss just as acutely now. I take her hand in support and she laces our fingers together.

"I'm so sorry. I can only imagine how hard that was. And that's when you decided to become a nurse?"

A small blush colors her cheeks.

"That didn't come until a bit later. My family wanted me to become a doctor. I come from a long line of doctors. Neurosurgeons. Trauma surgeons. If it's a surgery specialty, someone in my family specializes in it. It was always assumed I'd join the family business, so to speak."

"Wow, that's impressive," I say. "When did you decide to become a nurse, then?"

I feel bad for grilling her about her background, but the more I learn about this woman, the more interested I am, and the more questions I have.

"I was an intern and one day we were doing rounds. And there was this kid having blood drawn. The nurse was telling him a joke to distract him. Logan was afraid of needles and needed to be distracted, too. And it just reminded me of how much time the nurses spent with Logan. How they'd bring him things to play with. They always spent the most time with us and I realized what I wanted to do. I switched tracks that day."

"That was brave of you to make that change." The music catches my attention, one of my favorite slow songs. "Will you dance with me?" I ask Carmen, standing and setting my wine glass down on the bar so I can hold my hand out in invitation. Her smile is bright.

"I'd love to." Her hand is soft in mine. She stands and I lead her to an open spot on the floor, pulling her into my arms.

"I'm going to admit, you've snuck up on me," I say as we sway to the music.

"Snuck up on you, how?"

"I didn't really think I was going to end up having a crush on someone here." Everything I learn about Carmen makes me feel more and more drawn to her. Anastasia's honey brown eyes and smile flash through my mind as Carmen's fingers play with the ends of my hair and I want her to run her fingers through it, but she restrains herself.

"Parker, are you telling me you have a crush on me?" she teases.

"That's exactly what I'm telling you." This time, I don't care about the cameras. I press a kiss to her lips, keeping it relatively chaste. Her lips are pillow soft and I know, with time, I could become addicted to them.

We part. One of the members of production has been sitting off in a secluded corner and comes over to let us know our time together and out of the house is over. And I remind myself this is a show and at the end, I'm going to have to pick only one person.

CHAPTER TWELVE

43 DAYS UNTIL PROPOSAL

C UT OFF AT THE shoulders in the short mirror, I try to tie the
tie on the suit I was instructed to wear today. The wardrobe
team allows me to be myself when it comes to clothes, for the most
part, but sometimes, I have to dress according to the date we are
going on.

"We will get to the field at eleven for the group date. The ladies
will show up at 11:05. You will have six minutes to greet everyone.
The girls will go off and get dressed for about twenty minutes and
then we will begin the date!

"After that, you and the winner of the competition will get
cleaned up and you will have a date with her. We will provide you
a light snack. You'll have, at max, two hours and thirty minutes with

her. Like always, you can end the date whenever you'd like. You're also allowed to eliminate her if you feel the need to do so at the end of the solo date.

"It tends to be very dramatic when it happens and the audience will love it when they see it happen to Lucy," Philip says, ticking things off his list as I try to tie my tie while partially squatting.

"Got it," I tell him simply, annoyed they'd think I would do anything just for ratings.

Once my tie is tied, I put my hair up into a low bun, the bane of the hairdresser's existence. She offers to style it for me every day, promising to not make it look too done, but I just know it won't feel like me, no matter what she does.

When it's time, and to avoid seeing the girls before the date, Philip leads me through a back door to a gate in the fence, hidden by a faux wall production created. My car is waiting for me.

Inside the car are various cameras strapped to the backs of the front seats so I can film my thoughts before or after the dates, should the mood strike. Sometimes, they give me scripted things to say so they can cut them in where needed.

"Good morning, Parker. How are you?" the production assistant assigned to ride with me today asks, her Boston accent thick.

"I'm good, thanks. How are you?"

Luckily, she always gives me the *Reader's Digest* version of her day before lapsing into silence. There are few things I dislike more than feeling like I have to fill the air with words. There is enough pressure on me to keep up the conversation during dates, the last thing I want to do is ride in the car with a constant diatribe.

We pull up in front of a local college's football stadium and I wonder what they will be doing today. Without waiting for the driver to open the door, I get out of the car. It disappears the second the door slams and I make my way to my blue mark at the end of a red carpet.

Almost every date I've been on has involved a red carpet for the ladies to walk down. I think it's incredibly cheesy, and probably a little bit of a pain for whomever has to deal with it, but I know there's no point in my objecting. The show is going to do what it's going to do. The thoughts of the leading man certainly don't matter to them.

At exactly 11:05, the limo carrying Victoria, Anastasia, Mia, and Aisha pulls up. Anastasia is the first from the car, her long black hair swinging freely. Her smile is perfect, and pulls one onto my face every time.

I find no matter who's in the room with me, if Anastasia is there, all I want to do is look at her. And talk to her. But the conversation with Carmen was so easy and flowed on our one-on-one date the other day, I was shocked when the date ended and I realized I had barely thought of Anastasia. Her perfume envelopes me moments before her arms do, pushing all thoughts of Carmen from my brain.

"Fancy seeing you here," I tell her as I take a deep breath in, hoping we'll be able to go on a truly solo date soon.

"Are you stalking me? You're being really obvious about it. Stalking, by its nature, is a more low-key endeavor," she jokes with a smile I want to kiss.

"Maybe I want you to know I'm stalking you, otherwise where's the fun?" I say with a wink.

"I think staying hidden *is* the fun. But I wouldn't know. You're the professional here."

I kiss her cheek before reluctantly pulling out of her embrace, the other girls waiting for their turn to say hi.

"I didn't know I was going to have a performance review today, but I'll take the critique under advisement for the second half of the show." I can hardly believe we are already three weeks into the filming schedule after Jasmine being sent home at the elimination last night. It feels like it's gone so much faster than when I was in *House of Deceit*.

Then again, on *House of Deceit*, a week was actually a week. Here, we are filming a "week" of the show every five days. The blistering pace makes it seem like more time is passing than it is.

Victoria all but elbows Anastasia out of the way as she goes to hug me. Her perfume almost gives me a cavity. It's too sweet.

"Hello, sexy. You look so good, I want to climb you like a tree," she whispers before taking my earlobe between her teeth.

I jerk back from her. Her expression is a little annoyed before settling into something, I believe, she intends to be sexy but makes it look like she has gas.

"You look good enough to eat. I got carried away," Victoria says.

Anastasia shifts and it catches my eye over Victoria's shoulder. Her expression has darkened, and she looks about ready to attack. Unsure if she's feeding off my discomfort at the situation, or if jealousy is starting to get the better of her, I move on to the other two girls before anything can happen.

"Hi Mia. Aisha. Thank you both for coming," I say as I hug both ladies. It feels off to hug them, a lack of connection becoming harder and harder to fight as I'm required to keep people around so the show is longer than a few weeks.

"You didn't thank me," Victoria says, batting her eyelashes. I can tell it's meant to be funny, but the edge to her tone hints maybe it's not.

"Maybe he was too shocked at the fact you were sucking on his ear like a poorly aimed vampire," Anastasia says, sarcasm dripping.

My jaw wants to drop at the unexpected biting remark while the caveman inside me glows at the show of jealousy. But Victoria's back tenses and I can feel the moment starting to devolve.

"Why don't you shut up? I was having a moment with my boyfriend," Victoria seethes.

"Your boyfriend? You mean the guy who probably wouldn't recognize you if he passed you on the street for all the time you've spent with him?"

"Woah, now. My memory isn't that bad," I joke, trying to defuse the tension while sliding myself a little closer to both women, prepared to intervene, but neither of them hear me.

"Don't think I didn't notice how you threw yourself on him when you got out of the limo. Desperate much?" Victoria cocks an eyebrow at Anya, crossing her arms over her chest.

One of the camera people moves, and I see how it catches Anastasia's attention. Her entire body language changes. The annoyance melts from her face in a split second.

"Whatever you say, Victoria," she says, backing down and trying to blend back into the group.

Wanting to drag the attention away from her, I step in.

"We are probably behind schedule now. Maybe we should get back to it?"

Production steps in, ushering the ladies into the changing room. I'm taken to the sideline where I'm given a stopwatch, whistle, and a clipboard.

"What are they going to be doing? For the competition?"

"The pacer test," Philip says.

"The pacer test? Like from fifth grade where they have to make it from one line to the other before the beep?"

"Yup!"

"What does that have to do with finding love?" I ask, trying to give him back all the things he just gave me.

I also want to ask why I needed to wear a suit for this, but I just let it go.

"They want to show the lengths the women will go to for your attention," he says, like he's talking to a particularly slow person.

"By making them run?" Rolling my eyes, I put the whistle over my head before shoving the other two items back into his hands. "I'm not holding these."

"Fine. Get on your mark, please. In the middle of the field." He hands me a card. "You're going to be reading this."

I do as he tells me. The sun is heating me up, and I'm wondering why we can't have a normal type of date. With the sound of an air horn rending the air in two, the women come running out from the tunnel and everyone is dressed in white. Which is weird. Until they get closer to me. Wedding dresses. All four of them are in wedding dresses.

And without warning, I'm back to watching Brittany walk down the aisle toward me in her grandmother's vintage wedding dress. She looked so happy and I loved her so much, but it didn't keep my heart from racing. My hand unconsciously rubs my sternum, trying to calm my body down, but it's not working. After months of sessions, I admitted to Sharon this would happen every once in a blue moon. She suggested putting an ice pack directly on my chest, calming my nerves down and giving my brain something to focus on when it was more intense. But I don't really think saying "Hey, I'm mid-panic attack. Can I get some ice?" would be very effective.

"Hi, ladies. In today's challenge for a one-on-one date and a chance to fan the flames of our desire, you will be running a pacer test. This sound"—I pause until the loud, high-pitched tone sounds around the stadium—"will tell you to go. You will run ten yards. For everyone who hasn't crossed the line before the sound emits again, you'll be eliminated. The pauses between beats will get shorter and shorter until, finally, one of you is the winner. Any questions?" It all comes out stilted and monotone as I just try to hold on and get through this circus.

They all tell me no, or so I assume as their voices are just indistinct sounds at this point. Anya pauses for a second, her eyes searching my face as I fight to breathe. Her eyebrows slant over her eyes.

"Are you okay?" she mouths and I nod minutely. She stands there for a second more and all I can do is hope she moves to the competition.

The last thing I want to do is call production's attention to me. Thankfully, she turns and moves to the line with the other girls. With the first tone, they are off.

They run back and forth. Back and forth. My heartbeat steadies as woman after woman end up on the sidelines waiting for the competition to end.

By the time Anya is crowned the winner, her face is red and sweaty, but the smile she gives me banishes the last of the panic and a fluttering of excitement takes its place.

The art museum is metal and too modern outside for the warmth and beauty of the art inside. Anastasia moves around the room, looking at various paintings. Some she merely gives a glance, but others she'll stand at for longer. We stood at one called *The Whispering Forest* for almost half an hour. The forest gave off an enchanted feeling but with a hidden undercurrent of danger. Like there might be monsters and it would depend on the person venturing into the depths of the trees on if they were dangerous.

But I don't mind. I'm just happy she won us some much-needed alone time. Or as alone as we can be during filming a show like this. Production is giving us space, filming from further back. But the mics mean it's just a facade.

"Do you like art?" she asks, moving onto a picture showing a scene from an 1800s picnic.

"I like art, but I don't really come to museums or anything. I couldn't tell you about influences or brush strokes or color composition. Just if I like it or not."

"Sometimes I think it's better to enjoy things than critique them." She takes in a painting, but all I can do is take in her.

"Do you go to museums often?" I ask.

"No. I don't have a lot of free time. The bakery takes up pretty much every minute."

"Is it everything you want it to be?"

She doesn't look at me, but I can see the edge of a smile.

"Yes and no. It's the hardest thing I've ever done. So many people say 'Do what you love and you'll never work a day' but every day I've worked doing this has been the hardest I've worked in my entire life. And some days, having to create on a deadline and to someone else's vision can suck the fun out of it for me. But to follow a dream? I wouldn't give it up for anything."

"That's how I feel about my company, too. It's nice to have someone understand the demands of being a business owner."

"What do you think they are talking about?" she says, indicating the painting we are standing next to.

"Oh, that's easy. This guy here"—I point to the painting, playing along—"the one in the top hat? He's telling her about dirigibles and how they are going to change the way people travel."

"Do you think that's why she's rolling her eyes?"

"Oh, absolutely." I move closer to the painting and clear my throat. Raising my voice an octave, I make up the painting's dialogue. "*Victor, I told you already, I'm part of the team that invented them.*"

Snickering, she moves closer. With a dropped voice, she joins in on the fun. "*But Martha, you don't understand. We would be able to fly thirty miles in an hour!*"

"*I wish you would fly thirty miles away from me and never come back. Maybe then my 'best friend' Sally can move in.*"

"*Well, I'm sure the stable boy would really miss me.*"

"*Scandal!*"

She giggles and the sound is perfect. I needed this. Despite the panic seeing the women in wedding dresses gave me earlier, this is easy. Simple. Pressure free, in spite of the cameras.

"Anastasia, I—"

"Anya, please. Anastasia makes me feel like I'm about to be grounded or something."

"Anya, I don't think I told you how beautiful you look tonight," I tell her. Her jeans and white t-shirt are casual, but they are perfectly tailored to her, keeping her from looking anything but put together. My hands twitch, wanting to run down her curves.

"You didn't, but I decided to forgive you and not hold your terrible manners against your parents."

"I'm sure they appreciate that."

"Can I ask you something? Something you might not want to answer?" she asks, nervous, but I know I'll tell her anything she wants to know.

"Yes, I'd still like you if you were a worm. I would make sure you had the best worm terrarium."

She snorts, a hand flying up to cover her face. "That wasn't going to be my question, but I think I can breathe easier knowing that."

"What's the question," I tell her, taking her hand and leading her to another painting.

"Do you want to talk about what was going on today?"

"What was going on today?"

"Parker, you had a panic attack. I've had them a few times in the past and I recognized the signs."

Not wanting to look at her, embarrassed she was so easily able to see what was happening, I try to decide how much I want to tell her. Fear gnaws at my stomach. Fear she'll leave. Fear she can see how broken I still am.

"It's no big deal."

Her heels click against the floor as we move from painting to painting in silence. It's not an awkward silence, but it is a heavy one. I can feel it pressing against me, tightening around me like ropes.

"There was this one time I was asked to enter a cake into a competition that had the ability to change my entire career. I had carte blanche to create anything I wanted. The prize was a quarter of a million dollars."

"What happened?" I ask, curious how this well put together woman could ever fail at such a competition.

"Every day, I would try to sit down and come up with a design and new flavor combination. Every day I would think 'Maybe tomorrow' and then, eventually, tomorrow was, well, *tomorrow* and I had no idea what to do. In a panic, I put together a cake that looked like a novice had done it. I couldn't get my hands to stop shaking.

"When they started the judging, and showed mine on the screen for the audience to be able to see, there were some snickers. And then a few people outright laughed. It got so loud in my head and I thought my lungs would never be able to draw in air again." She continues moving through the room until she's standing right in front of me and a sculpture titled *A Symphony of Dreams* that has two lovers entwined on a bed, but the man has wings.

The moment grows and I can almost feel Sharon's eyes boring into me telling me to take a chance and open up.

"The thought of my ex-wife and how things ended kind of blindsided me. And a part of me is scared it would happen again."

She nods, reading I don't want to go too much further into depth with the camera crew around us. I am counting down the minutes until I can get away from all the cameras.

"It's understandable some things would remind you of something so monumental in your life. Especially on this journey. I won't hold it against you, considering I made the choice to come here after a guy I had been flirting with all night at an event ended up having a girlfriend. I wouldn't say I was in the best head space to apply," she jokes. "I'm glad I'm here, though." She touches my hand before moving off to another painting and the ropes of pain and hurt and betrayal from Brittany's abandonment loosen around me just a little.

The fact she's not running away in the opposite direction is leeching the worry from me.

"I signed up after my therapist said something to me."

"You're in therapy?"

"Going on nine months," I tell her. One thing I decided when I finally took Charlie's advice and found Sharon was, I would never hide the fact I needed the help. "Don't worry, she'd give me a gold star."

"Do you have a little chart where you collect your therapy gold stars?"

Her quick wit and joking manner are quickly becoming my favorite things about Anya. Even when we are discussing something heavy, she has an ability to put me at ease.

"Right beside my bed."

"It's good to see your accomplishments daily."

"That's what I think, too." I grab her hand, interlocking our fingers. "You're very easy to talk to."

"I'm just trying to lure you into a false sense of security so you'll keep me around, the audience will fall in love with me, and I'll be the next lead on *House of Desire* so twenty men can fight for me."

"Sounds like I might need to learn how to fight, then."

Her eyes rake down my body and I heat under her gaze, the desire to kiss her almost taking over.

"You might want to get on that."

Pulling my shirt off over my head, part of me wishes I had kissed Anya before she got into her car. But there was something holding me back. It felt too soon, and the thought of messing things up with her makes my anxiety spike.

Flipping on the light, I begin to undo my belt as I move through the house.

"Hey, good lookin'," Victoria says from the bed, naked but for the sheet draped over her.

"How did you get in here?" I say, shocked, but trying to lock down my face, not giving her any reaction.

"I know you're feeling the connection between us and I didn't want to wait for the Desire Suite dates."

After her little ear biting event at the group date, I knew I would be eliminating Victoria this week. When the pacer test got down to Anya and her, I was very worried I'd have to spend the night on a date with Victoria. I move toward the front of the house and I hear her get off the bed.

"Parker! I love you!" she yells at me, annoyance tightening her tone.

I rip the door open, calling for anyone from production before turning back toward her, thankful she brought the sheet with her.

"How could you possibly love me? We've barely spent any time together! And most of the time wasn't even one-on-one." I move out of the house, with her following.

"What do you mean how could I love you? You're hot! And funny. And I know you love me, too. You don't want to tell everyone else for the show, but I know it's true."

"Victoria," I say, voice steady, as members of production start to come around us. And camera people. "I appreciate you have feelings for me, but unfortunately, those feelings just aren't reciprocated. I don't want to hurt you, and you're a lovely woman, but I just don't think you're the right one for me. I think it's time for you to go home. I don't want to lead you on."

The veil of civility drops from her, and standing before me is a goddess of rage.

"You think I should go home? You think one of those other *bitches* is the right one for you?"

She grabs up one of the flower pots that sits in front of the pool house and hurls it. The ceramic pot shatters, scattering dirt and flowers everywhere.

"Victoria, I think you need to calm down," I say, mentally kicking myself. The knee jerk comment slipped out despite the fact I know it's the worst thing you could ever say to an enraged person.

As she picks up and throws another flower pot, I hear the back door slide open as some of the ladies join the show. Intending to keep them safe, I move more toward the property line instead of the house. When the pot shatters on the ground, a part of my brain marvels at the fact the sheet is staying where she tied it. I hear one of the members of production send out a call to get the local police department sent to the house and I worry about Victoria, despite the fact she's throwing things at me.

"I don't know why I came here! You didn't even give me a chance! No one ever gives me a chance!" she yells, throwing one of the lounge chairs into the pool.

A few of the girls chuckle at the sight, drawing her attention and ire. Before she can make a move toward them, I step back into her path, drawing her focus once more.

"You're right. I didn't give you a fair shot. I'm sorry. Unfortunately, I'm only allowed to go on so many solo dates and they are always determined by winners of competitions and whatnot. I would have picked you, otherwise."

Anya comes into view, still dressed from our date, and Victoria's eyes harden as she catches sight of her.

"You stole my date! It should have been me!" She starts storming toward Anya, but I keep myself in front of her.

"It should have been you. Maybe they'll let us do a picnic here," I say.

"Are you trying to placate me?" she screeches, turning her hateful gaze back to me.

Sirens tear through the air as the police near, red and blue lights flashing in the night sky. Two cops come through the front door of the pool house, taking my secluded entrance while movement from another two coming out of the mansion catches my eye.

"Ma'am," one says with a thick handlebar mustache. "You're going to have to get dressed and come with us tonight. We don't want any problems."

Tears start streaming down Victoria's face as she takes in the scene around her.

"I just wanted someone to love me," she cries.

"I know. Everyone does. But we can't destroy property. Why don't we get you dressed and then you can come with us and relax for the evening, okay?" he says, his voice low and even.

She swipes at her tears before moving into the pool house. Once she's out of sight, I turn toward the other cops.

"What's going to happen to her?" I ask.

"It'll depend if the owners of the property want to press charges, but either way, she's going to spend the night in a jail cell," the officer says.

"I don't want her to go to jail," I say.

"That's not up to you."

Victoria comes out of the pool house, this time dressed in actual clothes. Thankfully, the cops don't have her in handcuffs as they escort her from the property.

"I'm sorry for making a scene," she apologizes as she stops in front of me.

"I'm sorry I made you feel neglected. You'll find the right person for you."

The other ladies part, allowing the cops and Victoria to move through the house, and as she leaves Anya locks eyes with me and I simply shrug, unsure what else to do.

CHAPTER THIRTEEN

ANYA

30 DAYS UNTIL PROPOSAL

There are only seven of us left. Isabella, Jasmine, and Bethany H.'s eliminations were all uneventful compared to Victoria's meltdown in our third week of filming. Then Aisha decided to leave, tired of the entire competition. Apparently, she realized dating the same man as eight other women wasn't something she wanted to do.

I couldn't say I blamed her. It's been a whirlwind of a month and we have an entire month to go. The whole situation is weird and pressure filled, but there's something about Parker that keeps me coming back for more.

After our solo date almost two weeks ago, I thought he was going to kiss me, and when he didn't, I figured I was going home. But he called my name, asking me to accept his flame, and gave me a smile that turned my insides to molten lava.

Sam the Butler comes into the game room with the silver serving platter and dome, while Zoey and I are playing pool.

"Anastasia, I have a note for you," he says, removing the dome.

I drop my cue onto the table, disrupting Zoey's shot and receiving a disgruntled "cheater".

I rip through the thick envelope and read the words quickly.

"We're going on a group date. We need to wear swimsuits and something we can hike in. I hate hiking. I want to be a hiking girl but I'm not," I complain, but I'm still excited for a chance to see Parker.

And if swimsuits are needed for us, hopefully they are needed for him as well.

"Who else is going?" Zoey asks.

She's only had one solo date with Parker, and while I don't think she expects to make it until the end, I know she has a bit of a crush on him. How could you not? He's beautiful.

"You, me, and Carmen. This should be fun," I say, rolling my eyes.

When I got out of the shower after the cooking date I lost to Carmen, Zoey was waiting for me. We decided to take some tea outside and sat with our feet dangling in the pool. And then Carmen came home gushing about how great the date was. Zoey was outraged on my behalf, disliking Carmen in solidarity, and offered to 'accidentally' knee Parker in the dick. I reined her in on that one, but it was a nice offer all the same.

"Don't worry. I'll drown Carmen if I have to," she says.

I laugh, hugging her to me, as I go to find Carmen and inform her about our date.

After two hours, I'm hot, sweaty, and bramble scratched, but as I look out over the valley with the sound of a waterfall behind me, I don't care. The waterfall cascades over a hundred feet into a secluded lagoon that reminds me of the one in *The Little Mermaid* movie where Sebastian sings "Kiss the Girl" to Eric.

There's two camera women with us this time. The much smaller cameras they have are almost small enough to ignore. They move off to the side to get their equipment set up while we all look at the lake.

"This is amazing," Parker says, awe in his voice. We all stand there, enjoying the view for a moment before he claps his hands, the sound jarring. "Who wants to go swimming?"

"I didn't come up here just to look at the scenery!" Zoey says, dropping her small backpack production had provided for us onto a large, flat rock. She pulls off her orange shirt, exposing the simple black bikini top she favors. As she shimmies from her shorts, I see she decided to go with her flowery bottoms.

She walks cautiously into the water until suddenly she drops from view. Sputtering as she breaks the surface, she calls out for us to be careful of the drop off.

As Zoey swims around, Carmen rips off her clothes, showing her tight body and small, but high sitting boobs. While her swimsuit is technically a one-piece, the strategic cutouts make it feel like you're getting an illicit look at her body.

Jealousy crawls through me as Parker watches her get into the water. I can't say I blame him. My eyes are glued to the sway of her hips, the bottoms of her suit only covering half of her ass, at most.

Taking a deep breath, I rip off my shirt, showing my top. I'm not proud of it, but I definitely picked the one with wiring much like a bra, bolstering up my chest. I could absolutely do a good *Baywatch* run in this top.

My string bottoms hug my hips. While mine cover a bit more than Carmen's, they aren't as full coverage as Zoey's. The cobalt blue color of my suit plays off my skin tone beautifully.

"Are you going to come in or just watch us like a pervert?" I tease Parker.

"Both," he says, drinking in my curves, and making my skin heat. "Definitely both."

"Let's go then," I say.

With a smirk, he rips off his shirt and my jealousy disintegrates along with my brain.

I've known he was in good shape, but I didn't realize how perfectly chiseled his body is. His hard chest flows into an impressive set of abs. But even lower, and more mouthwatering, is The V. His swimsuit is sitting low on his hips.

I know I'm staring. My brain tells me I should look away, and probably wipe the drool inevitably falling from my lips, but I can't. I'm too busy begging the universe for the string holding up his shorts to fail.

Zoey lets out a wolf whistle behind me, snapping me from my stupor.

"I like the way you look at me," he says, his voice low.

With a Herculean effort, I pull my gaze up to his equally mesmerizing eyes.

"How am I looking at you?" I ask, as if I don't already know.

"Like I'm the answer to every question you've ever had."

"Cocky much?"

"Yes, but I'm not wrong."

I sniff, unwilling to admit he's correct, and turn toward the lagoon. His rough hand grabs mine, sending my heart skipping, and we walk into the water together.

Zoey floats on her back. After the initial sharp drop off, the water is no deeper than six feet in the area we are in, but Zoey is unable to touch. Parker stands just fine, but I'm on my tiptoes. Carmen squeals about something touching her leg, using it as an excuse to drape herself over Parker. He holds up Carmen and I decide to float like Zoey, so I don't have to watch it.

"Do you want a family, Park?" Zoey asks, out of the blue.

"Oh, um, yeah, I do, actually, but they aren't a requirement. I'm happy to just be an uncle as well. Whatever my partner wants, but I've always liked kids." His answer starts a little stilted, but I chalk it up to nerves about opening up. It's obvious to me that Parker is a private person and being on this show must be incredibly difficult for him.

"How many kids do you want?" I ask with interest.

"Two? Again, it'd depend on what my partner wanted, since she's the one who would be carrying them. Bringing another life into this world isn't a decision I take lightly. They, and their mother, would always be my first priority."

It's a good answer. An amazing answer. One thing I've picked up about Parker is how deeply he cares. And not just for the people he is close to, but any person.

He reminds me of my father.

Growing up, Dom and I never had to wonder if our dad would be at a game or a teacher's conference or waiting for us when we got home from school. Our parents were deeply involved in our lives, and if I were ever to be a parent, I know it would be the same for me.

But I've never really thought about having kids before this moment. I always assumed I would have them, but I've never been with someone I wanted to take on the commitment with. Even if it doesn't work out between you, once kids are involved, you're stuck with the person in some regard.

Forever.

I take in Parker for what feels like the first time. I see past his stunning face and I know he would be an amazing partner. An image of a blond-haired, green eyed little boy sitting on his shoulders flashes through my mind and warmth blooms in my stomach.

"What about you ladies? Any desire for kids?" he asks.

"I had a hysterectomy when I was younger. I had really bad endometriosis and there was no other option. I could adopt, sure, but I think I'd prefer to be child-free. Then I could pour myself into the kids of my sisters and friends," Zoey says, in her matter-of-fact way.

"I'm sorry you had to go through with that. Having that decision taken from you was probably hard," I say, swimming over to her, wrapping her in my arms.

"It was at the time, but I've worked through it in therapy. I'm not one to let something I can't change bring me down." She pats my arm in silent thanks.

"Sounds like a good viewpoint to have," Parker says, shrugging out of Carmen's grasp, and coming to give Zoey a hug. My arms drop from my friend and I move out of his way. Watching Zoey and Parker does not make me crazy the way seeing him and Carmen does.

"If you give me a few minutes, I can make up a big sob story so you keep this hot bod pressed against me," Zoey says, waggling her eyebrows up at Parker suggestively.

He lets out a bark of laughter before hugging her even tighter to him and my insides melt like a marshmallow over a campfire.

We all move around the living room in our cocktail dresses. The first night, this room felt so small, almost claustrophobic with all twenty of us and the production crew. Now thirteen are gone? It feels bare, almost. Zoey, Leslie, and I sit on a pair of couches, talking, as we wait for Parker to join us. The other ladies are mingling about, but we three tend to hang out together the most.

Leslie started joining Zoey and me at dinner, enjoying talking about something other than this show. She's lamented multiple times about us being on different coasts. I guess with her event planning business, she needs a baker she can consistently rely on and suggest to her clients.

"I thought I had died and gone to heaven. I've never dated a man with a six pack before. And the fact it was pressed against me? *And* he was wet? I almost came on the spot," Zoey says to Leslie.

"Girl, with love, if you tell me this story again, I'm going to stab you in the eye with my stiletto. I'm sufficiently jealous, okay?" Leslie says, partially joking.

"That's a very specific place to threaten to stab her," I say, trying to dig the cherry out of my drink.

"I feel like the eye would be the one place a stiletto could puncture."

"I don't know, I feel like with enough pressure, it could go through other places. Like the stomach, perhaps?" I suggest.

"Just in case my opinion matters, I would like it to be known I don't want to be stabbed, regardless of the place," Zoey calls out.

Her tongue wiggles around, trying to find her straw without looking but it continues to elude her. Finally, she pulls the glass away from her face, grabs the straw, and puts it into her mouth, going cross-eyed as she watches it.

"Your opinion doesn't matter in this case, but thank you for voicing it," Leslie says, laughing at her straw antics.

Jacob Jacobson comes into the room and we all quiet down, immediately moving toward the middle of the room. We have done this enough now that production doesn't have to herd us any longer.

"Hello, ladies."

"Hi, Jacob," we all intone.

"Welcome to the week five elimination—"

"Cut!" a member of production calls out, cutting Jacob off. "This elimination will be week six of the airing schedule. Go again."

Jacob's smile plasters itself on his face once more.

"Welcome to the week six elimination night cocktail party. Parker will be joining you in a few moments. You will have one hour to make a lasting impression. I'll see you soon," he says, and leaves.

Within thirty seconds, Parker is walking in and he smiles at all of us.

"Looking lovely tonight, ladies. Anya, could I talk to you?"

"Sure," I say, Zoey and Leslie both making kissing sounds as I follow him outside to one of the couches, flipping them off behind his back.

Before I can sit down, he grabs me, pulling me into a hug. His spicy smell envelopes me and I press my face against him, taking a deep breath.

"I missed you the past few days," he says, surprising me. Unless we are on a date, we don't get the opportunity to talk to Parker.

"You just saw me two days ago," I tease, but if I'm honest, I missed him, too.

"And? I can't miss you if I've seen you already in a week?"

"That's not what I said. I'm sorry, you just took me off guard. It's nice to be missed," I tell him. And it's true. It is nice to be missed. Maybe I just hadn't realized how much he's enjoyed our time together.

"Tell me something. Anything. I want to keep talking to you." He pulls me down onto the couch, making sure our knees touch as he rests his arm across the back, looking at me. Cameras move around us, but I ignore them, trying to focus on Parker.

"Zoey is trying to teach me how to play pool because she wants us to go to bars and hustle people."

He chuckles, tucking his hair behind his ear.

"Why does that not surprise me? Just be careful. Some people get real upset when they get hustled."

"You can be our bodyguard."

"I would be honored," he says, putting his giant hand over his heart.

His thick, wavy hair falls forward and temporarily obscures half of his face. Without my input, my hand reaches up and tucks it back for him, but instead of immediately letting go, I linger.

I've thought about having my hands in his hair many times. I never had a thing for guys with long hair before, but with Parker? It works. I couldn't imagine him with short hair. It's softer than it looks. Silky, almost. His green eyes search my face as I continue to stroke the strands in my hand.

"I love your hair."

"You can touch it whenever you want."

"You might come to regret telling me that," I sigh.

"I don't think I will."

Reluctantly, I pull my hand back. "Are you nervous about tonight? I don't think I could send people home week after week. I don't like hurting people's feelings."

"No, I know exactly what I want to do. Who I want to keep around. It's not as hard as you'd think. The hard part is keeping people around when you don't see a future with them because the show needs to have contestants."

"If you could have it your way, how many of us would you have left at this point?"

"Two."

There's no question in his voice.

"Wow, that's very definitive." Even though I'm pretty sure I'm one of the two, a small, annoying piece of me is jealous the answer isn't one. And that I'm not the one.

"I believe there are people in this world you click with and you just know there's something there, no matter how much time you spend with them."

"And you've felt that with two of us?" I ask, my heart beating as I let myself finally consider he could be as attracted to me as I am to him.

"No, I've felt that with one of you. The other one, there's a curiosity there, but it's not as strong."

"I still don't think I want to be in your position."

Tenderness softens his face. His fingertips drag up my thigh, leaving flames in their wake. "I would do it all over again, I think."

My eyes fall to his lips. His plump, soft looking lips. I can't wait any longer. I start to lean toward him, but the sound of the glass door sliding open stops me.

"Fucking hell," I say, dropping my head. Heels click against the stone behind me.

His fingers settle under my chin, raising my face to look at him.

"I'll see you back in there, yeah?" he asks.

"I'll be there."

He kisses my cheek before I stand, ceding my seat to Leslie standing behind me.

"Sorry, girl. They sent me out here."

I squeeze her arm as I move past. "It's okay, I understand."

Disappointment has me turning back only to find Parker's green eyes set on me.

Minutes tick by as the girls rotate out to talk to Parker one-on-one. When Carmen sashays her way out the door, the last of us to go, I feel my nose wrinkle.

"Hide it a little better, babe. A camera is probably on you right now," Zoey says under her breath as she brings her new drink to her lips. Taking her advice, I paste on a smile and wait until we are told to find our places for the elimination ceremony.

"Ladies, it's time. Parker, do you have anything you'd like to say?" Jacob Jacobson asks, standing to Parker's right, like always.

"Every week this becomes more difficult. I never thought it would be this hard to decide who to send home. You're all changing me for the better."

"If you don't receive a flame tonight, your time on *House of Desire* will be over. Parker," Jacob says and then steps back.

Taking a candle from the basket, Parker lights it and turns toward us.

"Anya," he says and a huge smile lights my face at being called first. It doesn't necessarily mean anything, but after our talk earlier, I'm wondering if it does as I walk up to him. "Anya, will you accept this flame of my desire?"

"I'd love to," I say, taking the candle from him as he presses another kiss to my cheek. I want to turn into him, let our lips meet, but after my brief moment of insanity earlier, I know that I don't want the other women around for our first kiss.

I move back to my spot as Parker lights another candle.

"Zoey," he says.

My blue-haired friend moves to stand in front of him.

"Zoey, would you accept this flame of my desire?"

"Absolutely," she says, taking it with a smile. He doesn't kiss her cheek.

After Zoey, he calls up Carmen, Leslie, and then Olivia before Jacob steps forward.

"Parker. Ladies. It's the last candle of the night," he says before stepping back once more, a languid smile on his face. It looks like he has no thoughts going on in his mind, a robot in standby mode.

Emily and Mia step forward as the last two while Parker lights the last candle.

"Emily," he calls and she steps forward. "Emily, will you accept the flame of my desire?"

"I will," she says, giving him a small hug before joining the rest of us.

"Mia, I'm sorry, you have not received a flame tonight, and your journey will end here," Jacob says, and that is the key for us to break from our stiff positions. We all blow out our candles as Mia says goodbye to Parker.

One of the members of production carries a tray with seven glasses of champagne for our end of elimination toast. Mia waves goodbye to us and heads out of the mansion, Parker walking her out to the limo. Returning, he grabs his glass of champagne from production, lifting it up.

"Here's to another week looking for love," he says simply, and we all clink our glasses, mentally preparing for the week ahead.

CHAPTER FOURTEEN

PARKER

24 DAYS UNTIL PROPOSAL

I SIT IN A waiting room, tranquil wall colors and music making me think of Sharon's waiting room as I wait for Anastasia. I was a little weary when I pulled up to the therapist's office, but when I really started thinking about it, I decided starting therapy a little early wouldn't be a bad thing. Especially in this situation where we are both performing for cameras.

No matter how much you want to act normal, you're still aware of being watched. Plus, the stress of normal life is missing from these encounters. Trying to date with jobs and friends and kids. Any responsibilities that are a normal part of everyday life.

Anastasia steps from the car and her simple outfit takes my breath away. Black cut-off shorts hug her hips and the soft, white tank top ends a few inches above the waistband, the skin there enticing.

Her red lips beg me to mess up her lipstick.

I've wanted to kiss her since the first night she ended up sprawled at my feet.

I don't know why I keep hesitating. I can tell she wants me to and yet, for some reason, with her, I don't want it to be filmed. I want it to be just ours and I know that's not a possibility.

"Hey, there," she says, pushing her sunglasses up into her hair, pulling it back from her face.

"You're enchanting," I tell her, no hint of hyperbole.

"I think you might have gotten hit on the head. How many fingers am I holding up?" She doesn't raise any fingers but looks at my lips, her mouth parting slightly and I almost give in to what we both want.

"I need you to get used to me complimenting you." I take her hips in my hands, pulling her closer to me and she wraps her arms around me, her hands settling at my lower back.

"Compliments make me feel weird."

"Because you get tired of hearing them all the time from men like me?"

"There's no one like you."

It takes everything in me to not puff my chest out at her compliment.

"Are you ready to get some couple's counseling done?" I ask, trying to diffuse some of the sexual tension.

"Hell yeah. I'm going to win therapy. Let's do this." She gives me a quick squeeze before taking my hand and leading me into the office that's waiting for us.

Production already has cameras set up to catch all the angles needed for the show. Once they give her the cue, our therapist walks in.

"Hello, Anastasia, Parker. I'm Dr. Jones."

Dr. Jones is grandmotherly. Graying hair, settled lines. Her face is welcoming. Soothing. There's something about it that makes you want to pour your heart out. Ten-year-old Parker wants to crawl into this woman's lap, let her stroke his hair, and kiss his scraped knee. She was made to take care of people; that much is obvious.

"Please make yourself comfortable," she says, indicating the inviting couch while she takes the single chair, opposite. "Our goal here today is to build intimacy between the two of you. With all these cameras around and the fact your time together will be watched by millions at home, that creates an environment for inauthentic behavior. We want to strip that away. Hopefully, if you make it out of the show together, it will set the beginning of a foundation for your relationship."

Anya nods her head and I relax a bit, realizing she might not make me divulge everything about myself on national television. The cameras are small in the corner of the room, no people manning them this time. But that doesn't mean I'm not aware of them.

"Let's start with a simple exercise. Parker, tell me what you've noticed about Anastasia in your time together."

Clearing my throat, I decide to turn my body to Anya and she mimics the gesture.

"I've noticed you're funny. And smart. And you always try to make sure everyone feels included on our group dates. Your confidence was a little shaken at some point, but you're trying not to let that experience win. And you're so beautiful, sometimes it makes my eyes hurt to look at you."

Her eyes water a little but she reins in her emotions and mumbles a bashful thanks.

"Anastasia, what have you noticed about Parker?"

"You're caring. And thoughtful. Protective of all of us. You enjoy touching and being touched. And despite being the lead here, I can tell how lucky you feel any of us would want to be here for you."

Warmth spreads through my limbs and my heartbeat slows at her kindness melting even the barest hint of trepidation from my body. Even though we've not known each other long, it's nice knowing someone can read me even a little.

"Well done, both of you. How did that make you feel?" Dr. Jones asks.

Not wanting Anya to feel put on the spot, I go first.

"Really nice. Like a hug on your worst day." I reach out and squeeze her knee.

"It made me feel seen."

And just like that, I feel a small sliver of my heart become hers.

"The next exercise is going to be a little more personal. I would like you both to go through your values. This can be anything like what you expect in a relationship, political, or religious views, anything you consider a deal breaker. The goal of this is to understand the person across from you in a way that would help you to know if you're compatible.

"Many of my clients in my practice have diametrically opposed ideals which, understandably, can cause a lot of tension. Parker?"

I take a deep breath and release it slowly, counting, just as Sharon has taught me.

"Loyalty and reliability are the most important things to me. I want to know I can count on you and for you to know you can count on me. No matter what it is, if you need me, I'll be there and I would want that from a partner.

"People matter to me, as you said. I believe everyone should be able to live the life they love, so long as it doesn't cause physical or emotional harm to someone else, whatever that may be. My only deal breaker is someone who runs away at any sign of tension." I say the last staring into Anya's beautiful eyes and I can see the understanding in their depths.

"Great. Anastasia?"

"I agree, completely, on letting people live the life they want. A deal breaker for me is someone that's a yeller or lets their anger out in an aggressive way. As far as the traits most important to me? I need someone willing to share themselves with me. Their thoughts and fears and hopes and dreams. I want to feel like nothing is off limits for us to talk about and for them to know they can ask me anything.

"I think, maybe, the reason I stopped looking for a partner, is that..." She pauses, looking up at the ceiling as she breathes in deep, but I hear the wobble in the sound and see tears gathering in her eyes.

"Anya, you don't have to say—" I start, not wanting to see her in pain.

"No, I want to tell you." She clears her throat as she gets her emotions under control and I reach out to take her hand, and wait.

I would wait however long she needed and not begrudge her a moment of the time. "Freshman year of college, I had a boyfriend who was a yeller. He would yell and rage anytime he was angry, and I was convinced one day he was going to hit me. But any time I would try to sit him down and end it, he would tell me how he couldn't live without me and if I left, he'd take his life.

"It took a long time to accept I couldn't stay and try to save him from himself. When I left, he didn't follow through with his threat, thankfully, but after, I knew I couldn't be with someone who would use my love for them against me. He effectively trapped me and I can't do that again. And I sure can't be with someone who yells at me. I want someone who can communicate."

Her use of the word trapped worms its way inside me, making me hear Brittany's voice for a moment as my heart breaks into a thousand shards at Anya's pain. The situations are completely different and yet, the outcome was the same.

I lift the hand I still hold and press a kiss to the back of it.

"Very nice," Dr. Jones says while Anya and I maintain eye contact. "How are we doing? Do we need to take a moment?"

"Whatever you need," I tell Anya.

"I'm good. Let's keep going," Anya says.

"The next exercise is going to encourage being grounded in the moment with the person. One of you will be blindfolded while the other will have options of various different items they can use on the other to play on one of the other senses. The blindfolded person is going to communicate what they are feeling. Which of you would like to be blindfolded first?"

"I will," I say.

She nods and hands me the black silk sleep mask I put on. Shuffling sounds echo around the room as Dr. Jones presents the various options to Anya.

She giggles at one and the sound brings a small smile to my face after everything she shared.

A light touch runs up my forearm, making me jump from the suddenness.

"Whoops, sorry. Did I scare you?" she asks, nervousness in her voice.

"No, it just startled me. Is that a feather?"

"You got it. I figured I'd start easy."

"That's nice of you," I smile. Part of me wants to rip this blindfold off so I can see her, but I'm too invested to see what she chooses next to end the game.

"Parker, what does the sensation make you think of or feel?" Dr. Jones prompts.

"Um, I don't know, really," I admit, almost sheepishly.

"That's okay. Try to focus on how you feel in your body on this next one."

Anya moves around more and suddenly there's a smell wafting directly beneath my nose. Following Dr. Jones's instruction, I pay attention to how I feel. Comfort and love swaddle me and I smile at the memory the smell conjures.

"That smells like my mom's famous pumpkin loaf," I tell her. "It makes me think of when I'd fall asleep on the couch after Thanksgiving lunch, the adults in the room talking around me."

"Famous, huh?" Anya teases. "Do you think she'll share the recipe? I haven't found one I'm in love with yet and seasonal treats are always a big draw."

"You'll have to ask her yourself."

"Deal," she says, and I feel her shift away from me, presumably to grab something else.

This time, something touches my bottom lip. She lets it rest there, light as a feather, the coldness bright against my warm skin. The scent of the strawberry hits me and suddenly I'm envisioning us in a candlelit room, but I don't think that would be appropriate to say here.

Sticking the tip of my tongue out, I taste fruit and as I open my mouth, she brings the berry forward, letting me bite into it. The sweet juice runs over my tongue and when her breathing hitches, part of me wishes I could see her.

"I feel"—I pause, searching for the word that could encompass my need for this woman— "hungry."

The couch shifts as I feel her stand, her footsteps muffled against the carpet. Her body heat warms my arm and I want to turn toward her, but I sit still, waiting to see what she does. One hand settles on my thigh, a little high but not as high as I want, and the other on my shoulder.

A gentle breeze streams over the shell of my ear as she blows out her breath and I harden as my mouth drops open.

My cock tries to stray to the thought of her breath on my ear as she straddles me, as I thrust up into her, but my brain begins throwing thoughts at me about how we are not alone and we are being *filmed*.

"Anya," I whisper, letting her hear the attraction flowing below my belt.

"Okay, I think that's good," Dr. Jones says, pulling us both back into reality.

"Sorry," Anya says, settling back onto the couch. Her cheeks are flushed with embarrassment when I remove the blindfold from my eyes, handing it to her to put on.

"Don't be," I tell her, giving her a reassuring smile. "That was my favorite one."

"Anastasia, go ahead and put the blindfold on and I will get the new options for Parker," the kind doctor says, ignoring the obvious sexual charge in the room.

"Which one made you laugh?" I ask her as Dr. Jones removes the tray before I can take note of all the other items.

"There was a slap bracelet. I was obsessed with those growing up and I just wasn't expecting to see it here. It was funny to me."

A new tray is set in front of me, filled with various options but like Anya's slap bracelet, my tray holds a little toy car in addition to the chocolate, whipped cream, strawberries, velvet, burlap, a hairbrush, and various bottles with different scents.

Wanting to start gently, I pick up the velvet. The soft fabric slides against my fingers as I drag it down Anya's neck. Goosebumps emerge on her arm.

She shifts on the couch and I have never wanted to read someone's mind more than I do in this moment.

"That reminds me of my favorite zip up sweatshirt my parents bought me one Christmas."

Putting the velvet down, I grab up the bottle that says 'teakwood' and wave it under her nose.

"That smells like you," she says, no hesitation, and I melt. The scent is featured heavily in my favorite cologne Charlie helped me pick and I love that she associates the smell with me.

Putting the bottle back down, I lean next to her and decide to follow her lead and be a bit bolder with my last sensation. A little nervous, I run my lips gently up her jaw until I get to her neck, placing a soft kiss to the pulse point, fluttering beneath my lips.

Her soft intake of breath sounds in my ear as she moves her chin infinitesimally, giving me better access.

My hands want to reach out and grab her, pressing a hard kiss against her slightly parted lips, but I don't.

I control myself even though I want to do nothing more than lose all control.

As I settle back, Dr. Jones lets Anya know she can remove the blindfold. With shaking hands, she reaches up and removes the silk, finding me immediately, heat in her eyes.

"Alright, I think we can call this session a success. The intimacy definitely seemed to have deepened, wouldn't you say?" Neither of us say anything. Anya's face is pink and she avoids looking at the therapist. And I'm trying to keep my dick from moving in my pants. Nodding our agreement is all we can do. "It was great meeting you both," she says, pushing herself to her feet.

We follow suit as she walks to the office door, holding it open for us.

"Thank you for your time," Anya says as she leaves the office.

"Parker, I'll see you in twenty minutes," Dr. Jones says, pulling me back into the real world as effectively as if she poured ice cold water over my head and I have no idea how I'm going to do that exercise with someone else when all I want is Anya.

CHAPTER FIFTEEN

ANYA

14 DAYS UNTIL PROPOSAL

IT FEELS WEIRD TO be standing outside my bakery, barred from going in until the camera is set up inside to film Parker and me arriving. I'm used to being the one in charge here, and to have that stripped from me is leaving me feeling a bit on edge. Not only that, but I've also been without Zoey's company in the down moments of the show.

When we all left the *House of Desire* mansion for our hometown dates, we knew we wouldn't see each other again for the show until the elimination after the Desire Suite dates next week. As Parker leaves each hometown, he'll either break up with the person, or ask them to join him back here in California for the Desire Suite dates.

While we all waited for Parker to join us at our homes, we were kept in local hotels with no one but a few production members to talk to. It's been a boring few days.

The sound of a car door shutting grabs my attention and I turn toward the noise to see Parker moving through the parking lot. I haven't seen him since last week's elimination, leaving me, Leslie, Zoey, and Carmen as the final four. He walks toward me and something in my chest settles, and I realize how much I missed him.

We get the signal the cameras are ready, but I don't care, as he takes me into his strong arms.

"Are you ready for this?" I ask him as he kisses my cheek in greeting, the cameras following the movement, I'm sure.

I want to grab his face and kiss him, but when his eyes flit to someone behind me for a split second, I keep my hormones under control.

"You're not going to make me bake something difficult like a soufflé or something, are you?" he asks me, a small amount of trepidation on his face.

"I was going to have you make a custom eight-tier wedding cake."

"Perfect. That's definitely within my capabilities."

"I figured as much," I say, smiling at him, butterflies fluttering around in my chest. He nudges me with his shoulder as we turn toward the bakery. "I believe I have a promise to fulfill and I think it should take the form of cupcakes," I say, reminding him of the group date from a few weeks ago.

"I was afraid you'd forgotten."

"Never."

The familiar weight of the door handle settles into my hand. Cool metal welcomes me home and I feel a lump in my throat. Baking is my favorite thing in the world and I have been missing it every day of this journey.

"Welcome to the Whimsical Whisk Bakery," I say, pulling open the door.

The inside of my shop is spotless, and I can tell my family has worked tirelessly to get everything ready for this moment.

Not only is the space cleaned, but the pastries, cupcakes, and cookies look like they were put together with the exacting precision of a surgeon. A lump forms in my throat at the beauty. At the outward showing of love staring back at me.

"This is really nice," Parker says.

"Thank you. It's my baby." He must hear the change in me, because his rough, warm hand grabs mine, squeezing.

"What's your favorite thing to bake?"

Setting aside the emotions so I don't cry on television, I look up at him, squeezing his hand back in thanks but not letting it go. "Out of the normal offerings? Or in general?"

"Mmm, both."

"The cupcakes are my favorite of the usual fare."

"They'd be mine, too. Really, I love anything cake based." He smiles and my world stops for a moment.

"Other than that, I love making cakes where the person gives me creative freedom. Whatever flavor I want. Whatever decoration fits the theme they're thinking. There's nothing like losing yourself in designing something new and different. And picking flavors to go together? That's my favorite thing. I don't let it send me into a panic spiral anymore."

Pulling on his hand, I lead him to the kitchen through the double doors behind my counter. When I walk into the space for the first time in weeks, I know I made the right choice with the rearranging I had the football players do that I won at the auction. I look around the space, seeing the efficiency of the setup.

Letting go of the stunning man's hand, I move to the hook by the door and grab the two aprons hanging there, handing one to Parker. I try not to laugh as he settles the sunshine yellow fabric over his head, tying the ties around his back. The color is so bright and happy. It almost looks out of place on this man who has given off slightly sad vibes since the day I met him.

"What kind of cupcakes are we making today?" he asks.

"The crowd favorite S'more to Love cupcake."

"That sounds amazing. I hope part of the baking process is taste testing the end result."

"Quality control is always important, and if you're a good boy I'll make sure you have the best one in the batch," I tease.

He cocks an eyebrow at me with a sexy smirk and I can feel my face heat.

"Guess I'll need to be a good boy, then," he says and I almost combust on the spot.

Clearing my throat, I begin moving around the kitchen. And talking. And talking. And talking some more. I get into the excitement of sharing my passion for baking, but Parker doesn't seem to mind. He asks questions here and there, seeming to catalog the steps in his mind. I grab two of the bowls, handing them to him while I grab up the others.

"Why do you weigh everything instead of using measuring cups?" he asks, as I lead him over to the mixer.

"Precision. Depending on how you fill the measuring cup, there is variability in the amount of the ingredient you're getting. If you weigh it, you'll always be sure what you're creating comes out the same every time. When someone comes into the Whimsical Whisk, it's because they are craving something we create. I want it to taste the same every time."

I pour both of my bowls into the mixing one, indicating Parker should do the same.

"That makes sense," he says, pouring the sugar in with the flour.

Before I can say anything, he flips the switch to high and the beaters fling the dry ingredients all around. Lunging over, I flick the switch back to off, puffs of flour floating in the air. I look up at Parker and his face is covered in flour, his mouth hanging open.

"We don't typically turn the mixer on high," I say, laughing at his stunned face. "Or at least, not at this point."

He turns to me and with the most sheepish grin I've ever seen. "Whoops."

I don't care the room is a mess. Happiness bubbles from deep within me at this man who exudes confidence despite being covered in flour.

"You have something on your face, right there," I say pointing to one spot, with a giggle.

"You don't say," he answers, deadpan. "You have a little something right here," he says, grabbing a handful of flour and lightly tossing it in my face.

"Rude," I say, grabbing my own handful and flinging it at him. We pause for a moment, looking at each other, both of us a mess, until we break.

Handfuls of flour are flung as he chases me around the small room, but I grab up an empty cookie sheet, blocking his projectiles. He scoots closer to me, causing me to back up until I realize he has me pinned. My back presses against the wall while my chest rises and falls with my panting breaths. He stalks closer, the bowl of what remains of the sugar and flour in hand.

"Don't you dare," I say, holding up my cookie sheet in warning.

He moves closer, gabbing my wrist of the hand holding my only weapon, but with his body looming over me, I forget our game and drop the cookie sheet without a thought. The clattering doesn't even register with him this close to me.

Parker releases my wrist and trails his fingers up my arm until his hand is resting against my neck, his thumb stroking my jaw.

"You have some sugar just here," he says before lifting his thumb to his mouth. His tongue flicks out, licking the sugar crystals from it, and my entire body warms. "Delicious."

I can't wait another second to kiss him. Kissing him is almost all I've been able to think about since our couple's therapy session when he kissed my jaw. I fling my arms around his neck, pulling his mouth down to meet mine. His thick arms wrap around me, pulling me against his body. He tastes of sweetness as my tongue traces his lips, asking for entrance which he gives.

My fingers find his hair band and tug it free, before fisting in the soft strands.

A moan escapes me and his hands move over my ass, squeezing, going down to my thighs, encouraging me to wrap my legs around him, which I do. Eagerly.

He grinds his impressive erection against my center, making me pant with desire.

"Parker, I need more," I say against his lips, and like a man starving, he shoves his tongue back into my mouth, tasting me with a white-hot passion as he carries me to the workbench we had been using.

He sets me on the edge before swiping all the instruments and bowls to the floor, causing an even bigger mess. The naked hunger in his eyes as he moves to capture my mouth again while he shoves my legs further apart, settling between my welcoming thighs, pushes any thoughts of cleaning from my mind.

Movement catches my attention over his shoulder and I pull back before his lips can make contact, green eyes questioning.

"Parker," I say, panic setting in as the camerawoman moves to get a better angle of our desperation. My need for him is making me forget we are always being filmed.

He looks over his shoulder, looking for what upset me, and his face darkens.

"Get the fuck out of here," he yells, anger thundering in his voice.

My body tightens at the volume while the woman squeaks and scurries from the room, leaving us alone even though she'll probably get in trouble for doing so.

"Anastasia, I'm sorry. I shouldn't have yelled, but the thought of them recording you made me panic a bit." He leans his forehead down, settling it against mine as his hands move up and down the outside of my thighs, calming instead of heating. "Plus, I've been wanting to kiss you since I first saw you and they ruined it."

"I have thought of almost nothing else in weeks," I whisper, anxiety calming inside me. "And they didn't ruin it."

It's true. I don't regret this moment of passion, even though it will be aired for millions to see. There's no way the footage won't be used. It's too good. Too hot. But I couldn't have lasted another day without his lips on mine.

He pulls back, looking at my face to see if I'm telling the truth or simply what he's wanting to hear.

"It was a fantastic kiss," I tell him, grinding myself against him for a moment to emphasize my point.

"The best I've ever had." His fingers dig into my ass as he grips my hips tightly, grinding himself against my soaking core so hard, I'm afraid he's going to feel my arousal through his pants. As he hits the perfect spot, making me gasp, I can see he's considering throwing caution to the wind and continuing what we had started. It would only take a second to free him and pull my panties to the side before he could plunge his thick cock into me.

But the thought of someone hearing him give me pleasure, or worse, capturing it on camera, stops me.

I reach up, cupping his cheek as I give him a soft kiss. He gives me a small smile and steps back so I can shimmy from the table.

Looking around the kitchen, I cringe.

"This is going to be fun to clean," I say. There is flour and sugar *everywhere.* I don't think a single surface was untouched in our fight, but even still, I can't bring myself to regret it.

We move around the room grabbing up all the different bowls and spoons, dumping them in the sink to be washed. I go into the cleaning closet to fill up the mop bucket for Parker while I grab as many cleaning cloths and paper towels as I can hold for myself. Making relatively quick work of the job, we clean the entire space until it's sparkling once more.

"Does this mean I won't get a cupcake today?" Parker asks, as I take his messy apron from him and throw them both in the basket to be washed.

I grab his hand and pull him through the double doors back into the front of the shop, the cameras waiting for us. Pushing open the case, I grab one of the cupcakes we were going to bake before our food fight.

"For you," I say presenting it to him as I slide the glass closed once more.

He takes it from my hand and breaks it in half, holding a piece out to me.

"I think we both deserve a treat," he says as I take it.

The cake is delicious if not, ever so slightly stale, telling me it was probably made yesterday so there wouldn't be any rushing this morning. But even despite that, Parker groans as he takes a bite.

"This is amazing," he says, giving me a kiss. The nonchalant gesture makes it seem like we've been trading kisses for far longer than the hour since our first, but I'm not upset by the easy comfortability.

"You're going to have to make these for my birthday every year until I die," he says, shoving the rest of the cake into his mouth, chewing greedily.

"Deal," I say as I grab his hand and lead him from the shop with the thought of years of making him birthday cakes glowing in my chest.

CHAPTER SIXTEEN

PARKER

THE HOUSE IS A light yellow. As we drove in, I noticed every house is painted one of five different colors. White, gray, blue, cream, or black. There were no other options in the neighborhood. All the houses are single level with well-manicured, but small, lawns.

But Anastasia's parents' house is slightly different from all the others. Theirs, instead of a cream, is more a pale yellow. Instead of a single level, there seems to be a small amount of space above the garage. Where everyone else's lawns are well manicured with perfect rows of bushes under the windows, a riot of color and unrestrained flowers sit.

The house feels happy. Loved. Like a family that has so much love it spills out to be seen by everyone that drives by.

I feel myself smiling at the structure that is so different from anything I've ever lived in before.

While my current house is beautiful, there's nothing about it that screams love and joy. It simply looks perfect and cold, like marble.

Cameras wait for me on the lawn, set to film me from the moment I step out of the car.

Settling into Parker, *House of Desire*, contestant, I grab the flowers from the seat next to me. I went to three flower shops after leaving the bakery, but I think the ones I picked are perfect. The blooms match the colorfulness of those in front of the house so well. When I saw the bouquet, I knew it was the one I had to bring with me for this date.

Our earlier kiss enters my mind as I open the door, ready to see the stunning raven-haired beauty who continues to draw me to her, and I wonder if something permanent could come from this show.

The black front door opens as I reach for the doorbell, and Anya stands in front of me in a blue dress the color of the cloudless summer day.

She smiles up at me, and out of reflex I bend down to give her a kiss.

"You look like a dream," I tell her. Her hand snakes out and gives me a sharp pinch on my forearm. "Hey! What was that for?"

"Just wanted you to know you weren't dreaming," she says, her smile beaming.

"Thanks for that."

"Any time. Are you nervous?"

"Should I be nervous?"

"I dunno," she shrugs. "You're going to be grilled. I haven't brought someone home in longer than I'd like to admit."

"I can handle anything they throw at me. Don't worry."

"Would you like to come in?" She moves to the side and I step into the small entryway. "Are those for me?"

"Um, actually, no. They are for your mother."

"You're going to kick Dom out of his spot as the favorite. Come on." She grabs my hand and leads me through the house.

Just like outside, the inside is exuberant in showcasing the love of the family living within its walls. Pictures overflow the walls with every member in various ages and activities. The walls are various shades and colors, but they all go together instead of making the space feel chaotic.

I lean to look harder at one picture where she's maybe seven years old and missing her two front teeth. A boy, who I assume is Dom, has his arm slung around her. They are both covered in streaks of mud, grass stains, and are soaking wet.

"This is my favorite," I say, touching the frame with the tip of my finger. "You both look so happy."

"I was. It was the first year we had a slip-n-slide and that was the first time we got to use it. I think we slid down that thing a hundred times."

She grabs my hand, linking our fingers, and pulls me toward the right, through an arch, and down a step into the wide living room.

"Everyone, this is Parker," she says by way of introduction, dropping my hand so I can move into the room.

The cameras are set up, but this time they are on tripods so as not to impede us in the space.

"Hello, Parker. I'm Gwen. Welcome to our home."

Gwen's delivery is slightly stiff and has me fighting down a smile. Anya rolls her eyes and I assume she tried to tell them to act natural. Awkwardness aside, it's easy to see where Anastasia gets her beauty from. Gwen's black hair matches her daughter's, except the gray streaks through the strands.

"It's a pleasure to meet you," I say, bending down to brush a kiss against her cheek. "These are for you." I offer her the flowers as I pull away and see the same smile I've seen on Anastasia's face.

"My goodness! They are so beautiful. I must find a vase for them. I'm sure it's collecting dust since my son never brings me flowers," she says, giving the evil eye to Dominic.

Where Anastasia favors her mother, Dominic favors their father. Except his stature. That seems to be all his own. Anastasia stands taller than both of her parents, but where she's a few inches taller, Dominic towers. I think his arms are even bigger than mine.

Anastasia snorts with laughter and I try to hold in my own chuckle.

"Mama, I'm *busy*! Does it not count that I pick you and your drunk friends up from Bingo?"

"Maybe it'd count more if you didn't get drunk as well, causing us all to have to call your father."

"Let's all remember Parker doesn't need to know about our apparent alcoholic tendencies," Anya tells them with both mortification and love in her voice.

"Oh, I like to get as full a picture as I can," I tell her. Her scowl directed at me merely makes me laugh.

"Please ignore my wife. She receives plenty of flowers from me," her father says, stepping forward, offering me his hand.

"I have no doubt, sir. It's a pleasure to meet you."

"Likewise. My name is Carl. If I could just say, I might be biased, but even without the show airing yet, I know Anastasia is the best person you have left."

"I agree with you completely," I say before leaning toward him conspiratorially. "But don't tell anyone else I said so. At least until the end of the show." I try to pull my hand back, but he holds tight and I don't want to yank it from his grip.

"Are you going to propose to my daughter?"

"Dad!"

Anya's father might only come up to my collarbone, but in this moment, he makes me feel like I'm eighteen again.

"I can't tell anyone who I'm picking, I'm sorry."

"Dad, let the guy go," Dominic says, nudging him. Her father gives me one more glare before letting me go and moving off to a recliner.

"Hey, man, I'm Dominic." His grip is strong but not in a trying to be intimidating kind of way. "I loved *House of Deceit.* You and Charlie were my favorites."

"Hey, good to meet you. And thanks for saying that. I might be biased, but Charlie was the best one on that show."

"Who's Charlie?" Gwen asks, coming back into the room, the flowers in a vase she sets on the mantel.

"Parker's ex-girlfriend," Dominic says.

"Parker's best friend," Anya tells her at the same time.

"You're friends with your ex-girlfriend? Anastasia, did you know this?" Gwen asks looking between us and I feel my heart sink.

The last thing I want them to think is I'm not serious about their daughter.

"It was a fake relationship, Dominic," Anya says, with a glare before turning to her mom. "He and Charlie are just friends."

Her knowledge of the situation makes me nervous. We hadn't really talked about my friendship with Charlie, and I'm not so delusional to think some women won't feel threatened by my closeness to her.

"Anya is right, Gwen. Charlie is just a friend." I look down at Anya. "Did you watch the show?" I ask her, nervous.

For some reason, all I want for her to say is no. That she has no preconceived notions of me. That she isn't judging me for the edits Frank, my wrangler and the decider of what clips were aired, had put in the show.

"No, but Lorelei told me you were going to be the lead of this show. Once I was accepted, she told me about Charlie just because she knows whomever you choose will be compared to her and wanted me to be prepared. Other than that, and telling me you're a good guy, she didn't tell me anything about you as a person," she reassures me, squeezing my arm.

"If you want to talk about it, just let me know."

She leans forward and kisses my bicep and my heart flutters. "I'm good."

Dinner is fantastic. Gwen pulled out all the stops, making various family recipes. Anya and Dom tease her about the effort she put into the meal for the cameras. Blushing, she swatted both of them with her towel as Carl set the various dishes on the table.

As the meal came to an end, I felt the air shift.

"So, Parker, tell us something about you. I feel like we've been talking all night," Gwen says, putting her knife and fork down in exchange for her glass of wine.

Wiping my mouth, I prepare for the grilling Anya warned me about and that I have already received at Leslie and Zoey's houses. Luckily, I'm much more prepared now than I was in the beginning.

"What would you like to know?" I ask.

"What do you do for a living?" Carl asks.

"I own a construction company. We specialize in custom homes. We are a one stop shop for people, so when they come to us, they know the entire process will be handled with the amount of care you want in your forever home."

"That must pay very well," Gwen says and I smile at her.

I don't have any notions my ability to afford a nice lifestyle for myself and a future partner isn't a consideration in a parent's mind.

"I'm very comfortable. It does require a lot of long hours, though."

"Anya's bakery requires long hours, too. She works very hard for her business."

"Papa," she says, dropping her face in her hands, embarrassed, a blush creeping up her neck

I press my leg against hers under the table, offering silent comfort.

"I have no doubt she does. It looked like an amazing shop and I could taste the love she puts into her cupcakes," I say, causing her blush to deepen and my chest to warm at the sight.

"Would you expect her to give up her dream for yours? Where is your company even located? If you don't even live in the same state—"

"Dad," Anastasia interrupts, "he lives here. He wouldn't expect me to give up my bakery."

"She's right. If it's something she's passionate about, I would support her in whatever way she needs. In fact, after tasting one of her cupcakes this morning, I have every intention of instructing my team to use her for the cookies and cupcakes we give to our clients when they move in. Unfortunately, I can't talk to my business manager until I'm off the show since our phones were confiscated, but it will be a change I implement immediately."

I didn't mean to say this. Even though it's true, I don't want Anastasia to think I'm simply trying to win points with her parents. Her baking is so good, everyone should try it. No matter if it works out between us or not.

Her hand slides onto my thigh under the table, giving it a squeeze. I press my elbow to her arm for a moment before we both retreat to our own space again. Catching the look her parents share, I know it's time for us to split off. Production requires I have one-on-one time with at least one parent for each woman so they can get footage of me talking about my feelings more. When it happens, and with which parent, is up to them.

"Parker, would you mind joining me for a drink outside? I'd just like to spend some time with you one-on-one," Gwen says.

"It'd be my pleasure." I stand from my chair before bending down and placing a kiss atop Anastasia's head. "I'll be back," I tell her.

"I'll be here."

Anya's mother grabs her glass and the half empty bottle of wine from the table before making her way through the kitchen and out the sliding glass door leading to the backyard. The space is simple, but inviting. She sits on an outdoor couch as I take a chair next to her.

"Do you want to know how long I've been married, Parker?" she asks, topping off my glass of wine.

"I'd love to," I say, taking a sip, wondering how this conversation will go. The talk I had with Leslie's father about blood lines and how his daughter is meant for society, not working, could have gone better. But I don't think Anastasia's parents have an elitist bone in their body.

"I have been married for forty-seven years. Anya's father proposed to me when I was just sixteen. Our parents wouldn't hear of it, of course, but they just assumed our engagement would end when our relationship took its natural course. As one does, during those years.

"But we knew what we had was real. Anastasia wants that. She doesn't need the ring or the paper or anything, but if she commits, if you do this with her, that'll be it. Are you prepared for that?

"Are you prepared for commitment?"

I consider the question thoughtfully. While I don't think I know any of these ladies well enough to get married tomorrow, I consider if I even *want* to be married again. Something I had considered in an abstract kind of way is now not an abstract thought.

Marriage doesn't mean the person is going to stay.

"I'm prepared to see where things go because I don't think I can say I'm prepared for marriage at this moment. You might not know this about me, but I was married before. I didn't take that commitment lightly. I didn't take the ending of it lightly. And I won't enter into another relationship lightly."

"Why are you on this show if you're not looking for love?" she asks, frankly. I appreciate her directness.

It's a fair question and until this moment, I couldn't admit the answer even to myself.

I stare out at her backyard, feeling like I'm on Sharon's couch during a therapy session. Keeping my eyes straight ahead, I tell the shadows and darkness my truth.

"Because I hoped I would find someone who made me think I deserved it."

CHAPTER SEVENTEEN

ANYA

4 DAYS UNTIL PROPOSAL

There's not a single camera in the room. Not a single other person. Nothing. I'm completely alone, waiting for Parker, and a part of me wants to run around the room naked and screaming just because I can. But a knock sounds at the door of my villa within the tropical inspired resort I arrived to the night before, and I know my Desire Suite date is about to begin. My hand shakes so much as I reach for the door handle, I almost can't grasp it on the first try. Despite Parker's enthusiastic request for me to continue on the show with him in the last candle ceremony, I'm still nervous.

The Desire Suite dates are the last dates before the finale of *House of Desire*, when the proposal will happen. While the purpose of this last date is for the couple to get to know each other without any cameras around, it has become assumed sex happens more often than not. And while I'm attracted to Parker, because I have a pulse, I'm just not sure I can have sex with someone I barely know.

Sure, we've done one therapy session together that was way more effective than I ever anticipated. And sure, he's met my parents. Something someone hasn't done in quite some time. *And* they loved him.

But there's an intimacy in sharing yourself with someone I'm not sure I want to do yet. I'm not a virgin, by any means. I've had one-night stands and friends with benefits arrangements. Mutually beneficial situations where there were no feelings on either side. The person was no one to me, romantically.

But Parker?

Parker could be someone to me romantically, and once sex is involved, you can never go back. That and he's still, technically, dating Carmen and Leslie for the show. I want to be able to cross that line when I know he's just mine.

So, I stand here, hand on the handle, until finally I twist and pull the door open. My heart skips a beat as I feel the string of fate, creating a new path I can't turn away from.

"Hi," I breathe, looking up at him, almost regretting my relaxed t-shirt and sleep shorts when I see his form fitting Henley and black jeans.

"Finally," he says, grabbing me around the waist and pulling me toward him for a hard kiss that makes my toes curl.

He walks me backward and I hear the door slam behind him. I break the kiss and look down at the bag in his hand.

"Do you want to set that down in the bedroom?"

"Sure, I'll be right back," he says, kissing the tip of my nose.

I look around the room, making sure it's perfect like I have been doing for the past hour. Soft music plays from the hidden speakers around the living room. Fake candles litter the space, presumably to offer guests the choice of ambiance without the threat of fire, giving the living room a nice glow. In the bedroom, I have the few floor and table lamps on as well, their light turned down, creating a cozy effect with the fluffy bed and velvet floor to ceiling curtains.

The light over the dining table and wet bar is dark for now.

"Have you eaten?" Parker asks, coming back into the room, now in a pair of gray sweatpants and a white undershirt, making my mouth water.

Seeing him in casual clothes removes any regret and I appreciate the small gesture. With each passing moment, I'm feeling more and more at ease.

"No, but I could eat."

"You look like a bunny rabbit that's being told to grab a carrot out of a trap," Parker says, coming over to me, rubbing his hands up and down my arms. "Are you nervous?"

"Very."

"What can I do to help?"

"Hug me?"

Before I can blink, I'm in his arms. His teakwood scent engulfs me and, while still nervous, I calm. I feel Parker settle in to holding me, setting his cheek on the top of my head. And that's all I need.

Pulling back, I smile up at him.

"Thank you for that."

"The first one is on the house, but the next one will cost you."

"Mmm, while worth it, I didn't bring any money with me."

His large hand reaches up, cupping my jaw. His thumb rubbing my bottom lip and making me want to squirm, but I hold still.

"There are other ways you can pay," he says, pulling my lip down. "Like you could do my laundry."

I shove him off me as we both laugh at his antics.

"I'll keep that in mind. You mentioned food."

"I changed my mind. I think we should stare lovingly into each other's eyes for the night."

"Sure," I say, making my tone serious. "Or, we could order some pie."

"Sold." He grabs up the menu and quickly scans it. "Let me know what you want for dinner. I'll call the front desk."

"Oh, I want the French Dip. I'll always say yes to a French Dip."

He looks back at me, the receiver held to his ear. "That's always a solid choice. Hi, yes. I'd like to put in an order for room service," he says into the phone and puts in our order.

I move to the couch, pulling a blanket over my legs and snuggling into the soft space.

"What do you want to do after dinner?" he asks, joining me on the couch.

"I thought maybe we could just relax and watch some movies? Or is that too boring? What did you do with the others?"

I want to kick myself for the last question. Not only is it not my business, I also just don't *want* to know. Thankfully, he acts like I didn't even ask.

"Will you snuggle with me during the movie?"

"Hmm," I hum, tapping my mouth with my finger, considering. "It's going to cost you."

His eyes light up at my joking tone. "Oh, yeah? Have some laundry you need me to do? Or maybe some floors that need to be scrubbed?"

This is the most at ease I have seen Parker this entire time. While his kindness and humor remain unchanged, there's a looseness that makes him even more appealing. Makes me fall for him even more. This could be our lives, if we left this show in a relationship. Spending time together after work, relaxing. The image paints itself in my mind and my heart starts to race.

"A kiss." I may not be ready to have sex with him, but that doesn't mean I don't want him to touch me.

"Easy," he says, almost lunging across the couch and planting a noisy, wet kiss on my lips. "There you go."

I wipe away his affection with the back of my hand and he rests his hand on his chest, fake affront on his face.

"You didn't let me finish."

"Deepest apologies, please continue," he says magnanimously.

"I want you to kiss me like you did in the bakery." All humor drops from his expression and his eyes burn into mine.

"Like the bakery, huh?" Unlike last time, he moves slowly, with purpose. A squeak escapes me as he grabs my ankle and pulls me toward him, laying me out on the couch. "I can do that."

He moves over me, holding the majority of his weight off me. I run my hands up his back, feeling his muscles twitch and pull him down on top of me.

"I don't want to crush you," he whispers as I spread my legs, letting him settle between them.

"You won't," I say before I capture his mouth.

Everything about it is perfect. We take our time tasting each other until he pulls away panting, making his way down my neck, littering kisses as he goes. He follows the neckline of my shirt until he's kissing the swell of my breast, pulling the fabric down ever so slightly, bearing more skin to his attentions.

My nipples pebble beneath my lace bra, and I can tell he's aching to suck them into his mouth.

My pulse thunders as I take a deep breath and twine my fingers in his hair, holding him to me tightly, higher than I want him to be, but not yet crossing that line. As his hands move under the hem of my shirt and tease the under-side of my breast, I consider throwing all my plans out the window and letting Parker take me.

That is, until the knock at the door has us springing apart like guilty teenagers.

CHAPTER EIGHTEEN

PARKER

"Room service," the voice calls out.

"Coming," Anastasia says, her voice husky with lust as she pulls her clothes into order. I would normally get up and get the door myself, but my raging hard on is probably not something the poor resort employee wants to see.

"Good evening, ma'am. Where would you like me to put this delicious food?" he asks, pushing the silver cart into the room.

"The table would be great, thank you," Anastasia says. Awkward silence fills the air as we wait for the server to finish placing the dishes on the table.

"Is there anything else I can do for you?"

"No, thank you so much." Anya holds the door open for him. By the time he pushes his cart out of the door, my erection has deflated enough I can stand up.

I move over to the table and pull out her chair.

"After you," I say.

"Why thank you, sir."

As we eat, we talk about small things, and I get a small glimpse of what it could be like to date Anya out in the real world. How much she loves her family and friends. How she does everything she can to be at Dom's games or have a monthly dinner with her parents. And every minute I realize how grateful I feel.

Grateful to be having dinner with this woman.

Grateful she was giving me a chance.

Grateful for the impulsive decision that led me here.

"Have you ever broken a bone?" I ask, taking a sip of my wine Anya had in the room.

"My best friend bet me I was too chicken to jump off the swings. But what she didn't know is I had been doing that with Dom whenever our parents would take us to the park. No matter how much we got yelled at about it. So, I got going really high and when I released, I could tell I had gone too high and panicked."

"The worst thing you can do," I say.

"Pretty much. I landed weird and had to catch myself. The momentum or the angle, I dunno, whatever it was, caused my arm to break. I was in a cast for eight weeks. In the summer. I couldn't swim, so you can imagine how upset I was."

"Swimming is the best part of summer. I always hated how itchy casts would get."

"What have you broken?"

"I broke my leg. It was during rugby. A guy on the other team was trying to tackle me and the field was muddy. My foot sunk down into the mud just enough that when he hit me, I twisted and my foot stayed where it was for a second longer than it should have. I was in a cast for twelve weeks, I think? I can't remember. Long enough," I told her, the phantom pain echoing in my leg for just a moment.

"Ouch," she says, wincing in sympathy and touching her leg. "Do you still play?"

"No, I gave it up about a year ago? Mitchel and I just had too much to do when our business really started gaining traction. Plus, I'm not twenty-one anymore and the hits were starting to wear on my body."

"A good problem to have. Sucks about your leg, though."

"It's fine now." I push my plate away from me. "Ready for the movie? I was thinking a slasher movie, so you'll get scared and want me to protect you. And me, being the big, strong man I am, will hold you in my arms." I give her a cheesy grin as she laughs, and while I make the suggestion sound like a joke, a night with her in my arms for a few hours is exactly what I want.

"Fine, we'll watch that, but then you have to watch *Titanic* with me."

I want to groan. That was Brittany's favorite movie. She loved the love story and the great tragedy of Jack's death. We watched it so many times I could almost recite it.

I want to tell her no, tell her there are too many memories and I want to be in the moment with her, but when she looks at me like that, it doesn't matter. But I hear Sharon's voice in my head, telling me even though it'll be hard, choosing to leave the past in the past will help me start to heal.

"Deal," I say choosing to enjoy this moment with Anya, even though it's the most complicated decision I've made.

"I should warn you; Dom and I used to watch slasher movies and make fun of them. I might not be cowering like you're hoping for. But if you get scared, I'll hold your hand," she teases, moving over to the couch.

Anastasia is leaned against me, eyes tight on the screen as Rose tries to break the handcuffs keeping Jack tied to a pipe in a room filling with water. Both of my ass cheeks and my arm are numb, but I don't care. She's comfortable and that's what matters.

She hadn't been kidding about laughing at slasher movies. And after listening to her mock the various characters for how they run, their decision-making abilities, and the quality of their screams, I ended up joining in and instead of being mildly uneasy from the jump scares, I was laughing along with her.

"Isn't this romantic?" she asks, a sigh in her voice.

"I feel like the whole ship sinking situation really puts a damper on the romance."

She sits up, staring at me with a look of shock on her face. I take advantage of her movement and shift. Pins and needles prick as the blood rushes into my extremities.

"*What* are you talking about? That makes it even more romantic!"

"I would be a little upset about having to die for someone I met two days before."

"Hey, Parker?"

The tone of her voice removes every bit of teasing out of my body.

"Hey, Anastasia?" My lungs feel like they are struggling to draw oxygen into my body.

"Wanna make out?"

Her blunt question has my thumb pressing the pause button. I turn on the couch and give her every ounce of my attention.

"I've wanted to do that since I knocked on the door. Earlier was not even close to enough, but I figured pouncing on you again would be a little overzealous," I tell her.

"I wouldn't have minded."

"The food would have gotten cold."

She shifts on the couch, moving toward me. With a question in her eyes, she puts a hand on my shoulder, forcing me to turn away from her so she can straddle my lap.

"Is this okay?" she asks, settling her weight onto my legs. My hands go to her ass and drag her over my hard dick. She rocks against me again, this time without my help, and I groan.

"Does that answer your question?" I ask her.

"Yes," she whispers, staring at my mouth.

"Good."

I tangle my fingers in her hair, pulling her full mouth down to mine. She tastes lightly of the cookies and cream she had while we watched the slasher flick earlier. Every time I kiss her, she tastes of sugar and chocolate and I become more and more addicted.

Her tongue runs across my bottom lip.

Tentative.

Seeking.

But that just won't do. Changing my grip, I angle her face. Her lips part, welcoming me as I delve deep inside, our tongues tangling in passion and need. Anya moans into my mouth and I release her hair, running my hand down her back, pressing her to me.

As my hand finds her ass once more, I give her a smack.

She pulls back, both of us panting.

"So, you thought dinner getting cold was more important?"

"I'm an idiot with no excuse," I say before I dive back in, lifting her slightly and pressing her back to the seat of the couch, settling between her legs.

"Parker, wait," she says, squirming, and I push back off her immediately, sitting on my haunches, looking down at her.

"Are you okay? What's wrong?"

"No, I'm okay, I just," she stutters, "I don't—"

"It's okay," I say, running my hand on the outside of her calf, reassuringly. "We'll go as far as we are both comfortable with. No further."

"I knew you'd understand. I just wanted to say it."

"Just tap me," I say as I settle back over her, her thighs tightening around my hips.

"Kiss me," she begs.

"Yes, ma'am," I respond as I take her swollen lips once more, knowing she's the one I have to pick at the finale.

CHAPTER NINETEEN

M Y PALMS ARE SWEATING, breathing shallow.

"The cameras are ready. Just to recap, she will show you three rings for each woman based on their answers to the questions during the application process.

"You have to look through all of them and pick one for each woman. We will have both available tomorrow in case you change your mind on who you're picking," Philip says, tapping away at his phone, oblivious to my panic. "Are you ready?"

While he seems to be giving me a choice, it's only for appearances. I have no choice. This was in the contract.

"Let's get this over with," I say, making to grab for the door handle, but he stops me.

"We would prefer more of an excited, 'so happy to be here' kind of attitude."

"Got it."

The sun is bright as I open the door, and head inside the high-end jewelry store. It's empty but for the associate behind the counter. And the camera people.

And the members of production.

Really, it's just empty of other customers.

"Hello, and welcome to Timeless Jewels," the associate says, holding her hand out for me. She reminds me of the associate who helped Alec find a ring for Charlie, but where Alec was calm and excited, I'm a walking panic attack.

I walk over to her, a smile on my face for the camera. Maybe if I fake it, eventually the calmness will filter to my insides.

"I'm Parker," I say shaking her hand. "Thank you for having us."

"It's our pleasure to mark this momentous occasion in your life. We've preselected some rings for you to review." She pulls two black velvet covered trays, three rings on each one. "This one is for Carmen and this one for Anastasia," she says, indicating, first the left and then the right.

But I didn't need any help determining which set was for which woman. The ones for Carmen are large and flashy while Anastasia's are more intricate and unique.

Letting go of Leslie at the last elimination was difficult, but ever since the first night, I knew it was going to come down to these two ladies. While I'm ring shopping, Philip told me they are both trying on various gowns for the finale.

The associate goes through the rings for each woman. There's a lot of 'emerald cut' this and 'pave band' that and it all begins to blend together.

Without much thought, I pick out a ring for Carmen I know I'll never give her.

I look at the rings for Anastasia and there's something about them that, while beautiful and something I could see her wearing, I know they aren't really *her*.

The one on the right keeps pulling my attention. I know it's the right choice out of these available options.

"This one," I say, pointing to it.

"Stunning choice, sir. Whichever lady you choose will be incredibly lucky."

I wipe the sweat beading on my forehead and thank her for her time, all but running out of the store.

My fingers tremble as I try to tie my bowtie for a third time. My day started at three in the morning when I decided sleep was not in the cards for me. Could I see myself with Anastasia? Yes. Absolutely. She's smart and funny and caring and I would be lucky to call her mine.

A camera moves to catch me untying the tie again.

What if everything I like about Anastasia has been for the show? I pause before starting my fourth attempt. Worry seeps into every crevice and strangles any other thought.

What if Anya has been pretending this entire time? I think about each of our times together, and how hard it is to deliver all the lines production requires of me. If she's pretending every time we are together, I'm almost impressed by her ability.

But the Anya I saw at the Desire Suite date was the same one I've seen the entire show. Other than the time with her family and at the bakery when she was telling me everything about her craft, that was the most relaxed I saw her.

Bowtie finally tied, I pull the ring box out of my pants pocket. I have opened it five hundred times since I picked it out yesterday.

There are so many things that could go wrong today. So many reasons I shouldn't be doing this. But I have to. It was in the contract. An engagement at the end of the show is required.

They don't care if it will last.

They don't care how either of us feel about it.

They don't care.

But I do.

And I don't know what to do because at the end of the day, I'm a hypocrite. I worry about Anastasia's honesty with me, how much of what I saw was for the cameras during all of these dates, these moments, that have been manufactured.

And yet.

Even how I reacted or didn't has been manufactured to an extent. How can I be mad if she did the same? Anastasia doesn't know the real me, though.

And I can't get engaged to someone who doesn't know what she's getting. Because eventually, she's going to figure out what I am. Boring. Predictable. All the things Brittany accused me of and I never wanted to be. And what I said to Anya's mom was the truth. Marriage matters to me. Commitment matters to me.

I wonder if I should change my mind. If I should propose to Carmen instead. Not because I actually *want* to be engaged to her, but because it won't hurt as much when it inevitably ends.

When she leaves.

I want a real relationship with Anya outside of this show. I want to call her and ask if she wants me to pick up pizza after she has a hard day. I want her to call me when something needs to be fixed around her shop.

I want to take her on dates.

Real dates.

But how do we do that, how do we go backward almost, if we are engaged? I wish I could talk to her so we could get on the same page. Tell her, even though I'm putting a ring on her finger, I want us to go slow. To give this a real shot.

That I want to be with her.

I should have talked to her about this during our Desire Suite date, but I was too busy kissing her.

"Are you ready?" Philip asks, popping his head into the room. Startled, I look up at him and pray I'm not about to ruin what this could be.

"Yes," I tell him, despite feeling the exact opposite.

The silence is oppressive as we ride down in the elevator. Once in the car, Philip debriefs me from the front of the car, as if this situation is completely normal.

"Carmen will come first. You'll reject her. There will be about thirty minutes, give us time to reset anything that we need, and Anastasia will arrive."

"Sounds good."

"We'll be there in fifteen minutes, so let's get some lead up shots."

He begins reading through the paper on his clipboard and I answer, as best I can. We pull up to a scenic view, the stage set.

"Got it. I'll let him know," Philip says into his phone as everyone puts the final touches on the camera set up while another wires me with a microphone.

"We are changing the order. Carmen's car is having some issues and Anastasia's had already left to get to the staging area."

I simply nod. Nothing I say matters at this point. The driver opens my door and my heart races as I step out into the early evening sun. I'm moved into position and everyone moves around, disappearing to give us the illusion of privacy.

I stand in the middle of a semi-circle of roses and other flowers I don't recognize. Candles flicker around me even though it's daytime. Before I know it, the black limo pulls up. The driver gets out, opening her door.

Just like the first day, I see her shapely leg first before she reaches out a hand to the driver to help her stand.

Anastasia is beautiful as she climbs out in her champagne dress that's covered in beads and sparkles. As perfect as she looks, the smile she gives me is radiant. Her heels crunch against the gravel and this time there is no twisting ankle sending her into a sprawling heap. She stretches out her hands once she's close to me and I marvel again at the softness of her skin before leaning down to give her inviting lips a kiss.

I linger for a moment, just in case it's the last time she lets me kiss her.

The ring in my pocket is heavy.

And the uncertainty of this moment makes my stomach turn.

"Hi," she says, breathless.

"How are you feeling?"

She bobs her head from side to side, a considering look on her face. "I'm nervous. Excited. Scared. Pick an emotion and I've pretty much felt it at some point today."

And this I understand. It has felt like I didn't control my body or emotions all day as I've readied for this moment.

"I might have cycled through a few of them myself."

I brush my thumb over the back of her knuckles and look at her perfectly manicured fingers.

"Parker, I—"

Worried that if I don't start talking now, I'll never start, I cut her off.

"Anastasia, getting to know you over the past few months has been one of the simple pleasures of my life. You're smart and funny and kind and stunning. But as beautiful as you are on the outside, you're even more beautiful on the inside. I am so incredibly humbled you chose to take a chance on this show and me."

"I wouldn't have wanted to do it with anyone else," she says, smiling, but this time it doesn't reach her eyes. In fact, other than her initial smile, all of her expressions have been more mask than real after I kissed her. As if she's having to school her features in what to do instead of showing what truly churns inside her.

My nerves explode at the change in her but I push it aside, telling myself she's just as nervous as I am. Releasing her hands, I grab the ring from my pocket while I get down on one knee. Her eyes widen as I move, tears brimming.

I open the box and take a deep breath.

"Anastasia, I know you wish for a partner. I can't promise this will be perfect, but what I can promise is that I want to be with you and see where it leads. The first night I saw you, all I desired was you. Will you please accept this ring as a symbol of the undying flame of that desire?"

The last words are not my own, the show preferring to bring it back around. This is *House of Desire* after all. Shouldn't desire be mentioned in the proposal?

But I don't care that I didn't *technically* propose. Because if I ever did ask someone to marry me, they would never have to wonder if it's real or not. And so long as a ring ends up on a finger, I doubt production will nitpick this nuance.

Her perfectly manicured hands come up and cover her mouth as a single, perfect tear streams down her face. Much like night one, I see disaster about to strike but am powerless to stop it.

"I can't," she says.

The world stops spinning, I'm sure of it.

"What?" I ask past the ringing in my ears.

"I'm so sorry. Parker, please, stand up."

"Not until you say yes." I almost beg her. Beg her to accept me. To want me.

To choose me.

"I can't say yes. I'm sorry, please," she tugs on my arm and I surge to my feet, the protective walls I've built around my heart slamming back into place. I hadn't realized until this moment how thoroughly she had crushed them.

"What do you mean you can't? Don't you want to see what could happen between us?"

Hurt and embarrassment turn to anger bubbling in my guts, and it's all I can do to continue standing there.

"Of course, *of course I do*. But we don't have to be engaged to do that. And I like you, Parker! I have the biggest crush on you and after our Desire Suite night I realized what I'm feeling is real. It's *real,* but I can't say yes to you when I'm not sure you're fully ready for the commitment of trying to make this work.

"We will have even more pressure put on us because of the audience and tabloids. And if we both aren't ready to give this everything we have, we will be torn apart and I don't want that for either of us. It's too much pressure. I need you to understand. Please."

Tears gather in her eyes, but they do nothing to stop the snort of dismissive laughter.

"Do you really think I believed it would be a *real* engagement?" I step back from her, crossing my arms over my chest. "I had to pick between you and Carmen so, here we are." Vile words spew from my poisoned heart, and I see as they destroy her. But I can't take them back.

All I can do is protect her from the broken shards of myself.

"Parker—" she says, stepping toward me, but I take a sharp step back.

"Just go, Anastasia," I interrupt. Her mouth keeps moving, but I can't hear the words over the sound of my thrumming pulse. Honey brown eyes search my face and she nods at whatever she finds.

As if time is slowed, she takes a step away from me and my chest tightens. My greatest fear turning into reality.

Another step back, eyes still locked with mine, and my heart skips a beat.

A third step, and all the oxygen is sucked out of the entire world.

She turns around, her dress swishing around her feet as they carry her away from me. She looks at me one last time as the limo door shuts behind her and I die, my heart rending in two, while I watch her drive away from me.

CHAPTER TWENTY

ANYA

I TRY TO HIDE the tears pouring down my face at his cruelty, but it's impossible. Cameras are mounted in the corner pointing right at me. Every moment of this heartbreak is going to be shown to the country. I know the audience will love Parker. They are going to call me stupid and delusional for rejecting a man like him. But they could never understand.

As I wipe my tears, a part of my brain wonders if the harsh words he spewed is the real Parker. How, if I just saw the real Parker, was he able to seem so kind and loving every other day? It doesn't matter that I want to be with him in the real world and give this a real shot. No matter how much I worried this would be the outcome, I know I made the right decision.

The worst part of it all is I didn't know I would have to reject him until after he left our Desire Suite date so I couldn't warn him. So that we could decide what to do together. If I had known before, I could have told him. Asked him, if he picked me, what we should do.

But I didn't know.

I didn't know until I watched him walk away from my suite in the morning, every footstep recorded by the cameras twenty feet away. After such a perfect date, I knew I wanted more of this. Chances to wake up beside him. Kiss him. Getting to know every inch of him.

But a ring on my finger would make me feel like we were still performing for an audience that doesn't care that we are real people with real feelings.

The member of production in the front seat deems I have had enough time to wallow and opens the partition. Her face is placid. Calm and uncaring my heart is sitting, broken and bleeding, inside a horseshoe of roses.

"Anastasia, why did you reject Parker?" she asks, looking at something in her lap. Probably the clipboards they always carried around with them.

"Because I like him," I tell her simply, proud my voice is not warbling with tears.

"Wouldn't that be a reason to say yes?"

"I don't want him to propose to me because I'm one of two women left at the end of a competition."

"Oh, I'm sorry. Can you give that answer again? We don't like to call it a competition. We prefer journey." She sits there, guileless eyes looking at me, like it's a perfectly normal thing to ask someone going through heartbreak to reword their answer to a question so it can be used in a sound bite.

But I guess, it is normal here.

This isn't the first time I've been asked to say something again or move my head or my hand or stand differently. Over the past nine weeks, it's like I've been a really bad actor and was improvising until suddenly I was given one line of a script.

"I don't want him to propose to me because I'm one of two women left at the end of this journey," I say, emphasizing 'journey' so I don't have to repeat myself again.

"Great. And did you have sex with Parker last night?" she asks, making a mark on her clipboard. I scowl.

"That's not your business."

"Does it bother you he, most likely, had sex with another woman so close to when you'd be seeing him?"

"That's not your concern, either."

"I'm afraid it is," she says before turning to the driver. "Can you circle around? We have a few more questions to get through before she can go into the hotel."

I hear the click, click, click of the turn signal as the driver takes the car around the block and I almost want to laugh at the absurdity of this situation. Here I sit, in a beautiful gown with tear-streaked makeup, wishing I had a chance to talk to Parker alone, and these people want to continue interviewing me.

"Now, would you say, despite your rejection, you're glad Parker picked you?"

Emotions all over the place, a giggle escapes. I'd like to think it's better than tears, but that's probably not true, since this will absolutely be cut and shown in a way that does nothing but make me seem petty and mean.

For the first time in nine weeks, I make the decision not to play the game. I ignore the question, leaning my head against the seat, and I hope they are giving Parker the space they refuse to give to me.

SIX WEEKS LATER

CHAPTER TWENTY-ONE

PARKER

I FINALLY FILMED MY last interview for the start of season promotion and all I could think about since I've left the mansion is Anya walking away from me. In one week, people will be able to watch me fall for her and then ruin everything. A part of me is still upset I will never see her again. Never get a chance to tell her I'm sorry for the things I said.

And never get to tell her I understand.

But the most important part would be apologizing.

My car pulls up to the *House of Deceit* mansion that was my home for twelve weeks so many years ago and in this moment, I realize how far I've come from the man who had a casual flirtation with someone that has become like a sister to me.

Tires crunch against the gravel as another car pulls up and I know that it's Charlie's. I'm glad the interviewer tonight wanted to film the segment instead of having a live meeting. It made it so I could be here for my best friend's movie premiere based on her book of our time in this house.

Plus, Alec will be proposing tonight.

A twist of jealousy in my belly sets my face in a frown. Unlike with my proposal, I know exactly what the answer will be tonight.

She gets out of the car, and stares up at the house for a moment while I walk up behind her.

"Are you ready?" I ask.

"How was filming? I didn't think you'd be here!" she exclaims, her arms wrapping around me, mine doing the same automatically. As much as I don't want to be at a party for hours, I have missed her.

"Filming was fine. I got in last night. We taped the last talk show spot instead of doing it live. Something came up for the interviewer."

She looks at me for a moment and must see the heartbreak written there. I haven't told her anything about the show and what happened, but it doesn't matter. She's always been able to read me so well.

"I'm here to talk. You've barely answered my texts since you stopped filming. Alec was willing to kidnap you to get you here tonight for me," she says.

"I don't want to talk about it. Plus, tonight is about you. Are you ready? Alec is waiting."

"Yeah, just taking a second to appreciate the view."

I give her a moment, but when I feel rain starting to fall on me, I take her garment bag and lead her into the house.

On the table in the entryway is a card and she squeals as she reads it. Taking my cue, I bend down and kiss her cheek.

"I'm going to go put this in the kitchen. See you in a bit."

Charlie peels off toward the interview room where Alec is waiting for her. When I let him know I'd be able to make it, he texted me all the details, making sure I'd lead her there once we were in the mansion. I walk through the various rooms and head back to the bathroom so I can get dressed in my tux.

Philip arranged everything for me so I wouldn't have to worry about what I'd wear. I make a mental note to thank him again as I unzip the garment bag and see everything is perfectly pressed.

Once I'm dressed, I walk through the house, reliving the memories. Nostalgia tightens my throat as I think about the time when the girls all put on a talent show, threatening our manhoods if we weren't there. Chuckling, I make my way to the living room, sure Alec is almost done proposing, and stare outside the glass doors.

Her sniffles of, hopefully, happy tears have me turning around.

"So, did you say yes?"

Her jaw drops and she swats my shoulder. "You knew?"

The fact she is surprised by this makes me throw my head back and laugh for the first time since Anastasia rejected me.

"I went with him to pick out the ring. We flew Courtney out to help, too," I tell her.

"I can't believe you lied to me, your fake girlfriend! And I will be having words with Court."

Knowing we don't have a lot of time, I place my hand on her back and begin leading her back to the dressing room.

"Don't be too mad at her. It was for a good reason."

I stand outside the room, keeping anyone from walking in on her, as I hear people setting up and a few early arrivals. The door flings open and all I can do is stare.

"Tell me I look beautiful," she says, with a megawatt smile.

"You look beautiful," I tell her and mean it. The eggplant purple dress stands out against her freckled skin, clinging to her curves. A slit hits high on her thigh as the skirt flows down to the ground.

While she's stunning, always has been, the happiness bleeding from her turns her into nothing short of an enchantress. My throat tightens again as my heart clenches. The joy of watching the person I love the most find her happiness fills the cracks inside me with light.

I wouldn't be standing here without her.

I wouldn't have met Anastasia without her and that would have been a loss no matter how it ended.

"Good job," she says, taking my arm, and leading me to the backyard where the guests will arrive. "This is going to be fun!"

As the stars of the movie arrive, I almost have an out-of-body experience. Seeing someone who is supposed to be playing me is wild. While I think he looks nothing like me, Charlie and Courtney both have sworn up and down I'm completely, and emphatically, wrong.

"Congratulations, man," I say, shaking Alec's hand as he comes out of the house into the backyard.

"Thanks. I hope you know you're required to come to the wedding," he says, making sure his tux is perfect. Like he'd ever have a string out of place.

"I wouldn't miss it for the world. Just tell me when and where. You know I'll be there."

Tank and Lorelei walk on the red carpet, posing like professionals while the photographers take picture after picture. Alec and I watch them as they make their way to us.

"Did you ask her yet?" Lorelei asks immediately, clasping her hands in front of her chest and basically bouncing with excitement.

"Ask who what?" Alec says, annoying her immediately.

"I'm going to call Dad and tell on you for being mean to me."

"Don't you think you're a little old to be a tattletale?"

"You only think that because I'm his favorite," she says, sticking her tongue out at her brother.

Charlie comes through the back door, a glass of champagne in one hand and a whiskey drink of some sort in the other. She hands it to Alec without a word as she greets Lorelei and Tank, thanking them for coming.

"So, are you going to tell me the news or are we supposed to pretend like we don't see that rock on your hand?" Lorelei asks, causing Charlie to laugh, her happiness infectious.

"Lorelei, guess what! I'm engaged," she says, thrusting her hand out. Lore squeals, grabbing her hand and getting so close, I think for a minute she's going to kiss the ring I helped pick out.

"Alec is going to be so upset you're off the market. Did you tell him you'll have to dump him now that someone's going to make an honest woman out of you?" Lorelei teases.

"He was heartsick, but I believe he'll get over it."

"Ha. Ha. Ha," Alec says, dry as the Sahara, taking a drink.

As the ladies fall, almost immediately, into talk of what type of dress Charlie should wear for the ceremony, I excuse myself and head inside looking for the bar.

"Whiskey, neat," I say, sliding next to a woman in a yellow dress.

"Parker, I thought I recognized your voice. It's so good to see you," Carmen says, turning toward me.

"Carmen? What are you doing here?" I ask, kissing her cheek in a surprised greeting.

"I'm here with a date. The actor who played Alec reached out to me on social media and we just kind of hit it off."

"That's great," I say, taking my drink from the bartender, while slipping a tip in the jar on the counter. "Listen, I never got a chance to apologize for not picking you. You're an amazing person and obviously there was chemistry between us, but there was always just something holding me back. I wish I could have been more straightforward with you on the show."

"Oh, sweetie, it's totally fine. We never would have worked anyway. I can see that now, even though I thought we'd be perfect together then." She takes a drink of her cocktail and gives a little wave to someone over my shoulder, probably her date, but my eyes stay on her.

"What do you mean? Why wouldn't we have worked?"

"Because you still need to get over your ex-wife," she says, her tone implying I'm an idiot for not seeing that.

"I am over my ex-wife."

"You might be in here," she says, tapping my forehead, "but you're not in here." Her hand settles on my heart and all I can do is stare at it, confused.

"I don't love her anymore," I tell her, agitation starting to take over at having to repeat myself.

"I didn't say you did, but that doesn't mean you're over the pain she's caused you in here." She taps my chest with one long nail. "Until you do, you'll never be able to fully love anyone."

She gives me a sad smile, and walks away. I down my drink, wiping my mouth with the back of my hand. I want to take a second and go find somewhere to sit in private to digest what Carmen just told me but I can't. This night is about Charlie and the last thing I would ever want to do is not be around to celebrate her.

Making my way through the considerably thicker crowd, I head back outside.

A waiter offers me a glass of champagne, which I take. Charlie greets everyone, but I only say hi to the people I know. After what seems like hours, I look over at the red carpet and standing in the shadow, just before she steps into the lights, is Anastasia. My heart seizes while pins and needles dance up my left arm. For a moment, I consider she's a hallucination brought on by a stroke or heart attack, but quickly rule that out.

"Is that her?" Charlie asks and all I can do is nod. We watch her make her way down the carpet. The photographers take her picture and she smiles, but it's not the smile she's given me so many times. Charlie shoves me as Anya gets to the end of the lights, almost tripping me while whispering, "Go talk to her!"

Throwing back my glass of champagne, I make my way toward her, straightening my jacket. My palms start sweating. What if she doesn't want to talk to me? All I want to do is apologize to her, but Charlie's movie premiere isn't the time to have the conversation we need to have. And since Anya doesn't like having the spotlight on her, would I be trapping her into a conversation? I should turn around and go back to Charlie's side, but the draw to Anya is too strong.

"Hi," I say. Completely moronic.

"Hey," she replies. Her eyes dart around the party as she shifts uncomfortably. She looks everywhere but at my face and my fingers scream to make her look at me.

But I don't touch her.

"You look beautiful." And she does. Her cream dress is stunning and hugs every curve.

"Thanks." When her honey brown eyes finally flick up to mine for a moment, I almost drop to my knees to beg her forgiveness. "You look pretty great yourself."

"What are you doing here? Are you with someone?" I ask, thinking of how Carmen has already found someone else, and my blood pressure starts to rise.

"Do you not want me here? I can go," she says, starting to move away from me. My hand whips out and stills her.

"No, stay. It was just curiosity, not an attack. Sorry."

"Oh. Lorelei invited me."

I whip around, looking for Alec's devious sister. She gives me a mocking wave and blows me a kiss. Apparently, Anya has shared *something* with her since we stopped filming. I glare at her before turning back to the most beautiful woman in the house.

We stand there awkwardly for a moment, just watching each other.

"Well, I guess—"

"Would you like to meet everyone? My friends?" I blurt out, interrupting her. "Or I could take you to the bar? Get you a drink?"

"I'm confused. Don't you hate me?" she asks, a tinge of anger to her voice and guilt dumps into me.

"I don't hate you. I could never hate you. Anya, I'm so sorry for the way we left things and I want to talk about it with you, apologize for real, but I don't want to do anything that ruins Charlie's night. Please believe me."

Her honey brown eyes search my face.

"I'd love to meet Charlie, if that's okay?" She shifts, still uncomfortable, but I see a little bit of hope on her face. Relief almost makes me drop to my knees, but I keep myself standing tall.

"And I know she would love to meet you," I say, offering my arm to help her across the grass. She looks at it and I wonder if my words from the failed proposal will keep her from touching me. As her fingers settle on my elbow, I reach over with my other hand and rub them gently over hers.

I go slowly with her, aware her shoes are tall and probably hard to walk in. Charlie and Alec moved inside while I talked to Anya, but by the way my best friend's face lights up as we move closer, I know she was watching the exchange through the glass. I widen my eyes slightly at her for a moment as we step into the house, trying to tell her not to embarrass me too badly.

Anya drops my arm the second we stop moving and I want to grab it and put it back, but instead I introduce her to my best friend.

"Charlie, Alec, this is Anastasia Reynier. Anya, Charlie Price and Alec King."

"Hi, it's so nice to meet you. Thank you so much for coming tonight," Charlie says, reaching out her hand, *House of Deceit* persona firmly in place. "I love your dress."

Bypassing the hand shake entirely, Anya lurches forward and envelopes Charlie in a one-armed hug. I've never been more jealous of Charlie. Ever.

"Lorelei loaned me your book and I *loved* it. It was so funny and cute and loving. I couldn't put it down. And the scene in the library? Whew. That was so hot." She says the words so fast they all run together and I almost have to bite my lip to keep from laughing.

I've watched people fawn over Charlie before, but this was by far the cutest instance.

"That's so kind of you to say," Charlie says, pulling back. "And that moment was even hotter in real life," she says, winking.

"Oh my God," Alec mumbles, dragging his hand down his face at his soon-to-be wife's antics.

"So. Did you win sweet Parker's heart at *House of Desire*?" my best friend asks, giving me a once over and I can see she is putting the pieces together of what might have happened on the show. I shouldn't have given Anya the option of meeting her. I should have taken her right to the bar. "I was considering not watching the show when it starts next week in deference to my friend here," she says, turning her gaze to me, "but sorry, bud. I'm watching every damn second of it."

"Cool. Sounds great," I say, mortified.

"I can keep a secret, I know about the NDA," she says, turning back to Anya. "You made it to the end, didn't you?"

"Okay!" I say, as Anya opens her mouth to respond, nervousness and trepidation on her face. "That's enough of that. We don't want to spoil the show for you."

And I don't want our last time together to be in her mind for the evening.

"You're a killjoy and I'm going to replace you as my male best friend. I think it's time for Keith to get a promotion."

"Keith locked you in the barn to get some peace and quiet the last time you visited," I remind her. The old rancher from *House of Deceit* loves Charlie like a daughter, no matter how much she pushes his buttons.

She waves away my comment. "I could say five words to that man and you'd think I tied him to a chair and forced him to listen to me read *The Odyssey* or something."

"He said you talked for three hours straight!" I say, laughing.

"He's dramatic. Don't worry about it. He'll be happy to replace you at the top spot. I just know it." She turns back to Anastasia, clapping her hands together. "Do you want to sit by me for the movie? I can tell you all the good secrets."

"Yes, please!" Anya says. taking the hand Charlie offers her, my friend leads her to seats in the front. Alec moves closer to me, both of us watching the women get settled in the chairs.

"She's the one, then?" he asks.

"Yeah. She's the one."

"I heard it didn't go well from one of my old co-workers on the show. I didn't tell Charlie anything," Alec says.

I look at him out of the corner of my eye before turning my attention back to the women.

"I don't think it could have gone worse."

He claps me on the shoulder, giving me a squeeze. That's about as affectionate Alec and I get, even though I consider him to be like family for loving Charlie.

"Whatever you two need to work through? I promise, it'll be worth it." He pats me on the back once more before following Charlie's path, kissing her on the cheek as he joins her.

Charlie doesn't stop talking to Anya, but she reaches back and takes Alec's hand all the same.

I walk out the back door for a moment and pull out my phone to dial the most important number I have in my contacts.

"Sharon? It's Parker. I need to set up a session."

CHAPTER TWENTY-TWO

ANYA

THE LINE GOES OUT the door of the bakery and the thought I might not have made enough for today worries me. Ever since the season of *House of Desire* started airing two weeks ago, we have been busier than usual. While, luckily, most people found my fall out of the limo to be charming and *not* humiliating, I know I would be willing to sacrifice my dignity all over again to have this amount of people in line.

"Anya! Girl, this is insane! Do you need any help?" Lorelei says, pushing through the door.

"Hey, there's a line!" one disgruntled customer shouts as Lorelei moved to stand at the end of the counter near me.

"Yes, and you're doing a great job standing in it. I'm a mobile order. Relax," Lore says with an eye roll. Feeling harried, Mom and

Dad unable to help this morning, and Liam already at school, I accept her offer.

"Yes, please. Do you want to work the register or bag things?" I ask, pulling out four cupcakes for the older woman on the other side of the counter.

I wasn't expecting this kind of increase in customers so early in the season. I talked about my business in the beginning introduction interview, but I assumed it wouldn't be until week eight in the airing schedule when they show the hometown dates, I would begin to see a pickup in business. However, apparently the town was so excited for a local businessperson to be featured, they wanted to offer their support.

I think they also hoped they'd be able to determine if I was the winner by Parker sneaking around here.

But he's not here and I have mixed emotions about it.

A part of me still wants to believe that him lashing out was not normal, brought on by my rejection and the immense amount of stress and the emotional situation we were in. Out of all the time I've spent with Parker, that was the only time I've seen him act that way. Even at the movie premiere, the Parker I saw was the carefree one I met in the Desire Suite date.

That doesn't heal the hurt his words caused and that is the part currently holding me back.

"I'm going to do the cash register. I used to work at a little restaurant in high school to make some extra money."

She sets her incredibly fashionable, but probably thrifted or second-hand bag, right on the floor by her feet. She takes a second to go through the different options on the iPad and then she's jumping in.

Soon, we are in a rhythm. I pull treat after treat from the case. She rings them up as they order. By the time I'm done boxing, their credit card is being swiped and they are out the door. It takes two hours and a few trips to the back to restock every cookie flavor, the croissants, and half of the cupcakes before we are through the line and finally able to take a breather.

"That was intense," Lorelei says, grabbing two bottles of water from the case and bringing me one. I tap in my code, marking the two items as free for inventory, and then crack open the lid, drinking down the cool liquid.

"Thank you for helping. I don't think I would have made it through without you." I flip the 'Open' sign to 'Closed' and we move into the back of the shop and grab two stools I have pushed against the wall and out of the way for slower days. "Shouldn't you be at work or something?"

"Probably, but I didn't have any client meetings today, and I was supposed to meet Charlie for breakfast over in this area. I wanted to talk to you."

"Okay? What about? You could have just called me," I tell her.

"No, this is an in person conversation."

"Yes, I will run away with you, but I just think Tank is going to really be upset and we should tell him where we are going to be so he can visit in off season."

She snorts, swatting my arm.

"That's not what I was going to ask."

"Seriously, what's up?"

She turns toward me on her stool and her eyes go big and a bit watery. Sniffling, she grabs my hands. A little concerned she's going to ask me for an organ or something, I brace myself.

"You're starting to freak me out," I tell her.

"Will you go to Charlie and Alec's wedding with me?"

"What? Why? Why isn't Tank going with you?" I take a drink of my water before getting up and grabbing us each a broken cookie I couldn't sell. I hand one to her as I take my seat again.

"They planned the wedding for Friday night so Tank could be there and fly back on Saturday for the game. I guess Alec's mentor knows the owner of a hotel in Hawai'i or something and he put in a few calls and got it all arranged and they did one of those wedding packages so the planning took pretty much no time. But that's beside the point." She waves her hand through the air. "The team they are playing hasn't won a single game, their starting quarterback got hurt, and their offensive coordinator was just fired so the league has decided to flex the game and now they are playing Sunday at noon, Saturday is no longer an off day, and he can't leave."

"But why would I go? I only met Charlie one time three weeks ago," I say, confused.

"Because you're my friend and I have a plus one and Charlie *loves* you and she maybe thinks you and Parker need to talk." She mumbles the last part so quickly I can't make out the words.

"What was that last bit there?"

She sighs. Her shoulders drop and the tears well up and I know I'm going to end up agreeing just to keep her from crying.

"When Tank told Alec he couldn't be his best man any more after the schedule change, Charlie said I could bring a friend and then mentioned you and how it'd be great because at least you would know people. And then she talked about how she watched you and Parker at the movie premier and she could see there was something there. And she loves Parker, so she'll do anything to make sure he's happy."

"I haven't seen Parker since then and the entire night it was awkward! All he wanted to do was get away from me, I'm sure." My heart starts racing at the thought of seeing Parker again, and I can feel my resistance crumbling.

"That's not how I heard it, but either way, I agree with her and you're my friend. It's my brother's wedding and I need someone to dance with and pretty much everyone else will be taken. I would go with you to Dom's wedding last minute if you needed a date."

That, paired with the single perfect tear running down her cheek, and I know she's got me. Whenever Dom gets married, I would want someone to dance and eat cake with too.

I sigh heavily and wonder how much I'm going to regret this decision.

"Okay, I'll go. But only if my dad can watch the shop. And I can find something to wear. When do we leave?"

"Five a.m." she says with a worried look, but I just roll my eyes at her.

"I guess I need to call Dad. And go shopping before everything closes," I say. My mind begins running a mile a minute, thinking of all the things I need to get done before we can leave.

"I know it's super last minute and I *might* have taken it on myself to buy you some new clothes, including a dress to wear before coming here."

"Sounds like you were very confident I was going to agree. I think I might need to reevaluate our friendship." I pause, sitting up straighter. "Wait, were those tears to guilt me into saying yes?"

Her beaming smile is all the answer I get as a mixture of anticipation and nerves settles in.

CHAPTER TWENTY-THREE

PARKER

OUR PRIVATE JET DESCENDS toward the runway, the blue water glittering like the ring on Charlie's finger. Between Alec's directorial debut being a smash hit at some festivals and making him the person to get, and Charlie's book being a bestseller for months, they decided to treat the small guest list to our own flight.

Charlie's dad snaps pictures through the window, his camera strap around his neck.

"I have a surprise for you at the resort when we get there," Charlie says, dropping down in the open seat next to me as we taxi to the area where we'll deplane. She's dressed in a soft cream dress, which I'm assuming is going to be a theme throughout the weekend.

"Isn't this your wedding? Where people give *you* gifts?"

"Societal norms aren't the boss of me."

"How could I forget. What is the gift?"

"Now where's the fun if I tell you?" she huffs.

"I can still be excited even if I know what it is."

"Mmm, maybe on other things, but not this one. Just trust me. Do you have your speech written, best man?"

"Do you have your vows written?" I ask, smirking at her.

"You should know I expect magic, so get it done." I give her a sarcastic salute as she gets up and moves back to her seat in the front next to Alec.

Shifting down into my seat, I close my eyes as we taxi to the gate where five black sedans are waiting for us.

"Damn, girl. Got that white glove treatment going on," Courtney says.

"We just wanted to make sure everyone was taken care of," Alec tells her.

The drivers help us all with our bags and the moment we are situated, our caravan takes off. Lush greenery surrounds us as we make our way to the resort, but I hardly notice with my cramped position in the furthest back seat of the car.

"Now, Parker. How was filming *House of Desire*?" Charlie's mom, Deborah, asks, turning to look back at me.

"It was great. The ladies were amazing and we had a really fun time," I tell her with my interview voice firmly in place.

"The girl who fell out of the limo is very beautiful. And funny, too! When they were in the cars on the first night, they would show these clips of them inside the cars and all the others were really boring, just talking about the house. But she was talking to the girls in her limo. She just seemed really nice."

"She was a stand out in the group, that's for sure." I still need to apologize, but after I got her number from Lorelei, every time I pick up the phone to do it, I almost end up in a ball on the floor in a panic.

"Are you still single?" she asks, a hint of intrigue in her voice.

"You know he can't tell you that, Deb," Charlie's dad says. "Stop pestering the boy."

"I'm not pestering him, am I, Parker?"

"No, ma'am. I just can't answer the question. Don't want to give away any secrets."

"Oh, yes, yes. We wouldn't want to get you in trouble. When you were on *House of Deceit* with Charlie, I wished you could both win. I liked you the most after my daughter. I thought your little romance with her was very sweet. I thought she'd be coming home with a boyfriend.

"I guess she did come home with one, didn't she? Once Alec showed up. Oh, she told us all about how you went and punched him in the face and drug him all the way across the country. That was just so sweet of you, looking out for her like that. I don't think I've ever had someone punch another person on my behalf."

"I probably should have handled it in a different way, but he's stubborn."

"He'd have to be to stand up to our Charlie," her dad says, affection shining through his voice.

We pull up in front of the hotel. Getting out of the car takes me a moment as I unpretzel my limbs, blood rushing back into my legs that fell asleep about fifteen minutes back. People stroll all over the resort. Within seconds, I spot ten different flower patterned shirts on guys as they seem to be heading toward, my guess is, a luau.

A hotel employee greets Charlie, handing her an envelope, and she nods.

"Alright, everyone. The front desk has your keys. Everyone has already been checked in. We have the rehearsal later this afternoon. If you need to attend, you've already been talked to. Otherwise, we'll see you at the rehearsal dinner tonight!" Charlie says. We all start making our way to the front desk, but Charlie grabs my arm, stopping me.

"I already have your key and I wanted to give you that gift."

"Lead the way," I say, grabbing the handle of my bag and following behind her.

The air is thick with humidity. I'm glad the shirt I'm wearing is breathable as the salty ocean breeze blows through, cooling me down.

"What is this present, anyway?" I ask, trailing behind the tall redhead. Just like everywhere else we go, heads turn as people check Charlie out.

"It's a surprise. You'll see soon."

She makes a turn and goes down a sidewalk between two cream-colored, two-story buildings that look out on the ocean. Arriving at a door, instead of putting the key in the door, she knocks.

"Is this not my room? What are we doing here?" I ask her, but she just gives me a look of annoyance before knocking again.

"My God, be patient," Charlie says as Lorelei rips open the door. I catch a glimpse of the beach through the window, straight back.

"Oh, hey! Where's my brother?" she asks, inviting us in with a sweep of her arm.

"He's helping get people settled. I just thought I'd stop by to say hi. Wanted to make sure you got settled in this morning." Charlie gives her a knowing smile as we move into the room. The room is smaller, but comfortable. Sounds of metal hangers clinking inside the closet draws my attention. I'm surprised there's someone else here since Tank isn't coming.

A hand grabs the bi-fold door, pulling it closed.

Suddenly, I'm looking into my favorite pair of honey brown eyes.

"Oh, hi," Anastasia says, no surprise in her voice.

"Parker, did I mention Lorelei brought Anya as her date?" Charlie asks, and I can hear the smile in her voice.

I gape at Anya, my mouth opening and closing like a fish out of water. All the apologies I've mentally written flood my mind and I want to say them all. Or move across the floor and pull her into my arms and kiss her.

"I'm going to give you two a moment to talk. Here's your room key." She slips a plastic card in my hand, grabs Lorelei's arm, and then heads out the door.

"I didn't realize you were coming," I tell her and at the split second of worry in her eyes I realize how my words sound. "I'm glad you're here," I amend, truthfully.

"I couldn't say no to Lorelei when she asked," she says.

We stand there awkwardly for a moment.

"I want—" I start.

"Don't you—" she says.

I give her a small smile. "Sorry, go ahead."

"Don't you have a rehearsal to get ready for?"

Hurt wraps itself around my heart like ivy and squeezes.

"Yeah, I need to go get settled and wash the flight off. I'll see you at the dinner?" I start making my way to the door, wanting to give her the space she obviously wants.

"I'll be there," she says, following me down the short hallway.

"See you then," I say, keeping my eyes on her until the door cuts off my view of her beautiful face.

"You will be helping people to their seats tomorrow. Family in the first few rows, everyone else can go wherever," the wedding planner tells me. Her blond hair is piled on top of her head in some kind of up-do, but at the moment, it looks more like someone stuck her finger in a light socket. "You will be walking Courtney down the aisle. She'll be on your left. The music will take a pause and then when it starts again, that is your cue. Walk at a normal pace."

Her large eyes almost look bugged with nerves as Courtney and I acknowledge her instructions before she moves off to Alec and Charlie's instructions.

Courtney nudges me with her sharp elbow, and I lean down for what is sure to be an entertaining comment.

"Do you get the sense she might hang upside down from a rafter in her spare time?" she whispers.

"I thought she might be having a sexual relationship with a barista who hooks her up to an espresso IV at night instead of sleeping."

"That's also a valid thought," she says, watching Charlie try not to roll her eyes at the woman. You'd think Charlie and Alec were heads of state with the number of instructions they are receiving instead of walking down the aisle in front of less than two dozen people.

"How did you like your surprise?" Courtney says, nudging me again. If she keeps doing that, I'm going to end up with a bruise on my arm.

"I wish Charlie would have warned me so I could be a bit more prepared. She didn't seem very excited to see me."

Her heart-shaped face radiates laughter. "Did that one sting, oh mighty sun god?"

I scoff, crossing my arms over my chest as Charlie practices walking down the aisle.

"Maybe."

"So sensitive when women don't throw themselves at your feet. Someone is very used to their pretty privilege."

"What the fuck is pretty privilege?"

She rolls her eyes at me like I should have any idea what she's talking about.

"Just what it sounds like. You are a striking man and because of that, you've probably never struggled getting female attention. You were just the lead on a nationwide franchise. They don't exactly let ugly people be the lead for that show."

"You think I was on *House of Desire* because I'm pretty?"

"Did they ask anyone else from your season of *House of Deceit* to do it?"

"Not that I'm aware of. No one said anything."

"Because Charlie is in a relationship. You're the only other one. Beyond the brooding, broken hearted thing, it's cause you're sexy as fuck."

I watch her, considering, and she doesn't break eye contact while my brain works through it.

"Okay, you might be correct."

"I am correct, but I'm glad you got there," she says with a smirk, patting my arm.

The wedding planner claps her hands, calling for attention. "Well done, everyone! You should have your wedding schedules in your email! If you have questions, let me know! Otherwise, I will see you all tomorrow. Have a great time at dinner!"

"That was a lot of exclamation points in her tone," Courtney says, and I snort a laugh as she walks over to her husband, who's waiting for us to be finished.

As a group, we make our way to the restaurant, everyone chatting and laughing, but all I can do is think about the fact Anastasia will be there. And I'll be able to talk to her.

All I see when I open the door is Anastasia in her red jumpsuit that drapes down her back, leaving the skin bare. My fingers itch to stroke her down her spine.

"This'll be fun," Courtney says, patting my arm as she moves past me.

Anya throws her head back and laughs, touching the arm of one of the guests and a small piece of me wants to knock the guy to the ground. Charlie walks up, and everyone looks at the bride. Except her.

She looks at me.

Her gold spike heels almost have us eye to eye and all I can do is smile.

"You look breathtaking," I tell her, wrapping her in my arms, unable to stop myself. She tenses for a moment before relaxing and putting her arms around me.

"Lore went on a bit of a shopping spree for me," she says into my ear before quickly pulling back. "One day you're going to run out of synonyms for 'beautiful'."

Her joking tone makes my chest tighten with hope.

"Maybe you'll inspire me to create new words."

"Merriam-Webster will be thrilled," she says.

I take a risk and grab her hand and lead her to a chair as the group all starts to take their seats. Dinner is a fun affair, but by the end of it I'm half hard. Our hands touched when I passed her the butter. My thigh pressed against her as I grabbed the bottle of water to refill our glasses. Her breath caressed my ear as she told me a secret. By the time Alec stood up to give a speech, I was two seconds from coming in my pants like a horny, virgin teenager.

Alec clinks his knife against his champagne flute, standing.

"Hi, everyone. We just wanted to take a moment and thank you for spending the next few days with us while I marry the love of my life. Charlie and I love you so much and we can't wait for tomorrow!" He bends down, giving Charlie a kiss as Anastasia looks up at me, smiling as she claps.

I want to kiss her in this moment, feel her soft lips, but I know I can't.

"Excuse me, sir, madam. Would you two like anything to drink from the bar?" the waiter asks, breaking our eye contact.

"Another glass of wine would be great," Anya says, standing from the table to join the mingling that is starting to happen.

"I'm good, thanks," I say, knowing I have to get out of here before I do something really stupid like try to kiss her. And to go rub one out.

I stand, my hand brushing Anya's bare lower back, and I know that's all I can handle.

"I'm going to turn in for the night," I tell her. "Have fun, okay? I'll see you tomorrow."

"Are you sure?" she asks, giving me an awkward hug.

"Yeah. It's gonna be a long day. Sleep good."

I move over to Charlie, giving her cheek a quick kiss. "I'm heading out. I'll see you tomorrow."

"It's still early. Where are you going?" she asks, taking a break from her conversation for just a second.

"I need to go blow off some steam."

She looks me up and down before looking over at Anastasia.

"Blow off some steam. Got it. Have fun," she says, giving me a wink before going back to her conversation.

With her dismissal, I give Anya one last wave and begin making my way out of the restaurant, my only goal to get back to my room.

CHAPTER TWENTY-FOUR

ANYA

PARKER WEAVES THROUGH THE tables of the resort restaurant. A few heads turn, following him through the space, and I can't blame them. The energy that pulses off of him demands attention. Pair that with his imposing frame and rugged good looks, and he's bound to draw a few gazes.

I've had to work the entire day to keep my eyes from falling on him every time he was nearby.

"Are you nervous?" I ask Charlie as she and Courtney join me for a moment. The restaurant gave us a section of tables and all the remaining guests are moving around and mingling as the evening starts to wind down. My feet throb in time with my pulse and I can't wait to get these shoes off when I get back to the room.

"The only thing I'm nervous about is crying off my makeup," she says with a smile. I watch Alec and Lorelei talk to Charlie's parents, and the conversation has brought out the groom's smile.

"While we have a second, I just want to thank you, personally, for letting me come. This place is amazing and I'm honored to get to be a part of your special day."

"I'm glad we have a chance to get to know you better," Charlie says. "Lore only has good things to say."

"Especially since Parker is head over heels for you," Courtney says, smiling as she takes a sip of her drink.

"Courtney!" Charlie exclaims.

"He's not head over heels for me."

The girls look at each other, the look they share saying more than words ever could. Charlie sighs as they look back at me.

"Anastasia, listen, Parker didn't tell me what happened between you until I pushed and even then all he said was he was a world class asshole." I shift my weight back and forth as she takes a hold of my hand. Her blue eyes hold me prisoner. "I know I'm his best friend, so you might not believe me and I wouldn't blame you, but I have to help him if it's in my power. I can see how he looks at you. And I can see the connection between you both.

"Whatever he said, probably hurt. And I'm not dismissing your very real pain or saying that you don't deserve an apology. But what I am saying is that in all the years I have known Parker, I have known him to be an incredibly kind, compassionate, loving man.

"There are things in his past—"

"I know about Brittany leaving him," I say, trying to get this conversation to end because I know she's right about the man Parker is. But that doesn't mean his words didn't cut me.

"He has been working so hard to get past that and he's not perfect. I have a feeling that whatever happened, it tied back to that for him. All I want is for you to give him a chance to apologize. That's it. If you don't want to have anything to do with him after that, then everyone will respect your choice. We won't try to force you into the same room together.

"And just so you know, I was in your place, so I know how it feels. When Alec and I started, he said some things that hurt more than I'd like to admit and yet here we are. If you still care for Parker, I promise you that he can be the best thing that's ever come into your life. I know he is for me. We wouldn't be standing here right now if Parker hadn't stepped in to help me. I hope you won't hold it against me that I'm doing the same."

A lump forms in my throat at the bright love in her eyes for Parker and I know she's right. We need to talk. I want to give him the benefit of the doubt and trust the man I have seen in every other moment since I met him. But he definitely has some groveling to do first.

I open my mouth to agree to giving him a chance to apologize until Lorelei lets out an ear-splitting squeal.

Charlie drops my hand as we look around for the reason behind her reaction and that's when I see Tank hobbling across the restaurant on crutches with a boot on one leg. Lorelei runs to him, weaving her arms around his midsection, giving him a hug. They talk for a moment before coming back to join the rest of us.

Charlie, Courtney, and I push up from the table and go to meet everyone in our group.

"What did you do?" Alec says.

"One of the guys stepped on my foot just right and somehow broke a bone in my foot. The doctors said it'll heal just fine and there shouldn't be any lasting issues, but I can't bear weight on it right now so I can't play. Since I'm on the DL, the coaching staff was okay with me flying out here for your wedding and not being on the sideline."

"We are so glad you're here, Tank!" Charlie says, giving him a hug.

"Sorry, about the foot, Bruiser," Courtney says.

Everyone mingles for a second as I make my way over to Lore, grabbing her hand.

"Hey, I'm going to go talk to the front desk and see if I can get my own room so you two can have some privacy," I tell her in a hushed tone.

"What? No! You don't have to do that. You're welcome to stay with us."

"Yeah, Anya. I'm not kicking you out. I can get a cot or something," Tank says, his arm around his wife's shoulders.

"You're going to sleep on a cot with a broken leg? Not on my watch. I'll just go talk to them," I say, folding my arms over my chest.

"I'll go with you," Lorelei says.

We say our goodbyes to the group and start to make our way out of the restaurant. Right as we are about to cross the threshold, Charlie yells at us to wait, and makes her way to join us.

"I'm coming, too, and don't even say anything. I'm the bride and I can do what I want."

She links her arms with both of us and we all traipse through the resort to the front desk. I was worried I'd feel like an outsider at such an intimate affair, but everyone has been so phenomenal at including me. Especially Charlie.

A waterfall is in the middle of the open-air reception, the sound tranquil. Palm trees dance in the slight breeze and music from a luau carries through the night air. All the receptionists are in cream-colored flower shirts and the women have their hair pinned back on one side, a flower tucked behind their ears.

"Hello. How may I help you?" one says, her teeth perfectly white and even in her perfectly placid smile.

"Hi, my name is Charlie. I'm the bride for the Price/King wedding. We have a bit of a situation with an extra guest showing up and we need to play musical rooms just a bit. Do you have any rooms available we could rent for the weekend?" the beautiful redhead asks, her voice and body pulling the attention of the male receptionists.

"Unfortunately, we are all booked up this weekend with four different weddings and various other groups. We would be happy to arrange other accommodation on the island on your guest's behalf if that is something they would prefer?" the woman says, her sanguine smile not budging an inch.

"No, that's alright. We want our family to all be here together. Thank you, anyway."

We all move off to the side so other guests can be assisted and huddle in a small circle.

"Okay, what are the options. I'm trying to think if anyone booked a two-bed room that maybe we could move around," Charlie says, tapping her finger to his lips.

"I don't want to inconvenience anyone. I wasn't supposed to be here, anyway. I can go to the other hotel, hang out, and then meet up to go back home. I really don't mind."

"No, absolutely not," Charlie says, her tone stubborn.

"There's always Tank's cot idea," Lorelei says.

"Parker," Charlie says.

I hesitate. Charlie's words from earlier run through my head and I realize how perfect of an opportunity it would be if we could have some privacy to talk.

"If you don't think he'll mind…" I say, trailing off. Part of me wants to still go to the other hotel, but the thought of being able to talk, to finally get past this, is too attractive.

"He wouldn't mind." She pulls out her phone and taps in a number before holding it up to her ear. I don't know if I'm more impressed she actually has someone's phone number memorized in this day and age or if I'm mortified that I'm basically forcing myself on him. She makes a noise of annoyance as I hear his voice mail click in, her call unanswered.

"Damn Viking. I'll text him. In the meantime, let's go get your stuff."

Like a puppy, I follow them back to our room, Charlie tapping away on her phone.

"Any luck?" Tank asks from our couch, his leg propped up on the coffee table.

"No. I'm going to have her room with Parker," Charlie says, not taking her eyes from her phone.

Tank snorts a laugh and mumbles something I think sounds like "This should be interesting" but I'm not sure. I make my way to my luggage and begin repacking all of my clothes and toiletries. One thing Mom taught me growing up was to never leave a suitcase packed when you get to your destination. That causes wrinkles and just delays your ability to get dressed and move on to the fun part of the day.

As I pull the zipper around, Charlie moves to me and hands me a key.

"He's in one of the small villas over on the ocean side. Room 1217. Do you need me to show you?"

"No, I know where those are. You're sure he'll be good with it?"

"Trust me, he'd be offended if we *didn't* let him help when he's in the position to do so." She opens the door for me.

"I'll see you all tomorrow, then. Have a good night."

"You too! And tell Parker to call me in the morning when he's awake."

"Will do," I say.

I make my way through the resort, pulling my suitcase behind me, following the signs to the villas, until I find his room. Knocking to warn him I'm coming in, I insert my key and push through the door. The first thing I notice is the sound of the waves crashing against the shore through the open wall. Floor to ceiling glass panels are pushed over the left. Two chairs are out on the lanai for relaxing during the day. A sumptuous couch faces a blank wall except for a console table that, if I had to guess, holds the TV. Moving toward the living room, I pass a partially open door.

The sound of grunts meet my ears.

"Hello," I call out, but no one responds. "Parker?" Wondering if I'm somehow in the wrong room, I push open the door, and come face to face with Parker's naked, beautiful ass.

His back muscles move and flex as he strokes himself aggressively. His moans are sexy and more intoxicating than all the alcohol I had at dinner. Eyes shut, his mouth hangs open as I watch him pleasure himself in the mirror, the sight the most erotic thing I've ever seen. I wonder who he's thinking about, what made him so ravenous he had to take care of himself, and a small, infinitesimal part of me hopes it was me.

"That feels so good. Don't stop," he moans. Giving himself a few more strokes, with a groan, he comes.

The handle of my bag drops from my fingers as I watch him, my thighs slick with my wanting, but at the sound, his green eyes snap open, finding me.

"What the fuck!" he says, ripping a towel off the counter and wrapping it around his waist.

"Sorry, I, well, you see, Tank, he. And I. So here. That looked like it felt good." I feel my face heat at that honesty and babble some more. "I'll give you a minute to…" I gesture at him before deciding the best thing I can do is shut the fuck up and go wait for him.

Water starts to run as, I assume, he washes his hands and before I can get myself back under control, he's standing in front of me, his naked chest a complete distraction.

"What are you doing in my room, Anastasia?" he asks, his voice curious.

"Did you not get Charlie's texts? She tried calling and texting you."

My heart is racing so hard I'm afraid I'm going to pass out. It takes every single iota of self-control I possess to not jump him right here and now.

"No, I hadn't seen them."

"Well, sure, your hands, or hand really, was full."

"Jesus. Why are you here?" he asks, his tone merely curious. His arms flex as he pulls his hair up, tying it into a bun at the base of his neck, a single strand hanging loose and covering his face. My hands want to tuck it away. They also want to take off his towel, and so I wrap them around myself to keep from doing either of those things.

"Tank showed up. He broke his foot and now he's here and I was going to stay with Lorelei this weekend but he's here and he can't sleep on a cot and I'm not entirely sure I want to sleep in a bed with both of them although they are both very attractive and that wouldn't be a bad thing if this was a porn but it's not, a porn that is, and so Charlie said you wouldn't mind if I stayed with you," I ramble.

"You want to stay with me because this isn't a porn?" I can see him trying not to laugh, so I close my eyes and take a deep breath and try to bring my racing heart under control. And to banish the attraction coursing through my blood like I just downed eight espressos in one go. Once I feel like I'm semi back on solid ground, I open my eyes again.

"Charlie suggested, since you have this room to yourself, I could stay with you. If that's okay."

"Oh, well," he scratches the back of his neck and looks around, obviously uncomfortable with the entire situation.

"I could sleep on the couch!" I offer. "It looks comfortable enough."

"Don't be ridiculous, you're not going to sleep on the couch. You can sleep in the bed. With me."

We make eye contact and my stomach floats. This is a bad idea, I know it is, but my stupid, traitorous mouth simply says, "Okay."

CHAPTER TWENTY-FIVE

As the sun comes up, lightening the sky outside, the ceiling becomes visible. The ceiling I've stared at almost all night. When I wasn't tossing and turning, that is. At first, the sound of the ocean kept me awake. Parker preferred to have the windows open, letting the ocean breeze sweep through the space. For someone who doesn't sleep with any white noise normally, this was incredibly distracting to me.

But the noise didn't hold a candle to the distraction that was sleeping next to Parker. The last time we slept in a bed together, his strong arms were wrapped around me and we didn't know what was to come the next day. This time, there was no snuggling. No gentle kisses on my shoulder. No marriage proposal waiting on the other side.

There was only a divider made of spare pillows that I wanted to rip away.

Every time my eyes closed, Parker's face as he spilled his seed in the bathroom would dance across my mind. My fingers ached to take care of myself. At one point, I considered going into the bathroom and following Parker's lead. But I couldn't do that.

What if he heard me?

And worse, joined me?

Or even worse, didn't join me?

My libido was firmly on team "join me" and my mind waffled between the two.

"Psst. Parker?" I whisper into the dawn. Even though he still has some groveling to do, I've softened a lot since my talk with Charlie.

"What?" he whispers back.

"Are you awake?"

"No. I'm asleep."

"Can you be awake?"

"What's in it for me?"

"The pleasure of my company?"

"I don't know if that's sufficient. Your inability to lay still and loud thoughts kept me up most of the night and I needed my beauty sleep. I'm in a wedding today."

I rip away the pillow blocking our faces, his already turned toward me humor lighting his eyes, and glare at him.

"I've got news for you. No one cares if you look pretty," I inform him.

"Untrue. There are going to be pictures of this event and I have to stand up next to Alec."

"Tank is here, now. Maybe he'll demote you."

"He texted me last night to let me know I'd still be best man."

"Oh, so that text you got," I joke and know it was not the right thing to say.

His eyes darken, tongue peeking out to wet his bottom lip. My gaze tracks the movement, wanting to lean over to kiss him. The memory of his hands on my body as he kissed me on the couch during the Desire Suite date makes me shift toward him, ever so slightly. Enough that, if he wasn't interested, could be taken as me getting more comfortable.

"Anastasia," he whispers, but my name is heavy with implication and desire.

"We should go get breakfast," I say, flinging the blankets off me. Almost jumping from the bed, I storm out onto the lanai, to get some air before I do something stupid like beg him to kiss me.

Footsteps sound through the villa, and I feel him standing behind me.

"I can't go get breakfast. I'm supposed to meet up with Alec and all the guys soon. We are grabbing food and going golfing. I'm sorry." He whispers the last part and it sounds sincere.

His fingers blaze a trail of heat down my arm, but I don't look at him. When he hugged me last night, it took me by surprise, but my body quickly remembered how much it loves being in his arms. And if I look at him right now, I might kiss him.

I feel him press against my back, wrapping his arms around me.

"I'll see you later, yeah?"

I nod and his lips press a kiss where my neck meets my shoulder, branding me. My mouth opens in silent exclamation. I want him to continue, but his arms drop from around me, the door opening and shutting gently a few minutes later.

Stomach grumbling, I move into the room, grabbing up the phone and pull the menu toward me.

"Kitchens," the man says, the sound of lots of people moving coming through the receiver.

"Hello, I'd like to place a room service order, if that's okay?"

"I'd be happy to take care of that, Mrs. Hightower. What can I get for you?"

I pause at his assumption that I'm Parker's wife, butterflies swarming in my stomach, but decide to leave it uncorrected. "Could I get the kalua pork eggs benedict, please? And some of that green juice? And a side of hash browns."

"No problem. We'll have it to you in thirty minutes." He hangs up the phone without saying goodbye.

My morning passes in a haze of relaxation. I take a nap on one of the loungers, trying to catch up on the sleep I didn't get last night. Looking at the time, I know I can't put it off any longer and go to get ready to watch two people declare their love for each other.

"I don't think you're supposed to look that good. You might upstage the bride," Parker says as I move toward him.

My silk, emerald dress has flowers all over it, skinny straps that crisscross over the back, and is my favorite thing Lorelei bought for me. She refused to take my money when I offered to pay her back for everything she bought but that just means I will be baking her things for free for the foreseeable future.

"You look pretty great yourself," I say, smiling. His tuxedo fits him like a glove and I catch more than one set of hungry eyes on his ass.

He offers me his arm. "Let me show you to your seat."

"Thank you," I say, linking my arm with his.

There are five rows of five chairs, split in groups of two with the aisle going down the center, and I wonder how I'm so lucky to be here. Ignoring the awkwardness between me and Parker this has been an incredible getaway and I'm glad that I agreed to come.

Parker leads me to the fourth row and puts me on the seat farthest from the aisle Charlie will be walking down. He takes my hand from his elbow and keeps a firm grip on it until I'm standing steadily in front of my chair. I turn back to him and I'm almost struck stupid by how beautiful he is.

His hair is tied back in his low bun, but a few strands have freed themselves to frame his face. The straight nose and stubbled jaw line are softened by his full lips and the faint laugh lines around his eyes.

Our eyes don't leave each other as the moment stretches, crackling like a fire between us. The wind blows, pulling my softly curled hair across my face, but before I can fix it, Parker's fingers are there, pulling it back and tucking it behind my ear, his thumb running the length of my jaw.

My eyes fall to his parted lips and for a moment, I think he's going to kiss me.

I want him to kiss me.

But before we can linger any longer, one of the guests I've not met calls his name and the moment melts like a snowflake on pavement warmed by the sun.

"Save me a dance?" he asks, giving the universal 'one moment' sign to the other guest.

"I'm sure I can find a slot for you," I say, imagining his strong hands pushing me around the dance floor.

Without another word, he nods, turns, and leaves.

Time seems to be moving at a normal pace again. I look around at the beautiful venue Charlie and Alec have chosen for the ceremony. While a simple affair, the backdrop is anything but.

A custom arch flows like a cresting wave with pink and purple flowers covering every square inch. The sun is setting behind us, giving the altar, and the sweeping view, a beautiful glow. Waves crash below the cliff, adding to the ambiance of the day. Lorelei mentioned the official, as well as Charlie and Alec, will be wearing small microphones that will play to speakers hidden discreetly below a few of the rows of chairs so everyone will be able to hear the ceremony.

But the beautiful venue can't keep my eyes from Parker forever. I watch as Lorelei touches Parker, a gentle hand on his, and for the first time since we left the *House of Desire*, I want to bat it away. The irrational spark of jealousy leaves me fuming as he walks her down the aisle to her seat in front of me. He kisses the back of her hand and I can't help but huff. Did he not want to kiss my hand?

The trail his thumb made along my jaw warms with his phantom fingers and I try to tame the dragon within me, fighting to free itself.

"You look great," Lore says, looking back at me.

"All thanks to you," I tell her, tamping down the jealousy.

"How was last night?" I think of Parker in the bathroom once more and feel the blush walk up my neck. "That good, huh?" she says with a smirk.

"It was no big deal."

"Uh huh."

With such a small wedding, it only takes about ten minutes to get everyone seated and the music that has been gently playing changes as Alec follows the officiant down the aisle. As if by magic, Courtney appears at the top of the aisle, her plum, floor length lace dress with sweetheart neckline amplifying the petite woman's curves, her arm through Parker's. A tissue peeks out of her bouquet clutching hands. She smiles and winks at a man, I'm assuming her husband, as she makes her way down the aisle and stands waiting, tears already gathering in her bespectacled eyes.

When they get to the front of the aisle, they split off. Parker slots between Alec and Tank who's sitting comfortably on a chair.

The music changes again and the officiant gestures for us to stand. Notes of the song waft on the air as Charlie comes to stand at the aisle, her smile visible from space.

Her dress is magnificent. Instead of stark white, she's chosen a beautiful cream that warms her skin. The A-line shape has a gentle flare from her hips, crystals and pearls becoming denser the farther down the dress you look. A deep V cuts the otherwise plain neckline, but the thin straps are covered in tulle that travels over her shoulders and fall like a cloak trailing behind her. Crystals and pearls decorate the tulle as well.

Riotous curls bounce all over, the ones near her face pinned together in the back, letting us see her stunning face. The makeup is light but impactful, accentuating her love soaked beauty even more.

Her father stands beside her, precious in his tuxedo, as his lip quivers.

They take their first step down the aisle as the music swells and I turn my head away from the bride.

My favorite part of any wedding is to watch the groom watch his soon-to-be spouse walk toward him. Alec's face is filled with awe at the ethereal beauty of the one he gets to call his. His eyes never stray. His intensity never lessens. His devotion is evident and steals my breath from my body.

What I wouldn't give to have someone look at me the way Alec is looking at Charlie.

In the blink of an eye, Charlie and her father stand before Alec. He tries to say something but simply lets out a great, gasping sob before throwing himself into Alec's surprised arms. The men hug and Alec's lips move as he whispers something to his soon-to-be father-in-law. The older man nods before pulling away, kissing his daughter on the cheek before taking his seat next to his wife.

"Honored guests, we are here today to celebrate the love Charlie and Alec have found within each other as they stand before you ready to make a promise, through the good times and the bad," the officiant says in a friendly voice.

He continues on, but I lose focus as my eyes move from the happy couple to Parker, standing strong beside his friend, and I can't help but think of when he was down on one knee in front of me.

How fast my heart was beating.

How I wanted to pull him to his feet.

How I wanted it, for just a second, to be real.

CHAPTER TWENTY-SIX

PARKER

I TRY NOT TO shift too much as the officiant talks about love and sacrifice. How partnerships are forever.

Over the years, I have been to exactly one wedding since Brittany left. One of my cousins was getting married about a year after I found myself in a house that would never know her again.

My parents didn't mean to cause me pain.

But pain was all I felt.

And everything I was trying to drown.

I was drunk before the wedding even started. Watching as my cousin made her way down the aisle, I couldn't stop swaying. My dad's hand was rough as he caught me when I almost took a tumble, scoffing behind me. But I had told them. Over and over I told them I didn't want to go to a ceremony celebrating the thing that was ripped away from me.

"But it'll be good for you to get out of the house," they said. They probably wouldn't think the six shots of whiskey I took to even get myself into the backseat of my dad's old Explorer would be good for me, but what they didn't know wouldn't kill them.

This wedding is different, though.

Listening to this man talk about the beauties and hardships of tying yourself to one person doesn't make me want to scream. In fact, Brittany's and my wedding doesn't even cross my mind.

All I can think about, all I can wonder, is if I'm ever going to do this again.

I want to look at Anastasia. It takes everything in me to keep my eyes off her.

Every minute golfing and getting ready I thought about Anya. About sleeping next to her. About how soft her lips looked this morning, even when she was scowling at me.

I shouldn't have kissed her neck. But I was a man possessed and I couldn't have stopped myself even if I tried. Her standing against the backdrop of the ocean, staring out, she looked so lonely. Like she needed to be held.

And my arms couldn't do anything but give her what she needed. If I'm being completely honest with myself, as Sharon is teaching me to do, I wanted her in my arms. I've wanted her in my arms every night since our Desire Suite date.

Having her only a foot away from me all night, unable to touch her, unable to kiss her, was excruciating. It took every ounce of my self-control to not pounce on her as she walked up the pathway.

"Alec, if you'd please?" the officiant asks.

He reaches into his pocket and pulls out the note cards he had been agonizing over on the golf course. Not because he didn't have them written, but because he was worried he would lose them. He checked his pocket for them every thirty seconds, not listening to us he'd probably feel better leaving them at the room.

He clears his throat and begins reading.

"Charlie, before you I didn't believe in fate and never really thought I needed a partner in life. After we lost my mother, I think I subconsciously decided to not prioritize love after that, after watching my dad lose the love of his life. And then I met you. And you make me believe in all of those things. In everything good in the world. You woke me up to the beauty that is living a full life. Loving you is why I was put here on this Earth and I can't wait to spend the rest of my life fulfilling that purpose."

A few sniffles from the audience reach me and I see Courtney hand Charlie a handkerchief to dab the tears in her eyes.

"That was beautiful. Charlie?"

She doesn't pull out a piece of paper or note cards. She just smiles at Alec.

"All I've wanted, my entire life, was a love like my parents'. One that weathers storms and brings light and life into a home. But now I've met you, now that I have you, all I want is our love. You have believed in me when I didn't. Loved me when I couldn't. And stood beside me when you couldn't stand in front of me. You've shown me I'm strong and capable. But there's no one else on this planet I want to be weak with. I love you and I will until I take my last breath and beyond."

Listening to my best friend swear to love Alec for life, I realize something I hadn't at eighteen. That love doesn't require unwavering strength and stoicism. That sometimes, the strongest thing you can do is be vulnerable. And maybe that wasn't a lesson I was ready to learn, open to learning, until now.

The officiant pulls my attention back as he starts the part of the service we have all been waiting for.

"Alec, do you take Charlie to be your lawfully wedded wife? To love in sickness and in health. To cherish always?"

I can't see his smile, but I can hear it in his "I do."

"Charlie, will you take Alec to be your lawfully wedded husband? To love in sickness and in health? To cherish always?"

Her smile is beautiful and brings a tear to my eye.

"Hell. Yes."

"With the power vested in me, I now declare you husband and wife. Alec, you may kiss the bride."

He grabs Charlie's face and pulls her in, kissing her to the wolf whistles of all the guests. As they part, they look out onto the faces of those they love and see love shining back on them.

"May I introduce, for the first time, Mr. and Mrs. Alec King."

Raising their hands up, Charlie gives a whoop of happiness before taking her flowers back from Courtney and making her way up the aisle. I offer my elbow to the sable-haired spitfire and as we make our own way up the aisle, I catch Anastasia's eye and give her a wink.

Pictures take forever. After all the wedding party shots are done, every guest is allowed to take a picture with the bride and groom, if they'd like. It's a nice touch and I make a mental note of how relaxed the entire thing is with such a small group.

When Brittany and I got married, she wanted to have everyone she had ever known in attendance. I think we had over two hundred guests between family and the entirety of our graduating class. All I remember from that night was not even getting to sit down to eat or having more than a single bite of cake. All I wanted to do was to celebrate with her.

Spend time with her.

But instead it was like a second prom.

As the pictures finish, Alec and Charlie go off to the dressing room for a moment, having mentioned they would be changing before the reception. They had mentioned this to the guests as well, telling them they were welcome to change if they'd like to be comfortable. Charlie has always been incredibly caring about other people as long as I've known her and on this day, that's supposed to be all about her, I love seeing she's being true to herself.

The reception is set up in a pavilion on the resort's property. Instead of separate tables, there are two long ones pushed together so we can all dine together as a family. It reminds me so much of *House of Deceit* and the meals all of us contestants would share every night, I get teary with nostalgia.

Courtney and I wait for Alec and Charlie at a distance from the party. Waiters serve the guests, seated at the table or mingling around the dance floor. The set up is simple, but romantic.

Flowers and candles are placed around while strings of overhead lights give the entire place a glow. Anastasia walks toward her chair, smiling and laughing at something Charlie's father says to her as she passes.

"Not that my opinion matters, but I like her. And Lore said she bakes like an angel. She's already agreed to let me help some at her bakery when I visit," Courtney says, standing next to me.

I watch Anya ask Court's husband if anyone is sitting in the seat next to him and when he indicates it's free, she takes it, drawing the friendly man into conversation.

"Your opinion matters," I say, looking down at the short woman.

"Not as much as Charlie's."

"I don't think anyone's matters to me as much as Charlie's." I think about that before correcting my statement. "Except Anastasia's."

"Can I give you an unsolicited piece of advice?" she says, grabbing my arm and turning me toward her.

"You act like I have any say in the matter."

She snorts with laughter. "That woman over there? She doesn't realize it yet, but she's in love with you. And I know you're in love with her. If you realize it or not, or are willing to admit it to yourself yet, I don't know, but that doesn't change the truth of the matter. Whatever you need to do so you can be with her? Do it. Don't hold back and try to protect yourself. Give her everything you have."

"And what if she doesn't want everything I have?" I ask the dark night. If I make eye contact with her, it'll make it too real. Too honest.

"Then that's her loss, but she does."

Before I can say anything else, like dispute the fact I'm in love with Anya, Charlie and Alec appear.

"What the hell are you wearing?" Courtney says, laughing.

Charlie is in a white set of footsie pajamas while Alec's look like a tuxedo.

"Do you know we had to have his made custom? What kind of world do we live in that doesn't have tuxedo onesies but does have a tuxedo t-shirt?"

"A terrible one," Courtney says, sarcastically.

Charlie looks at Alec with love and adoration written all over her face. "The first gift he ever gave me, other than picking me for the show, was a set of gold footsie pajamas."

"Isn't that precious. Alright, let's get this show on the road. I'm starving and I want to get drunk and make out with my husband on the dance floor," Courtney says, and we all start walking toward the pavilion.

Everyone stands, cheering, as they see us arrive. Charlie and Alec go to the head of the table on the right while Courtney and I take the left. Once we are all seated, the dinner is served. Drinks, conversation, and laughter all flow until finally, the DJ announces the first dance. They sway to the music, oblivious to anyone else in their vicinity.

"At this time, Charlie and Alec would like everyone to join them in their dance."

Courtney's husband immediately gets up from his chair, coming over to his wife beside me and holds out his hand. "Ready to shake a tail feather, my love?" he asks.

"Let's do this," she says, putting her hand in his. Before she lets him pull her to her feet, she whispers to me. "Go ask her to dance or I'll castrate you."

Not wanting to test her, I stand, making my way to the woman who has held my attention all evening. I'm almost nervous as I make my way to her.

"I think you promised me a dance," I say, holding out my hand. She turns and looks up at me, smiling, and I feel my lips turn up in answer.

"I guess I can suffer through one dance with you," she jokes.

Her hand feels perfect in mine as I lead her to the dance floor. Her arms come around my neck and I can smell her perfume. It begs me to press my nose against her wrist. My hands settle on her hips and while all my self-control goes to keeping myself from smelling her like a creep, I'm unable to stop them from sinking slightly lower than appropriate, and pulling her tight against me.

The music fades in my ears and all I know is Anastasia and how good she feels in my arms. How much I want her to stay in my arms.

"Anya, I need to apologize to you. For everything that happened at the finale." She looks around nervously but relaxes when she realizes that no one is listening to us. She nods at me and I take it as a signal to continue.

"'Sorry' doesn't even begin to cover the regret I have for the things that I said. I'd like to say that moment isn't the person that I am, but the fact that it even happened means somewhere deep inside me that man is in me.

"My ex-wife left me. She rejected me. And I thought I was over it, but when you started rejecting me, my fight or flight kicked in," I tell her, realizing in this exact moment Carmen was right. "That doesn't make what I did right, or okay, and I am so sorry I caused you pain. I am working to heal the parts inside me that led to that reaction. I will do everything I can to do better.

"Because I want to see where this can go. For real. I even considered picking Carmen because you were the one I wanted for real and I didn't want to propose when I knew neither of us were ready for that and breaking up with Carmen after the show would be easy. But I couldn't reject you. I couldn't let you feel that way and I figured after the show we could talk about what we really wanted and move forward. And then I hurt you even more. Will you ever be able to forgive me?"

We continue moving around the floor, but I know the song is coming to an end and I desperately need to know where I stand with this woman.

"Can I tell you why I said no?" she asks, her tone gentle.

"Please," I beg.

"I wanted you for real, too. When I went on the show, I never thought I'd actually fall for you. I couldn't say yes because I want my first engagement to be real.

"You had to ask someone to marry you, but I knew how much pressure would be on us. Getting engaged when we hadn't even gone out on a real date? I couldn't do it. I wanted us to see what happened between us in the real world. I rejected you, hoping we could agree to date."

Hope, light and bright, flickers in my chest.

"We both did what we did because we wanted to date in the real world?" I ask. A part of me needs some reassurance that I heard correctly.

"Sounds like it," she says with a smile.

"And you forgive me?" I ask, daring not to hope.

"I forgive you. But this is going to be the only time."

I nod in understanding. And I do understand. I would never want to hurt her and if I can't fix my broken edges enough so I don't cut her, then I don't deserve her.

"Can I ask you on a date now, then? I still want to see what could be between us."

Her face falls.

"I think we should just be friends first. We were on a show where emotions were running high and we deserve to get to know one another without cameras in our faces."

My heart falls a little, but the fact she didn't say no keeps me hopeful.

"You can never have too many friends," I tell her, and her smile seals one of the cracks inside me. The song changes to something faster paced, but we continue swaying at the edge of the dance floor. I will dance every minute of this reception if she will let me hold her in my arms.

"Beautiful wedding," she says, conversationally. "Charlie's dress was gorgeous. She looked perfect."

"Not as perfect as you."

Her blush is enchanting and when her lips part, I lean down. But as our lips are about to touch, she pulls back.

"Just friends, remember?" she says. I refuse to let the disappointment last longer than a few seconds.

"Sorry, yes, just friends," I tell her. My arms relax just a bit, letting her gain some space but not run away.

"It's not that I don't want to kiss you, Parker. I do. But maybe that would make things too blurry?"

Her words make me bold.

"What if, maybe, we have a 'what happens at the wedding, stays at the wedding' night? When we get back home, friends only."

I can see her thinking, mulling over my proposition.

"Tempting. I'll let you know."

"Deal."

The night continues. Drinks flow and the dancing goes from cute and fun to down and dirty. Courtney gets drunk and makes out with her husband on the dance floor like she promised, grinding on him like they are going to make baby number two later tonight. Charlie dances around like a demented show girl, Anastasia trying not to get hit by a flying limb as she dances with her and Lorelei. Tank stands near them, swaying on his crutches, his attempt at dancing with his wife. Alec sits at the table, nursing a drink, but his eyes don't leave his bride.

"She is an awful dancer," I say, taking a seat next to him, my words slurring ever so slightly.

"Absolutely no sense of rhythm, but I didn't marry her for her ability to dance."

"That's obvious. Congratulations again."

"Thank you," he says, finally looking at me. "How's staying with Anastasia?"

"Absolute fucking torture, thanks for asking."

His mouth lifts in a bit of a smirk.

"That's how I felt every time I had to watch Charlie and you flirt for the audience."

"I'm surprised you didn't beat the shit out of me for kissing her, regardless that it was to sell the 'romance' to the people at home," I admit. Somehow, we've never had this conversation before and maybe their wedding isn't the place, but here we are.

"Because that would have hurt her chances. And I couldn't step foot in the house or I'd be fired."

"That didn't stop you later though," I say, referencing when he went in to protect her from the villain of our season that was oddly obsessed with her. And then them having sex in the library.

"I was still trying to follow the rules when you kissed her. I loved her by the time I went into the house."

We fall quiet, watching the group dance for a bit longer before Alec finally decides to take my best friend back to their room to sleep off her over exuberance. The rest of the guests begin leaving and I go find Anastasia as she says goodnight to Lorelei.

"Ready to go back to our room?" I ask, as she turns to me. Her cheeks are flushed and she's a little sweaty, but she's gorgeous.

"Yeah, let's go."

She puts her hand through my arm without a thought and I have to remind myself we are just friends as she leans against me on our way back to the villa.

CHAPTER TWENTY-SEVEN

ANYA

"Do you want to shower first?" Parker asks as the door shuts behind us. His bow tie is hanging around his neck, the first three buttons of his shirt undone. All I want to do is to get him completely undressed, but I had to be a dumbass and say we should just be friends. But with his green eyes looking into mine, I knew that if I didn't keep that separation between us for now, I would fall too hard, too fast, and the hurt part of me wants to make sure that he really means it when he says he won't hurt me like that again.

Then again, he did propose a friends with benefits like situation while we are here and I'm not dumb enough to pretend like that isn't *incredibly* appealing.

"Yeah, that'd be good," I say. He gives me a nod, opening the bathroom door for me before walking into the room, taking off his jacket as he goes.

I press my back against the bathroom door for a moment after shutting myself in the room and try to remember how to breathe. And then, an idea takes form. Before I can stop myself I go out to find Parker sitting on the couch, legs splayed, with a drink in his hand. He looks up as I approach, and the want in his eyes emboldens me.

"Could you unzip me?" I ask, turning toward him. Could I unzip myself? Yes. But in my tipsy state all I want to do is push the bounds of his control, hoping he'll snap and try to kiss me again. I want to take him up on his proposition, but I don't want to be the one to break first.

He stands, grabs the zipper, and with excruciating slowness, draws it down my back. One finger traces down my spine, goosebumps erupting in its wake.

"Thank you," I say, my voice husky as I hold my dress to myself.

"I'm here to be of service," he says, voice rough.

Moving into the bathroom, I drop my dress before turning on the water, giving it a moment to warm as I look at myself in the mirror. Eyes bright, cheeks flushed, hair in slight disarray. Alluring. But not alluring enough.

The water sluices over my body as I wash myself, imagining Parker's hands are the ones spreading the soap suds over my skin. I finish my shower before I can do something stupid like invite him in, and wrap up in a towel.

"Your turn," I call as I move into the bedroom nook. I can feel his eyes on me as I grab my pajamas off the bed. I turn around to see him walking on silent feet to the bathroom, shutting the door behind him. Part of me wishes that he had come over here and ripped the towel from my grip, but of course he didn't.

He's going to follow my lead.

As I hear him move about, I try to keep my thoughts from his naked body and how he looks as he pleasures himself. I crawl into bed, feigning sleep, but my arousal is making it hard to focus.

The shower shuts off and I realize that I trust Parker to not let this affect our relationship. That when he says we can be friends and get to know each other when we get home, even if we do this. That his feelings toward me won't change, his interest won't lessen, just because we have sex. But I'm going to have to be the one to initiate anything.

Throwing back the covers, I stand from the bed, hastily pulling my clothes off my body. I lay down on my side, leaning against the headboard, my legs spread. I consider touching myself so he can find me, much like I found him.

I hear the curtain being ripped back, the metal rings holding it to the bar clinking as it collects on one side. Thoughts of Parker's wet body fill my brain once more and my mouth waters.

Shaking my head, I lay on my back above the covers, one arm behind my head while my other sits on my stomach. His footsteps echo against the floor, my heart racing as they get closer, and I hear them stop as he catches sight of me. But I don't take my eyes off the ceiling.

"I have an IUD," I tell him, simply.

"Anastasia," he says, but I can hear the lust dripping off my name. "What are you doing?"

"Taking you up on your offer," I say, finally looking at him. I pull my knees up, setting my feet on the bed before letting my knees fall to the sides.

His knuckles are white on the towel, but I can see that he's hard.

"You've been drinking," he says, his eyes on the space between my legs. "I'd be taking advantage."

I wait a beat. Two. I slowly close my legs and flip over to my stomach as if I'm going to go to sleep. I hear him take another step toward the bed and smile. Feeling powerful, I slowly raise my ass into the air in invitation, until I'm on my knees with my chest still against the bed. The air is cool against my exposed core, but I don't care. Embarrassment should be flooding me at such a wanton, desperate display, but all I feel is an insatiable hunger I know will never abate.

This is a bad idea.

I know it is, but maybe if we don't talk, don't make a big deal out of it, we can just enjoy the pleasure.

"Take advantage of me, Parker." Before his name has left my lips, I hear his towel drop to the floor.

The bed dips as he moves behind me. His fingers brush my ankles before traveling up, drawing all rational thought from my brain.

Tomorrow is going to be a nightmare. But his large hands grab my ass cheeks and bare me to his gaze.

I jolt as if tased as his tongue swipes through my pooling wetness.

He jostles slightly behind me as I feel him kneel, knocking my legs a little wider as he settles in. The head of his cock brushes my opening. Once. Twice. Three times, allowing me to move away, and when I don't, he pushes in.

Just an inch. Barely inside me.

Not enough.

Never enough.

But I say nothing. I don't moan at the slight stretch, no matter how much I want to, as he pushes that inch in and out, giving me just a taste of what I want.

His hands continue their exploration of my body, traveling up my back and fisting tightly in my hair. But only for a moment. He's edging me in every possible way. Continuing their journey, the exploring, his hands find their way down my arms and settle on my wrists. Pausing the slow movement of his hips, he grabs my wrists. With little effort, he raises my upper body off the mattress before settling my hands against the headboard.

Warm fingers encircle mine as he makes sure my grip is tight before letting his hands explore my breasts. With the lightest pressure, his fingertips circle the tight points of my nipples. The sharp, and sudden, twist makes me want to cry out at the delicious pain, but my teeth clamp together, locking the scream down like gold in a vault.

My pussy throbs with anticipation as his hands make their way back down to my ass once more. He lets out the softest moan as he spreads me again, my inner thighs soaked from his ministrations.

Grabbing handfuls of my hips, he thrusts into me and a silent scream escapes as his thick cock slides home inside me. He pauses, letting me adjust. I feel the addiction take root as he pulls out with excruciating slowness.

The headboard slams against the wall as he thrusts back into me, the sound of our hips meeting echoing around the otherwise silent room. More prepared, the pain diminishes into pleasure. I want to moan. Beg him for more. But I don't, not wanting to break our silent agreement.

As he pulls out again, I squeeze my muscles around him, making him suck in a breath as he withdraws.

The move seems to push mild mannered Parker down, a wild, rutting man left in his place. He shifts behind me before slamming into me. Again and again and again.

The wall gets marked up as he takes me ferociously. My legs quake while sweat starts to bead along my spine. Our sawing breaths cleave the air as he punishes me. I won't be able to walk tomorrow, but I don't care as my orgasm starts to build.

Feeling my body begin to tighten, one of his hands drops as he begins playing with my clit, gathering my wetness on his fingers. The pace is relentless as Parker takes me, but I meet him thrust for thrust, hungry for everything he gives.

The wood of the headboard groans beneath the onslaught of his thrusts, but I barely hear it as his hand that was playing with my clit makes its way to my ass.

Circling the hole, his fingers drive me wild as they seemingly ask for permission. My head nods my enthusiastic consent as the tip breaches the entrance. I begin pushing myself back onto him, taking his finger deeper as my grunts start to come unbidden.

My muscles tighten as the crest of ecstasy nears.

Right as I fall over the edge, he adds another finger, filling me to the brim, causing me to explode.

My vision goes spotty as a guttural moan rips from my throat, the orgasm claiming my body as thoroughly as Parker claims me. After what feels like an eternity, I settle back into my body as his strokes become undisciplined. Frantic, even.

Leaning over me, he grabs onto the headboard. His sweat soaked abs flex as he drives himself into me as hard as he can, growling in my ear. I feel his cock thicken and with the first pulse of his release inside me, his teeth clamp down where my neck meets my shoulder, where he kissed me so tenderly earlier, pulling a shout of pain and pleasure from my mouth. His teeth push me into a second, smaller orgasm as he fills me with every drop of his come.

He rests against me, panting. My limbs shake, trying to keep us from falling to the bed. Parker pulls out of my aching body, but despite the soreness I want more. His feet pad to the bathroom and I hear the sink turn on as I drop down to the bed, unable to move.

The bed dips when he comes back. I cry out as he gently drags a warm washcloth between my legs.

"Sorry," he whispers before placing a kiss on my lower back. I don't know if he's apologizing for the soreness he caused or for giving in in the first place, so I don't respond but I spread my legs a little further, giving him better access. I start to drift off as he takes care of me and seconds before I'm pulled beneath the surface of consciousness, I could swear I hear him whisper, "I don't think I can let you go."

CHAPTER TWENTY-EIGHT

PARKER

I CHECK MY PHONE for the seven thousandth time in the span of the forty-five-minute meeting, Mitchel giving me the side eye as the client asks a question I don't hear.

"I'm sorry, what?"

"While yes, it does increase the cost some, bathrooms can be extremely difficult to add in later considering plumbing needs. I know it seems like an extravagance, considering it's just the two of you that will be living in the home, but when people visit they'll find comfort in having the bathroom in the room. It also allows for if an adult child ever needs to move back in, they can have their own suite. Or if you have live in help. It's a huge selling point if you ever need to put the house on the market," Mitchel says, saving me. "You can never have too many bathrooms."

"I think he's right, babe," the blonde woman in the tight pink dress tells her husband, laying a hand on his forearm.

"Okay, let's do that then. Was there anything else we were needing to make a decision on today?" he asks, checking his Rolex with impatience.

"No, that's all for now. We are going to get a few permits in line, submit the plans to the city. All the formalities. Once we have everything back, we'll break ground."

"This is so amazing," she says, clapping her perfectly manicured hands, the light catching on her giant diamond ring. I stand from the table, everyone following my lead.

"Mitchel has everything under control on your house. And I will personally be calling the city to see if we can expedite a few of the steps. They know we offer quality in every step, so we can normally fast track a few things."

I reach out and shake both of their hands. Splitting off to my office while Mitchel shows them out, I check my phone once more and the lack of a text makes me crazy. After our night together, which turned into an incredible morning, and the agreement to remain friends, I'm trying not to let my seeming obsession overtake me.

All this weekend did was strengthen my conviction I want to attempt a relationship with Anya, but if she wants to be friends, that's what we'll do.

No matter how much it kills me.

"What the fuck, dude," Mitchel says, shutting the door as he joins me. "They are spending five fucking million dollars and you wouldn't stop checking your phone. Which is happening almost constantly since you got back from the wedding the other day."

"I might have hooked up with someone and I gave her my phone number and I'm waiting to hear from her," I tell him, leaning back in my chair.

"Well, well, well. You little slut," he says, shimming his shoulders. "Someone from the resort? How did you meet her?"

"It was a wedding guest."

"Oh?"

"Lorelei brought Anastasia."

"The girl from the show?" I nod. "The wife is rooting for her to win, you know. The press prefers Carmen, but she and you would never pair together long term."

I drag my hands down my face before letting out a growl of frustration.

"Does everyone watch this stupid show? I swear I didn't realize how many people were going to watch it. The cleaning guy the other day stopped me in the bathroom to tell me how stupid I was for sending Jasmine home. I was just trying to take a piss!"

"We just want to support you. You know that. Do we need to start hiring more hermits? Perhaps send a company wide memo to not talk about it?" he asks, suppressed laughter on his face.

"You're fired."

"You can't fire me because you can't stop looking at your phone for five seconds to even listen to a client."

"Why are you in my office?"

"We need to go over the progress updates for the week."

My hand reaches for my phone, but I successfully stop myself, keeping the slightest shred of my dignity, and focus on Mitchel once more.

Five minutes before close, I sit outside the bakery, knuckles white as I grip the steering wheel. I've been staring at the front door for the past ten minutes, but I can't bring myself to get out.

"Just go in there. Just get out of the car," I say to myself in the, thankfully, empty truck. "Open the door. Open the door. Do it. Do it now."

My hand reaches out to the door handle, finally breaking through my nerves, and I make my way up to the bakery, remembering the hot kiss Anya and I shared the last time I was here. As I reach for the door, a man walks out.

His silk shirt is peacock blue, unbuttoned to below his sternum. A thick chain hangs round his neck with a diamond studded seventeen. Even without pads and a helmet on, I know Miles Lawson when I see him.

"Amazing catch the other day," I say as I pass by him, through the door he holds open for me. It's probably a regular occurrence to see Dom's teammates around here wanting to support his sister.

"Thank you for saying that. Our quarterback put up an amazing toss," he says before releasing the door and heading on his way.

A kid stands behind the counter, his mouth hanging open and a napkin in his frozen hand.

"You alright, kid?" I ask him, hoping he hasn't gone into shock or something.

"That was Miles Lawson. He signed this for me. He shook *my hand*." Awe drips from every word and I understand the feeling. My father took me to a few training camp sessions for the professional football team in Illinois. We would go for a few days and watch the teams practice, most of the players giving autographs and taking pictures after they were done for the day.

"His hand was huge!" he says with a giant smile on his face, before suddenly realizing I might need some help. "Oh, hi. Welcome to the Whimsical Whisk Bakery. Unfortunately, we are sold out today, but I can give you a coupon for another day for the inconvenience. We've been really busy since the owner was on some dating show. My mom watched it, but she said I wasn't allowed to." He rolls his eyes to show me what he thought of that rule and I try not to smile, liking the kid. "It's not like I don't know what boyfriends and girlfriends do. I have a girlfriend and we even kiss sometimes."

"Kissing is a lot of fun, but maybe there are some other things she didn't want you to see. Those shows aren't really good for showing what relationships are really like."

"Yeah, maybe. Were you wanting that coupon?"

"Actually, I was here looking for Anastasia. Is she here?"

"She's in the back. She's really popular today. Are you going to ask her out, too?" He takes off his apron and hits a few buttons on the iPad before moving to the front door and flipping the sign to closed.

"Too?" I ask.

"Yeah, Miles asked Anastasia out on a date."

"He did? What did she say?" Equal parts jealousy and nerves hit me with such a power, I almost get lightheaded.

"I don't know. She made me go in the back and wash dishes, but I told her to not let him leave before I could get an autograph. But I listened at the door and heard him ask her. I couldn't hear her, though. Don't tell her I was spying, okay? I don't want to get fired. I really like this job."

"It'll be our little secret," I promise. "Do you think you could go get her for me?"

"Sure! I'll be right back."

He goes through the swinging door to the back room and I hear him call out to Anastasia.

"Anya, another guy is here to see you," the shop boy says.

"What's his name?" she says.

Hearing her voice makes my insides twist and I shove my shaking hands into my pockets. Maybe Courtney was right about how I've never had to work for women before. I don't think I have ever been this nervous. Even when I asked Brittany out for the first time, I didn't have a single nervous flutter in my entire body.

But now? I'm nothing but nervous flutters.

"I don't know, I didn't ask."

"What does he look like?"

"Tall. Blond. Kind of like a biker that's all dressed up for work."

I smile at the kid's assessment of me and it calms me. That is, until she pushes through the door. All I can hear is her moaning in pleasure and I have to focus everything I have on not getting hard.

"Parker? What are you doing here?" Her cheeks pinken and I have to redouble my efforts to think of anything *except* our time together.

Willing my body to relax, I give her the smile that has always made women melt.

"I was in the area and thought maybe I could take you to an early dinner or something. You know, as friends."

"Oh, I actually have plans tonight," she says, wringing the towel in her hands.

"No, you don't. You were telling my mom earlier how you were going to get ahead on the baking for tomorrow."

She looks at her employee, glaring.

"Those are plans, Liam."

"Not fun plans," he grumbles and I have to trap my laugh as she puts her hands on her hips, giving him a no nonsense look.

"Shouldn't you be heading home? Your mom will kill me if you're late again."

"Crap!" he says, before diving under the counter, coming up with a backpack and slinging it over his shoulder. "Nice to meet you." He pushes through the door, sprinting off to the left.

"He's funny," I tell her, wishing I could kiss her lips and we could finish what we started the last time we were here.

"He's a pain in my ass. But I love him. I really do have things to do tonight. I keep selling out since the third episode aired last night and I'm trying to get things ready tonight so I can bake more tomorrow morning," she says, apologetic.

My heart drops, but I try not to show my disappointment.

"No problem. It was super last minute anyway. Just thought I'd ask. Have a good night."

I turn toward the front door, keeping my body relaxed. Unbothered. A friend wouldn't have their heart fall into their stomach at a rejection.

"I was going to run to the store later," she says, stopping me as I start to push the door open. I turn my head back to her, willing her to continue. "I didn't order enough of a few things. I'm still trying to get a grip on the new demand, so I need to go to the grocery store. We could go now, if you want."

"You want me to go grocery shopping with you?" I ask.

"Friends go shopping together. I just need to grab a few things. You don't have to go, I just thought I'd ask." I see doubt creep onto her face and want to squash it immediately.

"Yes, let's go grocery shopping. Do you want me to drive?"

"That'd be great. Let me grab my purse."

She goes into the back as I grab my keys from my pocket. I wish I had brought a change of clothes to the office so I wasn't still in my uptight work clothes, but I can't seem to care.

I'm with Anastasia and that's all that matters.

The store is bustling with people stopping by before heading home from work. Everyone has a frenzied air about them, like they want to go in, grab what they need, and leave. But Anastasia takes her time. She lets people cut her off or anticipates their movements and stops short, allowing them an unimpeded path.

One of the wheels on the cart I'm pushing is spinning like a top and completely useless while another one randomly gets stuck, making an annoying noise as it drags across the floor.

"I think you picked the most messed up cart in the whole bunch," I tell her as she reaches up for a thing of honey, her shirt riding up and letting me see an inch of her skin.

Only an inch, but an inch is enough to make my mouth water.

"You could have grabbed another one, but you were distracted by that balloon."

"It looked like a penis and I was shocked they'd sell it."

"It was obviously a mushroom."

"A penis mushroom."

"You're ridiculous," she says, putting the honey in the cart before making her way down the aisle. A woman passes us and her eyes widen as she does a double take, but luckily, she doesn't say anything.

I should have considered people might recognize us. It happened a bit after the finale of *House of Deceit*.

No one else pays us any attention as we go through aisle after aisle. I'm surprised by the normalcy of the entire situation. I realize I haven't been grocery shopping with another person since long before Brittany and I got divorced. We would go together on Sundays when we first got married, but eventually, she got tired of my impatience to leave and I got tired of her needing to read every single label.

After a particularly nasty fight in the middle of a store, we decided it would be best if she shopped on her own and I would make sure to bring everything in from the car and put it all away where it belonged. It worked for us, but I see now the casual intimacy we lost in not doing such a task together.

But Anya could read every label twice and I wouldn't care.

"So Miles Lawson was at your shop today. That's pretty cool," I say with exactly zero preamble. She looks at me over her shoulder, raising an eyebrow.

"He's my brother's teammate. They come around every once in a while."

"In silk shirts?" I mumble under my breath, feeling childish for being jealous.

She turns around, putting a hand out to stop the cart, making people break around us with scoffs.

"Go ahead and ask," she says in an accusatory voice.

"Ask what?" I say, trying to feign ignorance, but I can tell she sees right through me. I know I'm going to regret this, but my jealousy won't let me move off this path. "You're going out with him, huh?"

"I haven't decided. He broke up with his girlfriend while we were filming, but I'm not really sure about it."

"Friend to friend, you should go. He seems cool in the interviews I've seen." I've been possessed. That's the only explanation for the suggestion coming out of my mouth. I want her to sit at home and pine for me until she finally gives in and lets me take her out.

"Fine. Maybe I will. It's not like there's any reason I should say no."

Her nostrils flare and I can tell I'm barreling down a dangerous path, with warning signs flashing, but I continue anyway. Like a complete and utter moron.

"Good."

"Good." She turns away from me in a huff.

At, possibly the worst time, another woman walks past us that looks like she should be in a swimsuit magazine and gives me a thorough look before winking at me.

I can see the flare of jealousy in Anya and the raging beast of a man inside me swells with pride while the civilized part of me is annoyed I enjoy it. Especially after I was the one that suggested she actually go out with Miles.

A hypocrite through and through.

"Looks like you could have a date of your own if you wanted," she says, sniffing with indignation and turning around, stomping through the crowd to get to the next thing on her list.

The shopping trip continues and we start talking again, but now the conversation is stiff and stilted and I hate myself for ruining our outing with my jealousy.

CHAPTER TWENTY-NINE

ANYA

M Y MAKEUP AND HAIR are done, but I'm still in my robe trying to decide what to wear.

"Why am I so nervous?" I ask Dom as he lies on my bed, throwing a baseball in the air. Where the baseball came from, I have no idea.

"Because you're excited?"

I am, but the nerves seem to be winning. I look at him, holding two different hangers in my hands. "Which one of these?"

I first put the plain black t-shirt dress in front of me before switching it for the red pantsuit I had worn to Charlie's rehearsal dinner.

"Why did you say yes?" he asks, without answering my question, just like I ignored him.

My thoughts go back to the grocery store and the jealousy I felt watching women check out Parker.

"I think because I just need to know what could have been if Miles hadn't had a girlfriend when I first met him. That I didn't just fall for Parker because he showed interest in me after all that, but because of *him*." I move the clothes in front of me again. "Which one?"

"Where's he taking you?" he asks, without looking at the options.

"He didn't say."

"And you didn't ask?"

"I was too busy looking at the hundred thousand dollars' worth of diamonds hanging from his neck when I video called him to say yes."

He sits up with a grunt, taking a chug of water from his water bottle on my side table.

"Lawson does love his jewelry. He's probably taking you somewhere fancy. He's pretty known for that in the locker room."

"Oh God. Am I going to be talked about in your locker room?" I ask him, my voice whiny. "Why are you letting me do this?"

"Relax, he doesn't talk about his dates. And if I remember right, you got me grounded for two weeks the last time I tried to tell you who to date. Plus, Mom told me you're a grown woman and to leave you alone, so I'm staying out of it."

"I'm just going to text him."

Throwing the outfit options on my bed, I grab up my phone, typing out a text to Miles.

Anya: *Hi Miles. It's Anya. For our date tonight, where are we going? I'm trying to make sure I dress appropriately.*

Miles Lawson: *We are going to Harbor View Bistro. Can't wait to see you.*

"He says we are going to Harbor View Bistro. Isn't that supposed to be fancy?"

"You know that blue dress you have that makes you look like a '50s housewife minus the mood stabilizers?"

"I'm afraid to say yes to that."

"Wear that. With those shoes with the things." He wiggles his fingers around in the air. One thing I'll say about Dom is he's very supportive, even if not always effective support.

"The shoes with the things?" I ask, rooting around inside my closet, looking for the dress he suggested. "This dress?"

"Yeah, that one. With the shoes."

"Oh my God, *what* shoes?" I ask, hanging the dress on the hook, before turning back toward the closet looking at my shoes.

"Get outta my way," he says, standing from the bed and shoving me out of his way.

"Dominic, you dick!"

"It's Stylist Dominic," he says, rooting around in my closet, pulling out my nude pumps with ankle straps and tosses them at me.

"You couldn't think of the word strap?" I ask, hanging one off my finger.

"Bite me. I'm pretty, not smart."

"Are you pretty, though?" I ask, and he flips me off as I grab the clothes and move into my bathroom, shutting the door to change.

I put on the dress, and I know Dom was right in picking it. While it has a sweetness to it, the deep V neckline shows enough cleavage so it crosses the line from sweet to sexy. I put on the shoes Dom picked out and check myself out in the mirror.

Looking polished and feeling hot, I give myself a wink in the mirror before opening the door.

"What do you think?"

"Lookin' good," he says, flashing me a thumbs up. I move to my closet once more, grabbing out a cream pashmina just in case it's cold in the restaurant.

My phone vibrates, the screen lighting up with a text from Miles.

Miles: *Arriving in thirty seconds*

"Okay, he's about to be here. Lock up when you leave, yeah? Let us get away before you head out."

"Have a good time," he calls out as I head for the front door.

Miles raps on the door twice and I pull it open before it stops echoing in the entry.

"You look beautiful," he says in way of greeting.

"Thank you. You look very nice as well," I say, taking in his green suit that looks like a second skin. His cream knit shirt shows the ridges of his muscles. Everything about his outfit looks brand new and perfectly coordinated and stylish. I almost feel frumpy next to his outstanding style.

"How was practice today?" I ask as we make our way to the car.

"It was good. Just a quick run through. I'm sure Dom told you," he says, opening my door for me.

"He didn't mention it," I say, not really sure what to talk to him about. The car ride is full of awkward silence as we make our way to the restaurant.

Harbor View Bistro comes into view and the evening is perfect. Sky painted in burnt oranges and pinks as the sun sinks down, the water is bathed in gold as it crashes on the shore. I shut the car door behind myself and even if this date is a dud, I'm very excited for the experience.

"Welcome, Mr. Lawson. We have your table ready. Would you please follow me?" the hostess asks rhetorically. A part of me wonders if it bothers Miles to have people recognize him. It must be oppressive to have the spotlight on him. It's been unnerving whenever I'm out in town and someone stops me to talk about *House of Desire*.

She turns and guides us through the dining room. As we turn the corner from the entry, the glass wall comes into view and the stunning sunset.

And right in front of the glass wall is Parker and a stunning woman with soft looking, blonde hair. I stop in the middle of the restaurant, staring. Miles runs into me with an oof.

The sound must carry, because I'm now looking into Parker's shocked green eyes, his jaw dropping. While he was the one who pushed, saying I should go out with Miles, I didn't expect for him to go on a date, too.

Especially at the same restaurant as my date. Too many emotions run through me as I stand here, unable to break eye contact.

"Something the matter?" Miles says, putting his face in my line of sight so he can see my face while his hand gently rests on my arm.

"No, nothing's the matter," I say, and finish making my way to the secluded, semi-circle booth the hostess is standing by.

"How's this?" she asks, placing the menus down at each place.

"It's great," I say, scooting in on one side while Miles comes in from the other.

"Perfect. Your server will be Frances and she will be right with you." And just like that, she's off.

"This is amazing," I say, trying to pretend like my world didn't just implode. The dining room is dimly lit with candles, the walls painted a darker shade of green, enhancing the coziness. I open the menu, but the words all blend together.

"Everything is good, but you really can't go wrong with the filet mignon with truffle butter. I've also heard the lobster risotto is delicious."

"Both of those sound delicious. Do you come here often?" I ask, searching for a topic of conversation I can focus on.

"I've been here a few times. Do you think we should get some wine with our meal?"

"Good evening," our server says, walking up at the perfect time to keep me from having to respond. "My name is Frances and I will be taking care of you today.

"Our specials tonight are a delicious grilled swordfish steak served with a tangy mango salsa, and paired with a coconut rice and sauteed broccolini. The second special is a succulent rack of lamb encrusted with rosemary and garlic, cooked to your preference, and served with a rich port wine reduction sauce. On the side are creamy mashed potatoes and roasted Brussels sprouts."

I think of Parker picking Carmen's meal over mine and going on a solo date with her. But before the memory can make me spiral, I lock it down.

"I'm going to have the filet, medium-rare. Bring me whatever wine the chef suggests," Miles says.

"And for you, ma'am?" she asks, turning to me.

"If you had to pick between the lobster risotto and the lamb special, which would you go with?"

It doesn't really matter. I'm not going to be able to taste any of it anyway, knowing Parker is twenty feet away enjoying the company of a beautiful woman. I take a peek at their table and the woman is basically vibrating with happiness at whatever Parker is saying and he gives her a small smile.

"While our normal menu items are tried-and-true staples of our dining experience, I do think the lamb shines."

"Let's do that. Medium, please? And I'll have a glass of wine the chef suggests, as well. Thank you."

She gives us a nod, taking our menus before hustling off to put in our orders. Another server brings over bread and butter, filling our water glasses at the same time.

"I saw some commercials for *House of Desire* the past few weeks. How was that experience? Media days are my least favorite days of my career, what with all the people bossing us around on where to be and what to say."

For the first time since I saw Parker, I really focus on Miles.

"We had a lot of that, too! Throw in having to try to do natural reactions four or five times so they could get the shots they wanted. It's hard to look genuinely shocked on the fifth take of a disagreement," I tell him and he smiles. It's a great smile and a small piece of my stomach flutters at having it pointed in my direction.

And so our date goes, on and on. We go back and forth asking questions as we eat some of the best food I've ever had.

"What sorts of hobbies do you like to do in the off season?" I ask Miles, trying to find some common ground.

"I typically visit various golf courses or go out on a friend's yacht for some relaxation and sun. Do you often get out on the water?"

"My bakery takes up a lot of my time and I don't have any friends that own boats. What's your favorite golf course?"

The fun I've had has really surprised me. I didn't think I'd be able to focus on anything other than Parker over by the window, and while I did glance at him a few times, I've enjoyed talking to Miles. But it's become evident that there's a large divide between our interests the longer we talk. He's a lovely guy, funny and smart, but I know that we aren't a good fit. We stand from the booth, I can't wait to get home and change into my comfortable clothes.

Miles leads me from the dining room and I am counting down the last twenty minutes of this date to get me back to my house. We walk across the parking lot and he grabs my hand, linking our fingers. I look down at my hand in confusion.

"I had a great time," he says and I look at him like he might have gotten a concussion between the table and here. There's no way he enjoyed that date.

"The dinner was great," I hedge.

We arrive at his car, but instead of going around to his side, he gives me a dazzling smile.

"Can I kiss you?" he asks.

CHAPTER THIRTY

PARKER

"My husband is going to be thrilled with the decisions we've made. And thank you, again, for meeting me here tonight. I know it was out of your way."

My anxiety has been at an all-time high since I saw Anya walk in with Miles Lawson. I might have pushed her toward him, but I was hoping that she wouldn't go. Because I'm a selfish bastard.

And I know I need to get out of here and do damage control. There's no way she didn't think I was on a date.

"I'm always happy to work around your schedule, Mrs. Day. I'm glad the court case worked out for your clients. I will get Mitchel on all of these items. In two months, you should be moving into your forever home."

She claps and bounces in her chair as I signal the waiter to bring our check. My leg is bouncing as I give them my credit card and get the bill taken care of.

"Are you ready?" I ask as I sign the receipt. I look up and see Anya's back as she heads out to the parking lot with Miles.

"Yes! I need to get home."

I get up from the table, holding out my hand to help her to her feet. Mrs. Day starts moving through the tables as I trail after her. The sky is dark outside of the lights in the parking lot. Anya is pressed against a white car as we walk by.

"Have a great night," I say, at the same time as I hear Miles ask if he can kiss Anastasia. It takes everything in me not to jump into the situation and tell him she's mine.

"See you later," Mrs. Day says before getting into her car and pulling out without any hesitation. Miles Lawson moves close to Anastasia.

"No, I'm sorry. I just don't think this is going to work. I wish you all the best, though," Anya says, and my heart soars as her eyes catch mine over Miles's shoulder.

"Okay, sure thing. Do you still want me to take you home? Or I can pay for a ride share for you and wait until it's here."

"That's okay, Miles. I've got her," I say against my better judgment.

Miles spins on his heel and takes me in. I see the moment when he recognizes me from the bakery.

"If that's not what Anya wants—" he starts until Anya cuts him off.

"It's fine. He's a friend. I don't want to put you out. Thank you for a lovely dinner," she says, putting her arms around him in an awkward hug, "and have a great night."

"Sure. You too," he says, and gets into his car. Anya turns to me.

"Where's your date?" Anya asks, the hint of jealousy warming me like a fire in the middle of winter.

"That was a work meeting. She is a lawyer and had to move the location of our meeting due to a mediation that went long. She hadn't eaten all day and wanted to grab dinner. She's married." I reach out and push back a piece of her hair, tucking it behind her ear. "You're beautiful when you're jealous."

She scoffs and crosses her arms over her chest. "I'm not jealous. Maybe you're projecting."

I can feel my cheeks stretch at the smile that lie brings to my face. "I'll go ahead and admit I was jealous. But I know I wasn't the only one."

Her eyes scan me and my work pants and tight button-down. Hunger, hot and crazed, enters her gaze, and I know we have about ten seconds before we are on each other. Grabbing her hand and leading her back to my truck, I thank every star in the sky I'm parked in the far back corner with bushes on two sides. I open the back door and shove her into the back seats, following behind her. The truck shakes as I slam the door, but I don't care because she already has her breasts bared to me, her chest heaving. A flush creeps up from her chest and I can't take it anymore. I have to taste it.

"We're still just friends," she tells me.

Her skin is soft against my tongue as her nails scratch against my scalp, sending chills down my spine and thickening my cock more than it already was. I'm straining against my pants, but I can't take my mouth off her long enough to free myself.

"Got it," I mumble against her neck.

Desperation I have never felt before lights my nerves on fire as her hand begins fumbling with my belt buckle. Grabbing a handful of my hair, she pulls me from her neck before pushing my hands down into the seat, telling me I can't touch her. She pushes me until my back is pressed against the door behind me, the handle cutting into my back, but I don't care.

She maneuvers one of my legs up onto the bench as she kneels on the floorboards between them.

The silence is getting to me. I want to hear her call my name as ecstasy relaxes her body into a puddle of orgasm beneath me, but I don't want this to stop and I'm afraid it will. I need to hear her beg and plead with me as I keep her on edge. But having her in my arms is more important.

I push down my needs.

My wants.

My desires.

And I take everything she'll give me.

My hips jerk as she palms my length, giving me strong, sure strokes. I watch her as she licks her lips, her eyes focused on my cock until, suddenly, she's swallowing me to the back of her throat. My head kicks back, smacking into the glass, as my teeth grind against the moan. Fingers aching to sink into her hair to control her movements, I claw my nails into the seat, keeping myself contained. I thrust up into her mouth. She can barely take my girth, but she does without complaint and my heart swells. Her throat constricts as I bottom out, her nose against my abs. The sound of her gagging on my cock makes me wild.

With a growl, I tangle my fingers in her hair and fuck her soft, warm, *wet* mouth, tears begin falling from her eyes at my aggressive pace. Her tears simply make me more unhinged until her hand goes down between her legs.

She rucks her dress up around her hips and I hear the wetness as her fingers slide into her pussy.

I thought I was at full capacity for how much I could desire this woman between my legs, but watching her pleasure herself as I brutally take her mouth, deepens the feeling.

She hums around my cock as her hand begins working faster and I know I won't survive unless I have her taste on my tongue right now.

Using my grip on her hair, I rip her off my aching member. It glistens with her saliva and the only way it'd look better is coated in the wetness between her lush thighs. I scoot down the bench seat, pulling her momentarily on top of me until I'm as stretched out as I can be. I grab her arms and pull her toward my face, needing her weight to crush me, but as she tries to seat herself, I realize it's futile. The space is just not big enough.

And that won't do. Not when she lets out the softest whine I've heard.

I gently push her back down my body while simultaneously wiggling my way out. Reaching behind me, I rip the door open. There's no way the paint isn't scratched from the bush, but I don't care as her eyes go wide as I step from the truck.

I pull her down toward me, her body mine as I move it this way and that until she's on her knees before me. Not quite the perfect height. That won't stop me.

Resting my knees on the frame of the truck, I'm thankful for the darkness surrounding us as I spread her ass and plunge my tongue deep into her sweet, pulsing pussy. I know she wants to moan, I can feel it gathering in her body as surely as her orgasm gathers. I try to drag her moan out, but much like our time at Charlie's wedding, she keeps her sounds trapped, almost like it keeps emotion out of it. I try to slow myself from devouring her too fast, but I can't stop the pace until her juices sluice down my chin, orgasm racking her body.

I pull back from her, panting, and look at the beautiful mess I've made of the even more beautiful woman kneeling before me. My dick is still hanging from my pants and leaking come with my arousal.

Grabbing her hips, I flip her malleable body over, laying her onto her back. I take my cock in my hand and begin stroking myself, pushing toward my own climax.

With the other hand, I spread her legs further apart, dipping my fingers inside her, and with a heavy exhale, the only sound I allow myself, I paint her soaked pussy in my release.

Lights glow from the front of Charlie's house. I hesitate to barge in on her evening, but when I open the door, I hear giggling from the backyard and decide maybe more than one opinion would be helpful in this situation. I make my way to the side of the house, letting myself in through the wrought-iron gate.

Lorelei and Charlie sit on the daybed that I fixed after Charlie and Alec broke it. A cell phone sits in a tripod, with Courtney and Molly, a former contestant from *House of Deceit*, on the screen.

"Well, look at this. What's going on here?" I ask, startling the girls, but once they see it's me, they squeal, climbing off the bed and launching themselves into my arms for hugs.

"Parker! I've missed you. What are you doing here?" Charlie asks, giving my cheek a peck.

"I wanted to talk to you about Anya, but I can call you tomorrow if you want."

"No! Absolutely not. Come sit with us," she says, grabbing my hand and pulling me over to the bed. Lorelei gets settled while Charlie pulls a chair over for me to sit on before readjusting the phone to include me.

"Hi, Parker!"

"Hey, Molly. How's Danielle?" I ask, referencing her wrangler turned fiancée from *House of Deceit*. "We missed you at the wedding."

"She's amazing," she says, her facial expression going goofy with love like it does every time Danielle is brought up. "We were so sad we couldn't go, but that convention led to a big contract, so it all worked out in the end."

"Congrats!"

"How dare you not acknowledge me. I thought we bonded at the wedding," Courtney says, fake pouting.

"How dare I acknowledge Molly first," I say, rolling my eyes. In this moment, I'm glad I came over here. These ladies are some of my favorites and they always have a way of making me laugh. "How are you doing?"

"I'm good. I just told Charlie we are moving out there! We sold this house and found one there. The moving trucks will be here in three days," she says bouncing.

"I don't think the state will be able to handle having you both here."

"Har har," Courtney says, flipping me the bird.

"Alright, so Anya. Go," Charlie says, wiggling to get comfy.

"We had sex at your wedding," I tell them, expecting looks of shock but receive none.

"Yes, she told us. What's going on?"

I would be offended she was telling people about our time together, but worry grips me. What if she needed to talk to them because she regretted it?

"Do you all just talk about me when I'm not here?"

"Self-absorbed much?" Courtney asks, making Molly snort with laughter.

Okay, maybe this wasn't the best idea ever.

"Lorelei could tell something was off with her on the car ride home from the airport and she told her everything, which prompted a girl's night dinner where she filled in the rest of us."

"Awesome. Are you all friends now?"

"Babe, you are mooning over her. Of course, we are going to befriend her," Charlie says, patting my arm. I love my best friend and her thoughtfulness. "Don't worry, she only had complimentary things to say about your sexual prowess."

"Thank God for that." I roll my eyes.

"So, what's the problem?" Lorelei asks. "Because we love Anya and if you fuck this up, we might shun you."

"We had sex again."

"That's not really a problem so long as she was consenting," Courtney says.

"It might have been in the parking lot of Harbor View Bistro. She went on a date with Miles Lawson and I might have been there on a business meeting."

That gets me the shocked silence I was expecting earlier until they are all talking over each other.

"I like car sex, but not at a restaurant," Courtney says.

"Guess the date didn't go well, then," Charlie snickers, covering her mouth as she giggles.

"I've never had car sex. I feel like I need to fix that immediately," Lorelei pipes in.

"That's hot," Molly says, simply.

Lorelei raises her hand like she's a student in class. I point to her. "I think my question is the most important one. How did you two end up together when she was on a date?"

I tell them everything and when I get to the part about offering to drive her home, Courtney cuts me off.

"And your offer to drive her home made her so horny she jumped you in the parking lot?" Courtney asks from the screen, reminding me she and Molly are there.

"I might have said something about her being jealous and she accused me right back and then she was checking me out. It devolved quickly from there."

"Yeah, that's definitely hot," Molly says, fanning herself dramatically.

"What should I do? I know she is attracted to me. And it always seems like she likes me."

"This is turning out like an angsty teenage diary entry," Courtney says, snickering.

"Diaries are for bad poetry you write while you cry on lonely nights when you think no one loves you," Charlie says.

"Maybe yours were. You were so dramatic freshman year," Courtney says as the other girls start to laugh as well.

"I was stupid and didn't have a fully developed brain!"

"At least they were just in the diary," Lorelei says, patting her arm in consolation.

"Oh, no! She had this boyfriend and she would give them to him!" Courtney cackles, falling out of frame.

"I hate you *so* much," Charlie says.

"You brought it up!"

"What's the likelihood you still have those diaries?" Molly asks.

Charlie huffs in exasperation. "Pretty high. I'll find them for you. It can be our next girl's night."

They all descend into a fit of drunken giggles and I just watch them, smiling. Part of me wishing I had more of a normal high school experience.

One that didn't end in marriage.

"Can we get back to the topic at hand?" I ask as they start to disintegrate into conversations about their various school age dating escapades.

"Oh, right. Sorry," Charlie says, wiping tears from her eyes.

"You need to ask her on a date," Charlie says, like it's the simplest thing in the world.

"But she wants to be friends."

"I hate to be the bearer of bad news, but having sex in a parking lot is not just being friends. Especially considering the feelings you both obviously have for each other. Do you want to just be friends?"

I know I don't, but it's not something I've wanted to admit out loud, fearful to push her away.

"No. I want to be with her. We can take it slow, but I don't want her to be with anyone else."

Charlie scoots to the edge of the bed and grabs my hands. "Then tell her that. Be an adult. Communicate. You've been working with Sharon on this. Now do it."

She's right. Like she is most of the time, not that I'd ever tell her that.

"When should I ask her?"

They all look at each other and without a word, seem to come to an agreement. Lorelei nods at Charlie who turns back around.

"Tomorrow, for sure. Just seal the deal. There's no way she's not working herself up into knots as well, but you want to give her a second to digest what happened."

Okay, I could do this. Now I just have to plan what I'm going to say to her.

CHAPTER THIRTY-ONE

ANYA

L IAM AND DAD WORK together in the front of the shop. Every day starts with a line of people and by lunch time, we are almost completely sold out. No matter how much I bake, it doesn't seem to be enough. The specialty orders are starting to come in more consistently as well, demanding a lot of my time. I don't mind, it's a nice problem to have, but I'm starting to wonder if it might be time to hire on some help.

Thoughts of Parker and our time in the truck distract me. I need to talk to him, tell him I'm not interested in only being friends anymore. Maybe we could get to know each other while we date, since that's what dating *is* for, after all.

I push the thought to the corner of my mind to ponder later and settle into a zen-like state as I decorate item after item.

"Anastasia," my father says, poking his head through the door.

"Yeah?" I say, looking up from the cupcake I was icing, the piping bag clutched in my hands.

"There's someone here who would like to discuss booking some custom items with you. Lorelei is with her."

"I'll be right there," I say, finishing off the cupcake, the last one for the order.

Not wanting to get icing on anyone, I move to the sink to wash my hands quickly. If Lorelei is bringing the person in, then I know there is going to be a good budget involved. And a fair amount of artistic freedom. Excited to see what the job could be, I pat my hair into place and take off my apron, dropping it on the worktable.

"Hi, Lorelei," I say, walking through the swinging door, but as I catch sight of her companion, I almost stop in my tracks.

"Oh my God," I whisper, walking up to the woman, holding my hand out for her to shake. "You're Ryan Jade," I tell her, like she doesn't know. "You're even more beautiful in person."

Her laugh is perfect, just like everything about her. Every strand of her blonde hair is perfectly styled. Her black t-shirt is tucked into a mini plaid skirt with thigh-high leather boots. Draped over her shoulders is an emerald trench coat that probably costs as much as one of my paychecks.

Striking turquoise eyes hold me captive.

"You're so sweet and absolutely stunning yourself," she says, her southern accent mesmerizing.

I must have died and gone to heaven because Ryan Jade just said I am stunning.

"This is amazing. I'm sorry, I'm a little star struck. I never thought I'd have the most famous singer in the entire world in my shop." I turn toward Lore.

"Why don't we go to the back and take a seat?" Lorelei says, noticing we have started to garner the attention of some of the customers. Phones are starting to point in our direction.

"Yes, please, follow me," I say, leading the way, my cheeks heating with embarrassment. "Be careful. There's icing everywhere," I tell them, not wanting Ryan to mess up her outfit.

"Oh my goodness, this is so cute!" she exclaims, pointing to the cupcake sitting on my prep table with a bubbling cauldron on it.

"Thanks. That's for a three-year-old's birthday. The little girl, Elli Mae, is obsessed with Halloween so she's getting a Halloween themed birthday party."

Ryan giggles at that, looking at the other cupcakes in the group. "My niece is in love with mail trucks, so my sister arranged for all these mail carriers to do a parade. She was so excited. It was a lot of fun for us adults, too."

"How cute," I say, showing her over to the table and chairs Lorelei convinced me to squeeze into the back for meetings just like this. Our knees are all going to touch, but having a space to talk to customers has been very helpful. "What can I do for you, Miss Jade?"

"Ryan, please. Lorelei has been posting all of your creations on her socials and she shared some goodies she had and I just knew I had to have you do my event."

I pull the notebook I keep on the table toward me, flipping to a new page.

"You know that Earl Gray cake you made for Alec? Ryan *loved* that," Lorelei adds.

"Yes!" she says, clasping her hands together. "That was the most delicious cake I have ever tried."

"I've tweaked that recipe a bit, and it's even more delicious now. Is that the flavor profile you're looking for?" I make note of her enjoyment of the cake for reference.

"Not this time. This is for my parent's thirtieth wedding anniversary next month and my mother doesn't really drink tea. The event is five weeks from Friday." I flip through my calendar and look at the red circles around that date.

"When do you need delivery that day?"

"By lunch time? Are you already booked?"

Lore leans over and looks at my calendar. "I forgot it was the wrap party."

"Wrap party?" Ryan asks, looking between us.

"I was on *House of Desire*. That is the day the finale will air and production is throwing a party. But that's not a problem. There will be time to do both."

"Are you sure? I don't want to crowd you. I'd offer to change the date, but my schedule is a little unwieldy at this time."

The genuine regret on her face surprises me. Others would know exactly what this would do for my shop and demand accommodation, at the bare minimum. But here she sits, sad her schedule is too busy to rearrange. For me.

"I'm sure. Now, we'd be happy to use any of our flavors and combinations of fillings. How many people?"

"There's going to be five hundred."

I look up at her, my eyes wide, before I look at Lorelei who nods, a small smile on her mouth.

"That's quite a few guests and a short turnaround time," I say, making the note.

"I'll pay you double, if I have to. They never got the wedding they always deserved. They have traveled around the world trying to make it better and helping with my career. I want them to be surrounded by all the friends and loved ones they've made enjoying your amazing creations."

I take a deep breath, telling myself I can do this.

"Then that's what they'll have," I tell her, touched she'd choose to trust me with such an important event, and we get to work.

After an hour of going through various options, I say goodbye to Lorelei and Ryan Jade. Holding my notebook to my chest, I give myself a second to let the excitement sink in. With this order, and the amount of profit I'll be making, I now have the budget to hire another baker.

"Is everything okay, honey?" Dad asks. Now the last customer has been served, I answer him.

"Ryan Jade wants me to bake for her parents' anniversary party. It's for *five hundred people*."

"That is amazing!" he says, sweeping me into a hug.

The bell above the door rings, and I turn to find Parker standing in my bakery once more. I'm not sure my nervous system can take any more surprises for the day, but he looks like he could be heading to a *GQ* cover shoot.

"Are you okay?" he asks, seeing me in father's arms.

"I just booked a life changing job," I tell him, a huge smile on my face.

"I knew it was only a matter of time," he says, giving me a hug before turning to Dad and Liam. "Carl, it's great to see you again. Liam, how are you doing?"

"Parker, would you like a cookie? There are a few left. My treat." My dad grabs one of the chocolate chunk with sea salt from the display case, putting it in a bag and offering it to him.

"I'll never turn down one of Anastasia's cookies. Thank you, sir." He takes the bag, immediately reaching in and breaking off a piece of the cookie.

"Are you just here to try to get free treats?" I joke.

"Yes. I'll see you later," he says, heading toward the door, but I grab onto his shirt, stopping him. He turns to me, smiling before coming back to me and placing a kiss on my forehead. "Can we talk? Do you have a minute?"

"She has a minute," Dad says, shooting me a wink.

Rolling my eyes, I grab Parker's hand from my shoulder and pull him behind me to the back table where I just had Lorelei and Ryan.

"What do you want to talk about?" I ask, my stomach sinking.

His leg shakes under the table as his fingers twist one of the bracelets tied around his wrist.

"I, um, well." He chuckles, fiddling with the bracelet around his wrist. "Sorry, I'm a little nervous. I know I said I would be fine being friends and I want to respect your feelings. I also thought if we were just friends, you wouldn't be able to hurt me, but at the end of the day, I care and you can hurt me. Watching you go out with other guys hurts me. I want us to be together, exclusively, so that we can figure out what this is. Would you like to go out on a date with me? As my girlfriend?"

I blink up at him, his rugged face full of earnest hope, and any regret I have felt since riding away from him in the limo disappears.

"I've been thinking about the whole friends thing, too." I smile at him. "I don't want to be friends, either."

He presses a hard kiss against my lips. "I think my heart stopped," he laughs.

"So...when are we going on this date?" I slip my arms around his neck.

"Is tonight too early?" he asks, running his hands from my hips to my lower back before settling there.

"My mom wants me to come over and spend some mother daughter time with her. What about Friday?"

"Friday sounds perfect."

"Then it's a date," I say as we grin at each other like fools.

The week seemed to slow down with the excitement for my date with Parker, but now I'm convinced time is passing in double time as I get ready. This time, I don't need Dom or anyone else's input on what I should wear on this date. There are no nerves. Just sweet anticipation. I keep everything simple since Parker told me to dress comfortably.

Favorite jeans.

Favorite blue t-shirt.

Favorite sneakers.

My phone dings that my ride has arrived. I grab a light jacket, just in case it's a little cold as the sun goes down, and head out the door.

"Ma'am," the driver says, holding my door open so I can climb in the pristine SUV, reminiscent of my time on *House of Desire*.

"Thank you," I say as I get in.

When Parker asked for my address so he could send a car to pick me up, I was skeptical. But once he explained with rush hour it would take almost two hours for him to get to me and take us where we were going, I agreed, insisting I would drive myself and there was no need to hire a car.

"But I want to be able to drive you home and I can't do that if you have your car."

How could I say no to that? I sent him my address and he ordered the car for me, letting me know what time it would arrive. When I offered to pay, he didn't even respond to my text.

I took that as a no.

"Can you tell me where we are going?" I ask the driver as he gets into the car.

"I was instructed to keep it a secret," he says, pulling out of my driveway.

Of course Parker thought of that. He wanted our location to be a surprise and no matter how many naked pictures I promised to send him in exchange for the information, he wouldn't budge.

Before long, the driver is pulling off the highway and I know immediately where we are going.

Anya: *You're taking me to an amusement park?*

Parker: *They say adrenaline can make you bond to a person or something. I figured it doesn't hurt to try. Probably should have asked if you were afraid of heights.*

Anya: *I'm not afraid of heights. Eyes on the road, mister.*

Parker: *Talk to text, babe. See you soon. I will kiss you in greeting.*

I smile down at my phone and know I am so screwed and probably half in love with this man already.

My driver pulls me up to the front of the theme park. Parker is standing there, looking hot as ever.

"I think I'm really becoming attached to those boots," I tell him as I get out of the car.

The biker style boots never really did it for me before, but tonight, between the boots and the unbuttoned flannel hanging over his gray shirt with the sleeves cuffed, I want to push him into the car and take advantage of him a little bit. His hair is, understandably, pulled back in his low bun, but I have every intention of pulling it free later and running my hands through it.

"I'll wear them whenever you want," he says, hugging me to him.

"I thought you promised me a kiss," I say, upset his lips are not already on mine.

"I didn't want to be too presumptuous," he admits.

"Presume away."

Permission granted, he leans down and gives me a firm but chaste kiss. Pulling away too soon, I look up at him.

"That wasn't near enough."

"I can't do what I want to do to you here. We'd get arrested."

"Is it really date night if you don't end up in jail?"

"There are families present."

"You're a real party pooper."

He kicks his head back laughing, and I press a kiss to his exposed throat.

"Okay, fine. We'll keep it PG. Now, what ride are you going to take me on first? And be warned, there is a correct answer."

"Adrenaline Alley," he says naming the multi-loop, high-speed rollercoaster Dominic and I rode so many times we almost threw up when we first moved here.

"Perfect place to start," I say, stepping back out of the circle of his arms. "Let's do this."

CHAPTER THIRTY-TWO

PARKER

The line to the ride is quick since it's the end of the season. Within ten minutes, we are getting loaded into our seats, but part of me wishes the line was a little longer because there weren't cameras on us. I could hold her hand and no one would be dissecting it in the morning. I could give her a kiss or put my arm around her, and a talk show wouldn't spend five minutes talking about all the other women I did that with and which one is the most important.

I could just be Parker.

On a date with my girlfriend.

And I sure don't think I'll get tired of thinking about how Anastasia is mine.

We get loaded into the front car, pulling the overhead harness down around our chests. Our feet are currently touching the ground, but once everyone is loaded, the floor will drop away.

"Are you a screamer?" Anya asks me, and all I do is raise my eyebrow. I know she didn't mean that how it sounded, right? "I love screaming."

"Could have fooled me," I said, laughing as she blushes and looks forward.

I reach out, touching her hand as the employee comes by, testing our restraints in an automatic fashion then sticking their thumb up to the one across the ride from him.

"Clear," the one in the booth says, monotone, and the floor drops away.

As we start making our accent, the chain click, click, clicking pulling us up the hill, Anya turns this way and that, looking at the lights of the park below us.

"It's so beautiful up here," she says, not paying attention to the ride.

We hit the top and crest. Turning to our right, we gain momentum and go through the first roll and that's where the scream is pulled from my throat.

I tried to hold it in, but it is no use.

Anastasia laughs and screams with glee as we are flung around, my head bouncing off the restraint like a ping pong ball between paddles. Our legs fling around through the corkscrew and after only sixty-four seconds, we slow, coming into the first pit stop on our way back into the loading area.

"I might be a screamer," I tell her and she throws her head back, laughing like a little kid.

Since the day I met her, this is the most unbridled joy I have seen on her.

No stress.

No cares.

Nothing.

I feel a spark of what could be an all consuming fire light in my chest. Despite the threat of possible rejection, I'm glad I took the chance to ask Anya to be mine.

"That was amazing. Do you want to go again?" Anya asks.

My brain feels bruised, but with her eyes shining so bright as we are released from our seats, I know I can't say no to anything she wants.

"Let's do it," I say, grabbing her hand and we run down the stairs and back through the queue, getting in line once more.

"I haven't been to an amusement park in maybe ten years. Thank you for bringing me."

She wraps her arms around my middle, hugging me tight. I hold her to me, planting a kiss on the top of her head.

"Maybe we should get season passes," I say, looking down at her. The offer was nonchalant, but I pray she can hear the promise in the words.

That I want her around long enough to even need a season pass somewhere.

"Sounds perfect." She stands on her tippy toes, pressing a soft kiss to my lips.

"Hey, the line's moving. Stop making out," the guy says behind us. Anya snorts and steps away from me, pulling me forward, but I glare at the guy who holds up both hands and doesn't say a word to us again.

We make our way through four more roller coasters before my stomach grumbles and I can't ignore my hunger any longer.

"Do you want to get something to eat?" I ask, knowing we are close to the food court.

"As long as I can get a funnel cake."

"I don't think it'd be a trip to the park without a funnel cake," I say, linking our hands together as we stroll to the food vendors. "You mentioned a big job when I stopped by the other day, but I didn't get a chance to ask about the details. What's the job?"

She pulls me to a stop, her eyes going big.

"*Ryan Jade* wants me to do her parents' anniversary party. For five hundred people! Lorelei sent some goodies to Alec. I'm assuming she was on a set with him or something? I didn't really ask, I was trying not to fawn all over her, but I guess she tried some of the desserts and the rest is history. I have to deliver it the morning of our wrap party."

The wrap party is going to be the bane of my existence. All the ladies from the season will arrive and we will have a group interview. Everyone wanting to know the status of my love life. Hopefully, I can tell them my heart belongs to the woman next to me.

"Who's Ryan Jade?"

Her mouth drops open and I rub my hand over my mouth hiding my smile.

"You know Ryan Jade. You have to. She is only the most famous pop singer in the world."

"Oh, yeah, I do know her," I admit. "My brother always thought she was super hot."

"She is even more stunning in person. If you broke up with me for her, I'd understand." She grabs my hand and tries to pull me toward the food again, but I don't let her budge me. Turning around, she looks at me, a question on her face.

"I wouldn't break up with you for her," I assure her

"It was just a joke, Parker. Come on, I can smell the funnel cakes and I'm starting to salivate."

Her dismissal is not enough for me.

"No. You need to hear me. I want *you*. No one else." I squeeze her hand, emphasizing my point. She drops my hand and then grabs my face. She pulls me down and gives me a loud, smacking kiss.

"Good," she says with a giggle.

"Let's go get you a funnel cake," I say, happier than I have been in years.

"Woohoo!" she says, pumping her arms in the air.

After the food, we go play some of the arcade games, letting our stomachs settle before getting on even more roller coasters. We run around the park like a pair of kids until the final announcement is made, kicking us out.

"Do you want me to carry your elephant?" I ask Anya. The stuffed animal is almost as tall as her. I was surprised when she won, not because I didn't believe she was capable, but because I know those games are rigged. But to get the big prize, she had to win three out of four times.

She won all four, just to prove she could.

"No, I'm bonding with it. Trying to get a feel for what it should be named. Do you have any suggestions?"

"Oh, I wouldn't even know where to begin. If it was mine, I probably would have named it Elephant."

"Not very creative."

I shrug my shoulders as I open the truck door so she can put the elephant in the back. She seat belts it into its seat and I shake my head in genuine affection before opening her door. As she steps up, she gives me a kiss. I'll never get tired of her quick little kisses.

"That was a fun date," she tells me. She shifts in her seat for a moment with a pretty blush staining her cheeks. "Will you take me home with you?"

The question is shy, but I immediately have to adjust my pants, immediately going to half staff.

"Hell, yeah," I say, giving her another kiss, and then closing her door. I hustle to my side, eager to get back to my place.

We drive the forty minutes back to my place in companionable silence. Anya looks out the window as my hand rests on her thigh. The casual intimacy of the gesture, and the fact she's letting me touch her in such a way, makes my eyes go misty.

I didn't realize how much I missed this. Hugging someone. Kissing them.

Touching.

But it's not just the physical things. It's everything. Mundane things. Even picking what's for dinner can be better with a partner.

There is a freedom in not having to check in with someone and being able to do anything you'd like whenever you want. But having someone care enough to wait up for you after a long day? To hold you through sadness? Stand beside you in your triumph? Someone who lets you be a witness to all the joy and pain in their life?

That's love.

And I realize I've missed having love in my life. Loving my friends and family and letting them love me. I've carried the burden of being alone for so long, not wanting to drag someone down with the weight of me around their neck. But I didn't give them what they needed, either.

In taking away their opportunity to be close to me, I took away their chance to fully love me and for me to fully love them.

And maybe we were lesser people for the loss.

The lessons Sharon has been drilling into my head week after week are starting to click. That just because Brittany left, doesn't mean I'm unloveable or undeserving of love. Her choices didn't determine my worth.

I squeeze Anya's thigh. Her beautiful eyes find mine in the dim lighting.

"I'm glad you're here with me," I tell her. She grasps my hand, holding it, without removing it from her leg.

"I'm glad you asked me to be."

We pull into my driveway and I park the truck, turning off the engine. "Let me get your door," I say, getting out and trotting around.

"Thank you," she says, squeezing my bicep as she gets out.

"Would you like anything to drink?" I ask, unlocking my door.

A car door opens and shuts out on the street, but right as I'm about to close my front door, I hear my name.

"Parker," the voice says, and my head snaps up, disbelief waring with shock inside me. "It's been a long time."

"Brittany." I pull the door open wider. "What are you doing here?"

CHAPTER THIRTY-THREE

S HE WALKS UP THE drive. Her hair is longer than I remember and as she gets closer, I can see the barest signs of age on her face. She lost the last visages of childhood but I still see the girl I married there.

"I'm here to see you. I was hoping we could talk."

I look back inside my house and there stands Anastasia, waiting for me. I turn back to my ex-wife.

"About what?" I demand.

"You know what about. I'm sorry to interrupt your date." If I didn't know every expression her face makes, I would have missed the infinitesimal smirk that passes over it. "I don't plan to be here very long, so maybe, if you could find the time?"

I look back at Anya as she moves closer to the door. My stomach twists and turns and the younger version of me, the one that was left behind, wars with the man I am now.

"It's okay," Anya whispers.

"Give me a second," I say to Brittany, shutting the door in her face, before turning toward my girlfriend who looks like she's about ready to bolt.

"Anya, I don't know what she's doing here," I say, panicked.

"It's okay. You should talk to her. I can just go home."

"Baby, please. I want you here," I say, almost begging her to stay, but I know, even if she does stay, the night is ruined. I'll be distracted the entire time.

"And I want to be here, but this is more important."

She goes up on her tiptoes and kisses me, but as she tries to pull away, I band my arms around her, holding her like I'm trying to fuse us together.

"Parker," she whispers, "you need to let me go. I'll talk to you later, okay?"

Panic grips me.

"Promise?" I can't let her go without knowing she won't disappear from my life.

"Promise."

I drop my arms and hold out my keys.

"Take my truck. I'll have Mitchel bring me to get it tomorrow."

She takes them, and opens the door, Brittany standing there with her arms crossed over her chest.

"Sorry to ruin your night," Brittany says as Anya walks past her, her voice the one I immediately recognize as her mean girl voice. Any time she was going to give someone a backhanded compliment, that was the voice she used. My hackles immediately rise. I open my mouth to say something, but Anya takes care of it.

"You didn't ruin it. I'll have plenty of other nights with him. He is my boyfriend, after all."

Brittany's arms drop when her dig doesn't land, but I don't care. I all but preen at Anya's claiming of me. I see a small slice of the smile she gives Brittany, and I'm just glad I'm not on the receiving end of it. I don't think I'd have any balls left.

"Do you want to come in?" I ask Brittany, stepping out of the way as Anya beeps my truck unlocked.

"Thanks, Parky," she says, using the nickname I haven't heard in so long. Anya waves as I look at her until the door blocks my line of sight.

My foyer is empty when I turn around. I move into the house, finding Brittany running her finger over the back of my leather sofa.

"How did you find out where I live?" I ask, anger starting to seep into my tone.

"Nice place," she says, looking up at the high ceilings. "It suits you."

"You're not here to talk about my house, Brittany. What do you want?" I fold my arms over my chest, closing myself off.

"How about a drink?" She flops down on my couch, making herself at home, and it sets my teeth on edge.

"Fine. But only if you tell me how you found my address." I move through the arched opening into the kitchen, grabbing two beers from the fridge. I take a long swig of mine and walk back to her, holding it out by the neck.

"Private investigator. I needed to talk to you and you changed your phone number." She grabs the drink from me. "Thanks," she says with a smile.

I take a seat in the chair across from her. Normally I'd be pissed about the extreme invasion of privacy, but it doesn't hold a candle to my worry about how Anya's feeling right now.

Brittany's had the upper hand since she showed up on my doorstep. But I know she won't answer anything until she's good and ready. Instead of peppering her with questions, trying to force her to talk to me like I used to, I just drink my beer and wait looking around the room like I've never been in here before.

The walls of my living room are a cream. Charlie hated the choice, but I thought it allowed for the architecture of the space to really shine. The mahogany-colored beams stand out, adding warmth. The deep leather of my couch matches, while the chairs Lorelei picked out are a forest green fabric and amazingly comfortable. The raw edged wood coffee table is made from a large tree my dad had removed from the backyard of my family home. It's the one piece I've taken with me throughout the years.

"I saw you on *House of Deceit*. You should have been the winner. That Charlie girl never would have lasted if not for you. But, then again, you weren't always the best observer of the people around you, huh?"

The dig lands, but I control my facial expression.

"The right person won," is all I say.

"Do you remember how we'd watch that show every week?"

"Yup."

"Did you think of me when you applied?"

"Once or twice," I tell her honestly, "but my time there has no connection to you."

She scoots back on the couch, laying one arm on the back as she takes a deep drink from her beer.

"When I saw you announced as a contestant, I almost swallowed my tongue. My Parker all grown up and on the show we always said we'd apply to."

"I'm not 'your' anything." I realize I don't want to go down memory lane with her. I want to be with Anastasia and finish our date.

"Don't you want to know where I've been?" she asks.

"I figured if you wanted me to know where you were, you wouldn't have left in the middle of the night and would have called at some point."

"I went dream chasing. After everything, I felt like I had a second chance at life. I had to take it while I could," she tells me with a smile.

"You couldn't've waited until the sun came up and told me you were going?"

"You never would have let me leave. I would have died in that town without doing anything."

"Whatever you have to tell yourself," I say, shrugging my shoulder.

My fingers itch to pull out my phone and text Anastasia and check on her, followed immediately by an emergency request to talk to Sharon tomorrow. I keep my hands still. Calm. Keep everything in. Just like I always have.

"She's beautiful," she says, trying to bait me in a new way.

"She is."

"You wouldn't have an issue pulling a beautiful woman. I mean, look at you. I'm sure you have people falling at your feet constantly," she says with a sly smirk and I know she's watched at least the first episode of *House of Desire*. "It's so funny you picked her. Considering you met her in the same way you met me. I guess we really do repeat our pasts, don't we?"

"What are you talking about?" I ask, not wanting to play her mind games.

"Don't you remember? You told Charlie about how we met, after all. You plowing into the cheerleading pyramid and knocking us over? You like to be the hero, dusting the dirt off the damsel in distress."

I snort. "Anastasia wasn't in distress."

"Wasn't she? I don't know. I saw a lot of distress on her face tonight."

I squeeze the beer bottle in my hand, as the need to call Anya nearly overtakes me. To check and make sure she's not going to leave me, too. All because of the woman sitting across from me that destroyed my heart all those years ago.

"Why are you here?" I ask through gritted teeth.

"I know I messed up with you, how great you were, and I'm hoping, maybe, we could pick up where we left off?"

I stare at her.

"You have got to be shitting me."

CHAPTER THIRTY-FOUR

ANYA

I SMILE AS THE door shuts, but the moment I hear the lock snick into place, my expression drops. Moving quietly just in case Parker hasn't moved away from the door, I press the truck's lock button careful to only hit it once and not let the alarm beep, and gently set his truck keys by the column so he'll see them, but they're hidden from the street.

Tears threaten, but I keep them in, pretending like I'm back in *House of Desire* and Parker is just on a date with one of the other girls. That there's a camera on me and I don't want it to catch me crying. Pulling out my phone, I scroll down and tap on the name I know will always pick up.

Always come get me.

"Dom," I say, choking back tears. "Will you come get me?"

Outside of Parker's neighborhood is a well-lit gas station. Instead of having Dom come to Parker's, I walk to the station, dropping a pin for him to find me once I'm there. The sound of his car's engine reaches me before I even see him. As the blue antique muscle car pulls in, his first purchase when he signed with the Thunderhawks, heads turn.

"Thanks for coming to get me," I say, climbing into the front seat.

"I'll have you know you interrupted a thrilling night of online Scrabble with Dad and buttered noodles for dinner."

"You are a ninety-two-year-old grandpa, trapped in a twenty-something's body."

"Twenty-something?"

"My mind is too preoccupied to remember your birthday right now."

My seat belt clicks as I fasten it. He pulls us out of the gas station, going slowly so he doesn't scrape the bottom of the car.

"Who were you with? Why did they leave you at the gas station? Did you forget how old they were, too?"

I lean back against my seat, staring up at the cream-colored ceiling above me.

"They didn't leave me at the gas station."

"Then how did you get here?" he asks, refusing to look at me, giving me privacy in case I'm going to cry. Our unspoken agreement all through life. We can cry with each other, without fear of being made fun of, and the other will not watch. The first time a guy stood me up for the winter dance in eighth grade, Dom sat in my closet to give me privacy while I cried and he told me jokes through the door to try to make me feel better.

"I was with Parker."

"I'll kill him," he says with no heat behind it. He knows I'd never let him fulfill the promise.

"His ex-wife showed up, Dom."

I know I shocked him by the complete and utter lack of any response. No sharp intake of breath. No laughing. No questions.

Nothing but the sound of the road and someone honking to our left.

A few tears escape as a flash of anger at the universe heats my insides. I feel like Parker and I have fought to get to this moment, without cameras and production assistants and a schedule, where we can try to give this relationship a chance. And the second we have a date, the best date of my life, the other shoe drops. My heart is breaking, worried this is going to end and I'll never get to feel Parker's lips on mine ever again.

When I can barely stand the silence anymore, I smack Dom's arm.

"Ow! What was that for?"

"I just dropped a bomb and you didn't say anything."

"What do you want me to say?" he asks, looking over at me as we pull up at a stoplight, the red glow falling on his face.

"Whatever you're thinking," I sigh. Maybe if he starts, I'll be able to figure out what to say. How I feel.

"I'm actually not really thinking anything."

"Not a single thought?" The light turns green and we continue on to my house.

"I didn't realize he had an ex-wife. How do you feel about that?" He keeps his tone placid and nonjudgmental.

"I don't mind. We all have pasts. His just involves a previous marriage," I say. And it's true. I don't mind he was married before. But I guess I never expected that past to show up on the doorstep.

On our first date.

"What's wrong then? And don't lie and say nothing. I know you better than that."

"I'm pretty much trying to figure out if I'm still going to have a boyfriend after tonight."

"He's your boyfriend? But he's back at his house with his ex-wife? And you're okay with that?"

"TBD on the boyfriend thing, but until I'm told otherwise, yes. It's new. Tonight was our first date being together. And yes, he's with her. In fact, I told him to talk to her. They have a history, not that I have any idea what that history is, and I could tell how torn he was on wanting me to stay and needing to talk to her. I made the decision for him."

Saying it out loud makes me feel like I made the worst mistake of my life.

"That's pretty damn understanding of you."

"If you had an ex show up on your doorstep finally ready to talk, wouldn't you want to take the opportunity?" I ask him. A part of me is really torn. Do I like that I'm not with Parker? No. I wish I could be there for him during this. But they need time to work through whatever happened, so Parker can finally have closure.

"I guess so, depending on the circumstances around the breakup."

We ride in silence for a while. I turn up the radio when my favorite song comes on, singing softly under my breath.

"What if I lose him?" I whisper when the song is over, putting voice to my biggest fear.

"If you lose him to his ex-wife, then I don't really think you ever had him to begin with."

We pull into my driveway and Dom shuts off the car, but neither of us get out. If I needed to sit here for two hours, he'd sit here for every moment.

And only complain when he got hungry.

"What do you want?" he asks, turning to look at me.

"I want him."

"Then just make sure he knows that you want him, even if you have to take some time and space."

I nod and undo my seatbelt and open the door. "Thanks for coming to pick me up."

"Make sure to leave me a five-star review on Uber," he says, turning over the engine.

My footsteps feel slow and leaden, but eventually I make it inside the house, Dominic waiting until I close my front door before he leaves, just as Dad taught him.

A shower sounds amazing and without waiting another second, I make my way into my bathroom. The pale-yellow room usually makes me happy. White tile goes halfway up the wall. At first, I hated how everything was original to the house built in the 1960s, but as I've lived here, the style has grown on me.

I reach past my white shower curtain with various colored flowers. Giving the hot water tap a quarter turn, I count to ten, and then continue turning, the water immediately steaming. Adding some cool, I find the perfect temperature. The water runs for a moment as I strip out of my clothes.

Stepping into the water, I think about what Dom said, and I realize he's right. If Parker wants to go back to his ex-wife, then there's nothing I can do about that. Nothing I would want to do.

I want Parker to be happy and if that's with her, then all I can do is remove myself from the picture.

CHAPTER THIRTY-FIVE

PARKER

M Y PHONE SITS ON my chest, hands resting on top of it, hoping it vibrates with a text from Anya.

When Brittany asked if she could stay in the guest room, my jaw almost dropped. She hadn't contacted me for *years* and now, not only does she want back in my life, she wants a place to stay? But then she gave me those big eyes she always did in high school, and my traitorous heart gave a small squeeze.

I showed her to the room before making my way to mine, making sure to lock the door so there would be absolutely no confusion about if she was welcome in my space.

And then I paced.

And paced. I debated texting Anya and asking her if I could come over to talk, but decided against it not wanting to pressure her. In the end I sent a short message telling her how great of a time I had with her and that I wished she was here before finally laying down around three in the morning.

The room lightens as dawn begins to break. Not able to wait any longer, I climb out of bed and into the shower after stripping out of my clothes. I had moved all of my meetings for this morning after Anya had agreed to go on a date with me. I didn't want to be presumptuous she would spend the night with me, but I didn't want to rush away if she was in my bed.

Who would have thought it would be Brittany in my house and not Anya.

I pick up my phone and send a text to Anya wishing her a good morning and asking if we can talk.

The smell of coffee and bacon meets me as I make my way down the hallway away from the sleeping quarters of the house.

"What are you wearing?" One of my old, long-sleeved winter shirts hangs off her body, hitting right below her ass. Her legs are toned and bare.

"Oh," she says, looking down at herself before turning her attention back to the eggs she's scrambling on the stovetop. "I hope you don't mind. I got cold and looked in the closet for another blanket. I didn't find one, but I found a box labeled winter clothes. I guess you probably don't need those much here."

"I do mind. Extra blankets are in the chest at the end of the bed."

"Just like our house," she says, smiling.

"It's convenient for guests."

Her cheeks turn a slight pink as she grabs a bowl from beside her, putting the eggs on it. On my island sits pancakes and bacon, along with a pot of coffee.

"I made breakfast," she says, stating the obvious as she sets the bowl next to the other plates. Steam rises off of everything. "There's coffee. I know how much you need your coffee first thing in the morning."

I look at the spread and despite the effort I see she put into the meal, I get angry.

Angry at her pretending like this is normal.

"I don't drink coffee anymore," I say, pettiness rising up and lashing out. I'm not proud of the small amount of hurt I put in her eyes, but I can't seem to accept her gesture.

"I see. The grounds must have been for your girlfriend, then."

I don't respond. She doesn't need to know anything about me and Anya. It's not her business. Not anymore.

"I'm going to work," I say, stating the obvious. Even without morning meetings, I'd rather be at the office than in this hellish situation. "When you leave, go out the garage. There's a panel on the left side when you look at the house from the driveway. Press the enter key and it'll shut the door. Remember, you said only one night." My tone is brusque, but I just don't care. Anya hasn't texted me and I know it's a direct result of the woman across from me.

Not only did she break my heart, leaving me a husk of myself, now, when I've finally found someone I can feel myself falling for, she pops back up.

"I remember," she snaps, crossing her arms under her breasts, pushing them up, showing me she's going bra-less this morning. In another life, that would have been enough for me to go to her and take her on the island, but now it does nothing for me. "Are we going to talk about what I said last night?"

"No."

"Okay. Are we going to talk about everything that happened back then?"

"*You* don't get to dictate this. *You* left. Not me. Leave your number on the notepad on the side of the fridge. I'll call you when I'm ready to talk. One more day without answers after ten years won't matter." I can feel my temper rising and I want to get out of here before I say something I regret.

My phone vibrates and I check it immediately, but it's just my ride share telling me they are outside the house.

"I'll talk to you later," I say in goodbye, heading for the front door. As I shut it behind myself, I see my truck still in the driveway.

My heart begins galloping thinking Anya is here, but when I look around, she's nowhere. The driver of my ride honks and I flash him a one moment signal. As I turn to lock the door with my spare set of keys, my foot bumps the ones I gave to Anya last night.

Squatting down, my joints crack like I'm a thousand years old. The metal is cold against my overheated hand. I wave off my driver, getting a double middle finger before he pulls away.

I look down the street like I can see the ghost of Anya leaving.

Every mile I drove into the office, I got more and more disappointed Anya didn't take my truck. I wanted a reason to get her to see me without me showing up at her bakery.

"What's your problem?" Mitchel asks as I stomp to my office, a warm coffee cup in my hand and a bag of fast food breakfast.

"Brittany is here."

Mitchel's eyes go wide as he follows me into my office, shutting the door behind him. He left for college after we graduated and wasn't there for the whole horrible thing, but on a few drunken nights, he definitely heard a story or two.

"Did she call you or something?"

I laugh at the absurdity of the entire situation. "No, because she wants to ruin my life all over again. She was waiting on my doorstep."

"Holy shit."

"And I was bringing Anastasia home for the first time after an amazing date."

His jaw drops and his entire facial expression is pretty much how I've felt since Anya and I pulled into my driveway.

"What did Anastasia say?"

"She told me to talk to Brittany. I gave her my car keys so she could get herself home, but she left them on the ground and must have had someone pick her up."

"Have you talked to her?" he asks, crossing his arms.

"She never answered my text from last night."

"What are you going to do?"

"I don't know. But I need to talk to her. Would it be insane to show up at her bakery? I think I'm still her boyfriend, but I don't want to overstep." Uncertainty at what to do and fear there's nothing I *can* do to rectify this situation has been making my stomach hurt since I shut the door on Anya yesterday.

"I don't think I'd show up in the middle of her workday. Maybe just text her a few more times and if she's still not answering, I'd show up at closing in a day or two. She might need a second to breathe."

"Okay, thanks. What do you need?"

We go over the details of a few different projects and the issues they are running into. Then we go through the list of new projects so I can add them to the map I like to keep marking of the different places around the city that our homes occupy.

"How far out are we booking?"

"Eighteen months," he says, checking his phone.

"Still?" I ask. That was the timeline before I left for the show and we hired additional people.

"We keep getting new customers. I've had to turn people away."

"Sounds like we need to expand the team again. Let's talk to finance and see where the budget stands." He taps on his phone and my computer pings with the notification of the meeting. "If there's room, highest priority is quality."

"Agreed. I can put out a call to the teams we already have and see if there's anyone they suggest."

"Let's check with the managers. See if any of the apprentices are ready to be promoted and prioritize those movements and then backfill them."

I check my phone as he makes notes. Still no message from Anastasia.

"She'll call," he says, catching me.

"I hope so."

"I'm going to get out of here. There are some emails waiting for you I need responses on."

"I'll look at them now. I'm going to visit the Valdez site this afternoon."

"Sounds like a plan. I'll let you get to it." He leaves my office and I pick up my phone again and type out a new text and send it. Considering how many times I've wanted to text her, I feel like I've shown great restraint to this point.

Parker: *I found my keys. I wish you would have taken the car.*

Anya: *I didn't want to inconvenience you*

I stare at the screen, reading her response a hundred times. How could she ever think anything regarding her would be an inconvenience?

Parker: *If you took a ride share, I want to pay for it.*

Anya: *That's not necessary. How did your night go?*

Fuck it. I press the video call button and it starts ringing. My heart pounds so hard against my ribs while I wait for her to pick up I'm afraid the bones will be bruised.

"You have flour on your nose," I tell her with a smile. She's beautiful. Disheveled hair. Tired eyes.

"It's been a busy morning."

"I thought I'd call you and answer your question. Last night was awful because you weren't there."

"You know that's not what I meant, Parker," she says. The lack of emotion in her voice is almost worse than if she were mad.

"I know, but it's no less true. It was weird, seeing her for the first time."

"Did you talk it out?"

Embarrassment. That's all I feel when I have to admit I wasted my night away from her.

"No. There were a lot of hurt feelings just seeing each other after so long."

"Hi, Anya!" Liam says in the background and her answering smile is bright and I wish I had received it.

"Hey, Li. Give me a second." She turns back to me. "Parker, I have to go. I'll talk to you later, okay?"

"Sure. Have a great day."

She hangs up quickly and I feel no better for the conversation. Not wanting to leave it like this, I text her the truth.

Parker: *I miss you.*

Tucking my phone away, I finish my breakfast as I sort through the various emails from Mitchel, vendors, and customers. Anything to keep my mind off of Anastasia and what she is doing.

My stomach grumbles hours later and I push back from my desk, trying to decide what I want to eat before my client meeting in an hour. Grabbing my keys from the drawer, I lock my computer.

"Knock, knock," Brittany says, standing in my doorway.

"You really need to stop showing up places," I tell her, rudely.

"I just thought I'd bring you lunch." She holds up a paper bag and I'm thrown back to our first month married when we would eat lunch together every day. "It's Chinese. I still remember your favorite food."

"I was just leaving to go to a meeting," I tell her, the smell of the food making my mouth water, but I refuse to give in.

"Oh, okay. I guess I'll just go then. I'll see you later?"

"Yeah. Later," I say, pushing past her. Leaving her, just like she left me.

Charlie: *Are you still coming to dinner tonight? Courtney and her family will be there. They got in this morning and are exhausted from unloading the moving truck.*

I was hoping for a text from Anastasia when I felt my phone vibrate in my meeting, but I guess I should have known better. It's been four days since our date and all of our conversations have been short and to the point. It's better than silence, but only just.

Every day after work, I've found myself sitting outside her bakery but unable to go in for fear of pushing her.

Parker: *I'll be there. Can Courtney make those cookies she mailed you that one time? Next dinner, perhaps?*

Charlie: *I'm surprised you want to eat anyone's baking but Anya's.*

Parker: *Yeah, I've got an update on that.*

Charlie: *Should I have the whiskey ready tonight?*

Parker: *Probably wouldn't hurt.*

She acknowledges my message with a thumbs up and I groan, thinking about telling her. The clock ticks a minute closer to five o'clock and I decide I'm done for the day. Keeping myself busy has only worked so well and I'm tired of fighting it.

"Mitch," I call from my office. He pops his head out of his office, taking a bite of a candy bar and raising his eyebrows at me. "I'm leaving for the day. If there's anything I need to do this weekend, shoot me a text. Otherwise, I'll see you on Monday."

He gives me a salute without saying anything and ducks back into his office.

As I make my way home, I think about going by the bakery but quickly realize a car accident has created a snarling mess of traffic in that direction, and I know with dinner at six, I'll be late if I make the detour.

Brittany's car sits in my driveway and I roll my eyes. After the first night, she gave me a sob story about not having enough money to get a hotel room, all the ones in the area being incredibly expensive. As I feel my heart rate spike, I know I'm going to have to kick her out this weekend.

And the fact that Anya hasn't talked to me much so I could tell her what's been going on and we could clear the air is sending me into a tailspin.

"Hey," Brittany calls out as I come in, shutting the door behind me.

"Hi."

"You're home early."

"I have plans with friends tonight."

She's standing in my kitchen, grabbing a beer out of the fridge, handing it to me. I twist off the top and take a long drink.

"Can I come?"

"No," I say, untucking my shirt as I make my way back to my bedroom. Her footsteps follow me down the hallway and I don't want to deal with this.

"Please? I'm so bored and you still won't talk to me."

I roll my eyes at her pushing. Before I would have given in.

"You want me to talk to you? Okay. Why did you leave, Brittany?" I ask, whirling around. "Why couldn't you talk to me? Tell me how unhappy you were? Why wouldn't you just *talk* to me?"

"Because you never would have heard me. It was the best thing for us!" she yells, equally as annoyed by the round and round we've found ourselves in. And yet, I can't bring myself to open up all of this pain again. I know it needs to happen. It has to happen. But the pain might end me.

"Yes, the perfect way to work through the loss of our *son* was to run away. Great choice," I say, emotion clogging.

My heart hurts. Just as it has every day I've thought of him, my son that didn't even live longer than a day.

"And your solution was so much better? To not talk to me or cry or even pretend like it happened? And it's not like I left the next day!"

"I had to keep moving or I was going to die with him. I'm sorry we still had bills to pay. I'm sorry I grieve differently than you."

"That wasn't the problem and you *know* it." She huffs as if she's just run a mile.

"Then what was the problem? Huh? What was it, Brittany?"

"I was *trapped*, Parker! He was gone and the entire reason I was still in that town, other than you, was *gone*. The only reason we got married was because I was pregnant. Did you really want to marry me? Did you? Because I don't think you did. I wanted to leave, go away to college, and that choice was taken from me when that double line showed up.

"And that was okay. I was so excited to have your baby. To be a family with you. And then we lost him and all I could think about was what we would be doing if he had survived. How I'd be taking him to preschool or shopping for clothes for him. Every milestone he never had. I was suffocating under our lost son and my dreams.

"I just wanted to feel something, *anything*. All I felt was this great gaping emptiness where my baby was supposed to be and I was so scared that's all I'd feel for the rest of my fucking life. All I could think about was how I wanted to go with him. To take care of him. To be with him.

"But I couldn't leave you. Until that was the only thing I could do, so I could maybe feel something again."

The ringing silence echoes after she finishes yelling and all I can do is nod while pushing the hurricane of emotions ripping through me to a distant corner of my broken soul.

"Sorry for trapping you then," I say, almost gently, shutting my door softly in her face.

CHAPTER THIRTY-SIX

"You're late," Charlie says, opening the door for me.

"Brittany is currently living with me and we got into a bit of a tiff. I brought wine," I tell her, shoving the bottle into her hands and pushing my way inside the door as she stares at me in shock.

I make my way through the house and to the kitchen where Courtney is standing at the island, nibbling on some cheese and crackers.

"Finally. I'm starving. Charlie, can we eat?" Courtney asks.

Her husband is sitting on the couch, playing with their son while he and Alec discuss something. The air is perfumed with Italian spices and I'm hoping for Charlie's homemade lasagna.

I call out a hello to the guys before pressing a kiss on Courtney's cheek and moving to the drink cart off to the side.

"Anyone need a drink?" A chorus of no's sounds, so I continue with making an old fashioned for myself.

"Hey, question for you," Court says, swallowing a bite of cracker. Charlie walks in and gently sets the bottle of wine on the counter. "Would you be willing to come by the house and price out a few things we want to have done around the place?"

"Not a problem. If you text me on Monday, I'll get you added to my calendar," I tell her, putting the glass decanter down.

"Amazing. How's Anya? Is she not coming?"

Not wanting to get into the current chaos with everyone, I say simply, "She's good. She's really busy with this huge job she landed. Actually, she mentioned wanting to hire some baking help. You should give her a call. I know you mentioned helping her at the wedding."

"That'd be perfect! Just give me her number," she says, picking up another cracker and cheese. "Charles, I need you to get the pizza out of the oven. Please? I'm begging."

Courtney's pleading seems to snap Charlie out of her shock. Moving to the oven, she pulls oven mitts out of the drawer and pulls the hot pizza out.

"You all go ahead and get started. Parker and I need to talk in private for a second." She puts the pizza on an awaiting cooling rack, drops the mitts on the counter, and grabs my wrist, pulling me out the back door.

"Start from the beginning," she says, crossing her arms and giving me a stern look.

I know I'm not going to get out of this, so I start from the moment I left her house last week, to my date with Anya, and the surprise of Brittany on the porch. By the time I'm done talking, I know we will be eating the cold slices of pizza that haven't been consumed yet.

"That's a lot," she says, moving us over to the sun bed, sitting on the end. I drop down next to her and we watch the water undulate for a few moments in silence before she speaks again. "You have to go talk to Anastasia. Knowing her the small amount I do, she's trying to give you space to work things out with Brittany. Maybe you need to do something a bit more drastic."

"Are you telling me to show up on her doorstep? Because I've been fighting the urge all week."

"You did it to help me and Alec get back together. Now do it for yourself. Unless you want to be with Brittany?" She looks at me, no judgment on her face, simply curiosity and love. My body relaxes as I realize my best friend isn't going to go anywhere. No matter what I do, she's going to be there.

"I love you," I tell her, overcome with her simple support, bumping her with my shoulder.

"I love you, too, my towering Viking."

"I don't want to be with Brittany. I just want closure."

"Then you need to talk to her. Really talk to her. Not yell. Not throwing things in each other's faces. Not be an asshole. Really talk. Because if you want it to work with Anya, with anyone, you need to be able to fully close the door on this chapter. You need to forgive the young man inside yourself that didn't know how to handle everything being thrown at you. You're not that guy anymore."

I nod, knowing she's right. Knowing all of my work with Sharon has avoided this moment but here, with my best friend, knowing she loves me for *me*, I can finally accept I did the best I could, and even if it wasn't perfect, that doesn't mean I'm not worth being loved.

Out of nowhere, my eyes fill with tears. I fight them, trying to keep them from falling, but it's futile.

For the first time, I cry for my lost son.

Charlie holds me as my grief pours from me in a raging river of tears. Her arms come around me as she holds me, being silently strong for the both of us. Time passes as the well of my sadness empties, and as I wipe my face dry, I feel the lightness starting to take hold.

"Thank you," I tell her, looking at her in the dim light.

"I will always be here, Parker. For whatever you need."

I nod, standing up, reaching out my hand to pull her to her feet.

"Should we go eat some pizza?" I ask.

"Hell, yeah," she says, and we walk back in the house hand in hand.

CHAPTER THIRTY-SEVEN

ANYA

MOM WORKS THE FRONT of the bakery today while Liam is at school and Dad is at a doctor's appointment. I sit in the back, trying to do all the planning necessary for Ryan Jade's party. Earlier in the week she stopped by to do a tasting, something I normally only offer for weddings, but considering the size of the party, I was happy to do it for her. My tablet includes all of my notes and various reference pictures I'll need for the day.

One of the buttercream shapes is new to me so I pull out my phone, trying to find a video that shows the technique so I can practice. I go to click on the video I found, but an unknown number pops up on my phone.

"Hello," I say, tentatively.

"Anya? It's Courtney, Charlie Price's, well I guess King now, best friend?"

"Courtney, yes! Hi. How are you?" I ask.

"I'm good, thanks. I'm actually calling for a favor, or really, offering a favor."

"A favor for me?" I stand up and begin pacing around my kitchen, a habit I've had since the first time a boy called my house to ask me out.

"Parker was at dinner at Charlie's house this past Friday, we missed you by the way, and he mentioned you had a big job coming up and you'd be looking for help?"

A small smile escapes. The fact he remembered our conversation touches me.

"Oh! Yes, oh my gosh, thank you for calling. I definitely could use some help. It's for next weekend and I am a bit overwhelmed to say the least."

"Awesome! Well, I need to finish settling my family into our new house and get my son enrolled in school. Do you think I could start with you on Monday or is that too late?"

"No, that'll be fine. It gives me time to finalize some designs and choices, and then we can hit the ground running on Monday."

"Sounds great. Thank you, for this. I've always wanted to work in a bakery. I figured this move would be the perfect opportunity," she says.

"Really, you're saving me. We'll discuss your pay and everything when you get here."

"Works for me. I'll see you on Monday, bright and early."

"See you then," I say, hanging up the call.

I stop pacing for a moment, a warm feeling creeping up. I pull up my texts and find the thread with Parker, tapping into it. It has been so hard not calling and texting him every second of the day, but I know he has a lot to work through with Brittany showing up. I can only imagine how hard that must have been for him and no matter how much I want him, he needs this time. Hopefully, getting the closure he's needed will only help us. If there's still going to be an us after all is said and done.

Anya: *Hi, Parker. Just got off the phone with Courtney. Thanks for telling her I needed help. Would you like to come over on Sunday, after Dom's game? I could cook us dinner and we could talk.*

I hit send, nerves running rampant through my body. Reaching back to tuck my phone in my pocket, before I can even put it away, it vibrates.

Parker: *Thank God. I've missed you. I'll be there.*

A small smile lights my face and I move around my day feeling lighter.

Lorelei and I walk in through the entrance designated for guests of the players. I decided to keep my outfit simple today and am wearing a t-shirt with our last name on the back and Dom's number and some plain jeans and tennis shoes.

"Do you think this outfit is too much? I was a little worried about it, but I wanted to try something different," Lorelei asks, spinning for me while we wait in line for security.

Her hair is streaked red today, paired with a mini skirt, thigh-high boots, and a strategically ripped up shirt. She looks much more like the other wives in this outfit.

"I think you look great. Your feet are going to die in those boots, though."

"No, didn't Dom tell you? Sasha invited us to sit in her suite today."

"And?" I ask.

"They have free food, a private bathroom, and an open bar," Lore says. "And the comfy seats."

"Okay, fine. I hate my brother. I would have worn something else if I had known. I'm a little surprised she even knows my name."

We place our bags on the conveyor belt as we move through the metal detectors, our conversation on pause.

"I heard through the grapevine she is a huge fan of *House of Desire* and has been obsessed with this season."

I roll my eyes as we collect our things. The Desire Suite dates aired two days earlier and my phone has been blowing up with interview requests, all of which I've rejected.

"Goodie."

"Don't worry, I'm sure it'll be fine."

"Do you want to know the only thing people want to talk about? Me falling after getting out of the limo."

She tries to keep in her laugh as we move to the elevator that will take us directly up to the suite area.

"It's important to be memorable, sweetie," she says, patting my arm.

"*Not* for falling down, Lore!"

"Well, okay, I'll give you that. Do you want to hear some gossip I've heard from Alec? To distract you?"

"Always."

"After the hometown episode was aired, people were crazy for Dom and they've thrown his name in the running to be a contestant for the next female led season."

"Could you imagine Dom on the show? How would that even work? Don't they film during season?" The thought of my brother being on a dating show makes me nervous for him. I know that professional football is all he's ever wanted to do and I would hate for him to get distracted from that for a show.

"Yeah, that's the only problem."

"The only problem after the fact he wouldn't want to do something like that," I tell her.

She loops her arm through mine and we make our way to our seats in Sasha's box, where she's chatting with a few other spouses I haven't met yet. She gasps when she catches sight of us out of the corner of her eye.

"Anastasia! I'm so excited to see you," she says, pushing through the group around her, flinging herself into my arms. The hug is a little awkward, but I return it as best I can. "Come sit with me."

She pulls back, grabbing my hand and pulling me away from Lorelei without even acknowledging her and we take two seats in the front row of the suite. Lore waves goodbye and heads to the bar.

"*Please* tell me you kissed Parker during the Desire Suite date and then tell me about it in excruciating detail. Also, girl. How embarrassing was it falling on night one?"

Annoyed I'm being asked that question, *again*, I keep my feelings from my face.

"More than you could even imagine," I say and then share a few details that, if they got out, would not be detrimental to anyone on the show.

With the anticipation of seeing Parker tonight, it feels like the game takes an eternity. But the time clicks down second after second, until finally we are at the two-minute warning and I can't wait any longer. I turn toward Sasha and grab her arm for a moment.

"Hey, I'm going to get going. Thanks for inviting me up here."

She gives me a hug. This time I'm ready and able to return the gesture in a relaxed way.

"Sounds good. Tell Dominic he did a great job."

I nod, surprised she knows his first name, but she's already turned back to watch her husband. Lorelei sees me moving and meets me at the top of the stairs.

"Leaving now? There's only two more minutes."

"Parker is coming over tonight. To talk."

Her gray eyes search mine.

"Is everything okay?"

"Hopefully."

"Good luck." She steps out of my way and I get out of the stadium as fast as I can.

CHAPTER THIRTY-EIGHT

PARKER

THE PENDING SUNRISE LIGHTENS the sky as my feet pound the pavement. When I woke up from a fitful sleep at five a.m., I quickly gave up on sleeping. Grabbing the first clothes my hands touched, I got changed, laced my shoes, and started a slow trot around my neighborhood.

Once I was properly warmed up, I started pushing my body faster and faster.

That was almost an hour ago and yet my brain can't think of anything but the fact that in a little more than twelve hours, I get to see Anastasia.

Sweat drips down into my eyes, stinging, but I keep going until my legs almost give out on me. Hands on my head, I look around and don't recognize anything around me. My neighborhood is like a labyrinth of loops and streets that double back on themselves. I pull out my phone and see Brittany texted, asking if I was okay. Apparently, she heard me leave the house.

As my lungs work to bring oxygen into my body after my excruciating pace, I know it's time.

Pulling up a map, I plot out my route back to my house, and start walking, giving myself time to get my thoughts in order.

Sun rays break the horizon as I open my front door, shutting it behind me with no thought to the noise. I know Brittany didn't go back to sleep. She's been asking me, almost constantly, if everything was okay, picking up on my energy since my dinner at Charlie's.

"Brittany?" I call out when I don't see her in the kitchen, her favorite place in any home.

"I'm here," she says, sitting up from the couch. "There's fresh coffee in the pot, if you want some."

Moving to the cabinet, I grab out a mug and pour myself some, long since abandoning my petty refusal to drink any if she made it.

"It's time to talk," I say, making my way to the couch, sitting opposite her. She fiddles with the blanket covering her legs. "And then you need to go."

"I know."

"I need to know why you left, Brittany. The whole answer. Please." If we had been having this conversation a year ago, I would have yelled or begged her for an answer, but I know now that won't change anything. Any of the hurt. Only getting through this will allow healing to begin.

She looks up at me and I see the woman I loved so long ago.

"Because I couldn't breathe. I would walk past the nursery every day and I would think about him, my sweet Wyatt, and how he was gone and I couldn't breathe. And there was a day I was trying to avoid walking past the room, and while watching TV I saw a commercial for the University of Illinois and I thought about my acceptance letter. It's the first time I ever thought 'I'm not trapped here. I don't have to stay.'"

"Is that when you decided to leave?"

"Not consciously, but yes."

"Why the middle of the night?" I ask, taking a drink of my coffee, giving my hands something to do.

"Because, despite everything, I loved you. I loved you more than I hated what we had become and I knew if you were awake, I could never walk away from you. I partially thought I wouldn't even make it out of the driveway."

"I called you," I say, but there's no accusation in my voice. I'm simply stating a fact.

"I know. Parker, I regret everything. I wish I had gotten help, worked through my grief. I did later, but it was too late. I am so sorry for hurting you. For leaving like that. For everything I said."

"I'm sorry, too. I was a crappy husband even before everything happened. I didn't know how to be an adult, let alone a partner, and so many things fell on you. And then everything with Wyatt happened. You weren't the only one who needed help. I didn't handle any of it well. I shouldn't have shut down." I try to blink back the tears, but I can't hold them in any longer and tears well in her eyes in answer. "The only way I could live from one second to the next was to turn everything off."

"Do you ever think of him?" she whispers.

"Always. Every day. I wonder if he'd have your smile and my eyes. How his laugh would sound. I've thought about all the parent-teacher conferences. The art projects he would have brought home. His first Christmas." I sniff, wiping at the tears that have started falling. "How we would have enrolled him in soccer or dance. Whatever he wanted. We would have gone to the park and I would have taught him how to ride a bike. I love him with every beat of my heart. Every time I close my eyes I see his face, every perfect feature."

She bursts into sobs as tears continue leaking down my face. I put my coffee mug on the table, and make my way to her, pulling her into my arms and we cry. Together, we mourn our son and all the heartbeats he never got to have. We mourn the end of us and as my tears subside, my soul feels lighter for the first time.

We pull back from each other, mopping up our faces.

With a tear-soaked voice, she brings us back to the present.

"You love her, don't you?"

I couldn't stop the smile that comes to my face if I wanted to.

"Yeah, I do."

"What if I told you it would be different with us? That we could move forward?"

My heart breaks at the sad hopefulness in her eyes because I can't give her what she wants. We can't go backwards, so I shake my head.

"It doesn't change anything for me. I'm hers. I never stood a chance against her."

She nods with dejected acceptance and pushes the blanket off of her, standing from the couch.

"I needed to know for sure. After I saw you on *House of Deceit* and then *Desire*, I couldn't stop thinking about how maybe you were in a better place, too. Even when I was getting the degrees and building a life for myself, I think I always had this hope that maybe we could find each other again."

"You never did tell me what you ended up studying," I say, because I am curious for a peek at the woman she's become in the aftermath of our loss.

She smiles at me and it's like the first one she ever gave me.

"My freshman year I found an amazing therapist and she suggested that I join a grief group for those who had lost children. I joined for a time and made a couple of friends. One day, I realized how much it helped me to help others. Now I'm a nurse in the NICU."

"That's amazing. I'm glad everything worked out for you," I tell her honestly.

"Me, too. I'll go get my stuff together." She stands from the couch, folding the blanket, before heading toward the hallway. Her steps pause and I look back at her, her eyes already on me. "Thank you, for letting me insert myself into your life. I know I didn't do any of this right either, and I'm sorry about that. I just want you to be happy, Parker. I hope you know that."

"I do. And I want you to be happy, too."

I stand and make my way toward her, holding my arms out to her, and as we embrace, it feels comfortable like a worn sweatshirt, but we don't fit together like we used to.

"I missed you, Parker," she mumbles.

I drop a kiss on top of her head. A goodbye to the past. "I missed you, too, Brittany."

The cold of the concrete has seeped through my jeans, my ass going numb an hour ago. A car makes its way down the street and finally it's Anastasia. I stand from my spot on the ground, making a mental note to buy her some outdoor chairs, and watch her come to a stop next to my truck.

"Hey, you're early," she says, and I feel a little bad for surprising her.

"I couldn't wait any longer," I tell her, honestly.

My eyes don't leave her as she makes her way to me. I always thought she was beautiful, but after not seeing her for over a week, I'm starving for every inch of her. She stops in front of me, tilting her head back just a touch to look me in the eye.

"I'm glad," she says. I give her a small smile, but otherwise make no move toward her.

"No hello kiss?" she asks, her voice soft.

"Are you sure?" I ask, hope sprouting inside me.

She lifts up on her tiptoes and gives me a chaste kiss.

With a deep exhale, I wrap my arms around her, pulling her hard against me as I press my mouth against her. Her arms go around my neck, pulling my hair free of its tie, her fingers tangling in the strands. My tongue swipes over her bottom lip asking for permission she eagerly gives.

The groan I release at her taste would be embarrassing if not for her moan as our tongues tangle together, my hands dropping to her biteable ass, gripping her so hard, I hope there will be bruises tomorrow.

With the self-control of a saint, I pull back, panting. "Should we go inside?"

"Definitely," she says, grabbing my hand and pulling me after her. As she goes to unlock the door, she wraps my arm around her. I let my finger trace the skin where her jeans rest, dipping just barely below the waistband.

"Are you hungry?" she asks.

"Not for food," I say, my voice rough, as I pull her against me once more.

My mouth brands her with the hot kisses I trail down her throat.

"Parker, before all of that, I think I need to know what happened between you and Brittany."

When I pull away, I don't let her go. Instead, I search her face. Her expression remains neutral and I know it's time. Because I want this woman, and there's no way to ignore the elephant in the room any longer.

"You're right," I say, giving her a soft kiss on the lips before spinning her to face away from me, my hands heavy on her hips, and I guide her through the house.

We take a seat on the couch facing each other, much like our first night in the *House of Desire*.

I close my eyes and take a breath. When I open them again, I'm settled.

Ready.

"I met Brittany in high school. From the moment I barreled into her cheerleading pyramid, we were basically inseparable. I loved her with everything I was. It felt like I was born to love her. Like the only reason I could continue breathing after meeting her was because my heart beat for her. Our senior year, we started to have sex. If there was time and even a little bit of privacy—well, you get the point."

My eyes lose focus as I fall back into the memory.

"One day"—I swallow thickly before continuing—"one day, she told me she was pregnant."

I remember the day perfectly, Brittany's panicked voice stopping my heart cold.

"We were nervous, but excited. Eventually. When we told our parents, they were shocked and disappointed. They made sure Brittany wanted to keep the baby and when we reassured them that we did, everyone started talking about marriage. I was never against the idea. I figured I'd end up married to her eventually anyway, so what did it matter if it was a few years before I intended to propose or not.

"She was a bit more hesitant. She always wanted to go to college and move around the country, exploring new places. She was going to backpack across Europe with friends for the summer while I stayed and worked my summer job. But I convinced her this was the best option. The sensible option. And she agreed. I didn't have a ring for her. I didn't even officially ask her. She said 'okay' and we were engaged."

Anya reaches out, touching my arm that's resting along the back of the couch, rubbing her thumb back and forth. The small sign of support bolsters my heart for what's to come.

"We graduated and got married. Rented our first apartment. It was a lot of changes. And throughout that, the pregnancy was normal. No one saw anything until it was too late. We were a week out from her due date, the final touches on the nursery being done whenever I'd come home from work.

"On one of the last ultrasounds, the technician must have noticed something because the doctor was called in immediately. After a few moments, they told Brittany to get dressed and brought us into their office."

Sadness drops my shoulders as I bleed for the kids Brittany and I were, and the crushing weight we were under.

"They had missed a congenital heart defect. He was given a month to live, but not more than a year. There was so much medical talk and after that, I could barely hear anything they said, but the gist was there were no options and my son was going to die.

"To say Brittany fell apart is, well, it's an understatement. As I held her, I knew I had to be strong for her, so I pushed down all my emotions. All my fear, my sadness, my worry. My grief. I shoved it all aside and held her. We were scheduled for her to be induced and within twenty-four hours, we were parents."

"What was your son's name?" she asks. My eyes fill with tears as I smile. It's a simple question, but it means more than any other.

"Wyatt Parker. Wyatt for Brittany's dad and Parker after me and mine."

She smiles at me, linking our fingers together.

"That's a handsome name."

I nod, my chin quivering.

I love this woman. This one with sadness, but not pity, written all over her face as I give her the darkest parts of me. As I share the only thing left of my son.

"He was alive for a day. He was so tiny in my arms. We never put him down. There wasn't a second of his life our arms weren't around him. I loved him more than anything in the entire world in those few minutes. Once he was gone, Brittany fell into a deep depression and I kept pushing everything aside and went back to work, making sure on top of losing our son, we didn't lose our house. I didn't know how to be a good husband even without all the grief. I know that now.

"Anyway, as time passed, we pulled apart from each other. It was impossible to know how to reach her across the chasm that was Wyatt between us. The angrier she got, the more I pulled away until all we were doing was fighting. And then one day, she left in the middle of the night. After a few years of trying to find her, I filed for divorce in absentia. It was granted after the appropriate amount of time given to let her respond.

"The day we found out about the defect is the same date, years later, our marriage officially ended."

My words trail off and she gives me time to collect myself, pressure free. I want to pull her into my lap, hold her, but I need a small amount of space. Just a little, to get the rest out.

"Why did she come here?" she asks, understandably. A tendril of guilt rises.

"She wanted to get back together." I search her face for how this makes her feel, but she's carefully blank.

"Do you still love her?" she asks. A fair question.

"She is the mother of my child. The person I expected to sit out on the front porch with every night. And I loved her. So much. It felt like I had always loved her. There will always be a soft spot in my heart for her, for what we shared and lost. For that time." I'm prepared for all the feelings that normally come with this story, but for the first time, all I feel is calm. Rightness. Like I'm finally ready to confront the pain of my past. "But that time is gone and when I look at her now, all I see is the boy she knew and the girl she was. She doesn't know me, now. She doesn't know the man her leaving helped to create. The one that has to fight to believe he's worth loving. I can't be that boy again. I don't want to be."

"Did anything happen while she was here?" Her voice is steady, but I doubt she feels that way inside.

"Nothing. She didn't try anything and I wouldn't have been open to it, but she did stay in my house. In the guest room. She never even crossed the threshold of my bedroom. But when she asked to stay, the part of me that remembers us together, that she gave me Wyatt, couldn't tell her no."

"I can understand that. But I'm glad to know nothing happened. Then what happened?" she asks, wanting me to finish the story as much as I want to finish it.

"Toward the end, before she left, our fights turned toward how I was trapping her. How boring I was. I ruined her life. I kept her from going to college. If we had thought of birth control at all, then none of this would have ever happened and she wouldn't know how much it hurt to lose a child. And I thought how right she was.

"I knew she wasn't on birth control but, like all teenagers, I just wanted to know what it felt like without the barrier. They weren't lying though when they said it only takes one time.

"The reason I ended up on *House of Desire* was because of something my therapist said. But I still wasn't ready. I hadn't healed from the abandonment and the angry words she had hurled at me. The lack of closure. And then I met you. And for once, I saw the light at the end of the tunnel. I never should have proposed to you. I should have told production to fuck off and do what I wanted, which was to ask you to be my girlfriend and date me in the real world. I'm so sorry, for putting you in the position of having to reject me. That wasn't fair of me."

Her eyes are filled with tears, but she reaches out, taking my hand.

"It's okay, Parker."

"No, it wasn't. I knew I couldn't give you the things you needed at that time but I just didn't want you to leave. I wanted to keep you and the ring was in my pocket and I didn't want to lose you. And that didn't work. But then I saw you at the movie premiere and I knew I needed to do what I had to so I could be a whole person again. I worked with my therapist three times a week for an entire month. We've finally downgraded to once a week lately. I'm not perfect. I'm not healed, I probably won't ever be after that loss, but I'm doing the work. And I'll keep doing the work, but I hope you want to give me a chance, imperfections and everything."

I lay myself bare to her and as she opens her mouth to respond, I cut her off.

"Actually, don't say anything. Not yet. Because this was heavy and a lot. I want you to take your time and really give it thought. Because if you want me, I want you to know I intend to keep you. Our wrap party for *House of Desire* is Friday, as you know, and if you want me, tell me then and be my date."

"If that's what you want," she says and then gives me a shy smile. "Do you want to help me cook dinner tonight? I was thinking the sausage and tortellini recipe I made you before."

"Sounds amazing," I say and we make our way into the kitchen. We spend hours cooking, eating, and just talking. The sun has long set when I make my way home, finally at peace.

CHAPTER THIRTY-NINE

ANYA

COURTNEY WRAPS THE LAST tray of un-iced cookies and other various desserts while I put the finishing touches on the five-tier cake. During one of our concept meetings, Ryan Jade had brought in photographs of her parents' wedding. Her mother's dress was encrusted in pearls, a family heirloom that was created by all the women in her family.

The champagne cake is filled with a pale pink strawberry buttercream, mixed with chunks of strawberries. It's covered in more buttercream with edible pearls spilling down the five tiers in a wave. Between the tiers are the same types of flowers that had been in the bridal bouquet.

It is one of the most beautiful cakes I have ever made.

I finish placing the last pearl, standing on my step stool.

My hand has been steady the entire time I've decorated this cake. Normally, the pressure makes me a little shaky, but ever since Parker and I talked, I have had a calmness inside. Climbing down my step stool, I stand back and just look at the cake for a moment, my eyes getting a little misty at the amazing work.

To say Courtney and I have been busy with all the baking is an understatement. The cupcakes were three different flavors for people who don't like strawberry. The designs on top were relatively simple for Courtney to do while Mom was completely focused on the ovens and swapping all the treats from waiting to be cooked to the cool down process while I worked on the cake. Dad and Liam handled the rest of the bakery like pros.

My phone vibrates and I smile at Parker's name on my screen.

Parker: *Send me pictures of the cake! I'm sure it looks amazing. Good luck today even though I know you don't need it.*

I send him a quick picture as Dom comes barreling into the back of the kitchen, grabbing the extra cupcake from the designated location. I always make sure to put one cupcake to the side for him any time he helps me, the flavor different every time.

"Wow, that's awesome," Dom exclaims, awe in his voice.

"Thanks. Delivery van all gassed up?" I ask, as I walk around the cake, making sure nothing else needs to be done.

"It's ready to go. Do you want to start loading up?"

"You're not coming," I say, looking at him. Lord knows I don't need him hitting on Ryan Jade. "I just need your muscles here. There will be people we can get to help at the venue."

He rolls his eyes at me as he shoves the last bite of cupcake in his mouth, cheeks bulging, and gives me a double fingered salute, which I return.

"Don't flip your brother off, Anastasia," Mom says, catching me. "And you let him help you."

Dom slaps a hand over his mouth to make sure he doesn't spit out his cupcake while he laughs at me getting scolded.

"Fine!" I say, throwing my hands up in the air, conceding to her wishes. "But if you're coming, then you're going to be useful and we are going to use your SUV to carry the supplies so Courtney can sit in the back with the cake."

Courtney snickers at our antics as she double checks the list of supplies to make sure I didn't miss anything. Having Courtney this week has been a blessing of the century. Once she stopped freaking out that Ryan Jade is our client, that is. Other than showing her my recipes and a single example of each design I was envisioning, she completely took over any task I gave her with minimal oversight, her knowledge as an at home baker, paying off in spades.

Everyone starts helping to load up Dom's SUV with boxes and bags. When it's time, we prepare to move the cake. Dom moves the van to the double doors in the back, throwing both open so we have plenty of room.

Dom steps to one side of the cake, me on the other, and Courtney on the back while Mom sits in the front seat of the van looking back to direct us.

"Ready?" I ask. They both nod, their faces set. "One, two, three."

We all lift the cake at the same time and take measured, steady steps.

"A little to the left," Mom says and we adjust. "Straight on. Straight on. And down."

The cake slides into the truck with not a single wiggle, the dowels I added for structural integrity holding up well. Courtney climbs through the side door on the back of the van to sit by the cake in case she needs to steady it. Mom gets out, hugging me as I go to get in the front of the truck.

"I'm proud of you, sweetie."

"Thanks, Mommy."

Dom pulls out of the parking lot first, and I move slowly behind him.

"Are you going to fire me if I tell you I might have eaten a cookie?" Courtney says from the back.

Her question pulls a surprised laugh out of me. "No, I always account for a few extra in case of breakage."

"That's good because today was fun and I don't want to get fired after only a week."

"Nah, don't worry about it." I go the speed limit the entire way to the planetarium Ryan has booked for the party.

"The drop off is always the worst part of the entire process as far as I'm concerned. It's so awkward. I hate standing there waiting for them to decide if they like my work or not and to pay me. And the small talk?" I watch Courtney shiver in the rear-view mirror.

"If you want, once we get the cake loaded on the cart, Dom and I can take care of it."

"And miss the possibility of Dom making an ass out of himself in front of Ryan Jade? Absolutely not. Is she as pretty in person as she is in pictures?"

I take a gentle left, getting honked at in the process. I don't mind, though. There's no way I'm going to drive with the pedal to the metal.

"She's even more stunning in person," I tell her as I turn into the planetarium's driveway, following the directions the event coordinator sent me via email earlier in the week.

Dom and I park, and a woman in a black pantsuit and white button-down meets us immediately.

"Right on time. Do you need a cart or anything?" she says, the second my door is open.

"Yes, please. My associate has a lot of boxes and other items," I say, pointing over at Dom.

While the woman scurries away to procure a cart for Dom, Courtney pulls out the one that's folded in the side of the van and expands it.

"Dom, can you come help me with the cake?" I call, locking the wheels of the cart. My brother comes over without a word, getting on one side while I take the other. "One, two, three."

We move the cake onto the cart, Courtney standing at the ready to steady anything. The woman arrives with another cart, moving it to Dom's car.

"Court, would you mind unloading the other car while Dom and I take in the cake?"

"Aye, aye, Captain," she says with a salute.

"Right this way," the woman says, leading us through the delivery door.

We make our way through a few hallways until we come to the sweeping space. People bustle around getting everything ready. I've never been in the planetarium without a show happening. With the lights on, it feels mundane compared to the magic of watching a meteor storm above you.

"Kind of drab when the lights are on, huh?" Dom says, looking around.

"Hush," I whisper, afraid someone overheard him. "And, yeah. But it'll be gorgeous when they turn on the sky. I've seen pictures of other receptions here and it's stunning."

Courtney catches up to us, the wheel on her cart squeaking. As I open my mouth to give her instructions, a voice with a soft southern twang rings out.

"Oh my *God*! Anastasia, that cake is the best thing I've ever seen!" Ryan says, scurrying across the floor. Even in the matching athletic set she's wearing and no makeup, she's one of the most stunning women I've ever seen. I look over at Dom and he's staring like he's trying to read a defense.

"You're drooling," I say before turning to Ryan as she reaches us.

Her arms are around me and she's pressing a kiss to each cheek.

"I knew Lorelei wouldn't steer me wrong with you."

"Thank you. You're so kind." Dom clears his throat and it takes everything in me not to roll my eyes. "This is Courtney, my other baker," I say, and Ryan gives her a polite smile. "And this is my brother Dominic," I tell her and he steps forward.

"Miss Jade, I went to your concert all three nights last year. Your shows are some of the best concerts I've been to in my entire life." I look at him, confused by his awestruck tone. He's met plenty of stars during his time as a professional football player, and he has *never* sounded like that when meeting someone.

She reaches her hand out to him, which he takes, but instead of shaking it, he holds it. She looks at him, a blush staining her cheeks.

"Next time, you'll have to come backstage. I could give you a tour," she says.

"It would be my honor," he tells her.

The silence becomes awkward for me as they continue to stare at each other.

"Sorry, I don't mean to interrupt whatever this is, but we need to get the desserts all set up." I take a look at my watch and time has flown. It's getting closer and closer to when I need to get home and change for tonight's event.

Where Parker will be waiting for me. And my answer.

I love him.

The caring, compassionate man I've seen from the very beginning. Even with no cameras, no need to pretend. No reason to lay his soul bare at my feet. And yet he did.

He's given me everything I needed to know the man I started falling for at *House of Desire* was real.

That the man I love is real and mine. My heart bursts with the knowledge. I'm all but climbing out of my skin with impatience to get to him.

"Um, yes," Ryan says, clearing her throat, dropping my brother's hand. "Let me go get your payment while you get set up. I'll be back in a minute." The last statement is more directed to Dom than me, and I try to hide my smile as she walks away.

"I'm gonna marry that woman," Dom says, reverent as Courtney snorts a laugh, pushing her cart up beside us.

"Maybe next time don't act like a worshiping fan right off the bat," she says, popping a brownie bite in her mouth.

"Stop eating things!" I say.

"Quality control," she says, eating another.

"Do you think she'll go on a date with me?" Dom says, straightening his shirt.

"I don't have time for your delusions. Can we get set up please?" I ask.

We begin moving everything around, decorating the table with all the creations Courtney and I worked so hard on. By the time I was putting the last cupcake on the table, Ryan was making her way back toward us.

"Sorry about that," Ryan says as she hurries back over.

"That's okay. How does it look?" I say, stepping back from the table and admiring the best display I've ever made.

"Perfect," she says, clapping her hands and squealing. "I have to get back to it. Here's your check." She thrusts the slip of paper into my hand. "You can expect to be *very* busy in the near future. Dominic, here's my card for that tour. Or anything else." She hands him a plain black card, and I think my brother is about to pass out on the floor in front of me, despite looking collected.

"I'll call you," he says, giving her a wink.

My mouth almost drops open at his suave flirting, but I don't want to embarrass him. Once she's gone, I turn toward him, smacking his arm.

"You better not fuck this up or I will kill you. And her fans will hate you."

"I have no intention of fucking it up. Don't you have some event to get to?"

I look at my watch and my heart rate picks up. "Shit! I'm going to be late."

"No, you won't. I'll take Courtney with me and she can clean up the kitchen," he says, knowing I'll never be able to relax if my bakery is in disarray.

"Hold on, now," Courtney says.

"Parker's waiting for her," Dom says, sharing a look with her and she smiles.

"I'll clean up," she promises. "For a fee."

"You got it," I say, grabbing Dom's keys from his hand and run for the car.

CHAPTER FORTY

PARKER

"Parker, it's so great of you to join us tonight. I know a lot of the fans at home are hoping for an update on your happily ever after since Anastasia's rejection," Jacob Jacobson says, the camera and bright lights on us.

The last episode of the show just finished airing and the first hour of the party will be live where various contestants will be interviewed.

"It's great to be here. All I can say is I hope my happily ever after starts tonight."

"Care to share a hint of what we can expect?"

"It's going to be a surprise," I tell him, itching to take off my suit, the tie almost strangling me.

"Alright, folks, you heard it here first. Parker is hopeful following the devastating ending of *House of Desire* where Anastasia, a crowd favorite from the beginning, turned down his proposal. We'll be back after this commercial break."

"And we're out," says the production member behind the camera. The red light flicks off and the tension in my shoulders drops.

I stand up from the chair, tucking my hair behind my ears as a production assistant removes my microphone.

"It was good seeing you, Jake," I say once I'm free. Zoey walks up, her hair now a deep red.

"Zoey, how are you?" I ask, wrapping her in a friendly hug.

"I'm great. It's good to see you. I'd ask how you're doing, considering the rejection the country just watched, but the look on your face tells me everything I need to know."

I smile at her. "I guess you'll just have to wait and see."

"Tell her to find me later, yeah?" I don't even waste my breath pretending to not know she's talking about Anya.

"Will do," I say, taking note of Charlie as she walks down the stairs. "Will you excuse me?"

"You look gorgeous," I say, holding my hand out to help her down the last few stairs. Her golden dress makes it seem like she glows in the dim light.

"I would tell you that you look good, but I don't want to inflate your ego. Where's Anastasia?"

"She'll be here soon."

And I know she's going to tell me she feels the same way for me as I do for her.

I've never been more certain of anything. And even on the off chance I'm wrong, I know I'll be able to survive this time.

"Where's your husband?" I ask, and she gives me a dreamy smile. She texted me, letting me know some of Alec's old colleagues got them tickets to this. There are other network people mingling around I don't know and am not too worried about meeting.

All I care about is Anya.

"He's finishing up a few things and then he'll be here. Do you want to dance in the meantime?"

"I'd love to," I say, offering her my arm.

I begin guiding her around the floor, one hand on her waist and the other clasping hers. The hotel ballroom is a popular spot for bigger events. The space was restored last year, updating some parts that had been damaged previously, but they were able to keep much of the original charm.

Four giant chandeliers hang down from the two-story high ceilings, adding to the glow of the candelabra sconces around the room. The arched windows reach almost to the ceiling, heavy drapes pulled closed to keep the affair private. In the corner, a band plays softly in the background as servers move around the room with hors d'oeuvres and flutes of champagne.

"You seem happy."

I look down into her deep blue eyes and see hope within them.

"I'm much better than I was."

"Did you work everything out with Brittany?" she asks, as I spin her out before pulling her back in.

"Yeah, I did. We both got the closure we needed."

"That's good, because the woman you're in love with is walking over here," she teases. I don't waste my time trying to cover up the truth of her words. I drop her hand and turn around to see Anastasia coming down the stairs.

Her black hair is pulled over one shoulder in a cascade of curls. Her red dress demands attention as it hugs every curve, the slit going indecently high. I can't wait to get my hands on her later.

Cameras focus on her entrance, wanting to get footage of the woman who broke my heart on the show.

"If she hurts you, I'll key her car," Charlie says, patting my arm.

"Thanks, but I don't think you're going to need to do that."

"Hi, Charlie. You look beautiful," Anya says, giving her a quick hug.

"You look exquisite," Charlie says. "Would you excuse me? There's a man with gray eyes I need to make out with."

And just like that, she deserts us. She climbs the stairs where her husband waits and makes good on her promise the moment she's in his arms.

"I was going to tell you how exquisite you look, but Charlie stole my line. Would you take a simple you made my heart skip a beat?" I tell Anya, holding out my hand in invitation to a dance.

"Ugh," she says, rolling her eyes. "I guess. But you're on thin ice." She smiles up at me and my heart freezes in my chest. "Hi," she says, softly.

"Hi. I missed you."

"I missed you, too." I pull her closer, uncaring of the people around us. "How did the delivery for Ryan Jade go?"

Excitement lights up her entire her being.

"She loved everything! She already posted a video on her social media, and Courtney said we were getting flooded with orders."

"That's amazing! I didn't have any doubt she'd love it. I'm so proud of you," I say, bending down and giving her a quick kiss, no longer caring who sees or if a camera is on us.

"Oh, and get this bit of salacious gossip," she says, dropping her voice conspiratorially. "I think Ryan Jade asked Dominic out on a date."

A choked laugh escapes me. "Are you serious? Dominic? Your brother, Dominic?"

"He told her how he went to all three of her shows last year, which was news to me, I have to admit. I didn't think he even listened to pop music. And then she said she'd get him backstage passes and take him on a tour of the entire thing."

"Holy shit. What if you end up being the sister-in-law of Ryan Jade?" I ask her, partially joking.

"He said he was going to marry her. Could you imagine? But Dom is one of the good ones. She'd be lucky to date him."

"But it worries you. I can see it in your eyes," I say as we sway to the quartet.

"She writes very autobiographical songs and her fans are intense, to put it nicely. If they don't work out, it could go very badly for Dom. So yes, I'm worried."

"I think that's a choice he'll have to make, but knowing Dom, even if they didn't work out, it wouldn't be because he was treating her badly."

"You're right. But as his sister, I'm supposed to be worried. I would hate to never be able to listen to her music again in solidarity with my brother."

"Yes, what a burden in exchange for his possible happiness." She smacks my arm, laughing.

We sway for a moment more and I can't take it any longer.

"Anastasia."

"Parker," she mimics, dropping her voice.

"Come to any decisions lately?"

She taps a finger against her chin, humming in contemplation.

"I might have."

By the sparkle in her eyes, I can tell she's going to make me ask directly. But I'll do it. I'll do anything she wants.

"What did you decide?"

Her eyes fill with tears, but I know this time it's not because she's going to walk away from me.

"Parker." She says my name with so much love, I know I want to hear her say it that way forever. Movement catches her eye as we notice a camera that has focused us.

I turn back to her. "Wait. I want this to just be ours. Come home with me after this and tell me then?" I whisper.

"Sounds perfect to me."

CHAPTER FORTY-ONE

T HE MOMENT THE DOOR to my truck slams shut, I yank Anya over to me and take her mouth in a searing kiss. There is no finesse in the kiss, only desperation until she pulls back from me. Once our dance ended, we mingled separately. My eyes couldn't stay off of her for too long and she seemed to have the same issue. Each glance had more and more heat until I was ready to combust right there.

"Drive," she commands, and I can't do anything but comply. We're leaving her car, but we'll worry about that tomorrow. Tonight, I need my hands all over her.

"Pull your dress up and spread your legs," I tell her as I pull out of the parking lot and get onto the highway. Her breathing stutters as she pulls at the material.

Cruise control is an amazing thing, the best invention on the planet, I decide as I reach over and begin running my fingers through her slickness before finally sinking two deep inside her.

Her moan is beautiful as she clenches around me.

"You're so wet for me," I groan as I curve my fingers, hitting the spot that makes her legs shake.

"Don't stop," she begs, nails cutting into my forearm.

She comes with a shout as I take the off ramp and book it to my house. My tires almost squeal as I turn into my driveway, slam on my breaks, and throw the truck in park. Anya pulls her dress down as she jumps out before I can get over to her door to open it for her. I need her like the ocean needs the shore.

"Kiss me," she orders, pulling me into the house the second I have the door unlocked.

From this day forward, she'll never have to ask me to kiss her ever again, I promise myself pushing her against the wall and kissing her with everything I am. Her hands go to my belt and she releases my throbbing dick.

I brace one arm against the wall and press my forehead to hers, groaning at how good her soft hand feels. Her honey brown eyes are focused on my face, drinking in my reaction to her ministrations.

"Fuck," I exclaim, as she adds pressure and twists her wrist as she strokes me. I kiss her, my hands going to her hair, taking control. "We are supposed to be talking."

"Talk later. What we need is to go to the bedroom," she pants.

If I was worried about her answer, I'd make us stop. But I'm not, so I bend down and band my arms around the backs of her thighs. She falls over my shoulder with a shout as I stand up.

"Parker! Put me down!" she giggles. She gives me a swift swat on the ass and I return it, getting a moan for my efforts.

"I'll put you down on the bed and nowhere else," I tell her, making my way down the hallway.

Kicking the door open, I move through the bedroom by the light coming in from the moon. Anya lets out an "oof" as I unceremoniously drop her down onto the bed.

"You have thirty seconds to get out of that dress before I rip it from your body."

I unbutton my shirt and drop it to the ground as I kick off my shoes.

"You promised to get me naked," she says and I pause, my hands on the waistband of my pants.

"I did, didn't I?" Pushing my pants down my legs, I stand naked in front of Anastasia. Her eyes take in every inch of me, heating my blood.

Man, I love this woman.

I grab her hand and gently pull her up from the bed and place a kiss on her lips. My fingertips trail down her arms before reaching back and taking hold of her zipper. Inch by excruciating inch, I unzip her dress. I think about the last time I did this and how different of a situation we were in.

Her dress pools at her feet and I'm transfixed by her beauty.

"Do you like what you see?" she asks with a smirk.

"The word 'yes' seems so inadequate right now. I could look at you like this for eternity and it still wouldn't be enough."

She trails her nails down my stomach, making goosebumps rise all over my body. My dick twitches with how much I want to be inside her, but I'm addicted to savoring this moment.

"One day, I'm going to get some whipped cream and cover your abs in it and then I'm going to lick it off."

"Promises, promises," I tell her with a smile.

I kiss my way down her neck, gently pushing her back onto the bed and settling between her legs.

"Tell me you want me," I whisper against her lips.

"I want you," she says, without a second of hesitation. The best words I've ever heard in my life.

I hook my arm under one of her knees, resting it on my shoulder. I settle more fully on her, pushing her knee to her shoulder. My other hand reaches down, aligning myself with her opening.

"Tell me to take you."

I tease her entrance, dipping the crown of my cock inside her.

"Take me, Parker. Take everything. I'm yours." The love in her voice makes my throat tighten with emotion.

I push inside her. She stretches around me and I have to take a moment so I don't come already, the tightness of her position almost too much.

"Parker, if you don't start moving, I'm going to cry. I need you. Please."

Pulling out and pushing in, my strokes are sure and strong like they were at the wedding, but without the edge of desperation. Love fills me as I take her, worshiping her.

"You feel amazing. I need to be buried between your thighs every day. It's heaven on Earth, I'm sure of it."

She reaches up and takes my lips.

"I'm so close," she says, matching my strokes. Anya's muscles tremble as I push us both closer and closer to the brink. I drink down her moans until, as her orgasm nears, her head kicks back, exposing her throat.

I nibble and kiss way down until I come to her nipples. Sucking one after the other into my mouth, I can feel her heart racing. When I pinch her nipple, giving it a small twist, I feel the moment crystalize and then break as wave after wave wracks her body.

"Parker, I'm coming, baby," she groans. "I'm coming for you. Only for you."

"You're such a good girl, taking your pleasure from me."

She relaxes as she comes down from her orgasm and my movements become jerky and undisciplined.

"I'm going to fill you so full of my come, it's going to drip down your thighs and you'll know exactly who you belong to," I tell her as I feel myself starting to thicken with my release inside her.

"Yes, please. Give me every drop, Parker."

I rut into her, my breathing turning choppy.

"You'll never take another cock, Anastasia. Mine is all you get. My come. My cock. My heart."

"I want it all. Come for me, Parker. Mark me as yours."

Her words break the last link of chain around my control and I bite her neck and shoulders as I come with a groan.

Her pussy squeezes around me as I tremble through my release. We both lay there, trying to catch our breath. My arms start shaking and before I can fall and crush her, I push up going to the bathroom for a warm, damp washcloth. I clean between her legs, kissing her soft thighs.

She grabs a handful of my hair, forcing me to look at her.

"That was amazing," I say, smiling at her.

"It's one for the record books. Do you want to take a shower with me?" she asks.

"Twist my arm."

I sit up, taking her hand, and pull her to the edge of the bed. Standing, I hook an arm under her knees and the other around her back. She lets out a squeal as her arms go around my neck.

"I can walk!" she tells me, kicking her legs.

"Then I don't think I did my job well enough," I say, kissing her.

I set her on the counter before turning on the water, making sure it is warm before picking her up again, and setting her inside the shower. She groans as the heat soaks into her. She tips her head back, wetting her hair.

"I love you. I want to be with you. I want this, you, every day," I say, not able to wait another second more without saying what I feel.

She looks at me, putting her hands on my shoulders.

"I never could have guessed when I went on *House of Desire*, I'd actually meet someone I could fall in love with. And this road has been rough and a little winding, but I would walk every inch of it again so long as this is waiting for us at the end. I have never wanted anything more than to be yours. I love you. And I want to be by your side every day."

Sweeter words have never been said to me. I bend down, taking her luscious mouth in a searing kiss, feeling so lucky that I really did find everything I desired.

EPILOGUE

ONE YEAR LATER

PARKER

"P ARKER, IT'S DONE," MITCHEL tells me, clapping me on the back, as I near my truck, ready to get home to Anastasia. It's been over a year since the finale of *House of Desire* and six months since she moved in. Every night I have raced home to see her as if it was the first time.

"It's done? It's a month early," I say, surprised, as excitement fills my chest.

"The team wanted to turn it around quickly. As an engagement gift to you."

"But I haven't even asked her to marry me yet," I say, laughing. His answering grin tells me how glad he is to see me happy after so many years in the darkness.

"No, but I know you've had that ring in your pocket since she moved in. So maybe it's time to put it on her finger."

"Maybe it is," I say, pulling out my phone. I dial a number I've had memorized. "Hey, I need your help." Within an hour, I'm standing inside the brand-new Whimsical Whisk Bakery as Charlie comes striding in.

"This is absolutely stunning, best friend," she says, taking in the space, making her way to the back to look around.

The space is incredible. The large windows allow the light from the setting sun into the shop. The herringbone pattern wood floor in a light honey color warms the space. A light green couch lines a wall, small tables set up in front of it. Bistro tables and chairs dot the floor, so people can hang out and enjoy the shop. The display sits on top of a L-shaped, white counter. Sitting on the back counter is a shiny espresso machine and various flavorings for Anya's concoctions. But the back is where the true magic is.

Since Ryan Jade's post, Anya's business has exploded to the point where she was unable to keep up with demand without working her fingers to the bone. Not only that, but people started asking if she offered baking classes, something she's always been interested in and that was when the idea took shape in my mind.

I wanted to create her dream bakery, and include space for classes.

Through the swinging back doors, the kitchen is easily double of the front space. In the back are four tables with six chairs each for classes. It's wired with a camera and TV so the students will be able to see what she's doing in great detail.

We also tripled all the equipment she had after guidance from Courtney based on their custom bakes wait list and the daily demand for their usual fare. She'll be able to hire more bakers for the day-to-day items and focus her attention on the classes and the custom creations like she wants.

"It's all thanks to you," I tell her, hugging her as she comes back to me. Her help on the decorating has been invaluable and I know Anya will love it.

"I did nothing." She waves away my thanks, but we both know it's not true. "Why am I here? It doesn't look like there are any finishing touches you need done."

"I think it's time I ask her to marry me."

Her eyes fill with tears and she clasps her hands in front of her heart. "I think you're right. What do you need from me?"

"I need a florist," I tell her and she smiles.

"I'll call Lorelei. She'll know just the one." She pulls out her phone and I know she will manage every detail for me.

Once everything is arranged, I head home, anticipation making me twitchy. The days stretch out before me. The countdown feels like it takes forever and is also no time at all. But finally, the day arrives.

My hands are shaking as I unlock the front door.

"Anastasia?" I call out, dropping my keys into the bowl on the entry table.

"Kitchen," she calls, and I laugh. I should have known.

Her arms are full of ingredients as she turns from the fridge, kicking it closed.

"I hope that chicken and lemon risotto dish sounds good. I've been craving it all day."

"Actually, I was thinking we could go out to dinner, tonight."

"Oh, that sounds perfect. But tomorrow we are having chicken. That burger joint is doing a fundraiser for the local school band if we wanted to go there."

I move around the island, opening the fridge door for her so she can put her armload of items back before I grab her and kiss her. I fall into the kiss, just like I have every kiss since she said she would be mine.

"We don't have to go to dinner," she says when she pulls back, her voice husky. It's tempting, but the ring in my pocket needs to be on her finger.

"We're going to go to dinner, not the burger joint, and then I'm going to bring you home and keep you up all night trying to break my record of number of orgasms I've given you in a night."

Her skin stains the prettiest pink and my dick starts to harden and I almost want to skip it all and ask her right here. Almost. But I know Charlie would kill me after all the work she's put in.

"That sounds like quite the plan."

"I'm going to take a really quick shower. Go ahead and get changed."

"What should I wear?"

"Something nice," I say, kissing her again before heading back to our bedroom. I make quick work in the shower, and wrap a towel around my hips as I step from the enclosure.

Anya stands in the middle of the room, a light blue dress on her that's almost silver.

"Is this nice enough?" she asks, spinning for me, her skirt swirling around her knees.

"It's perfect," I say, kissing her again, careful not to get her wet. "Go wait in the living room, I'll be right there."

I check my pocket for the ring box three times before I leave the bedroom, my light gray suit a perfect complement to her dress. I leave my hair down, her preferred style, and make my way to the woman I'm going to propose to.

"Ready?" I ask.

"Ready," she says, standing, tucking her phone into her pocket. The pockets were the biggest selling point when she brought the outfit home. She emphasized their existence multiple times when she tried it on for me. She sees the black silk in my hand and looks at me questioningly.

"Blindfolding me in public, now, huh? Was that time in our couple's therapy session on the show not enough?"

"Where we are going is a surprise."

"Okay, but just know, you have to use this tonight. I'm not going to be able to think of anything else."

"Deal," I say as she turns her back to me.

I get the blindfold situated and carry her to my truck, setting her inside. Within ten minutes, we arrive at her new bakery, one of the largest benefits of the new location. Charlie holds the door open for me as I lead Anya into the space, quietly blowing me a kiss as she leaves. Everything is perfect. The flowers and candles are exactly as they were when I proposed to Anya on the finale of *House of Desire*.

"It smells like paint, Parker. Not exactly an appetizing scent," Anya jokes.

"If you want to go somewhere else once you see it, we will."

"Can I take the blindfold off?"

I get into position behind her, getting down on one knee, the ring box in my hand. My heart is racing as I tell her to take off the blindfold.

"Yes. Take it off."

Her gasp is everything and I know I did well.

"Parker, what is this?" she says, looking around until she sees the sign. "The Whimsical Whisk Bakery? Is this mine?"

"Anastasia," I whisper, and she spins around, her hands covering her mouth as tears fill her eyes. "I love you more than I thought possible. Ever since I met you, I know what it feels like to have my entire being set aflame. You consume me. Every thought. Every heartbeat. It's yours. There is no one else. When you got out of that limo, it was like someone rang a gong inside my soul. And now I've heard it, I don't think I can go back. I want you to be mine every day for the rest of our lives. Will you marry me?"

Silent tears stream down her face, her hands falling down and showing me a smile that stops my heart.

"Yes," she whispers. "A thousand times, yes."

I surge up from my place, grabbing her into my arms, spinning her around. The ring fits perfectly on her finger and something settles in my soul, knowing this woman is mine. Forever.

"So, what do you think of your new bakery?" I ask after we stare at her ring for a few moments.

"It's amazing! Parker, when did you do this? *How* did you do this?"

"It was one of the jobs my crew was working on. I saw the location one day on my way to another job and I knew I had to buy it for you. You can either keep both locations open, or close the other one and move all of your operations here. But I think you should keep both. Start expanding."

"I can't believe you did this for me."

"I would do anything for you." I tuck her hair behind her ear as she looks up at me with love in her eyes. I plan to see that look on her face every day for the rest of my life. "Do you want to see the back?"

She nods enthusiastically before skipping away through the swinging door. I laugh, following her.

"Oh my God! I can do classes!" She runs past all the new equipment and runs her hands over the tables her students will be sitting at in the near future.

"I knew that was important to you. And you'll be able to hire more bakers. I have no doubt the additional capacity will quickly pay for them."

"I've had the money to hire more for a while, but there was no space. But now there's plenty! I love you," she says, coming back over to me, wrapping her arms around my middle.

"I love you, too. And I can't wait to marry you."

"Lots of changes tonight, but that's the best one of all," she says.

"Do you think we should start the marathon of orgasms here?" I ask, remembering our time in her bakery on the show. Her eyes darken and skin heats.

I begin undoing my pants, freeing myself. My hand strokes my dick as she backs up, raising herself up onto the working surface in the middle of the space. She spreads her legs wide, pulling up the skirt of her dress, baring herself to me.

"No panties?" I ask, feeling myself harden even more at her needy display.

"I knew I wouldn't be able to wait for you to take me."

I pull her to the edge of the table, line myself up, and thrust home, our moans echoing around the space.

"Say my name," I say.

"Parker," she moans. I pull out, slowly, enjoying every inch of her soaked pussy.

"Tell me you're mine," I command, thrusting in again, hitting the spot I know drives her wild.

"I'm yours." She leans back, resting on her elbows, hooded eyes watching as I take her harshly.

"You're mine. Forever. And you're going to come on my cock like the good wife I know you are," I tell her as I unleash myself on her core and she takes everything I give her, everything I am.

GWEN'S SAUSAGE TORTELLINI RECIPE

1 lb smoked sausage, sliced
1 tbsp olive oil
3 garlic cloves, minced
1 cup chicken broth
8 oz tomato sauce
2 tbsp tomato paste
1 tbsp Italian seasoning
20 oz cheese tortellini
1/2 cup heavy cream
1/4 cup Parmesan cheese
Crushed red pepper to taste (can omit)

1. In a deep skillet, heat the olive oil over medium heat and brown sausage
2. Add garlic to pan and cook for 30 seconds, until fragrant
3. Stir in all other ingredients
4. Bring to boil. Once boiling reduce heat to low and simmer for 12-15 minutes, stirring occasionally
5. Enjoy!!

ACKNOWLEDGEMENTS

O NE THING THAT I never expected about being an author
is how much I would love complete strangers like you.
I'm not being hyperbolic. I can't thank you enough for picking
up this book and giving me your trust to tell you a good story
for the first time, or coming back for more. It means more than
you could know and I'm so happy that you're here.

I want to give a huge, huge, HUGE thank you to my beta
readers, Melissa, Audrey, Aisling, Hannah, and Daytona. You'd
be holding a book in your hands without them, but it wouldn't
be this book. It wouldn't be a book I'd be as proud of. Their
hard work was so important.

A big thank you to all of my ARC readers who are too many to
name, but I appreciate every single one of you. Your reviews are an

important part of the book launch process and I'm so honored you donated your time to review *House of Desire.*

Courtney Parker. You're one of my best friends and a huge driving force behind every book I write. Thank you for helping me with ideas and some of the funniest lines and telling me I could do it when I texted crying saying the exact opposite. I wouldn't still be writing without you. 'Thank you' isn't enough but it's the words I have.

To my critique partner Dani. I'm so proud to call you a best friend and a writing partner. You're a soft place to land when my sadness, pain, happiness, and worry are too heavy to shoulder alone. Thank you for being there for the good days and the bad. I love you to the moon and to Saturn.

Paige, Emily, and Amber, y'all keep me sane during my corporate America work days. Without you I'd be crying in a ball in the corner of my room. It's hard to write when you're crying in a ball in the corner.

To Christie. Thank you for naming Dom. You couldn't have picked a more perfect name for him and I can't wait to explore him more.

To Carley and Jess at Under the Cover (an Indie Romance bookstore here in Kansas City that is worth the trip) thank you for all your support and love to not only me but every indie author that comes in.

To Makenna Albert. I don't think I could write a book without you. Thank you for all your help and support and advice.

To my weenie dog Frankie, aka Hotdog, who I lost during the writing of this book. Writing won't be the same without you snuggled under the blanket with me. Thank you for spending your life with me. Your kitty cat sister has taken over your spot, but you'll always be missed.

To my family. For everything. I hope that you skipped the sexy bits in this one just like in *House of Deceit*. If you didn't, lets pretend like you did. Deal? Deal.

About the Author

N.E. Butcher was born and raised in a suburb of Kansas City, MO. Recently returned home after 13 years away, she's enjoying putting down roots while spending time with her loved ones. When not daydreaming up stories, you'll find her engrossed in a gripping book, knitting gifts for loved ones, or embracing her creative side with home DIY projects.

An unabashed Taylor Swift enthusiast, N.E. Butcher finds inspiration in the singer's lyrics and melodies and always has her music playing in the house that she shares with two adorable cats.

Join her on a romantic journey as she delves into tales of love, heartbreak, and second chances, captivating your heart with every turn of the page.